SUMMERHILL

Mrs. Jeni,

Thank you for supporting
my book & for everything &
every memory from when
we were kids 💜

(Lolcy & I)

Ashdon B

Also by Ashdon Byszewski

The Gig Harbor Suicides

ASHDON BYSZEWSKI

SUMMERHILL

Printed in the United States of America

First Printing, 2023

ISBN 978-1-329-60599-2

Imprint: Lulu.com

Lulu Publishing

627 Davis Drive Suite 300 Morrisville, NC

27560 USA

www.Lulu.com

Dedication

For Angela, who is always in my corner and has seen the best in me even on my

darkest days.

Thank you for being the best friend I could have ever asked for.

And for one more girl-

you know who you are.

Content Warning

This book contains themes of homophobia, emotional abuse, sexual assault, as well as some sexually explicit scenes.

Pronunciation Guide

Niamh MacKenna - (Knee-V)

Cian MacKenna - (Kee-In)

Aine MacKenna - (Awn-yuh)

"I remember that it hurt.

Looking at her hurt."

- Rusty Borgens

"Our love is stronger than time, greater than any distance. Our love spans

across stars and worlds. I will find you again,

I promise."

- Sarah J. Maas

PROLOGUE

I'm going to be totally honest: I love morally gray stories.

Anyone can pick up a pen and write a story about a hero who is good, and a villain who is bad. It's not that hard. Take the majority of movies you watch: there's a hero who is innately good, a villain who is innately bad, they have an epic battle, and it ends with good triumphing over evil, and they call it a full circle story. And I mean, fuck, if it kept the viewers attention, made them laugh, made them cry, and really *feel* something, then it was a good story, right?

I don't think so.

Maybe I'm just twisted, but I think it's much, *much* more interesting to fuck with the characters. I like twists and obstacles and wrenches in plans. Wrenches in plans make characters more interesting. They make them memorable. Give them multiple hardships and multiple obstacles, combined with heartbreak or betrayal.

Make nothing black and white! Make everything challenging! Make the hero question everything they know!

The best stories, in my opinion, are the ones where the main character comes out of their trials heavily, thoroughly changed. The kind-hearted, sensitive, codependent maiden turned stone-cold, emotionless murderer. The heartless, sadistic villain falling in love, and not the cheesy kind: the kind that spans worlds and conquers death.

Let's say, for example, I wrote a story about a princess who's about to be eaten by a dragon. There's a witch holding her captive, and a prince who wants to rescue her.

So you have your elements all lined up: damsel in distress, dragon about to go to town, prince with intent of saving the girl, and a witch who craves death.

In a normal story, the prince would slay the beast in the name of love, save the princess, and kill the witch, too, for good measure. Everything lines up nicely, good wins over evil, the fucking end. But, see, I don't think that's very exciting. Some people like happy endings like that. Most people crave happy endings, because they expect them.

Good for them. Personally, I'm not a fan.

I like to surprise the reader with wrenches. I fucking *love* wrenches. I like nail-biting, edge-of-my-seat anxiety, twist and turns kind of stories.

I like surprises and crave the strange, the dark, and the unexpected like a moth to flame.

So switch it up a bit- let's say the prince shows up to the cliff edge, sword in hand. The princess is standing precariously over the edge, the dragon looming above her. The witch overlooks it all from behind the trees, fingers steepled together in anticipation of how this will all play out.

The prince goes to rescue her, aiming his sword at the dragon's throat. But before he can hit home, the witch whispers some incantation under her breath, and with a burst of light, the prince falls to the ground, dead. The witch darts out from behind the trees, and the princess and her embrace with the sort of passion that would put Jack and Rose to shame. The dragon takes off with the prince's corpse, and the princess and the witch escape into the forest to live happily ever after.

Big, gigantic wrench for you: turns out the dragon was just a front. The prince felt entitled to the princess simply because she was a princess, and he was a prince. It's how it was supposed to be. Right? Except the princess is queer, and she and the witch had been in love the whole time.

So they took matters into their own hands.

Big wrench for our prince: the witch used her magic to summon a fucking *dragon.*

The princess used herself as a lure.

And when the prince came to claim what he thought was rightfully his, they fucking killed him, and let the dragon have his body as a thank-you.

The end.

See, wrenches in plans are great. Morally gray stories are GREAT, because who does the reader side with? Who *should* they side with?

Some readers may side with the princess and the witch, because love conquers all, right? At least, that's what everyone feeds us.

Some readers may side with the prince, might feel sympathetic for the poor guy. I mean, shit. He got eaten by a dragon just for trying to rescue some girl. Sad, right? Maybe even a tad over aggressive.

I like stories that are questionable, because that's how life is. Neither right nor wrong, neither good nor evil, because let's be honest: nothing is ever *truly* black and white. Real life just isn't like that.

There are *always* wrenches. And they aren't always obvious, either.

They can be sneaky, devious little fuckers. They can sneak into a story without the reader noticing- unless they're paying very, very close attention.
Because in stories like this one, good does *not* always win.
Light does *not* always chase out the darkness.

And people you think are the saviors, the heroes, and the good guys might actually be the villain in a very, very clever disguise.
Wolves can fit surprisingly easy into the skin of a sheep.

The prince does not always get the princess, and the villain does not always have a horrible, gut-wrenching origin story that turned them evil.

Sometimes, people are just born like that.

Sometimes darkness is innate.

    And sometimes, in rare cases, such as in this story,

    there are external forces at work that neither the hero nor the villain ever see

coming.

    Sometimes, something

          darker

   and

               older

than any of the characters is at work.

    Sometimes,

a presence that has been there before

              any of the trees stood

before

the sun ever rose

and before

a certain town was

ever

built

is lying dormant,

waiting.

Waiting, and watching,

just waiting to wake up.

Waiting to wake up,

and very,

very

hungry

OCTOBER

CHAPTER ONE
NIAMH

"Are you still moping back there?"

My dad peeks over his shoulder momentarily, quickly returning his attention to the road after seeing me in the same position I'd been in when they half-carried me to the car over a day ago. I'm hunched into a ball as small as I can go, knees to my chest, hair in my face, hoodie up. Trying to contain myself, my anger, lest I explode. I hadn't left Saxon Beach without a little bit of a fight. In the span of a week, my entire life had gotten so colossally, enormously fucked up.

On Wednesday, I was expelled from my high school, along with my three best friends.
On Thursday, said three best friends, the same three I'd had since kindergarten, completely stopped speaking to me.

On Friday, my parents announced that we were moving. Not just moving away from Saxon Beach, California, the lively, sprawling beach city I'd grown up in, built roots in. No, that wouldn't be punishment enough.

No, we were moving to the tiny, rinky-dink fishing town off the coast of Maine that my dad grew up in. A little nowhere town in the cape.

Cape Summerhill: the complete and polar opposite of Saxon Beach.

I don't answer him, instead pulling my black, salt-stained hoodie farther around my face and gazing listlessly out the window. Strands of my loose, sun-streaked blonde hair tickles my cheeks. I'd refused to shower after the big announcement, which only resulted in me looking like a half-homeless street urchin. Hair unbrushed, dirty sweats and hoodie, unlaced Vans.

Nice.

I stare out the window, my reflection mirrored back at me. My blonde, nearly white sun-streaked hair is falling out of the halfhearted bun I'd attempted. My eyes, normally a bright, playful green, remain dull and unfocused. The dark circles underneath them are as deep as thumbprints. The billions of freckles that smatter across my cheekbones and nose, the same ones that prompt old people to call me "impish" and "cheerful" can't even give my appearance a boost right now. I look completely hollow.

My parents might call me dramatic, but they aren't the ones who got plucked right out of their senior year, their hometown, and their entire *life* just to get dropped in BFE, Maine.

I know I'm being a little shit by ignoring him. But I feel it's a little merited, at this point.

My mom whips her head around the passenger seat. "Niamh Erin MacKenna. You're acting like a toddler, and frankly, I could care less. But do *not* ignore your father when he's speaking to you."

My mom, Shawnie MacKenna, allows no room for further arguing. Her tone is sharp, how it usually is. Sharp and full of a thinly-veiled warning, like if I push back, she'll explode.
Maybe anger issues run in the family.

A retort forms on my tongue, but I think better of it and swallow it back down. Arguing with her never gets me anywhere except grounded for some bullshit reason.

Instead, I turn away from the window, stretching my legs out long in the backseat, scuffing my crusty Vans against the worn seats.

"What, Dad." I say tonelessly.

My mom just shakes her head.

My dad, Aidan MacKenna, unlike my mom, was raised in a very traditional Irish-Catholic household, where they always listened to and respected one another. My four uncles and two aunts are just as playful, charming, and upbeat as my dad. His temper is mild, his heart big, and his ears are always open.

How he and my mom ended up married is so beyond me.

He adjusts the mirror above him, his playful, alert green eyes meeting my own. I tell myself not to be a dick to him.

"I get that you're upset, Niamh. It's valid, my love. Just try to keep an open mind about it is what I'm saying. You get to start completely new here. You can remake yourself, if that's what you want. Do you know how rare of a chance that is?"

"I don't want to remake myself. I was happy back home." I bite out, tears threatening my eyes. Swallowing hard, I dissolve the instant lump in my throat until it scurries back to wherever it came from.

My mom laughs mirthlessly. "So happy that you decided to burn down school property?"

"Shawnie." My dad glances over at her. A gentle warning, because we still weren't discussing what happened, what I did.

They didn't even know what really happened. What I really did.
I swallow hard again, but this time, it isn't to chase away tears. It's to calm myself, compose myself, because they can never know what really happened.

Never.

My dad reaches back, squeezes my knee with his big, calloused hand. "I know you're hurting, Niamhy. But try to keep an open mind. Cape Summerhill is a beautiful, beautiful place. The surf is really good, and you get to go to my alma mater!"

"Yeah, cold East coast surf." I grumble out, crossing my arms tightly. Gone are my days of surfing in a bikini and being tan-year round from countless hours spent at the Saxon Beach pier with my friends. Makani, Booker, and Indie and I ran that fucking place. We'd earned our spot at the best wave in Saxon Beach.
None of which mattered anymore, because I didn't live there anymore.

"You have a 5/4, my love." He says in reference to the one hulking, thick wetsuit I owned for contests up North. A wetsuit with thick, thick neoprene and a hood, meant for the cold waters of Santa Cruz. Never for Saxon Beach.

"I don't even know anyone there." I retort.

Neither one of my parents reply.
I groan, leaning my forehead back against the window, fully prepared to pout my way into this new existence.

After another hour of uncomfortable silence and really scratchy, horrible radio, we cut off the main freeway, exiting slowly onto a causeway.

I peer out the window with vague interest. Saxon Beach is all palm trees, wide, open beaches, and gentrification. Like Venice Beach, but bigger. The causeway we're making our way across now is hard to make out in the thick, sideways rain that's been falling for the last few hours. But despite the quickly darkening sky, at the end of the bridge, I start to see what looks like hundreds, and I mean *hundreds* of acres of pine trees.

No town- just a million tall, dark trees.

"Is Summerhill in the forest?" I ask, my voice penetrating the silence that grew thicker than the fog outside.

My dad smiles at my sudden interest. Despite missing Ireland, he *loved* growing up here, always telling my siblings and I stories about the town that rested against the cold sea and the fog and the woods, separate from the rest of the world. The cape was a place, to him at least, that felt suspended from the rest of reality. Somewhere that felt all at once magical and alive, different from the rest of the world. A place where nature took rightful ownership of itself, he always said.

A town where the sea and the woods ruled over the people, not the other way around.

"Yes, my love. Remember what I told you? It's right in the middle of the woods. They built it that way on purpose, so that the forest borders the town on all four sides. The North Gate woods, the East Gate woods, the South Gate woods, and the West Gate woods. Cape Summerhill lies right in the center of them all."

I ponder this as the car slows, traffic halting us over the causeway. The rain seems to thicken, reaching a sort of torrential downpour. Briefly I wonder if the rain will bring the seawater up enough to be level with the bridge, causing us all to drown. Dismissing this thought, I wonder if Maine is one of those places that rains all the fucking time, a place where I'll always be cold. I *hate* the cold. Saxon Beach is warm year round: always sunny and seventy five ish, always pleasant. As a result, I detest the cold. Unlike my very, very Irish family, my skin tans easily, and my hair is a distinct shade of white-blonde, making me really easy to spot in family photos. A little brown, blonde, freckled creature amidst a sea of red headed, milky-skinned, elvish looking ones.

"Call your brother and sister before we get there, Niamh. Let them know we made it in one piece." My mom says without looking at me.

I pull my phone out of my backpack on the floor, shooting off a text to my brother and sister, Cian and Aine. Always getting the better end of the stick, such as being older than me, both Cian and Aine are in their mid twenties, living in Seattle and Santa Cruz, respectively.

Before I stash my phone away, I check my texts to my best friends- Makani Gonzalez, Booker Reyes, and Indie Via and I have been inseparable since kindergarten. We do everything together: surf every day before and after school, part-time jobs, and convince the others into doing stupid, impulsive shit. Generally wreaking havoc in the way that seventeen year olds do.

At least, we used to.

Except since we were a pack of four, people just called us "those fucking groms" or "the fucking rat pack" whenever we enacted one of our questionable, dumb dares. Never troublemakers- just "those four."

We dared each other to steal giant handles from the grocery store. We dared each other to graffiti every square inch of the Saxon Beach High School teacher parking lot. We dared each other to crash not one, but two of Makani's trucks while going offroading. We dared each other to chug hard teas until we chuked, and then showed up horribly, deliriously hungover to class on Monday. We dared each other to do things that we thought the other wouldn't dare try- and then proving each other wrong became the game. Our dares grew steadily more absurd, more public.

But we were a pack, and we never left each others' side.

Emphasis on *were* a pact.

We used to be inseparable. I thought we'd be friends close to forever. Indie and I talked about raising our *kids* together, for fucks sake. I had a ten-year pact with Makani: if one of us made it big in surfing, we'd just marry each other to reap the benefits, traveling the world together until we got too old. We wanted to surf. We wanted to have money. If one of us could achieve that, then both of us would, together.

Together, key word.

But now, all three text bubbles are green.

Message Not Delivered, my four texts to Makani read.

My heart contracts, squeezing my chest into a tight, tiny little crevice. I tell myself not to breathe, not to feel it too hard. I can't break down right now. Not in this car, not in front of my parents. I can't cry. I *won't* cry.

You're okay, Niamh, I tell myself. *You're okay. You're okay.*

My dad suddenly squeals- *squeals-* and points out the window as the car inches forward.

"Look! Look! We made it! Oh, hell, this is so nostalgic. I remember seeing the sign whenever we'd come back from a trip, and knowing I was home."

He smiles into the mirror, and my mom looks over and kisses his cheek.

"Happy to be home?" She smiles at him. He's silent, but I can tell by his voice that he missed it here. Maybe my colossal fuckup was just a really, really good excuse for him to move us back.

I follow his eyes in the mirror to where he's looking, and as we exit the causeway and onto a narrow, two-lane road that disappears into the towering trees, I see a giant, wooden sign.

Welcome to Cape Summerhill it reads, painted over the image of a lighthouse, pine trees, and patches of odd purple berries, framed by tiny white flowers.

Frowning, I pull out my phone again. A quick google search on Summerhill tells me they're elderberries. Growing wild on the cape, they're super rich in antioxidants and vitamins, good for boosting your immunity.

But it's the footnote underneath that catches my eye.

In Medieval times, elderberry was used as protection against witches.

The fuck?

I had a vague idea that Summerhill was slightly behind the times, being an island or whatever, combined with my Dad's thousand of magical, slightly creepy stories. But witches, really?

Kind of far-fetched, even for him.

I flick back up to the top of the article, where I see that the current population of Cape Summerhill is a whopping 1,200.

Jesus fucking *Christ.*

I lose service as we enter the woods proper, tall, ominous pine trees on either side of the highway, enveloping our car in darkness. All I can see out my window is that thick, bucketing rain, and a white fog that coats the air.

Groaning, I wonder what the fuck I'm in for.

Welcome to fucking Cape Summerhill, indeed.

CHAPTER TWO
TYLER

From the journal of Tyler Iris Lane
Friday, October 27th

Here's three truths about me, because I feel like writing it down.

I have secrets, I'm brash, and I'm exceptionally good at telling lies.

Three simple truths about myself, because these things always come in threes.

I'm secretive. A keeper of-

No, a hoarder of secrets. Like a dragon with treasure, I can be greedy, always wanting

more. Secrets are currency. I like knowing I always have things to hold over people's heads. And in

a town absolutely rotten with them, how could I not be greedy? I have so many things held tight

to my chest that I shouldn't know, and collecting them is addictive.

Magic is addictive, too, but I'll dive into that treasure chest later.

It's addictive, knowing things I shouldn't. Truly, it is. See, when people think you aren't paying attention, they let all sorts of things slip they wouldn't normally.
And I snatch them up happily.

I'm brash.
Not impudent or cocky, necessarily. There's a difference. They all think I'm harsh, just bordering on rude.
So I just let them. I really don't care what they think.
But it's one thing to be brash and arrogant and go around acting like you know everything. It's an entirely different story when you actually do know things that others don't. It's an entirely different story when you can hear people's innermost thoughts, see things happen before they unfold.
So maybe I am brash. Maybe I am arrogant.
But if I'm better than the rest of them, why would I pretend we're equal?

Fine. I might be a tad bit cocky. And harsh. And bitter.
I guess that does make me brash, damnit.
But at least I'm not dull.

A liar, however.
This one, I'm not proud of.
Which is unfortunate, because it's also the truest one out of all of them.

I wasn't always such a good liar. But I'm different. And being different in a town that hates anything they can't explain forced me to adapt.

It's a bit sad, if you think about it. I was born here. Generations of women in my family were born here, resided here. A few of them died here, too.

So I'm not leaving. They can't kick me out.

My grandmother says they're just jealous, that they wish they were like me.

But grandmother's are required to make you feel better.

So it's sad, sure. They all hate me and hate my grandmother, solely because we can do things that they cannot.

Solely because they are ordinary, and we are not.

Here's three more simple truths, because like I said, these sort of things always come in threes.

1.) I was born Tyler Iris Lane.

2.) I've been told I take after my mother. Her bigger-than-average, deeply sapphire eyes, her milky skin, her thick mane of brown hair. Her sharp features- the angle of her cheekbones, the slope of her nose. On her, these were called graceful. On me, they're called lanky. Impish. Like a baby colt where my mother was some sort of beautiful mare. Constellations of freckles invade my face, warring for space with the tiny crescent scars that line my jaw.

Mischievous, see?

3.) *I can hear and see things others cannot.*

I can make things move if I tell them to.

I can whisper things into the earth, and make them do my bidding.

I can make people stumble, and I can make them fall.

I can do all of these things, because all Lane women are born with gifts. All Lane women are born with something extra embedded in their veins, as sure as the blood that runs and the thoughts that whir and spin. On the outside, Lane women appear exceptionally average, just like everyone else. But on the inside...

Something equally bright and equally powerful rests in the space where their hearts should be.

Gifts. Magic. Witchcraft. Whatever they're deciding to call it today.

But don't trust what I say. I'm just a secretive, brash little liar, after all.

CHAPTER THREE

NIAMH

Bright and early- and I mean seven in the morning, rooster crowing kind of

early- my dad decides this is just the absolute *most perfect time* for us to head into

town, to *get our bearings.* He says it just like that, too, because he's genuinely excited.

He's big on positivity.

I wish I could say the same.

We've been here all of one night. Just getting to the new house last night was a

blur in itself. By the time we had entered the town proper, it was so dark I couldn't

even tell what direction we were going. I must had fallen asleep at some point,

because I woke up this morning on a deep-set, dusty blue couch, with zero

recollection of getting inside.

I can hear my dad bustling around somewhere in the direction of the kitchen, just based on his horribly off-tune humming of some punk song. Blink, if I had to guess. He really likes to relive his teenage years.

I sit up, scratching sleep crusts out of my eyes. My dad is *the* original morning person: it literally can't be past seven thirty, and yet all the windows are open, and I can hear him brewing coffee as he continues to sing. Back home, he used to have coffee ready by the time I got back from surfing, every morning without fail.

Shoving away thoughts of back home, I sit up, pushing my scratchy, still salt-crusted hair out of my face.

The room I'm in seems to have a nautical theme to it- all navy blues and creams, stripes and anchors. The couch I'm on is covered in about ninety throw pillows, all decorated with tiny anchors and lobsters. The walls of our new home are a deep brown, dark wood almost like a cabin. It's cozy and dark, like a writer's retreat, not a family home. Like the kind of cabin that people pay good money for to rent out as an Airbnb, marketed as "Isolating Getaway In The Forests Of Maine!"

Even though I've been determined to hate it because it isn't Saxon Beach, I can feel myself actually kind of liking it now that I'm looking around. It's obvious that watermen or women lived here, just based on the decor alone: all pirate ships, lobsters, bass and anchors. It's cool, actually. Very different from our modern, airy apartment back home: all white everything, open windows, huge balcony overlooking the Saxon Beach pier.

I remember my dad saying that the house came fully furnished, the old owners leaving all their stuff behind. They were the lighthouse keepers back in the day, I guess. Even though the sole lighthouse on Summerhill has long been out of service, according to my dad. It's clear who lived here though. There's no photos on the walls at all. Just paintings of pirate ships amongst choppy seas. Stormy tempests, mermaids.

It's kind of fucking sick.

This house is nothing like my real home, though. The thought alone brings my anger back to the surface. This is *nothing* like Saxon Beach, and it never will be. Back home, we lived within walking distance to the pier. I could walk to the beach. I never had to drive anywhere to go surfing. Saxon Beach is like seventy five degrees year round, and our apartment was all natural lighting, whites and yellows all around. Sunny. Open. And as cool as it is, this new place is *nothing* like home. It's dusty and dark and reclusive, logs and dark wood, fucking pirate ships and lighthouses.

And, I think obstinately, to top it all off, this place smells like fucking salt. Like brine and moldy wood.

"Dad!"

I slide off the couch, still in the same clothes as the last three days. Jesus Christ. I should change.

My dad waltzes into the living room, his pale, freckly arms absolutely drowning in an oversize fisherman's sweater. The deep blue of it makes his green eyes and his sandy red hair pop, and I tell him so.

He just beams at me, and seeing him so happy kind of holds the bitter edge of anger and hate off my chest for a minute. He's genuinely so happy to be back home. He really missed Cape Summerhill.

"Thank you, my love. Alright. Dress warm, we're leaving in five. I want to take you guys to this little cafe in town. It's where I would spend all my time writing as a teenager!"

He wanders off, permanently chipper, wondering aloud that hopefully said favorite cafe is still around. I nearly retort about how in a town this small, nothing probably ever closes or goes out of business.

But he's so damn *happy* that I force myself swallow it back down. I can't ruin his entire day. I just can't.

I already put him through enough.

Thirty minutes later, after a very long, very needed shower, I'm once again stuffed into the back of our faded blue Subaru outback that we've had since I was born, feeling suffocated. I've spent enough time in this car over the last three days to last me a lifetime, which I joyfully tell my parents.

Not surprisingly, I'm met with silence from both of them.

I try to contain my irritation at the weather. Another day promising rain, and already covered in thick, heavy fog again. The entire forest around us, as far as I can see, is bathed in hues of gray. Our house sits in a pool of fog, the tall, ominous pine trees behind it barely poking out the top. Gray sky, gray ground.
It's like a ghost world.

My dad was right about one thing, though: nature really does seem to take back its rightful place here. I didn't realize it last night in the dark, but now I can see that our new home sits just at the edge of the treeline where the woods start, miles and miles of woods just behind it. It's a little ominous, if I'm being honest. I've never been surrounded by this many trees before. I've never been in a forest, period. Saxon Beach is flat.

My dad's childhood stories of Summerhill play on a loop in my head as we pull out of the misty driveway. Stories of Summerhill's cold, churning sea, of its sheer cliffs that kids liked to jump off of, of its wide, dark miles of forest. A place that reminded him of Ireland, a little corner of the world that reminded him of another: a place so rooted in the outdoors and the unknown. For him and my grandparents, living in Summerhill made it easy to forget other places existed. So rooted was it in urban legends and ghost stories that it almost felt like a magical sort of place.

All small towns have their stories, but one in particular begins to wind through my head, the details turning themselves over and over in my mind easily. As if I could forget something so colossally *odd.*

It was a story saved for the rare rainy nights in Saxon Beach, the nights where Cian, Aine and I would curl up under blankets and very intricate pillow forts, begging dad for a ghost story, to which he'd happily oblige. He is an author, after all. He's the best at it.

According to my dad, Summerhill was built in the center of the forest by its founder, Thomas Summers, back in 1664. He arrived with a pair of seven year old twin daughters in tow, cute little blonde things named Abigail and Catherine. They built the town at the heart of the woods, and it was as tedious a process as you can imagine, and children were meant to be seen and not heard. As a result, Abigail and Catherine Summers were shooed away, mostly allowed to roam free nearby, so long as they came home by sunset. So they spent hours out in the woods, never too far from their settlement. Two seven year olds and a vast, uninhabited forest: their possibilities were endless. They played make-believe, inventing stories and epic adventures for the two of themselves, and dutifully arrived home every night, usually covered in dirt and mud.

My dad always liked to accentuate that part by saying they looked exactly like us three when we hadn't taken a bath in a while.

But the part that always raised the hair on my arms and made Cian hide his face in the blankets was this.

One day, my dad said, in the dead of June, Catherine Summers came home alone, bearing very obvious signs of shock.

When Thomas Summers asked his daughter where Abigail was, she became completely hysterical and upset, utterly inconsolable. She claimed that they had been playing in the woods, like usual. But this time, they'd gone a little farther.

And they'd found, she said, a large gate.

A towering, iron gate, standing alone in the center of the trees.

For someone so distraught, she described it in great detail: she claimed it was bigger than a house, and iron. Both parts of it stood wide open, and seemed to be facing South.

Oddly enough, and impossibly enough, she told her father that it had not been attached to a single thing but the forest floor.

Almost as if it had grown up from the ground itself.

Catherine told her father that she was unnerved by their discovery. It stood taller than a house, she said. It wasn't attached to anything.

And it disturbed her how it had just.... appeared without either of the girls noticing.

It was disturbing, and quite frankly, it scared her.

But not Abigail.

Abigail, she said, had been mesmerized by the giant gate. She had looked at it with awe, with excitement. Despite her protests, she said, Abigail refused to just leave.

So mesmerized was her twin, Catherine said, that she decided to walk through the gate.

Shaking myself from memory, I twist against my seat belt buckle, the hair on the back of my neck raising as I recall the next part.

After Abigail Summers ran through the gate,

She didn't come out the other side.

She was just.. gone.

Thomas Summers and the other founders of the town questioned Catherine repeatedly, conducted searches of the wilderness that surrounded them, and prayed rigorously, all while the poor seven year old just grew more and more hysterical. She kept repeating the same story over and over, and no matter who questioned her, it remained the same:

Her twin walked through the gate, and she did not come out the other side. She just vanished.

It was as if she'd just been plucked from existence.

She also said, through all her days of tears and all her grief, that it hadn't smelled right by the gate. That the closer they had gotten to it, the more rancid the air had grown.

My dad would use a low, scratchy voice for this part, mimicking some evil spirit. Cian usually slept with Aine or I after this story.

Catherine Summers described it as rotten, in that part of the woods. Rancid, and vile. Like the very air was dead.
Dead air, she'd called it. Because wherever that gate went, wherever it came from, it had made everything around it smell old. Old like the bodies they buried whenever someone in the settlement took ill.

The thing that had taken her sister felt old, she said.

A gate to nowhere, surrounded by dead air.

The Summers family ended up leaving their town-in-progress, giving it away to another family they'd arrived with.

They named it Summerhill, in honor of Thomas's lost child.

Once they'd finally explored most of the wilderness that surrounded them, they named each part of the forest around the town properly:

Naming each section after the fabled gate that had supposedly claimed Abigail's life.

The northern sect of the woods became the North Gate woods.

The east became the East Gate woods.

The western became the West Gate woods,

And then the South Gate woods.

The South Gate woods, where, according to legend, there existed a gate somewhere deep inside.

A gate that stood taller than a house,

Was made of strong, thick iron,

Grew up from the very dirt,

And stood wide, wide open.

A gate that appeared and ate a little girl.

As we meander down the tiny, two-lane highway bordered by towering pines and elms, I stare out at the woods bordering our new house. Images of a giant gate and identical twin girls run rampant through my mind.

Ghost stories, that's all. My dad might be a writer and fantastic storyteller at that, but he tries not to carry my grandparent's Irish superstitions or fears around with him. He's very, very rooted in reality, unless he's writing.

My Gran and Granda, however, brought everything from Ireland to the states with them. Every time I see them, it surprises me how little they've let this country change them. I've never heard their take on living in Summerhill, but I'll bet every cent of my college funds that if they heard my dad's story, they would find a way to rope the fae or unkempt spirits somewhere into it.

For once, I'm silent as we drive, and not from anger or unfairness. No, I'm full of thoughts as we cut through the fog to get to town.

Thoughts about the woods.

It's funny, because I've read my fair share of Slenderman stories. I've seen The Blair Witch Project hundreds of times.

But I've never actually *been* in the woods before.

And I'm seventeen- I'm way too old to believe in any of that shit anyways.

But staring out at the treeline right now as we zip by, with the fog and the impending rain darkening the sky...

I can't help but wonder if there's any truth to my dad's story.

I don't know how else to explain the feeling of being watched from all sides.

CHAPTER FOUR

NIAMH

The smell of fresh fish, brine, and the ocean carrying through the open air assault my senses headily the second I open the door.

It's much, much different from back home, where being by the ocean came with the smell of fast food and heavy layers of sunscreen. Saxon Beach has a boardwalk littered with tourist traps. But here, in Summerhill, it smells natural, like the ocean took the land back in its watery hands where it belongs.

Along with the smell comes the cold. I'm instantly grateful that I threw a giant, oversized green knit sweater on and my favorite black beanie. Running my fingers through my long, still-wet curls, I join my parents huddled in front of the car.

My mom turns to me.

"The coffee shop your dad wants to go to is down the street if you want to head over there. We're going to say hi to some old friends first."

Taking that as my cue to get lost, along with the fact that I really have no desire to be around her or here at all, I head off in the direction she pointed to, a five dollar bill stuffed deep in my pocket.

For about ten seconds, I question why my parents are letting me roam totally free in a town that I've never once stepped foot in.

But the more I walk in the direction she pointed to, I quickly realize why.

The fog refuses to let up, but I can at least see five feet in front of me now. And holy shit, it's like stepping back in time.

On either side of me, tall, peeling wooden buildings line the sides of the street. All clapboard, run-down buildings painted in dark browns, creams and blues, all in various phases of deterioration, like the strips of wood were no match for the brutal sea air.

I pass a *Dave's Finest Breads,* a tiny deli-liquor store combo, *North Gate Surf Shop, Al's Rare Books,* a laundromat, some new-age crystal store, *East Cliff Bait & Tackle,* and *Torah Shapes* before dead-ending a dock.

The harbor. Which means somehow, in my barely five minute walk, I missed the coffee shop. Nice, Niamh.

Completely alone, I stare out at the hundreds of skiffs and sailboats that line the dock's weathered, barnacled beams, and it finally sinks in.

This is my home now. This gray, foggy, tiny fishing town that has no idea I exist. This tiny little cape in the sea that contains: no friends. No pier surf break. No stupid dares with said friends. No comfort, no home. And no sunlight, apparently, either.

You know, my mind whispers rudely out of nowhere as I sulk, watching a pretty blue sailboat flap in the briny breeze. *You can be as angry or defiant as you want, but it won't get you back to Saxon Beach.*

I give my inner voice the finger, but it's right.

Being a pouty, obnoxious little shit won't get me home.

It won't make Makani, Booker, or Indie speak to me again.

It won't undo what I did.

The thing I did, the one that I can never, ever tell anyone.

The reason I put up with this move with little to no fight was because it was a complete and total scapegoat for me.

I swallow hard, rubbing a hand on the back of my neck. My hair is so thick and so curly-wavy that it's still wet, and I'm fucking cold.

I must have passed the coffee shop, that's all. I go to turn around, walking off the dock when movement to my right catches my eye. A crash of laughter accompanying it tears me away from any thoughts of caffeine, snapping me immediately to attention.

Running at a full sprint down the street towards me are two teenagers. Both of them carry a thick, hulking surfboard under their arms, and wear a thick, hooded wetsuit and booties. As they get closer, I can see that both of their boards are nearly ten feet long, single fins. One of them is glassed in a vibrant, iridescent shade of turquoise, the other a bright and cheery sunshine-yellow.

As they get closer, I realize they're twins.

They reach the end of the street, and the taller one, a boy, throws a half-assed glance both ways before darting towards the dock where I'm standing. His twin sister trails him on much shorter legs.
I don't have time to move out of the way or pretend I wasn't watching, so when they inevitably see me, I just freeze.
They stop, conversation halted. My first Summerhill natives, and ones that look my age at that.

The guy is at *least* six two, seriously, and built like a beanpole, and carrying the beautiful bright yellow board. Immediately I can tell he's one of those guys that can eat whatever they want without gaining an ounce of weight. His thick, gingery-blonde hair curls in perfect springs and coils all over his head, just skimming past his shoulders. His freckled, smiling face is deeply tanned, matching the exact shade of his hands.

A tiny smile ghosts my face as I note that his nails are painted blue, just like his sister's beautiful longboard, along with three blue rings accenting his fingers. His sister is clad in the same thick, hooded wetsuit, but her chin only reaches his shoulders. She's thin and dainty, but holds herself with a fierce confidence that I instantly am drawn to. Freckles dot her face just like her brothers, her hair that same shade of tawny auburn, like cinnamon and nutmeg and spiced tea, but hers falls in thick waves halfway down her back. She carries a board equally as thick and beautiful as her brother's, a swirling, bright turquoise. I wonder how the fuck she's holding it.

She can't be more than a hundred pounds, and that thing is built like a kayak. Built for easy paddling and smooth, sweeping turns. Built for grace and style.

I sigh internally, because I have neither. I shortboard. My boards are all as thin as a potato chip, thruster set ups, and meant for aggressive, sharp cutbacks, built for power and drive. I can't longboard for shit.

They stop, and I kick myself internally for just staring like a fucking idiot. *Act normal, Niamh, for fucks sake!*

"Sup." Is what ends up coming out my mouth, along with a halfhearted wave. Nice, Niamh. Nice.

But the boy looks at me, straightens, and smiles back: a smile so bright and so genuine, reaching the very corners of his eyes, that I feel myself relax without trying. It sets his entire face alight, warm and joyful and without hesitation.
He exudes charm and warmth with that lightbulb smile without seeming to try at all. And as I smile back at him, offering a hesitant, much smaller version of his own, it's impossible not to notice that his board matches the hue of his eyes exactly.

A bright, sparkling gold. Warm, like a hearth. Like the sun.

He smiles down at me, his perfect, charming smile, those eyes and that board a direct contrast to the weather.

"Damn. I thought we were the only ones who got up this early."

His voice is as bubbly as his smile, upbeat and light. He's so…. Chipper.

Okay, Niamh. Just be yourself. Don't be fucking weird.

"I just moved here yesterday. I'm getting my bearings." I say, echoing my dad's words from this morning. "I'm Niamh," I add hastily, fumbling with my sweater sleeves that hang past my fingertips.

He smiles bigger, and his sister finally does too, though hers doesn't reach her eyes like her brother's do. With a pang, I'm reminded of Makani and Indie. Indie was always the first to dive headfirst into any idea Booker or I threw at the group. Mak, on the other hand, usually ended up being the voice of reason, saving us from doing something stupid, even for us four.

My thoughts are interrupted when he speaks again.

"Kneeeeeeeeee-v." He sounds it out, stretching my name out long. "How do you spell that?"

"N-I-A-M-H. We're Irish." I say with a grin. Trying to tell people how to say or spell my name growing up was a giant pain in my ass. My dad could have picked something normal for my siblings and I, like Sean. Or Shannon. Bridget. Fucking Mary. But my granda was apparently a big stickler for tradition, so my big brother got Cian, my big sister got Aine, and I got roped with Niamh.

"Zeke Torah. This is my extremely talkative and welcoming twin, Marlo."

Marlo rolls her eyes at her brother and hefts her board up higher on her hip. "Um, I'm sorry. Not all of us can function without caffeine at the ass crack of dawn like some people."

She looks at me head on. "He's very chipper."

Zeke smiles again. "Professionally chipper. Where'd you move from?"

"Saxon Beach, California." My heart pangs in my chest.

Marlo looks up, scrunching her brows. "Is that in LA?"

"Kind of. Closer to Manhattan Beach."

"What grade are you in?" Zeke asks me. The wind starts to kick up as we talk, blowing my wet curls across my cheeks. Marlo's attention strays from the conversation, her eyes darting from us to the water every few seconds.

When I tell Zeke I'm a senior, he nods like he gets it.

"That sucks so bad you had to move during your senior year. Summerhill is such a small freaking town. But you'll get to know people quickly, so don't trip. Plus you're in our grade, and we're fun. The most fun, actually."

At this, Marlo just snorts, staring off into the water like her mind isn't quite there. I smile genuinely. He's just like Indie: a cheeky little fucker.

I mean, I get it. He's got that blonde-tipped hair that most surfers get from daily sun exposure. He's tan, he's got freckles. He's got a great smile. He has every reason to be cheeky.

He's cute, too. I catch myself thinking absentmindedly. Cute in the way all the guys back home are cute: physically, they're all tan and muscular and wear string bracelets and have no sense of style other than fading, old t-shirts.
But all the guys in Saxon Beach are one and the same on the inside: full of sun and salt and beer, loud and cocky, most of them battling what will end up turning into lifelong struggles with prescription pills. All less charming than they think they really are, but talented enough in the water that no one cares.
All one and the same.

Zeke's still talking.

"..... And it's actually really fun if you don't have a first period class because then you can just surf before and show up when everyone else has already been in class for an hour. But you'll get the hang of it. We'll see you around, yeah? If you need a tour or anything let me know. It's tiny here, but it's actually fun. Do you surf?"

Marlo snorts again. "Just because she's from California and blonde doesn't automatically mean she surfs, dude."

I'm loving this. I might be far as fuck from everything I hold near and dear, my life completely new and unknown, but Zeke and Marlo Torah have just become my beacon of shiny hope.

Hopefully there's shortboardable waves somewhere on this cape.

I'm about to tell them both that of course I surf when Marlo starts bouncing on the balls of her feet and glancing down the harbor impatiently.

"Dude. Wind." She says. Zeke smiles apologetically.

"Sorry. We're gonna miss our window for waves. We'll look for you Monday?"

Marlo waves at me and takes off. I nod at Zeke, my smile still glued to my face. He shoulders his big yellow board and takes off sprinting after Marlo, yelling over his shoulder,

"CheeEEEEeeHOOOoooo see ya Niamh!"

They sprint down the harbor, going fast considering how big those boards are. Once they reach the forest to the left, a giant hill coated in pine trees, they don't stop. They head right inside.

I wonder where the fuck the surf is, as all I can see from the dock is the hill, and miles upon miles of of woods. Maybe it ends in a cliff? Maybe that's where the break is?

Something tells me that surfing in Summerhill, Maine is going to be very, very different from Saxon Beach, and not just because of the temperature difference.

I watch them walk into the treeline until the bright yellow and blue of their boards disappear into the trees, then I turn and head back for town.

Between Marlo's confident, sarcastic attitude and Zeke's bubbly and easy way of conversing, I'm left in the best mood I've been in since the principal of Saxon Beach High School caught me lighting a goddamn building on fire.

CHAPTER FIVE

TYLER

It isn't that hard once you do it a couple times.

Magic is meant to look simple. It lures you in like that: a few handfuls of dried herbs here, a pinch of salt there, weave it all together with a spool of ribbon and some rhyming words.

To an idiot, it seems easy. Like just anyone could do it.

But real magic isn't like that.

Real magic is innate, something you're either born with or you aren't. And it's *strong.* It's consuming.

I toss my battered, dog-eared journal to the ground, instead focusing all my attention to my senses. For this late in the season, I'm mildly surprised it isn't freezing yet. The temperature is probably hovering somewhere around sixty.

I soak it all up, feeling the winter sun, or lack thereof on my face.

My bare feet, digging into the rotted wood of the park bench I'm laid out on. My back digging into that same wood.

The smooth, loose cotton skirt against my smooth, thin legs, just brushing the tops of my cold toes.

The breeze rustling my long, dark hair, carrying the smell of the sea, of brine, of salt and earth, and of pine.

I soak all of this in, and then I allow it to consume me.

I force my mind to go blank, only filled with the world around me. The smell, the taste, the feel. The flavor of a Summerhill afternoon in the dim winter light.

I wait until the sounds of people walking the path behind me, of children tossing a frisbee, and of the distant, powerful crashing of the waves down at North Gate beach to dull.

I wait until these all fade away completely, until all I can hear from every angle in my head is a dull, light buzzing. It reverberates deep in the back of my head, behind my eyes, in my chest.

Dissolving the world around me used to take ages.

It took a lot of strenuous, tedious practice to make it happen this quickly.

When a searing, burning heat lights in my chest, I open my eyes.

The lively, cold gray afternoon around me is gone.

Everything in the park is gone.

Even the miles upon miles of trees in the North Gate woods are gone.

Everything around me is gray and hazy, like I'm looking through a thick fog. Not like the fog that usually consumes this town- this fog is alive, brimming with magic, with things people can't normally know.
This fog is full of answers.

I'm completely alone in this liminal, in-between world. I have maybe two minutes before I'll lose my energy. Two minutes to use this carefully built playing ground.

Quickly and deliberately I drop to my knees, placing palms on the gray ground. Or ceiling. It all looks the same.

With a heavy, choking exhale, I push all the energy, that searing heat from my chest down and into my hands, willing myself to *see*.

I haven't done any magic in a few days. I've been exhausted, mentally drained from all the requests and visits this time of year usually brings. Around Halloween, when my grandmother and I celebrate Samhain, the town usually remembers that we exist again. That's when they come begging for our help. Whether it's others my age wanting to do some stupid things for the holiday, like begging me to conduct a seance or craft a ouija board for them, or people coming to us for a genuine reason: a sickness, a fight with a partner, mental turmoil that can't be cured, they're all the same.

They treat us like worms until they want something. Until they need us.

Nobody wants the help of a *witch* until they have no other options, apparently.

The vision comes slowly. This is the hardest part: the waiting.

It's always a slow build, and always so utterly, horribly seductive.

Real magic likes to see how far it can push you. How much you can take.

I breathe it all in, a stupid, sleepy grin invading my face, and will the vision to come.

"I Will It So. I Will It So." I whisper under my breath. Three times in succession, because magic loves to work in threes.

I breathe deep once, twice.

A third time.

Then, without any warning, my head is yanked back by an unseen force, and not at all gently.

My closed eyes are ripped open by an unseen wind.

And then it all comes at once, the magic buildingbuildingbuilding in a heavy, buzzing wave. My chest feels like it may burst. It rises in my stomach, building in the back of my throat, I want to open my mouth, to moan. It's that good.

But I force myself to clench my jaw shut, trapping the energy inside.

It works. Delicious, tantalizing heat, thick and real trickles down the back of my neck like oil, causing the hair on my arms to rise and my stomach muscles to tighten. That warmth spills down my neck, then my sides, then my hips. Like candle wax, or oil, or warm water, it pours over me, then starts to pool somewhere in the middle.

The magic slides its smooth, oily hands between my legs.

This is the hardest part, and why no average person can ever achieve real results when attempting to learn the craft.

Magic is too strong for the average human. It's dangerous for this very reason. It tries to seduce you.

And it's a very cunning, clever lover. It knows exactly how to make you feel, exactly where to touch you and where to leave its mark so that *you* will bend to its will, and not the other way around.

Conjurers aplenty have succumbed to it.

But I am not the average person.

I'm a Lane.

I withstand it, gritting my teeth, my body tight and awake and alive.

I fight it, and then I'm rewarded when a feeling I can only describe as a roller coaster drop consumes me, bringing with it a vision.

It used to be so hard to even get to *this* point. The first few times I attempted scrying, the magic coursing through my body was so strong and so potent that it took all of my willpower not to open my eyes, discard the oncoming vision, and moan. I'm being serious. Magic feels *delicious.*

Nobody prepared me for that one. I had to figure it out on my own, and then figure out some more by hunting for my mother's old journals. Not once did my grandmother ever mention the quick rush of heat that slides down your limbs when trying to cast, how it trickles down the small of your back and neck. Not once did she tell me how it makes your skin sweaty and flushed, your pulse race, and that place deep in your lower stomach tighten.

She most *definitely* did not tell me that magic can do all the things you do to yourself: but much, *much* better.

Magic can make even the strongest crumble. It's designed that way, designed to ensnare by seducing you thoroughly, by whispering things into your ears, pressing soft lips against your neck.

Reminding you that it is *always* in control.

And nobody told me how good that feels. Magic is a lover, and a good one at that.

Not that I'd know the difference. Being a witch in a town full of ignorant, backwards idiots doesn't exactly have people lining up at my door.
Whatever.

If you can't control it, you'll never get anywhere. It's too temptatious. According to my grandmother, more Lane women than we know of have succumbed to it, and been lost, their magic and minds along with it.

My mother being one of them.

But I'm not as stupid as she was. And, just days away from being eighteen, I'm way stronger than my grandmother. She barely does more than the odd charm here and there anymore. She isn't interested in big spells.

I'm the one really utilizing my gifts. I'm the one with potential, now.

The vision explodes behind my eyes like stardust.

At first, I see the same exact scene I've been seeing for a little over a year now. Every time I attempt to See, it's always the same. And like all the times before, I still have no fucking idea what it means.

A figure, a person, being chased by a mob into the woods. And the mob is beyond angry: they're *furious*. I can taste their need for bloodshed like wine on my tongue. It's that strong. Their wrath and their hate burns so sharply that I wonder, again, why they're chasing this person into the trees.

What did they *do?*

The trees overtake and swallow both the runner and mob.

This goddamn vision, the same one, for a year now. I'm no closer to knowing what it means, and it's just pissing me off more and more. I can't even tell if it's a vision from the past or the future, or just some symbolic, magical bullshit.

My own anger replaces their hate burning in my chest. I'm pissed off. I'm strong, and I work with my gifts daily, flexing them like a muscle. I'm strong, and I just grow stronger.

So why the *fuck* am I still seeing this?

My chest glows hot, my magic building again.

And then,

for the first time in over a year,

the scene changes.

The woods and the mob evaporate, and in their place is a girl.

A tall, tan girl, built like an athlete. I can smell the salt on her skin, taste the ocean on the strands of her white-blonde hair. She smells of clean sheets, the brine on the breeze, and the last sips of the sunset. Bright, fiery orange, deep, burning reds and yellows.

A girl from the sea. And a very, very angry one, at that.

Unfairness, grief, and sadness billow around her like smoke.

She's missing something.

Her scent changes to something tangy, replacing the ocean with something that makes my mouth water back in my physical body.

A secret.

She's hiding something, something big.

Something that reeks of magic.

Well, well, well.

Back in my physical body, my smile starts to stretch, and stretch, my eyes still shut

tightly.

But then she's gone, and I see

Fire.

Everywhere. Great pine trees up in flames.

And then,

An enormous iron gate, standing alone amidst the trees.

I see darkness, spreading through the woods like wildfire, the trees

disappearing anywhere that blackness touches.

Faces and hands materialize in the trunks of the trees, and laughter ripples

through the spaces between. It isn't kind.

And then again, the girl. Flames engulf her completely, and then she's gone.

In her place is that ominous, gigantic iron gate.

Then it's gone, and I see the girl walk into the woods,

and not come back out.

I smell *burning.*

I see the air still around the trees, as if someone pressed pause on time.

The air stills,

Deadairirdeadairdeadair

The breeze stopping,
the oxygen itself halting.

The trees.
With a jolt back in my body, I recognize them. Those are *my* trees. That's the South Gate woods.

This vision is in *Summerhill.*
This happens, or happened, in Summerhill.

Laughter ripples through the space I'm in- the same laughter in my vision.
You can't be harmed in the in-between, but still, I keep my hands flat to the ground just in case.

Shadows squirm along the forest floor, and then,

A deeply sweet, smooth,

Old voice,

A voice that is both old and cunning, but smooth and round as a stone

slinks

through the South Gate woods.

Something older than time itself, older than the darkness between the trees,

laughs

And for the first time ever, my physical body flinches.

With a snap, a lightning strike, a burst of raw, untethered energy,

it fades.

With a groan, I'm thrown back into the physical world. The euphoric, sensual rush of magic exits my body, quickly replaced with exhaustion. My head is absolutely searing with pain, which I know will fade within minutes. It always does.

Sweat runs down my cheeks despite the chill, and I stand on shaking jelly legs.

What the *fuck* was that?

I've been scrying since I first came into my gifts, and usually they come true. At the very least, they provide insight to things that come to pass, or things that once had. But today was different. Today was a new one. I haven't seen anything new in a year.

My grandmother, Eleni Lane, tells me every single time I complain about this that my mind is just blocked. That whatever the vision is doesn't want me to see at the moment, and that it'll come when it's ready.

I sit up on the bench, watching the people of Summerhill go about their lives around me. A few of them catch my watching, intense gaze, and hurry away. Stupid fucks.

I hate them all.

I rub my sweaty, pallid face with shaky hands, pushing sweaty strands of hair out of my face. My stomach growls.

I feel used. Battered.

Magic has a cost.

Once I feel I can stand, I follow the path into the trees, back into the South Gate woods towards home, thoughts of the blonde girl finding their way into every nook and cranny of my already-crowded mind.

Chapter Six

Niamh

Something about the thick, impenetrable fog makes me feel like I'm in a ghost world.

I tug my beanie farther over my ears and sigh dramatically, half-hoping my mom hears. We've been wandering around town for nearly three hours. Three. Hours.

We toured my new high school. We ran into a bunch of my dad's old buddies, who clapped him on the back and told him how much they loved his latest book. Said friends then insisted on taking us out for brunch, which is why I'm currently squished into a faded, dimly-lit booth at *Cape Cafe by the Bay,* pushing a mug of cold coffee around while my parents socialize.

All while the rain is finally pouring down relentlessly, bringing the mist off the harbor in stronger, saltier. Even though we're inside the coffee shop, I swear it still clings to my hair and my skin like alcohol when you're hungover.

When my dad orders a third cup of coffee, signaling that his social batteries are still going strong, I decide that there's only so much small town I can take for one day.

Our drive into town only took five minutes. Walking home shouldn't be much longer. Even though it's raining, even though I don't know my way around, I scoot out of the booth and tell everyone that I'm walking home. To my shock, my parents say okay and go back to their brunch.

Right as I open the door, my dad calls after me.

"Niamhy! Stick to the treeline, okay? There's a path that cuts through the East Gate straight to the house."

My dad's friends all laugh and call him anxious, and I leave.

And sure as shit, a path is exactly where I find myself twenty minutes later. A very muddy, worn footpath, exactly where he said it would be, starting at the treeline of the East Gate woods and heading deep within.

As the town of Summerhill fades behind me, taking with it the smell of freshly baked bread, fish, and hot coffee, I head into the darkness of the East Gate woods, following the path perfectly.

There's no signs, nothing to mark that I'm going the right way, other than the well-worn dirt path. I wonder who made it, and who walks it every day. As I pass through clusters of towering pines, bunched so close together that it forces me to stay

SUMMERHILL

on the path, the thick branches finally eat away the last of the rain-swollen sky,

swallowing me in darkness.

I'm totally, completely alone.

I can't hear a single thing but my own breath. The rain stills as the trees

swallow the last of the sky, and there's no animals, no chittering insects. I'm the only

sound on the path.

Unease begins to creep into my stomach. I've never been afraid of the dark. I was

never the kid that asked my dad to check under my bed or in my closet. Even with my

gran and granda's stories of the fae that snatch children away from their beds, or the

shifting, spindly beings that roam in the spaces between our world and another, I've

never been afraid.

Until right now.

An oily, slick feeling coats my throat and stomach. Fear.

The trees seem to close in on me, and the feeling starts to climb up the back of my

throat. My heart starts to slam against my ribs, and I look around at the trees, feeling

once again like I'm being watched. No, watched isn't the right word.

It's like I'm being assessed.

I force myself to swallow hard, as I always do when trying to tamp down

uncomfortable feelings. As if swallowing the rising fear will make it just go away.

I take a deep, steadying breath and pull my old ass wire earbuds out of my pants

pocket. Shoving them deep into my ears and pulling my beanie tight over them, I

68

quickly adjust the volume and cue something loud, something horribly twangy and acoustic to distract me.

A Hot Mulligan song comes on, and I relax a bit. Tades Sanville's twanging voice crying about a girl is currently louder than the erratic beating of my heart, and I welcome it.

I walk faster, ignoring the innate urge to run.

I'm humming the words to Deluxe Capacitor when I see it.

Just standing there at the end of the pathway, cropping up out of nowhere. A head-high, soaked wooden sign.

So faded and so withering that the words it bears are almost unreadable at first glance. I stop without meaning to, my ridiculous, cowardly heart thumping in my ears.

In what looks like hand painted, crude lettering, I can just barely make out the words *South Gate* scribbled on the plank of wood.

South Gate. Like the stretch of woods.

I recall everything my dad told me in all his many, many stories. The South Gate woods are the section most locals avoid. There's not even any houses built nearby. They're wholly uninhabited.

They're also the section of woods that, according to urban legend, are where the fabled gate shows up.

The gate that stole a girl from existence all those hundreds of years ago.

My eyes widen, my pulse a mere hummingbird's wings.

How the *fuck* did I end up in the South Gate woods? I left town in the exact direction we came from: East. In theory, I should've cut directly through the East Gate woods and dead ended at our house.

There is no way in fuck I could've veered this far off course. I've been on the path the whole time. I've been on the path. I have. Haven't I?

Setting my growing unease aside, I step closer and run my finger down the withering wood. The writing is crude and sloppy like a toddler did it. I'm properly mesmerized. This feels like something right out of a movie.

If Booker and Indie and Mak were here, we'd be daring the others to steal the sign and run.

My finger freezes on the letter S, and I realize what I'm doing. I quickly retract my hand with a small gasp. Like a kid who touched the stove when they know it's going to burn you.

For a millisecond, I almost expect something to happen. Something horrible or impossible, like a demon or a faerie materializing from a nearby tree and snatching me.

Almost.

"Fucking hell, Niamh. *Relax.*" I say aloud, pulling my earbuds out. My voice penetrates the heavy, thick silence that I'm in once more.

I look around me. Nothing but trees. It's wet, and dark, starting to get misty, and I really want to get the fuck home. My dad would definitely be worried if I went missing. My mom would probably just be annoyed. I mean, she's always acted that way no matter what I do. But this time, I feel like I deserve her anger a bit more than usual. I did burn down school property, after all.

The thought of what happened- of what I *did*- gets my legs moving again and releases me from the fear and unease threatening to choke me. I step around the sign and keep walking, following the path. So what if I'm in the South Gate woods right now? Where the fuck else am I supposed to go? Backwards? No. My current plan is just to keep going. Maybe the sign was placed in the wrong spot. Hopefully.

Hopefully I'll end up somewhere near my house, and soon.

Hopefully the feeling of dread in my stomach is just nerves.

I don't enjoy the feeling of being watched at all.

CHAPTER SEVEN

If she would have looked up

just once

she would have seen it trailing her while she walked the path

the path that was designed to twist and change

to switch direction on the hour

designed to mislead any who stepped onto it at all

if she would have looked up

just one time

she would have seen the large black mass that

                    skittered

and

                    crawled

from branch to branch

she would have seen it

                              giggling

to itself

as she walked on

completely oblivious

        if she had looked up just once

she would have seen the way that darkness engulfed every tree behind her hiding it in the shadows as it followed her

hiding it until it was nothing more than a pair of

white

unblinking

eyes

in the spaces between trees

no more than an idea

 a scribble of ink

and a pair of too-big eyes

if the blonde girl on the path had looked up just once

just once

she would have seen that mass of shadow

slither

down

     the branches

and

    shed

its skin

that mass of shadow gone

that scribble of ink gone

 and in its place a little girl

once it touched the forest floor

a little girl with doll-like curls resting beneath her white bonnet

curled perfectly around her cherubic

smiling

child face

a little girl in a simple gray dress

a simple clean apron

and a simple white bonnet covering those golden curls

the only thing that gave her away were her eyes

she lacked them

in their place were the same enormous

too-big

white eyes that did not know how to blink

     if the girl on the path had looked up once

she would have seen that little girl following her

ducking behind trees and peeking out

as if playing hide and seek

she would have seen how the thing that looked like a little girl followed her

with a grin that stretched wider than her face allowed

would have seen the pine needles and black dirt falling out of the corners of her small child mouth as she grinned

the thing on the path was enjoying this game of tag

it giggled to itself out of the child's mouth as it followed her

if she had looked up at any moment

she would have seen the little girl-creature scrabbling up the great thick pine trees with broken fingernails and child's feet

climbing up and down the great trees with speed that was much too fast for a child of her size

and when the thing that looked like a little girl grew bored of the skin it was wearing it shed it again

discarding her shape while the girl on the path below remained oblivious

this time

a large black goat stood in the spot the little girl had just been seconds before

a great big billy goat

nearly as big as a horse

and yet the way the beast held itself so

still

and unmoving

it seemed like something both wiser and far more chilling than the average goat

the great black billy goat watched her from the dark

and it knew that surely

without fail

that if the girl on the path deep leading deep into the South Gate woods had looked up at all

she would have seen it in any one of the skins it preferred to wear

perhaps it is a good thing she didn't look

the goat thinks

licking black goat lips.

it watches from the space between trees as she heads down the path

and it greedily

sips

lapping up

her fear that is spreading slowly and steadily

deep in the pit of her stomach

like a virus

the girl on the path is growing afraid

and the big black goat

drools

because it knows that she will taste delicious

between her fear and her innate

burning anger

she reminds it very much of a girl from many years ago

the black goat sheds its skin a third time

a small, simple brown this time

it licks sharpened teeth

all three rows

and stares at the girl's retreating figure through its big white eyes

it will leave her alone today

it decides

it will see her again.

Chapter Eight

Niamh

For the first time in over a week, I wake up to an alarm.

I sit up too fast, banging my head on the ceiling in the process. A string of obscenities leave my lips, even though the pain dulls within a second. Despite hating everything about the move, my new bedroom is actually super sick. It's in the attic, since the old owners had it converted to a fourth bedroom. It boasts a slanted, sloping ceiling, the same dark wood, and a single window: a gigantic, floor to ceiling pane of glass in the shape of a triangle, overlooking the East Gate woods below.

I hate everything about this move but the bedroom. The bedroom, I love.

I love it *too* much, apparently, because the thought of getting out of my wide, warm queen bed right now and going to *fucking school* seems like a really unfortunate fever dream.

Groaning, I pull the dense, bulky navy quilt back over my face, shutting out the mental images of Summerhill County High School. It had seemed okay enough. All indoors, which is like a foreign concept to me. Gigantic, modern. It was fine.

But I don't know a single goddamn person.

"Niamhyyyyyy!" My dad's voice floats up the drop-ladder to my room. "First day of schooooool!

I groan louder but toss the quilt off my face, staring up at the ceiling. The natural light is spilling in from the triangle window, coating the entire room in patchy gray. Fog again. Lovely. If I was back home, I would've already been in the water by now. I would've been surfing with Mak and Booker and Indie, and then gone to class whenever we felt like it, still wet. There would be no alarms. No low-sloping attic ceilings. No first day bullshit. No fucking fog and rain.

I finally unpacked all my shit from home- my tattered, ripped surf posters, signed by the biggest names on tour are covering every bare inch of wall. First and second place plaques rest above my bed. My board bag lies shoved in the corner, all eight boards stuffed to the brim. All my first place trophies line my shelf, boasting just how good I was starting to really get, and my hundreds upon hundreds of books are all haphazardly piled in my bookshelf, all sagging beneath the weight of billions of words.

When you have a well-respected novelist as a dad, you kind of grow up loving to read.

I roll over and grab my phone. One more time, I tell myself. One more time I'll check, then I'll get up and get ready.

Despite knowing the answer, I check my old group chat again, just to see. Well, not just to see. If I'm being honest, it isn't really just to check if any of my best friends texted me back.

It's so I don't have to think about whatever happened on the way home yesterday afternoon.

I scroll down to our text chain. Nothing.

All my messages to Makani still read as not delivered, all green. Booker's went through, but there's no reply, same with Indie.

Sighing, I sit up.

I miss them so bad that it physically *hurts*. My chest actually, seriously tightens for a second, and I have to force myself to swallow hard again and shove those feelings down. *Relax, Niamh.* I tell myself. *It's about to be your first day at a new school. Act normal.*

It'll be fine, I tell myself. It'll be good. And I don't need to make friends here. Mak, Booker, and Indie are irreplaceable. I don't want anyone else.

Anger sparks behind my eyes, burning the still-present lump in my throat. I don't *want* anyone else, and I don't want *any* of this. I didn't ask for this. This is so fucking UNFAIR.

But I did what I did, and no one can know.

Maybe Summerhill is a fitting punishment.

As I get dressed, my anger slowly dimming, my brain thinks of Zeke and Marlo. The friendly, freckled Torah twins.
I wonder if they'll actually look for me today like they said they would, or if I'll even see them at all. I didn't see them this weekend the few times we went into town. A part of me had hoped that maybe I'd see them when we went to the grocery store, or when I sat with my dad for nearly five hours at the cafe while he edited his newest book, but nothing.

As I stalk over to my mirror to do my hair, I kick something below my bed that crinkles. Something small and heavy. Picking it up, I can feel that it's a book, wrapped in brown paper and tied with a yellow ribbon, with a note attached to the front.

I smile despite myself. Over the weekend we crossed the causeway into actual Maine to see my dad's new office. As a published fantasy author, he prefers to write somewhere that he can separate from the rest of his life. I guess it helps him focus. The tiny, two-story building that overlooks the ocean with Summerhill a mere blip in the distance seemed to be just what he needed. There was a little bookstore attached, I recall.

The package turns out to be not a book, but a thick, black-leather bound journal. I place it on my desk and skim the note.

"My sweet, stubborn Niamh, have a great first day! Be yourself, and keep an open mind. You are strong, beautiful, and bright. Love always, Dad."

I force myself to take a deep breath, once again forcing the uncomfortable feelings down and back into the depths of my stomach where they belong.

The man might've moved me across the country, taking me far, far away from everything I love. But he bought me a journal.

My dad's been encouraging me to write for as long as I can remember. Not to be like him, he always says, but solely because I'm talented. Whenever I'd lose a surf contest back home and beat myself up, wishing I was more naturally talented, he was always right there to remind me that writing was an option for me if surfing was not. Mak and the rest of them liked my writings, but it was always surf surf surf skate do some fuckshit with them, so they never gave them a serious look. No one else ever saw that part of me.
But my dad does, and he always reminds me.

And, a little voice in the back of my mind adds on, *he never asked what* really *happened that day. He might have whisked you away to Summerhill, but he never once pried into what you did, what really happened.*

The corners of my mouth twitch into a frown, and I look in the mirror, tearing myself away from my thoughts. My dad's gigantic, oversized navy fisherman's sweater, the same shade as the night sky. My favorite black beanie. Baggy green corduroy jeans, scuffed black Vans. I leave my hair down, letting it fall naturally in its mismatched curls and waves halfway down my back, the colors fading from darker blonde to the sun-bleached ends. Miraculously, I still have my tan from back home, and combined with being freshly showered, my green eyes finally pop again, my skin glowing. I look healthy again. I look awake and alive, very different from how I did a week ago. It's almost like the fresh sea air and a few showers washed all the grief off.

If only they could wash off what I did.

What I can *do*.

And my dad might love me, but he can never know what I really did.

And if moving to Summerhill and sticking it out here, forsaking my old life completely is what it'll take to keep my secret hidden, then I guess I'll do it.

Fifteen minutes later, I'm standing outside the sprawling, open campus of Summerhill County High school. I'm determined to make it a good day, but god, the building itself is just a stark reminder of how very, very different it is than Saxon Beach.

For starters, the tall, dark stone building is surrounded by the gigantic pine trees that seem to cover this entire cape. Literally surrounded on all sides except for the front entrance, where the main street that leads to town starts. The sleet-gray and emerald green banners from the first day of school are still up, welcoming the new freshman by encouraging them to have 'Bass Pride.' The striped fish is etched in stone on the front.

Imagine having a fish as your mascot, Jesus Christ. Saxon Beach's mascot is a fucking *pirate*. Pirates are cool. Jack Sparrow is cool. A fish is fucking stupid, much to my dad's insistence that it is most definitely not. *"This is a town that makes its living off of fishing, Niamh!"* My mom had scoffed in the car on the way here. My dad just smiled at me in the rearview mirror. He wore his green *Bass Pride* sweater, asking me multiple times if I wanted him to come inside with me, to which I declined and asked him instead if he wanted his last child at home to be a social pariah.

I don't need him here, but I definitely wish I had *someone* with me as I linger by the entrance. It's daunting, being completely new. I've never been the new kid before. Makani, Booker, and Indie and I have been inseparable since kindergarten. I've never had to do the new girl thing.

I'm completely alone.

I should be with them right now. We should be sprinting up the stairs to class, just barely having got out of the water in time. Booker would be hauling ass in his white jeep, all of us trying to dry our hair in the open wind. We'd slide into our seats at the last second, dropping our backpacks on the floor, along with half the beach. Sometimes showing up hungover, sometimes with coffee from our favorite spot on the boardwalk in hand, but usually still with wet hair and sandy feet, smiling impishly like 'what're they gonna do?' Usually marked late, our teachers already fed up, but not one of us giving a single fuck.

Fuck. I'm not going to start the day like this. No.

I shake my head, attempting to clear my thoughts. Taking a deep, steadying breath, inhaling the crisp air of the ocean and the forest, I roll my shoulders back, and blink hard. Okay. Good. Let's go, Niamh. You're fine.

I'm supposed to meet with a guidance counselor to get my schedule before I go anywhere, so I make my destination the front office, wherever that fucking is. All around me heading up the stone steps and inside people are chatting with friends, running into teammates, and heading to their classes. Everyone I make eye contact with is smiling. Everyone seems happy.

No one's standing alone, just waiting.

As if soaking in my mood, the sky outside continues to darken, threatening heavy rain even at eight in the morning. The fog is light today for once, but regardless, I pull my beanie farther down on my cold ears. I'm fucking freezing, I'm in a completely new and foreign place, and this sucks so hard. In Saxon Beach, I had my friends. I had surfing. I knew who I was.

Here, in Summerhill, I have no fucking idea anymore. For the first time in my life, I feel deeply, truly lonely.

I stand there like a ghost for a few minutes, lost in my feels while everyone around me heads inside, until I hear an ecstatic, bright voice howl through the treeline and across the quad.

"NIAMH! HI!"

And sure enough, it's Zeke Torah.

Those corkscrew curls bounce against his shoulders as he tears across the quad to me. Even from a distance, I can tell that he's definitely tanner, at least from the neck up.

When he reaches me, he runs up and gives me a brief but very tight hug, crushing me to his lanky chest and absolutely towering over me in a gray beanie, plain black hoodie, blue jeans and black converse high tops. He carries a black JanSport that looks as if there's not a single book in it, and trains his gold, warm eyes down at me. His accompanying smile radiates charm and an unmistakable happiness: that buoyant, youthful type of joy you seem to cling to as a child.

As he pulls away from the hug, I catch the very distinct scent of sage and rain on his hoodie.

Between that surprisingly pleasant smell and the way his coppery curls poke out from under his beanie, I find myself doing what I've given dozens of other girls back home shit for: being speechless in front of some dude.

"Hey." I manage to get out, my traitorous heartbeat starting to quicken. "I wasn't sure I'd see you today."

Zeke just smiles again, flashing me that lightbulb grin that I'm coming to associate with him.

"Summerhill is tiny. Like actually tiny. I don't think I could miss you if you tried. But it probably helps that I looked for you."

He says this last part with a hand on the back of his neck, a different kind of grin coating his face: a nervous one. He shakes it off quickly, though, leading me inside Summerhill County High School.

Once inside, my searing loneliness begins to fade. Between Zeke's rapidfire questions for me and his unwavering, megawatt smile, I start to slide easily into the best mood I've been in for over a week. Talking to him comes easier, as if just being near him calms me.

The farther down the halls we walk, it's very apparent to me exactly how popular Zeke Torah must be. We can't turn a single corner without saying hi to someone, or getting pulled into a hug. And as I'm glued to his side, I also get introductions. Zeke introduces me cheerfully to everyone and anyone who will listen. A lot of the kids we stop and talk to look exactly like my old friends- all blonde-tipped, tan, surfy looking guys. The more people I'm introduced to, the more it seems I might fall into the kind of crowd I used to belong to.

The thought has my heart feeling some type of way.

The first bell starts to ring, and I interrupt Zeke and a short blonde girl quickly to tell him that I still need to get my schedule.

He nods knowingly. "Lemme grab Marlo real quick and we'll come with you. We both have a free first period. Might go surf with some buddies. Do you surf? You never told me. I feel like you do. You should come if you don't have a class." He cuts his glance sideways at me. "Tell me you definitely do."

I find myself smirking, forcing myself to meet his eyes. "Of course I do."

Zeke tips his head back and laughs. "You're fucking rad. I knew it. I literally told Marlo as we got in the water that day that there's no way that girl doesn't rip."

He motions for me to follow him, and I do. As we head towards a building marked ADMIN, he looks at me conspiratorially.

"None of the girls actually surf here." He whispers down to me, bending low to my ear as we walk. "They say they do, but they don't actually get in the water unless it's summertime and don't have to wear a wetsuit. They can't brave the cold water in the winter like an actual core lord. So I'm glad you're here to show them what's up."

His voice in my ear is giving me chills, and I angle my neck away from him when I respond.

"Good thing I'm such a core lord, then." I deadpan at him. He chuckles, slinging his arm around my shoulder like we're the best of friends. We walk towards the office, arguing about which type of board is better for a beach break, and I find myself genuinely growing happier and happier the more I talk to him. People like Zeke are my favorite. Easy to talk to, like you've been friends for ten years, not ten minutes.

Shockingly, without noticing it right away, I realize that I've been relaxing into my old self this entire time. Before I turned into this angry, secretive person, I was likable. I stuck to Mak and the others like glue, but we had other friends. I was the witty and sarcastic one, Mak the gentle and sensitive, Indie the reckless and confident, and Booker the impulsive and enabling. We had other friends between us four, and the old Niamh was well-liked. Being sarcastic and funny gets you places.

And right now, I feel a hell of a lot like the old Niamh.

And the best part? That little voice in my head says.

No one has to know why *you moved here.*

That thought alone propels my face into an enormous grin, the happiness flooding my heart with blood, hot and fast.

No one here has to know anything if I don't tell them. They don't have to know jack shit if I don't say anything. It's not like my parents are going to tell anyone. Zeke knows *nothing* about me other than the fact I'm new and I surf. I don't have to regale him with anything about my past if I choose not to. I can just be the sarcastic, charming new girl.

Easy.

We run into Marlo outside the office, looking absolutely stunning in nothing more than a thick, emerald green long sleeve shirt and baggy brown dickies and black doc martens. The clothes swallow her skinny, dainty frame, but the cleverly picked colors offset her fiery hair perfectly. Even her tan, freckled skin seems to glow. She totes a simple crochet book bag that overflows with notebooks and binders.

Like her twin, she also hugs me immediately, every bit as friendly as Zeke today. She then loops her arm through mine as we walk into the office.

The loneliness is but a distant memory at this point.

While we wait for the secretary to grab my schedule, Marlo tells me how they've been friends with literally everyone in their class since kindergarten. In a place as small as Summerhill, you get to know everyone your age pretty quickly.

In less than ten minutes, I learn that the Torah's live on the edge of the woods in the North Gate, super close to the water. That's where they'd been running to the morning I met them. They're water babies through and through. Besides being a major fisherman, surfer, and all around waterman, their dad, Jimbo, owns a surfboard shaping company in town. Everyone in Summerhill supports local, along with a lot of the closer towns over the causeway. Because of this, Torah Shapes does very well, and Zeke and Marlo have been in the water since before they could walk. Marlo tells me that her dad encourages them to surf as much as they possibly can, even letting them skip school if there's a good swell, or driving them off the cape to hunt down waves.

I've found my people.

After grabbing my schedule, the twins walk me to my first class. We stop just outside the still relatively-empty classroom, chatting about nothing. I've got five minutes before English, so I lean back against the wall, letting the twins talk. Marlo snatches my schedule mid conversation about local surf spots and scans it quickly.

"You've got no classes with the both of us, but PE with me. Drop that class and take surf PE instead. You get double credits, and you get to leave early every day."

She speaks rapidfire, just like her brother. But where Zeke carries an air of joy and cheer that makes his golden eyes pop, Marlo is all confidence, her aqua eyes stern and alive, a truly commanding presence for such a short person.

"We have a surf team, too. You should try out. We need more girls. There's just me and Layla right now, but we carry the team. Damn. You also have English *and* chem with Zeke. Damn."

She looks up at me, her face completely blank. "Don't let this degenerate distract you."

At this, Zeke laughs, and feigns right to grab Marlo in a headlock. She squeals in protest, dodging his gangly arms and boisterous self.

"Absolutely not. It's too early for this. You see what I have to live with, Niamh?" She grunts, emerging from his grip and smoothing her hair back down.

Zeke lets go of her, hitching his backpack over his shoulder. "Don't let her fool you. She's probably stronger than me."

"And better looking."

"Ohhhhhhhhhkay, dude."

Zeke looks over at me, winking. "This is where Niamh says 'I'd let Zeke put *me* in a headlock' and we run off together and leave you stranded here, and then I knock your books to the ground like a typical high school bully."

Marlo looks over at me, her eyebrows nearly disappearing into her hairline. I raise mine right back. Is Zeke... flirting with me? Interesting.

Interesting, and tempting.

I look at Marlo and Marlo only. "Maybe if Zeke takes me to surf with him, I'll let him put me in a headlock."

She smiles widely at me, aqua eyes flashing like I passed some unknown test. "That can be arranged."

Zeke's face erupts into an enormous grin again, dancing between boyish nervousness and that lighthearted happiness.

"Yeah, it absolutely the fuck can. But *I'm* going to be her favorite twin, so fuck off, Marlo. Also- fuck, I'm about to be late to math."

He runs off, those long legs carrying him halfway down the hall before he glances over his shoulder to wave goodbye to us, his smile directed at me.

Marlo makes to leave, too, but turns around at the last second.

"We'll come find you at lunch, okay? Also…. Niamh, I don't want to put any pressure on you, first day and all…. But holy shit, I have *never* seen him that nervous in my life, Jesus."

She waves goodbye as I stand outside my English class, leaving me with my head spinning, but not at all in a bad way. Two thoughts run through my mind on a loop:

1. Summerhill…. isn't terrible.
2. Zeke and Marlo are fucking wonderful.

I haven't thought about Mak, Booker, Indie, or what happened since I saw the twins this morning. Fucking hell. At this rate, how am I going to stay angry about moving here?

I *need* to be angry. Anger feels right.

Wait. What?

Another thought darts through my head, shattering the one about anger. My inner voice pokes around my skull all nosey.

What if, it says, *Summerhill is exactly what you need?*

CHAPTER NINE

TYLER

I peel my dirty, rain-soaked sweater off the second I walk in the doorway. The thin, milky white skin of my stomach immediately chills in its absence. I toss it absentmindedly on the floor, splattering mud inside the hut.

I've been told a number of times by my grandmother not to refer to our modest two-story cabin as a 'hut.' It doesn't come from a place of discontent. Honestly, I love the hut. It sits bordering the South Gate woods, which basically just ensures that no one is going to fuck with us. It's cozy, the fire is always burning, and it always smells of pine trees and the sea. Eleni and I have a pretty good herb patch going for this late in the fall, and our little patch carries the smell of rosemary, lavender, and mint up into my room if I leave my window open.

So yeah, I love the hut. Very much so.

But once, my sophomore year, Mia Fergor told everyone in class that I lived in a 'witch's hut' in the South Gate woods with my grandmother, and that she was the witch of the woods. That she was responsible for the three kids that went missing the year prior.

That she ate them, just like the Gate did.

My grandmother has lived in Summerhill her entire life, just as my mother did. She's just as much a staple of this town as any one of them. She belongs here just as much as the rest of them.

But she- and I, by default, will never be accepted because of who we are inside. Eleni to this *day* isn't accepted, just because of her practice. She doesn't hide her gifts. Everyone knows Eleni practices magic. Whether they call her a conjurer of the black arts, a devil worshiper, a witch, a magician, it doesn't matter. They know, because she lives out loud.

Living out loud, but as an outcast. Magic always comes with a price, usually in threefold. I guess living as an outcast is the cost for having the gifts.

But back to Mia fucking Fergor. After she made that comment, for weeks I endured the cringes, the sideways looks, and the general unease of my classmates whenever I entered the room. I did more than endure it- being me, I could *hear* their thoughts. I didn't even have to go reaching into their minds: so strong was their fear and their disgust that their thoughts came to me. I could taste their malaise.

Yet I did nothing, said nothing to confirm if the rumors were true or false. Here's three truths for you, Mia Fergor.

One: I do live in the South Gate woods. That much is true.

Two: Eleni is *not* the one that took whatever stupid fucks went missing in the South Gate woods. There are things in there that aren't so easily explained away. It'd be easy to use the town witch as a scapegoat.

But you'd have to be a genuine, spineless idiot to think that whatever is *really* in those woods won't hurt you. People that go in there usually know that there's a slim chance of coming back out.

There are things older than human beings, you know. There are magics and places even Eleni and I don't prod at or go looking for. You'd have to be a real fucking idiot to think that we're the only creatures that walk this planet.
All the stories about the South Gate exist for a reason, and there isn't a doubt in my adolescent mind that there's probably some dark, creepy shit in there that I don't ever want to meet.

That dark, creepy shit is not my grandmother.

And Three: You're absolutely right, Mia. We are witches.

Just not in the cauldrons-and-spells way you think. Being a Lane is very, very different than that. The magic that exists in Lane women is more like the branches of a tree.
It takes root in you the second you utter your first breath of life, and then it spreads. It grows the more you use it.
If you cut open my arms, my veins would have leaves and gnarls, stardust and sea salt.

When I finally ran into Mia outside of class one day that year, she had lifted her chin as if to say something.

I wasn't deterred even for a second. I had just stared her dead in the eyes and told her if she ever spread a rumor about Eleni or I again, I wouldn't need to use magic to shut her mouth. I'd bury her with my hands alone.

Then I walked away before she could respond. And guess what? The rumors stopped.

People went back to leaving me alone.

I think back to that day a lot. As tempting as it would've been to use my gifts against her, I didn't cave. Eleni would've been proud. That's one of her very, very few rules: No magic against anyone for ill intent.

That, along with no non-consensual love spells, and no fucking with what's already dead, because apparently any one of those spells cast can and will come back to you in threefold.

I still think Mia Fergor might've been worth the repercussions.

"Eleni!" I screech into the dim, dark hallway, shucking my wet undershirt off as well. I grab a clean sweater from the rack by the door, praying she won't walk in and see my top half completely naked. "I'm home!"

My grandmother doesn't respond, probably doing god knows what.

I roll my eyes to the ceiling, stalking into the hallway, running my fingers through my long, wet locks. My limbs are still shaking from my vision earlier, so I head for the kitchen intending to make a snack to replenish my energy when I hear my name. And it isn't in my grandmother's voice. It's deep, throaty. A man's voice.

No men live here.

I tear through the rest of the hallway, my long gazelle legs crossing the carpeted runner that leads into the kitchen within milliseconds. Every second that passes has my heart jacking up another notch, and I'm already uttering protection charms under my breath when

…..When I want to kick myself, seeing who's sitting at our kitchen table.

His bare, disgusting feet are propped up on the hand-knitted yellow placemats, those filthy toes dangerously close to a vase of fresh-picked lavender. His hands are up to the elbows in a box of my favorite rosemary and olive crackers. My best- and only-friend Felix laughs as he sees my expression, tossing a cracker into his mouth.

"You looked scared as shit." He snorts, spraying crumbs over his lap.

His slightly upturned hazel eyes crinkle with amusement, offsetting the streaks of red throughout his autumn-colored hair. He's always had this look of permanent mischief about him. Eleni says it's because he's more fae than boy, and she finds him endearing for this fact alone. I think it's because he goes everywhere with no shoes and likes to try and prank me twenty four seven. I want to throttle him half the time.

"Fuck off." I sigh, letting my heart rate settle to a normal pace again. I take a seat on the edge of the kitchen table, attempting to snatch the box of crackers. "Where's Eleni?"

He tosses another into his mouth before I can snatch the box from him, shrugging half heartedly and talking with his mouth full. "Not sure. She left pretty quick, said she had an urgent meeting with someone? Vance? No, Van Lot? No, Van…."

"Van Devon?" I offer.

Felix nods. "Yeah. She took one of the jar spells with her. Said she needed 'something more potent than last time.'" He curls his fingers around the air quotes.

Felix knows exactly what Eleni and I are. I've always had the vague notion that he grew up familiar with magic, whether it be on his own or in his family. Maybe Eleni is right, and he is more fae than boy.

Whatever the reason, he's never offered an explanation, and I've never asked for one. But whenever I use my gifts, or Eleni discusses business with him in the room, he doesn't act shocked.

Which is probably why he's my only friend.

At this comment, though, we both burst into raucous, full-belly laughter. It isn't uncommon for the occasional person to come by and ask my grandmother for a charm. Eleni's gifts are slightly different from mine. She possesses healing, along with sight. The simplest jar spells or charms crafted by her hands can cure most things that ail people. Common colds, unidentified spasms and viruses, heartache. She can see things, too, like I can.

I snort, handing the box of crackers back to him. "The Van Devon's can go fuck themselves."

This gets the giggles going again, and he laughs so hard his eyes start to water.

"Go.... fuck.... themselves......" Felix gasps out, tears starting to roll down his cheeks. "Y..yeah... because no... one else.... Can!"

It's no secret that even for all her shit-talking, Cathy Van Devon orders a spell jar from Eleni every two weeks like clockwork. An enhancing spell. A spell crafted to "boost mood and enhance performance." Is what Felix and I read on her package one time before Eleni had delivered it. It didn't take a genius to figure out what exactly she needed to *enhance.* Her husband is like twenty years older than her or something.

"Shame the poor guy can't get it up anymore." Felix finally gets out between wheezes for air.

I wipe tears away, massaging my now-sore abs. "Honestly, it's a wonder they're still married. I would've left ages ago."

Felix sprays crumbs across the table, then sobers up a little. "I wonder what Morgan would say?"

At this, though, I stop laughing instantly.

Morgan Van Devon, Summerhill's perfect princess, isn't exactly one of my favorite people. She's my age in school, and we've known each other since birth. But she's *exactly* like her mother. A grade-A cunt.

The Van Devon's are pretty much the top of the social hierarchy in our town. They're the richest by far, own the biggest house in the North Gate, two businesses on main street, and love to trot around their wealth like it's their entire personality. Sure, they throw charity events every once in a blue moon. Sure, the dance studio that Morgan and her mother both work at is *supposedly* a non-profit. But it all means jack shit when Mr. and Mrs. Van Devon act like anyone below their status level is a complete worm. Their son, Jonathan, isn't any better. I've seen him beat up boys half his age just for looking at him wrong. He's an asshole.

Morgan, on the other hand, I don't truly have any issue with. She's smart, wily, and intelligent. She speaks out, doesn't let herself get pushed around, and, supposedly, is a very talented dancer. But she also gives me the same side eye that the rest of them do in the halls. She also never says anything when people are shitty to me in town. She also has never once defended me when her brother or mom start shit with me.

So I'm indifferent towards her. But Felix looooooves to point out the one mishap I had. The one, *one* time I fucked up, and botched a spell.

Badly.

"Ty-leeeer and Morrrrr-gan, sittin in a tree. K-I-S-S-"

Without warning, I dive onto him, knocking him backwards out of the chair.

On the kitchen floor, I grab Felix in a headlock, and the vase of lavender falls over and shatters in pieces all around us. I'm at a slight disadvantage being that I'm much thinner, smaller, and lack the sinewy muscles he seems to keep building every day. But nevertheless, I manage to sit on his chest and pin his wrists with my knees. Mud from the ends of my skirt get on his shirt and neck, and I smile maliciously.

I get low and close to his face. My long, nut-brown hair tickles both sides of his cheeks, and I can smell the rosemary crackers on his breath.

In another world, I would've found this situation extremely attractive.

In another world, where Felix isn't Felix, my obnoxious best friend, and he isn't speaking about Morgan.

I will my voice to grow an octave lower, to be as predatory and haunting as the fog that rolls through the South Gate woods on a moonless night.

I will my eyes to deepen, hiding the pupils. Deep, endless pools of sapphire blue, looking right into him.

"What have we discussed, Felix."

His face is red, as I've got my knees on either side of his windpipe, but he's still laughing, the imp.

"WHAT HAVE WE DISCUSSED." I ask again, my voice dangerously low.

Measured, carrying the lilt it does when I cast. Like rose petals and silken sheets, carried on the breeze with a gentle hand.

Seductive, intentional. A cat and mouse game.

It seems to do the trick, because his laughter finally ceases.

"Don't go. All. Witchy shit on. Me." He coughs, and I shift my weight slightly. "You didn't mean to spell her. I know. I know. Now get off of me."

I get off of him, satisfied, allowing him to massage his neck.

What happened was this, because apparently I can never catch a break.

This February, a man named Moore Vanderhill found me on my favorite bench just outside the North Gate woods. He skipped any pleasantries and begged me to craft a jar spell for him- a love spell.
How he knew I was a witch, or how he even knew my name was beyond me.

He proceeded to tell me a sob story about a woman he was in love with who treated him like shit, apparently. He was completely and irrevocably head over heels for her, but I guess she had some issues and wouldn't commit to him. He begged me for something that would bridge the two of their souls, in making them completely each others until the end of time.

He begged for unconditional, true love, something both parties would die for.

And he was completely, dead serious about this, and willing to pay me.

The thing is, love spells are tricky, because it's the consent part that's hard. It must be freely, willingly given from both parties for a spell like that to work. Everything comes in threes- truths, lies, repercussions. And crafting a love spell without clear, verbal or written consent from both parties?

The repercussions on everyone involved could be deadly.

Blurring the lines between free will and force too much is honestly *asking* for some bad shit to happen. *Especially* when you ask an angry, spiteful eighteen year old girl to do it for you.

But when I explained all of this to Moore Vanderhill, basically telling him tough luck, hope you get your girl, buddy, he didn't argue with me or try to plead his case.

He just opened his pocket and pulled out a wad of bills, and smiled a sparkling, knowing smile at me.

Three thousand bills, to be precise.

It's not that I'm easily bought.

It's just that three thousand dollars could get me off of this godforsaken cape, and keep me off of it. It's not like Eleni and I are made of money- what my mom left me after she died barely covers our expenses.

Three thousand dollars could buy me a ferry. A train. A plane.

Three thousand could buy my ticket to a place far, far away from a town that hates every bit of me.

Three thousand dollars could buy me a new life, somewhere far, far away from Summerhill, Maine.

So I did it.

I crafted Moore's jar spell, exactly as he asked for it.

I filled it with not only my own innate passion and rage, but with all the things he'd asked me to put into it: his desire, his *want*.

It was so potent, I could taste searing cayenne on my tongue. He wanted this woman, whoever she was, desired her so deeply, that it scalded the inside of my mouth like hot tea.

As he'd found me on a waxing crescent, I put his spell on a shelf in our pantry for safekeeping until the next full moon. I intended to hand deliver it the morning of the full moon.

But the thing is, Eleni got to it before I did.

And because she's old and her eyes are going,

And also because I failed to tell her,

She didn't take it to fucking *Moore Vanderhill*. She delivered it to Morgan Van Devon. In person. On a full moon.

Who, of course, exclaimed in surprise that she hadn't ordered a spell jar, let alone did she know what the small mason jar, sealed in red candle wax and bound tightly with a honey-soaked ribbon even *was*.

My colossal fuckup didn't end there, though. Morgan, shockingly, had been willing to just let it go.

But Cathy Van Devon was livid, insisting that I was out to get her daughter. Because of course I'm such a desperate, lovestruck freak that I resorted to *spelling her* to make her fall in love with me, right? Obviously. Of course.

Eleni, thankfully, believed me, though she gave me hell for weeks for crafting such a strong, potent love spell without telling her. Such things could come back to bite me, she said. She was furious with me.

But no intervention on mine or Eleni's behalf changed Cathy Van Devon's mind. She turned everyone against us after that, making me more of an outcast than I already was. Eleni still gets orders, and people are slightly more kind to her. I say slightly because she isn't the one who has to go to a public high school where everyone fucking hates you.

The last eight months have been rough, to put it lightly.

Getting LESBIAN and WITCH scrawled onto my locker has really been the highlight of my school days. It's still happening, all these months later. Every time something like that happens, the anger that builds in my chest is so potent that it almost suffocates me. Felix has to get me to walk away before I do something stupid, like hex one of the idiots.

I started ditching school more these last few months. Thankfully, Felix is always game to come with me.

Here's three truths for you.

One: I'm *not* gay.

At least, I don't think so. I haven't kissed anyone.

Two: Before the incident this February, I'd never even *spoken* to Morgan Van Devon. Not once.

Three: Moore Vanderhill skipped town. Or disappeared. Or something. He never found me to collect his spell, and as a result, I never got my money.

Maybe he wandered into the South Gate. Maybe he just left.

Whatever happened, he disappeared.

But it doesn't matter now. Now, the entire Van Devon family hates me, along with the rest of Summerhill.

And yet Cathy Van Devon secretly orders from Eleni for her fucking limp-dick husband, all while slandering my name to anyone who will listen.

Since I can't really do anything about it, I make it a point now to listen to her thoughts whenever I see her in town. It brings me slight satisfaction seeing how actually horrible her life seems to be.

She's a pill-popping, boring, surface-level housewife.

Useless hag. Her life is so boring.

It brings me joy.

But now, of course, Morgan Van Devon's name is a touchy subject.

And of course, Felix being Felix finds every opportunity he can to make gay jokes to me.

At least the spell didn't work.

Thank fucking God.

CHAPTER TEN

TYLER

From the journal of Tyler Iris Lane

Friday, February 11th

<u>She</u>

<u>Will</u> <u>Be</u>

<u>Mine.</u>

a jar spell for Moore Vanderhill

Crafted on a Friday, during a waxing crescent.

<u>Ingredients:</u>

- *1 medium-sized mason jar*

- *Three shards of rose quartz, charged under a full moon*

- *Three shards of red jasper, charged under a full moon*

- Salt for basic protection

- Three dried sunflower petals for happiness & joy

- Three _dried_ rose petals for love

- Three _fresh_ rose petals for love

- Cinnamon for passion & intensity

- Cayenne for passion & intensity

- Pure rose oil for love

- Catnip for lust, desire, & attraction

- Patchouli for lust & love

- Three bay leaves for wishes coming true

- A single strip of paper

- Red ink

- White ribbon

- Two red candles

- A picture of your beloved

- Red ribbon

- Honey

Instructions:

- Light the first red candle.

- Take the strip of paper. Use the red ink to write your intent on this paper three times through. Think of the one you want deeply, with purpose, while you write. Do NOT lift your hand from the paper. Save any t's that need crossing or i's that need to be dotted for after you write it three times through.

- On the other side of the paper, repeat.

- After this, fold the picture of the one you want into the strip of paper. Bind them together tightly, and then bind them both with the red ribbon. Make it tight enough that they won't become unrolled.

- Place the bound object into the jar, thinking of her deeply while you place it inside.

- Place the rest of the objects into the jar, save for the white ribbon and the other candle. Think of her while you drop these inside.

- Coat the jar with the honey, making sure to cover the object inside entirely.

- Cap the jar, and use the last of the honey to soak the white ribbon. Wrap the ribbon around the jar tightly. Think about her while you do this.

- Place the second red candle on top of the jar, and light it. Best done under open moonlight, or near the sea. Let it burn down entirely, coating the jar entirely. While it burns, repeat the following phrase;

"My very name invokes ardor,

Love and lust align.

Every waking minute,

Her desire for me grows.

And soon,

She Will Be Mine.

She Will Be Mine."

- Repeat this phrase nightly, keeping the jar somewhere near open moonlight.

  Visualize her, and what you want your outcome to be while you speak.

- Repeat this process until the next full moon, or until your outcome is achieved.

Chapter Eleven

Niamh

As far as first days go, it could've been much worse.

Tolerable, if not dragging. Having classes with Zeke and Marlo made it a lot easier, though. I've never been a fan of school in the first place- my attention tends to wander, straying towards the water. Hence the several detentions that my friends and I got back home for ditching to go surf.

Oh well.

Even with all that being said, I have to admit though that it wasn't *terrible*. Having the majority of my classes with the twins made it almost an easy transition. None of my teachers made me do the stand up and introduce yourself thing, thank fucking god. Zeke and Marlo did it for me, making me sound cool and exotic.

He isn't Makani or Booker, and she isn't Indie. But today, they made missing my old friends- the giant, gaping cavern in my chest- feel less like an abyss, and more like a hole.

I'm bent low to the ground just outside the East Gate woods. I have to take the path home again, the same one I took over the weekend, since both my parents are at work. A ten, fifteen minute walk home, tops.
I'm re-tying the laces to my muddy Vans when I hear my name being called.

I raise my head, peering across the campus. Zeke is running in my direction, Marlo trailing after him on her much shorter legs.

"Niamh!" He announces loudly and cheerfully to the mostly-empty quad. "First day okay?"
He sits on the ground criss-cross, smiling up at me like he genuinely wants to know. As if he can't tell: he spent the entire day toting me around, introducing me to his friends, making sure I had everything I needed. A proper gentleman. Rare for a surfer.

I stand, wiping my hands off on my pants. "Thrilling."
Marlo stares over her shoulder at the town in the distance, where the mist from the harbor is finally starting to seep in for the afternoon. It's starting to match the darkening sky.

Her expression is bleak. "We were gonna see if you wanted to come surf, but it looks like it might get blown out from the storm now."

Zeke groans at this, tossing his head back dramatically. I can't help but empathize with the guy. I distinctly recall the time Makani and I paddled out at the jetty near my house a day after a big storm had come through. We'd both thrown up for hours afterwards.

"Does it storm pretty bad here?" I ask them. "Back home, if it rained a decent amount, we couldn't get in the water for like three days because of the runoff."

Zeke runs a hand through his perfect curls while Marlo pulls her phone out, her attention snatched away.

"Yeah, we get a few decent ones every winter and spring. The one that's supposed to hit this weekend is just a bunch of thunder and lightning with all the rain. Huge bummer. I really wanted to take you to North Gate. It's the best spot on the cape besides East Cliff, but that one really needs a West-North West swell. Also, it's a left, miss goofy foot."

Marlo doesn't look up from her phone as he talks, but there's a faint gleam in her aqua eyes as she continues to type furiously.

"You never surf East Cliff."

"Oh, I'm sorry. Says the one who only paddles out there at *all* if Kai is."

Her face glows, still buried in whoever she's talking to. It matches the shade of her coppery, fiery hair perfectly. "That is not even remotely close to being true."

"You have to jump off the cliff to get to the break. Marlo's a wuss." He lowers his voice. "Unless Kai's there."

"I can hear you, dipshit. Stop slandering my name to Niamh."

Zeke looks at me, and I smile despite myself as he chooses, wisely, not to push the matter. "You leaving right now?" He asks me.

Looking out past the school where the fog is starting to roll in quickly through main street, I wonder just how much time I have before the rain hits. I'd really, really rather not walk the path home at all. But especially not in the pouring rain. I think of my options while I stare off towards the harbor. Stay and hangout with Zeke and Marlo for a few more minutes, risking a very, very wet walk home. Or make some excuse and leave now, staying dry, but alone with my thoughts.

I pick at a loose thread on my sweater. My very dry, warm sweater. It takes me all of thirty seconds to decide.

We walk over to the student parking lot, which is really just a patch of grass behind the main building. Zeke and Marlo don't have a car either, it seems.

We sit three deep on a rotted bench as the sky continues to darken, Zeke on one side, Marlo in the middle, and me on the other end. I start to wrap my arms around myself tightly, but not before Zeke shrugs his hoodie off and hands it to me so quickly that I don't even have time to blink. I stuff my arms into it and hold it to my chest, smiling gratefully. When he looks away, I hold it closer to my face.

Based on my experience, there are two kinds of boys in this world. Boys that sleep with one paper-thin pillow, have navy sheets, spend more time at the gym than anywhere else, and think that having big muscles and being a better-than-average surfer should have girls falling over themselves trying to get with them. These types of boys smell like sweat and male arrogance. Having a sticker on the nose of your board shouldn't automatically equal having play. In Saxon Beach, though, it kind of does for most girls.

Then on the other end, there are boys that play guitar and have plants in their rooms, ones that make their beds, hug their moms, and listen to decently-good music. Boys that aren't afraid to paint their nails and show basic human emotion. They usually smell really, really fucking good, too.

Zeke's hoodie smells of sage, clean sheets, and jasmine. Something all at once feminine, and yet soft.

Motherfucker.

"So what're you guys gonna do instead?" I ask him. "Actually, what *do* people do here? Does everyone just surf? Or fish?"

Neither of them answer me right away. Marlo's still typing furiously on her phone, her tongue poking out one corner of her mouth. Zeke rolls his eyes, trying to peek over her shoulder to see who she's texting. She angles away from him, squealing, nearly falling off the bench in the process.

Their simple, playful interaction causes my heart to constrict again. Makani and I were just like this.

"If we don't surf, we die." Zeke says so simply and straightfaced that I can't help but laugh.

"I feel that." I chuckle. He laughs, and we catch each other's eye across the table. His golden, warm eyes glimmer, and I feel the moment stretch out long. My heart slams against my ribs, and I look away first.

This finally gets a response out of Marlo.

"He's just being dramatic. We tip cattle like normal, civilized small-town folk."

"There's cattle here?" I wrinkle my nose.

Marlo smirks at me, finally tucking her phone away. She tucks one strand of wavy, shiny auburn hair behind her ear, her eyes flashing at me with a look I can't name.

"No. Whenever we get bored, we just wander through the woods and dare each other to find the gate in the woods."

The way she says 'gate' causes adrenaline to flood my heart immediately, my brain honing in on the abnormal like a moth to light.

I think of the sign at the end of the path. The path that I have to take *today*.

The very path that changed on me, somehow, and led me in a completely different direction.

I try to contain my curiosity. Alerting them to my strange, unnatural experience with the South Gate woods….. And with *me*, in general, could very quickly write me off as Weird New Girl, which is the last thing I need. Summerhill is supposed to be my fresh start.

I feel my heart harden, some iron walls going up. No matter how cool Zeke and Marlo are, they can never know what I truly am.

What I did. *Can do.*

No one will know what I did.

No one. No matter how friendly, cute, or charming they are.

No matter how golden or sparkly their eyes are, or how much their hoodie smells like a fucking herbal soap shop.

They can't know.

So I act as if I've never heard of it. "What gate?"

I keep my voice lighthearted and curious, but sit on my hands so they don't give away how nervous I am, or that I'm lying. My dad can always tell when I'm lying, because I have the worst tell: I pick at my nails.

The splinters of the bench dig into my palms, into my short, jagged nails.

Both the twins look at me now, Marlo's bright blue eyes all at once alight and mischievous, her attention completely on me. Zeke, on the other hand, swears quietly under his breath, Hhs joyful, bubbly attitude gone.

"Oooohhhhhh," Marlo smiles deviously. "Shit. I forgot that she doesn't know about any of the legends." She glances sideways at her brother, who's looking like he swallowed wrong.

Zeke won't meet my gaze, but he meets his sister's head on, gentle anger carved into his features. It shocks me, seeing him look at her like that. My chest fills with quick, anxious energy, my heartbeat pounding.

I try for the role of curious and innocent newbie, poking his thigh across the table until he caves, finally smiling at me.

"It's honestly not a big deal, Niamh. It's just the layout of the town, like how they divided up the forest when they built Summerhill. We're on campus, which is in the North end of town. So the woods over here are the North Gate woods. To your left is the East Gate woods. North Gate is pretty fire though because it has the best surf on the cape."

I nod, following along. He still looks like he's upset, but selfishly I will him to continue.

"The East Gate and West Gate are just a lot of subdivisions. There's a lot more open land over there, less hills, and the trees are less dense."

He trails off here as if that's it, and Marlo goes back to her phone. I nod again, but inside I'm growing frustrated. He still hasn't mentioned anything about the South Gate woods. I could give a fuck about the layout of Summerhill. I want to know, without having to ask and look weird, why the path I took home changed on me. What's really up with that part of the forest.

I'm close to just asking the both of them something along the lines of 'what about the South Gate?' when I really look at his face.

Zeke's genuinely upset.

Luckily for me, Marlo's put her phone down and is staring at her twin in rapt attention, a wide, shit-eating grin on her freckled face. What comes out of her mouth gives me goosebumps through the hoodie.

"You can't forget the South Gate, brother. It's critical to her local knowledge."

Zeke looks at Marlo with that same gentle, below-the-surface anger right as the first clap of thunder rolls over our heads. I wonder why he's so bothered by the South Gate.

I can sense a sibling argument brewing just like the storm above us. God knows Aine and I had our moments- she's only six years older than me, but still. We fought dirty. Maybe that's how I ended up so tough.

"I'm not going to scare her on her first day. Drop it, Marlo." He says in a quiet voice, looking very much like he wants to leave. He won't look at either of us now.

My heart pounds. No, no, no. I need this. I need to know what they know. Because maybe whatever ghost story or whatever they're about to tell me will give me a hint as to how the actual fuck I ended up in the South Gate woods when I entered at the East Gate.

"Why would I be scared?" I ask them, almost at the exact moment a near-deafening clap of thunder rolls across the student parking lot. The sky is quickly turning the shade of a fresh bruise, and the wind off the harbor starts to pick up. I'm grateful as hell for Zeke's hoodie.

Although I'm kind of being a dick to him right now. I can clearly see he's upset, yet I keep pushing. Goddamnit, Niamh.

Marlo takes out her phone again, her grin only growing, completely ignoring Zeke's sour mood. She talks and texts at the same time, like she knows the story by heart.

"Basically, everyone avoids the South Gate woods. It's kind of our own urban legend." She sets her phone down, angling it away from Zeke, and pulls a notebook out of her bag, flipping to a quick pencil drawing of the town.

"North, East, South, West. Four parts of the same woods. It made for easy mapping when Thomas Summers was building Summerhill, placing our town right in the middle of the forest. But according to the story,"

She pauses for effect. "Thomas Summers came to Maine with two daughters in tow. Seven year old twins, Abigail and Catherine. I guess building an entire settlement was boring, because he let them run off in the woods all day by themselves. Top tier parenting, right? They were allowed to stay out as long as they wanted, as long as they came home for dinner. Things were going fine until the summer, when one day, only Catherine came home."

I do my damn hardest to not appear impatient. I know the story. know that Abigail Summers disappeared when she walked through the gate.

I want to know about the damn *path*.

Zeke is just shaking his head, looking away from both of us now. I wonder why he seems so disgusted, so removed from this. It almost seems like he's taking it personally.

Marlo continues, still completely ignoring her brother. Her smile is so maniacal I almost feel like I should be more scared.

"When Thomas asked his daughter where the other was, she became downright hysterical, claiming that they'd found, of all things, an enormous, hulking gate. She told him about it, down to the gritty details: that it stood alone in the center of the trees, that it just appeared out of nowhere, it was thirty feet tall, made of iron, with both doors wide open…. and not attached to a single thing but the forest floor."

She stops when her phone pings, quickly shooting off a text to whoever she's been hiding away from Zeke and I, then resumes her story without pausing to take a breath.

"She told her father that it scared her, but not Abigail. Abigail was enchanted by the gate, and urged Catherine to walk through it with her. She refused, insisting they should leave, because she felt that something wasn't right. So Abigail ran through the gate alone…. except she didn't come out the other side."

Despite having heard the story several times from my dad, hearing it come from Marlo's mouth gives me deep chills, icy fingers running down my neck and spine. It's one thing to hear the story of the Summers family as an eight year old on a stormy night, but quite another to hear it from someone my own age.

"According to the story, Abigail was just…. gone. She walked through the gate, and didn't emerge on the other side. Catherine said it was like she was plucked from thin air. Of course, in that time period, everyone wanted to blame witchcraft. They went so far as to involve the church, who couldn't seem to find the gate at all, nor another explanation. They questioned Catherine Summers time and time again, and still she repeated the same story, the same words over and over. She told her father and anyone who would listen that her twin had walked in, and simply vanished from existence. And," She grins evilly, "That it didn't smell right."

Zeke swears loudly and stands up, spinning to face his twin sister. Clear, bright anger contorts his freckled, tanned face, and his jaw is clenched tight.

"*Fuck,* Marlo, don't fucking scare her!" He spits out, his words sharp. Marlo doesn't recoil at all. It's almost like she expected this reaction.

It's the only time I've seen him raise his voice, or appear anything other than easygoing and chipper. This is clearly hitting way too hard for him. I wonder, again, what the hell happened.

I feel guilty for pushing him. Clearly this is upsetting to him, and I'm the asshole who kept pushing. A sudden desperate, immediate urge to see that lightbulb smile and happy face again hits me.

While he's busy giving Marlo the eye, I stick my muddy Vans out and nudge the back of his knee with my foot, causing his leg to buckle beneath him. A classic move.

He whips around, looking at me. "Hey," I say gently. "I'm sorry, dude. I'm just curious. I promise you I can handle creepy."

Zeke shakes his head and rubs a hand over his face, but he reluctantly sits back down in between Marlo and I. My heart does a little flip when he sits purposely closer to me. I nudge his knees with my own, and he gives me a grateful squeeze.

"Marlo, did you say it didn't.. smell right?" I ask once he's calm.

Marlo doesn't even look at Zeke as she continues. "In every history book I've found, every local account, her words are the same. She told her father and anyone who questioned her that it smelled rotten in that part of the woods. Like the closer they stood to the gate, the mustier and more rank it grew. She likened it to a dead animal carcass. Even Abigail had agreed with her before she'd walked through it. The people of the settlement started to refer to it as dead air."

Dead air.

Goosebumps ripple down both my arms under Zeke's hoodie right as a third clap of thunder tears across the field, and I jump visibly. Zeke immediately mistakes this for discomfort.

"Great. Now that we've scared the shit out of her on her very first day of school, welcome to Summerhill, Niamh. Can we go do something fun now? Like maybe not tell her shit that's gonna make her want to move back home immediately?"

Zeke stands up, clapping his hands together, then offers me a hand up. His features are tight, his body language very clearly, visibly upset, but I can tell he's trying to play it off as no big deal in front of me.

I want to ask him. I really, really do. My curiosity is piqued, deeply so. But I also don't want to pry. I barely know him. *He's sweet,* though, I think to myself as I watch him out of the corner of my eye. He's shrugging his arms into a windbreaker that he pulled out of his backpack, re-adjusting his beanie. My eyes linger on his fingers as he pulls it down over his ears, and I tear my gaze away before he or Marlo see.

His protective nature *is* sweet, because at least one of us seems aware of how disturbing the Summers story actually is. But all I gleaned from that was just that- it's a story. An urban legend. Every fucking state has urban legends. For fucks sake, Saxon Beach had the black eyed children. Appearing as toddlers or school-age children, supposedly they have black eyes and beg people to let inside. Makani and I broke into an abandoned hospital in downtown Saxon Beach one time looking for them. We never did.

And sure, the idea of a giant, towering gate in the woods somewhere is fucking creepy. Abigail Summers just….. getting deleted from existence is fucking creepy. But the probability of it being true? Hilarious. I've read enough of my dad's fantasy to know that shit like that isn't actually real.

I take Zeke's hand. A warm, calloused, tan one that doesn't let go of mine once I'm up. Marlo lifts her gaze from her phone just long enough to see Zeke's hand in my own.

"Stop flirting. I *am* trying to plan something fun, oh sensitive one. Were you aware that your best friends have the house to themselves for an entire weekend?"

Zeke frowns and drops my hand. "I've told you I don't like it when you call me that. Also, Kai and Colin have the house to themselves? When?"

"Keep up, brother. We're having a party."

Within a minute, the vibes of the previous conversation have all but disappeared, and Marlo reveals that two of their best friends from the surf team (*"They're* my *friends!" Zeke interjects*) do in fact have an empty house for the entirety of the weekend. A very large, expensive house. From what I can gather in between their snipes at each other and playful, lighthearted banter, it seems like Kai Bohdie, captain of the Summerhill Surf Team, and his older brother, Colin, are known for raucous, chaotic parties, one of which will be happening in two weeks.

"It's perfect." Marlo announces, tucking her phone back into her pocket, seemingly satisfied. "While you were busy being all I'm-A-Cancer-I'm-Really-Sensitive-And-Emotional man, Kai and I have decided on a weekend to boost everyone's post-Halloween depression. I'm showing up with a handle of Fireball to complete my mission since I failed at their Halloween party."

"And your mission is?" I ask.

Zeke just snorts, and not in a nice way. "Kai Bohdie."

Despite Zeke's sour mood, I feel all my fearful, curious emotions about the South Gate woods fading away. This feels *normal*. Planning my weekend with Mak, Booker and Indie was normal. Deciding where to go, what was happening, and who was going. Mostly, planning on how colosally fucked up we could get. Indie and I together are prone to very impulsive decisions, usually doing Booker and Mak proud. One time, we-

Were.

We *were* prone to impulsive decisions.

I allow myself one full minute of reliving the happy, alcohol-soaked memories from last year with my friends, then I shove them back down to the cavern in my stomach, where the anger and pain rests. I'm not doing this right now.

Marlo looks up at her brother, gauging his face before she responds. When he just rolls his eyes at her, she smiles and jumps up, grabbing her bag. The three of us leave the student lot as more thunder rumbles through the area, carrying into town behind us.

"She's been after Kai since like sixth grade." He says openly, once again perfectly chipper. Marlo doesn't interrupt him, but her face reddens slightly. "He's our captain, and he's my friend, but the dude is a huge frat star in the making. Apparently, that's what Marlo's into now. I try not to ask further questions that provide me insight into my sister's sex life."

He's definitely still upset with her.

And with that parting comment, Zeke hugs me goodbye, swifter than any of his previous ones and walks off towards town by himself, leaving Marlo and I at the treeline.

I feel like I did something wrong, and I tell Marlo exactly that while I untangle my arms from his sage-and-sea scented hoodie. I glance behind me, staring at the path that I have to take home. Her phone buzzes again, presumably Kai Bodhie.

"So I *am* trying to get with Kai, for the record, and no, dude, you're totally fine. Zeke's just being sensitive. Ignore him. It's not you. He acts like that whenever the South Gate gets brought up."

I bite my lip, going to hand her his hoodie back. I'm torn between wanting to ask why, and not wanting to pry. It seems like it's his business, so he should be the one to tell me.

Before I turn to go, about to make some vague, dumb excuse about needing to get home, Marlo hands me the scrap of notebook paper that had the map of the forest on it.

"Here's my number. Text me tomorrow, let's meet up before class. We need to plan for next weekend. And keep that hoodie. It probably smells better than any other one you've gotten." She smirks, like she knows exactly what I'd been thinking when I put it on.

I smile at her, but stop myself before I head onto the path proper. "Hey, Marlo?"

"Yeah?"

I choose my words carefully, trying to seem blissfully, ignorantly curious. "The urban legend, about the South Gate. Does it….? I mean…. Do people really go missing?"

Marlo half smiles at me, the darkening sky behind her making for a sinister backdrop. She leans on one hip, tucking a long, reddish strand of hair behind her ear, also seeming to pick her words carefully.

"If you're asking me if the gate is real, who knows, dude. I don't really believe in it, but a looooooooot of people here do. Mostly the older crowd, but some younger ones, too. Abigail Summers was never found- that much *is* real. And a few years ago, like when my parents were little, three kids went missing in the South Gate woods. They were never found either. But the woods here are enormous, dude. Whether or not they went missing because of some paranormal vanishing gate or not is up for discussion. There's a lot of trees out there, and it gets dark. People get lost in the woods all over the world. It's normal. But eeeevvveeerrryyyyyy single time someone doesn't come out of the South Gate woods, the rumors start. And then, on top of that, every once in a blue moon someone claims to have actually *seen* the gate. Enough people have made claims that now, it's sort of our own urban legend. The older people have a lot of their own names and explanations for it. Some like to say there's a witch in the woods. Some say it's a door to another world. Some say it's a door to Hell. Everyone over the age of fifty that you ask has a different name for it. I've heard The Demon Gate, Satan's Doorway, Solomon's Gateway, Solomon's Key. People at school just call it the South Gate."

After this nuke of information, she drops her voice, and this time remorse coats her words.

"So… shit. Okay, whatever, I'm just going to tell you. Zeke had a friend when we were eight that actually went missing. His name was Miles. He was more Zeke's friend than mine, but I still knew him. We were way too young to be going anywhere by ourselves, to be honest, but it's a small town, and we all had bikes, right? We used to bike to our friends' houses all the time. But one day, Miles just didn't come home. They lived over in the East Gate, close enough to border the South Gate. His parents looked for him and ended up finding his bike in the South Gate woods, which of course sent them into hysterics. There was this whole investigation, police from the mainland came over and everything, but they never found him. So now Zeke's suuuuuper touchy about anything having to do with the gate."

She trails off, turning to leave, but then turns back around, smiling softly. "I wouldn't ask him about it, if I were you. I think he likes you."

And on that parting note, she jogs off, and I'm left dumbstruck.

I turn around and stare out at the path in front of me. The East Gate woods.

The worn, dirt footpath that should, in theory, take me straight home. Less than a fifteen minute walk.

The woods where, according to legend, there lies a gigantic, possibly supernatural gate.

The woods where, according to legend, people go in, and don't come back out.

Chapter Twelve

Niamh

The rain starts not even five minutes into my walk.

It falls in the same thick, heavy ropes that I'm coming to associate with Summerhill, coming in a downpour of epic proportion. I try to stare straight ahead, walking quickly to avoid getting thoroughly drenched.

It's hard to go that fast, though, because this time, I'm determined not to miss a single goddamn step.

The path grows muddy quickly, soaking my Vans and the bottom of my jeans, but I can't find it in me to care. I barely glance at the trees around me, or the thin, barely-visible sky above me. I'm not going to get lost this time. I should make it home in like ten minutes, at this rate. Zeke's hoodie, my jeans, and my hair might all be sticking to my skin like saran wrap, and I might be blinking water out of my eyes, but dammit, I will *not* get lost this time.

As I continue my speedy pace, though, I almost wish Marlo hadn't told me the story about Zeke's missing friend, Miles.

Even though I don't fully believe in the gate- it doesn't mean I want to be out here in the dark. I can barely see, and it's wet and I'm so out of my element on this goddamn cape. Saxon Beach didn't have fucking *forests*. We had sand.

The numerous pine trees of the East Gate woods thin out the deeper I go, and I feel myself start to breathe easier. I'm soaked and starting to grow itchy and miserable, but this must mean that I'm getting closer to home if it's thinning out. Our house is in a clearing, so that makes sense. Yeah, they're definitely thinning out.

I take a right once I reach a crossroads, following the path into where the hulking pine trees continue to thin out. Heading East.
No crude wooden signs pop up. I'm in the clear. Fuck yeah, Niamh.

I relax, finally, and glance down at my salt-stained watch. In between the tide level that's still set to Saxon Beach, the glowing orange numbers tell me exactly what I need to know: There's thirty minutes until sunset. I should be home way before that, closer to ten or less now. Finally not worrying anymore, I reach into my soaked pocket and yank my earbuds out, sticking an earbud in. I cue up a loud, fast-paced Neck Deep song, shoving down thoughts of iron gates and missing kids, and instead hum along, cheerfully and peacefully soaking in my little nature walk.

After a few minutes I reach into my somehow dry pocket, hunting for a different playlist, when I hear a very clear, firm voice in the back of my head say *don't.*

Don't.

The voice is clear as day, as if it were a person standing next to me. My inner voice is usually calm and breathless, annoyed with me. This is still that inner voice: but it seems to come from somewhere deeper, right now. This inner voice is warning me to pay attention, to not look down.

I whip my head up, my pulse quickening. There's nothing there.

And then everything goes completely and utterly dark.

Completely dark, and not like the night.

Dark like someone reached up into the sky and picked the stars down one by one. Dark like the fucking End Times.

I can't see my hand in front of my face. I can't see my legs, or any of my body at all. Fumbling, breathing faster, I punch the buttons on my watch, triggering the underwater/night vision mode.

I can't see the glowing orange numbers on my watch.

I can't even see my breath fogging out in front of me.

A panicked, cold fear rolls through my body, and I freeze in place, the rain still dumping around me. All around me I can hear the quiet splashing of rain meeting mud, and my panicky, frenzied breathing. Frozen in place, I just stand there.

Every wet, frozen second feels horribly like eons.

I don't know what to do. I don't know what to do.

Then, in the same place that my inner voice came from, a feeling starts to take root. An old, primal feeling, designed to keep me alive, designed to propel my limbs to run from predators.

Danger.

I am in danger.

And then my inner voice speaks again in that same loud, commanding voice, as real as if it were coming from beside me.

It's the only sound that rings through the trees at all.

There's someone here.

I exhale into the dark with the force of a snail, my throat shrunken to the size of a paper straw. Fear, real and vibrant and warping my common sense floods my body instantly.

I stay frozen in place right as *something* moves behind me

Some*thing*, not someone. I don't know how I know it isn't a person. I just do. With a sixth sense that I didn't know I had, I stay frozen in place as something moves on the ground behind me.

No.

In front of me.

No.

Above me?

It keeps moving, and even without being able to see, I can feel whatever is here moving quickly, seeming to jump, or crawl, or fly up into the pine trees and back down. It must be an animal. I don't know how else it would be able to move that fast. Even though I know, deep down, that it is not.

Chills run down my arms and legs beneath my clothes as I feel the thing get closer to me again, the air itself dropping a few degrees around me. Whatever it is, it's something cold, and something I can't see. After a second, I catch the faint yet distinct scent of animal carcass.

Something that smells very, distinctly rotten.

Something that smells very distinctly dead.

My stomach clenches, my whole body locking up tight as the smell wafts right under my nose.

And then my body goes liquid, and I don't even have the decency to be embarrassed.

The only thought that takes space in my mind right then is this: My dad's superstitious, old, paranoid Irish parents were right all along. My grandparents' stories ring through my head as I stand in place, too scared to even breathe.

There are things in pockets of the world that we cannot see, whether it be because these things are good at hiding, or simply because they exist in in-between places humans cannot breach. Things that can roam to and from, things that can crawl back and forth between our world and their own. Wherever that world may be.

And most people assume that because we can't see them that they simply aren't real.

But just because we can't see something doesn't mean it didn't see us.

CHAPTER THIRTEEN

NIAMH

Fear has a funny way of making you remember things.

Some people freeze up when their brain perceives danger. Some people run. Some people shut down completely, their brain deeming the situation too traumatic to remain fully present. It's different for everyone. My brain has always chosen to remember fear in snapshots, similar to a film camera. Little detailed moments, highlighted in snippets.

All the memories I have of the scariest day of my life resides in stills.

Click.

Makani's smiling eyes on mine, the bare, tanned skin of his back gleaming gold under the late morning sun as we hop the chain-link fence into our school. He smells like banana sunscreen, and he has his shirt tucked into the back of his board shorts pocket.

Click.

Me reaching to the top and tossing the plastic container of lighter fluid down after him, then leaping down myself.

Click.

My blue tank top gets stuck on the wire, and without wasting a second, I yank it off completely and run after him in my bikini top and shorts.

Click.

Booker and Indie following after us, laughing.

Click.

Taking turns pouring the entire contents of the can onto the storage shed, the old, falling apart one holding the PE equipment. The four of us laughing at how bad it smells, like years worth of sweaty feet.

Click.

Booker's maniacal, shit-eating grin as he produces a white Bic lighter from his pocket. His dark, swoopy bangs fall into his eyes, and he pushes them away with one heavily-braceleted arm. Him asking us if we're really about to do this, the biggest dare we've done yet. Setting a fire.

Click.

Me snatching it from his hands, my own grin rivaling his, and flicking the tiny blue flame into existence.

Click.

Feeling everything at once: The heat of the late-October sun, still just as hot as it was in July.

Smelling the sunscreen wafting from everyone's bare, tan shoulders. We were still surfing in board shorts and bikinis in October.

Seeing the adrenaline and excitement in all three pairs of eyes looking at me.

And love.

Overwhelming, choking love from all three of them, intermingled with excitement and the thrill of doing something we should definitely not be doing. The excitement in those eyes sparkling like they did every time we enacted a dare, every time we did something we shouldn't do, like lighting school property on fire over the weekend because Mak had said I wouldn't do it.

Of course I had to prove him wrong.

Click.

Flicking the lighter to life again, and tossing it onto the soaked equipment shed.

But this is when my memories change.

Because I remember what happened next with frightening, crystal-clear recollection.

I know I'll never forget it.

Click.

The *nanosecond* that the lighter meets the soaked storage shed, I have a thought that comes from somewhere deep within. A thought that is angry and demanding, a thought that seems to bury its way under my skin, until *I* feel angry and demanding.

Big, I think. *Be big, be aggressive.*

I think it with a well of anger that feels all at once my own and not my own, coming from deep, deep beneath my chest, below the space where my heart lies. Somewhere innate and true.

Somewhere that burns brighter than a hot coal, and just as hot.

The storage shed immediately erupts into a roaring, violent bonfire.

And the longer I stare at it, feeling the flames lick my bare shoulders,

that violent, unchecked anger starts to simmer beneath my skin, consuming me. And I let it, because it feels right.

That is what undoes me.

The second I let it consume me, I'm no longer angry.
But I'm also no longer in my body.

I'm fucking celestial, I'm untied to Earth.

I'm a planet, a star, a nebula.

What happens is this.

The second I let the anger consume me, my heart *slips* out of its cage in my ribs.

It falls down into my stomach, then farther still.

Heat begins to slide down my back like oil, hot and tantalizing all down my spine, and then pools itself between my legs.

I remember gasping, my back arching on instinct.

It feels real, alive. Like whatever's happening is purposely trying to get a reaction out of me.

A warm, sweet weight rests at the base of my earlobes. Like someone's mouth, like someone running their lips along the back of my neck and the spot behind my earlobes.

My legs feel limp, and my lower stomach coils tight. It's too much, it's too much.

Endless, searing heat fills my body, along with it an overwhelming, planet-sized feeling of *good* washing over me.

I'm rooted to the spot, this ecstasy filling my body both inside and out. I'm aware of the shed burning, but it feels as if it's a world away.

Dizzy, tantalizing *want* courses through my skin, my veins.

It's desire.

No.

It's *need.*

I almost feel like *I'm* on fire, but I can't be.

The searing heat runs gentle, slippery fingers down my neck again, trailing down my arms, between my thighs-

I must have moaned, because this is when my three friends tear their excited, big eyes away from the complete bonfire of a storage shed and look at me instead.

And suddenly, I want *them* to feel how good I do. This feeling is unlike *anything* I've ever felt before. Ever.

I don't have the words to tell them, so I grab Makani's arm-

And the pained, agonizing scream that falls out of his throat is the single most horrible sound I've heard in my whole life.

A sound I won't forget as long as I live.

Click.

Booker is there in an instant, ripping Mak's arm out of my iron grip. Then he yells, too.

The consuming, beautiful feeling that had been flooding my body vanishes.

In the spot where I'd grabbed Makani, there lies a giant, hand-sized, charred black burn mark. His arm is waxy and blackened where I grabbed him, completely damaged beyond the tissue. A third degree burn.

Click.

They stare at me, all three of them. Makani is still screaming, clutching his arm in agony, while Booker and Indie just stare at me in utter shock.

In that instant, whatever bond that made us a four pack is severed. It is no longer us. It is them and me. It is Mak, Booker, and Indie against Niamh.

Amidst his horrified, pain-filled screams, Indie and Booker help Makani up, and all three of them stare at me as if I'm a stranger. As if I'm someone they don't know at all.

Click.

They run, both arms looped around Mak.

I stay.

Click.

The storage shed continues to burn, and when the Saxon Beach Fire Department show up, the SBPD along with them, I'm still there, sitting in the grass.

I don't talk. I don't say anything. My body feels oddly spent, my limbs jelly.

Click.

When my parents show up, I don't say anything. I don't offer them a single word. They've been on the receiving end of our stupid dares.

I let them think this is just another one of those.

And while we drive as a family to the Saxon Beach Police Department headquarters, I don't think of the world of trouble I'm sure to be destined for.

I don't think of the storage shed. I don't think about what the school is going to say when they find out.

I don't think about Mak's arm, or how I somehow did that.

I don't think about my friends at all.

No, what goes through my mind is one thought, and one alone.

How do I get that feeling back?

Whatever is on the path with me right now coats my mind so thoroughly in fear that I start to see in brief snapshots.

Click.

The thing on the path with me stops moving.

I hear whispering.

Click.

I hear bleating. Very shrill, distinct bleating. A goat.

Instead of snapping me out of my frozen state, all that sound does is intensify my fear, allowing for sheer, undiluted panic to seep inside instead.

I can't think. I can't think. I'm going to fucking *die* out here in the woods and I can't get air in holy shit I'm gonna fucking die ohmygod ohfuck whatisthat whatISTHAT

Click.

A cloying, heavy weight rests on the back of my neck, wrapping around from behind. It rests just below my hair, right at the space behind my ears.

I can't see at all, but I feel it perfectly. A tangible darkness.

And then it tries to *speak.*

Whatever thing is coiled behind my ears, intermingling with the rain on my skin and my tangled hair tries to speak to me.

The words that I hear are broken, raspy.
Choking and scratchy, as if it hasn't used its voice in some time.

But it shit sure tries, slipping across my skin and coiling closer to the openings of my ears.

And what comes out is something that sounds very much like *friend.*

The thing that is trying to worm its way inside my ears tries again, it's raspy, unused voice catching and scratching against its throat.

Friend?

It comes out scratchy again, and I can feel it try to smile against my neck.

And it is as it asks a third time that I know without question that whatever is on this path with me right is definitely not a friend.

Because human things- normal things- do not ask like that.

The primal, keep-Niamh-alive voice in my head is pulling all the fire alarms, running around and knocking on my skull, telling me to run.

Run, Niamh.

For once, I listen to it.

Run, Niamh.

So I bolt into a dead sprint, adrenaline filling my veins.

Like a hare, I dart through the woods, completely unable to see.

Unable to think about anything other than what the *fuck just touched me.*

As I run, I can hear something else behind me, following me. Something other than whatever was lying on my neck: something big, and heavy. Something that lopes along, and can't run as fast as me.

Something old.

Panting, tears flowing freely, I keep at a sprint, praying I don't smack headfirst into a pine tree. If I stop, I'm a goner. I know it without having to question it. Whatever is behind me wants to be friends, and I'm not in the habit of making friends with things that smell like death reincarnated.

I can taste my heart in my throat, my skin glowing hot and cold. I'm not crying anymore, I'm barely breathing. Sheer terror is the only thing propelling me forward. I'm a hare, I'm a fucking hare.

Oh my fucking God, I'm the prey. Oh, my fucking, *God.*

From somewhere far behind me, I can hear a goat's distinct bleating.

I yelp, picking up my pace into the darkness. My backpack slaps against Zeke's soaked hoodie, and my panting, labored breathing is all I can hear for a few minutes. Then-

Fuck. Is it gone?

Then, the darkness begins to subside just enough that I can make out the trunks of the pine trees again. The dark greens of their needles, the deep, rough browns of their bases.

Yes. *YES.* Fuck yes. Oh my god, yes. That's a tree. And that's a tree.

I'm still on the path.

Finally, and only because the stitch in my side is unbearable, I stop, heaving for breath.

I can see completely again. Waving my hand in front of my face, I can clearly see my bitten, jagged nails, and their chipped black polish.

I look down at myself. I can see my baggy, oversized jeans, now completely coated in thick black mud from my run. My socks and shoes are toast. Zeke's hoodie is so rain-soaked that it feels like an extra few pounds, combined with my sweaty skin.

My beanie nearly falls over my eyes, the ends of my white-blonde hair coated in the same mud, a few stray pine needles as well.

I slap a hand to the back of my neck, rubbing it. There's nothing there, other than rain and mud.

No…. *thing.*

Fully and completely unable to process what just happened, I continue down the path, my shaky, jelly limbs propelling my forward.

I feel my lips start to tremble as I battle tears.

None of this is fair. I should have never been put in this situation at *all.* I should be home with my friends, not walking in the middle of this weird ass, creepy ass, small town paranormal ass whatever the *fuck just happened* town.

Fuck Summerhill. Fuck the woods. Fuck all of this.

I'm looking down, trying to wipe my angry tears away without getting mud in my eyes, but when I look up, I see it.

The South Gate sign.

"This is not *fucking. Happening.*"

My voice comes out choked from tears and raw in my disbelief.

No fucking way. No fucking *way*. Summerhill could go fuck itself. This is *not* happening again.

What the fuck is up with this town?

I shut my eyes, rainwater sliding down my cheeks like tears. Anger, residual fear, and unfairness course through my body, and I'm exhausted.

When the urge to burst into wild, childlike sobs subsides, I open my eyes. The sign is still there.

Fuck. This.

Fuck getting home. Fuck Summerhill. Fuck this continuous, perpetual fog. Fuck the fucking state of Maine. Fuck living on a fucking cape. Fuck this stupid, creepy fucking town. Fuck the TREES. I want to burn them. All of them.

I never should've *been here*. I should be *home,* where I belong. I should be with Mak and Booker and Indie, without weird things happening to me. I should be home, and not getting chased by *something I can't fucking see in the woods.*

But even as I think all of this, my rage rising, one thought blares brighter than all the rest.

But something weird did *happen to you back home, Niamh.*

And you loved *how it felt.*

I let out a sob, anger and frustration tearing through me. I let them.

Any other day, I would probably fight the feelings, stuff them back down. But right now, I'm too tired to try. My energy is spent from my sprint, and a new emotion takes over instead:

Hopelessness.

My shaky jelly legs finally give out, and I fall to the ground, laying in a pile on the muddy path.

The path that changed on me not once, but twice.

The path where something that smelled very, very dead asked to be my friend.

The path that led me to this same sign not once, but,

"Christ."

My exhaustion disappears as I nearly jump out of my fucking skin, looking around for wherever the voice just came from.

It isn't the same voice as whatever spoke to me minutes ago. It isn't that inhuman, scratchy one. This one is different.

This voice is feminine, lilting.

I'm not religious, unlike the rest of my Irish-Catholic family.
But for the first time in recent years, I pray.
Please, God. Don't throw anything else my way right now. I can't do it. I literally cannot take any more right now. Please, God. I am not your strongest soldier. I'm seventeen. Please, God, do not give me anything else right now.

"You good?"

I scramble to my feet, mud sliding off of my clothes in clumps as the instinct to run floods my body for the second time today. I look around wildly amidst the fog, which rolled in thick while I was on the ground. The South Gate sign in front of me is now barely visible.

But there, behind the sign, is definitely a girl.

Her features are partially hidden in the fog, and all I can really make out is her outline- her hips, her shoulders, and what looks like dark, waist-length hair. As I swear at the scene before me, she leans against the sign and laughs, seemingly amused.

When I can't formulate a single word, she laughs again. A dry, quick chuckle, in that lilting, pretty voice.

"Where's the fire?" She says.

Her choice of words knocks the wind out of me, and my mouth goes dry. I realize that she must have watched my entire meltdown. She probably saw me fall to the ground, laying in the mud and rain like a fucking toddler having a tantrum.

She must see my expression, because she stops laughing and stands tall, crossing her arms lazily. I can see her fully now amidst the fog.

She's tall, taller than me. Thin and gangly, yet she looks strong, like she doesn't take shit from anyone. It rolls off of her in waves. Maybe it's just the way she seems so unafraid of the dark woods behind her, so unafraid of the way the shadows between the trees seem to move, shifting with the fog. She's pale like someone who's never seen the sun, her skin milky and porcelain. Contrasted with the dark brown of her stick-straight hair, which spills over her shoulders and far down to her waist, she looks more like a faerie or a forest sprite than human. Combined with her long, sapphire blue skirt and oversized gray sweater, I almost expect to see wings behind her. Or at the very least, horns.

She sees me assessing her, and I watch her face shift into a visible, coy smirk, one that reaches her eyes fully. And those eyes....

Her eyes are a dark, *dark* blue. Dark like below sea level dark, two twin sapphires glinting through the fog. Piercing, pulling eyes that look me over while I look at her, that smirk telling me that she knows exactly how to use those eyes.

She tilts her head to the side, and I'm reminded, strangely, of the way a cat looks at a mouse.

Hungry.

My adrenaline spikes again, my calves tensing, ready to sprint as if my life might very well depend on it. Fear is fucking crazy. I didn't think I had any more energy left in me, and yet right now my body floods once more with shaky, instant adrenaline. My vision pounds in tune with my hummingbird heartbeat until all I can see is the girl.

Something tells me she might run a bit faster than the thing in the woods.

But before I can make a decision, she laughs for a third time, and this time it's gentle, meant to dispel my fear.

"Relax," she says, leaning back against the sign again. "It's just an expression."

She tilts her head again, assessing me. Those deep, dark wells of blue look me over with curiosity and something else I can't name.

My adrenaline fades, and suddenly I can barely muster the strength to stand. It's like honey has been poured into my veins: I'm exhausted, more so than I've ever been in my life. I feel spent.

Trying to listen to the warning light in the back of my head, though, I take a few tentative steps away from her, attempting to control my slow, leaden legs. I wonder what she sees right now- a sweaty, muddy, disgusting urchin of a person. My hair is probably a wreck, coated in forest debris and limp from the fog and rain. I can feel my face covered in tears and dirt, not to mention my clothes. I look like a fucking heathen. Combined with what she definitely just witnessed, I'm shocked she hasn't asked me if I'm on drugs or something. But she just looks at me curiously, like I'm fascinating, but she's trying really hard not to care.

"Who.. are you?" I manage to get out, my voice cracking twice. I'm too exhausted to care.

She stands straight, stretching those long arms languidly. I'm still in shock that she hasn't said a word about my obvious breakdown.

My breakdown because I was *fucking chased by something I couldn't see that was trying to crawl inside of my skull.*

She doesn't move far from the treeline, but she leans back against another tree, close enough to where she could reach out and touch me if she wanted. She's still smirking, too. It isn't an unkind one, but it isn't nice, either. It's crooked, like she has a secret and desperately wants to tell me.

"She speaks at last. I'm shocked."
That sensual, lilting voice carries all the way into my head.

I swallow hard. Breathing shallow, I try to regain some moisture in my mouth. I could totally outrun her. I could one hundred percent outrun her if I needed to. But my fear is fading quickly, curiosity taking over.

I swallow. "I'm Niamh."

Then I want to kick myself, swearing internally. What have my gran and granda etched into my brain since I was a kid? *Never give them your true name.*

Then again, my grandparents were referring to faeries and dark creatures. This is very clearly a human girl.

The girl stretches one pale, cool hand out, and I take it without meaning to, my cold, filthy hand fitting in hers perfectly.
Her hand is rough, worn deep with calluses and ridged scars. She might be tiny, but she's definitely strong. Every breath that leaves her lips radiates confidence, just bordering on arrogance.

"Tyler."

When I don't say anything, she chuckles under her breath. "Can I ask what the hell you were running towards? Or away from, I guess?"

So she *did* see.

Her voice is silky and smooth, rose petals and gentle breezes. A direct contrast to her tightly bound muscles and deep, alluring eyes.

"I-." I say.

Do I tell her? Will she think I'm crazy? Will she tell people? But…. if there is something in there, I *should* tell someone. Right?

"There was something in there." Is what comes out. My voice shakes, but I speak my truth nevertheless. "I was just walking home… I just moved here…. and it went dark. Something was following me, trying to talk to me… I don't know. I don't know."

Fuck. That was elaborate, Niamh. Good job.

"So…. do you always take the path that cuts directly through the South Gate woods?"

After she asks, she glances behind her. I wonder what she's looking at.

Shifting, moving shadows, crawling between the trees.

Stop it, Niamh. Christ.

"I wasn't trying to. This is supposed to be the path closest to my house. It did that the first time, though. It switched up on me and led me here. I don't know how. These woods are weird."

Tyler fiddles with something at her side that I can't see amidst the fog.

"People don't really hang out in the South Gate, you know."

I look up at the hand painted sign, thinking about how fucking *angry* and I had been upon seeing it again. About how unfair and upsetting all of this is. Then I think of what happened the last time I'd gotten too angry, gotten too consumed in that emotion. Makani got burned.

I burned him.

I don't even know what to say to her right now.

"Yeah, I gathered that." I say. "People say that there's something fucked up about this part of the woods. I'm kind of inclined to agree."

Tyler meets my gaze but doesn't offer an opinion, then reaches her arm out, running her fingers down the wooden post of the sign. The way she strokes it is almost tender, almost affectionate.

A thought hits me.

"Did *you* paint that?" I ask her.

She snorts, dropping her hand immediately. "No. Some idiot kids from town did, most likely. Or maybe not. Like I said, nobody really comes to this part of the woods, unless they aren't trying to come back. Except," She tilts her head sideways again, "For you, apparently. If the path unnerved you the first time, why'd you come back a second?"

I can't help myself. "Do you believe in the gate?"

Tyler's smirk resurfaces, and she looks at me with newfound interest. "Yes and no. There's a witch in these woods. No one's told you yet?"

Before I can answer, she continues, ticking the facts off of her long fingers.

"Let me see. She crawls through the forest like a shadow, in and out of the gate. She can change her shape, taking the form of any one of her familiars: a crow, a hare, a specter, a black goat, to nothing more than black smoke that stays low to the floor. Her veins are rotten with forest dirt and pine needles. She whispers charms into the wind, calling wayward souls from their beds, just to carve their hearts from their bodies, fresh for her darkest spells."

Tyler cocks her head, considering me. "They also say," she whispers, "that she *moves* the gate. That she can pick it up and place it anywhere in the woods. They say that she moves it so that people are more likely to find it. She always knows when someone's in the woods."

I stare at her, my jaw on the floor.

"*And* that with just one kiss, she can pull your very essence, your very soul, your *humanity* through her lips and make you entirely hers, making you forget everything except for her. Everything, including how to pull air into your lungs."

I swear I stop breathing for a second.

And then Tyler bursts into laughter. "Oh my god." She clutches her side, pretending to wipe away a tear. "You should see your face right now. Holy hell."

She keeps laughing longer than I feel it's merited, considering what I've been through today.

I say nothing, trying not to look weak. Something tells me if I completely break down and cry right now, she'd run with it. So instead, I force myself to roll my eyes and scoff.

"A witch of the woods. How terrifying."

I try to come off as nonchalant and sarcastic, but my inner voice is shaking her head slowly at me, whispering *careful, Niamh.*
That same tiny voice that's buzzing around the back of my skull right now like angry bees, buzzing with more questions than answers. Tyler crosses and uncrosses her

arms, her shoulder grazing just below the letters. Her gaze is unreadable, her face half hidden in the fog again. Part of me wants to get closer.

Another wiser, instinctive part of me says to hold back.

"Believe what you want. I'm sure they," She crooks one finger lazily towards the direction I came from, towards town, "Will tell you all sorts of things. There's dozens of stories about these woods. It doesn't matter what the truth really is. The locals avoid the South Gate woods, at any cost."

Her voice is silk. Roses. Light and practiced and cunning. But underneath the measured words and careless tone, I detect something else. I don't quite catch it in time, though.

Weird.

"So you're not a local, I'm guessing?" I venture to ask, shifting my feet. All the sweat from the previous few minutes has pooled down my back, mingling with the chilly rainwater. I'm absolutely filthy, and a hot shower suddenly becomes the top of my priority list. After actually getting home, that is.

Tyler snorts, and I wonder what it is I'm saying that could possibly be so amusing to her. It isn't that she's making fun of me- it's something else I can't put my finger on.

"I used to be." She says, in that same measured, petal-soft voice. "They're assholes. It's whatever."

My curiosity spikes, but she's started to walk off, heading back into the trees. I think of how milky and clear her skin was, and then feel truly, genuinely filthy, like the forest picked me up, chewed me around, and spat me back at its feet. I need to go *home.* I need to get out of this goddamn fucking forest.

"Wait," I call into the treeline. I dart forward, running my hands down the sign, checking behind it.

Tyler's gone.

"Fuck." I say for the millionth time. I'm clearly lost, probably hallucinating, absolutely disgusting, and to top it all off, the town I'm now stuck in is rotten with urban legends. Demon gates. Witches in the woods. Fucking creepy inhuman things that follow people home.

A gate that deletes people from existence.

A sect of the woods that even the locals avoid.

Places and pockets of the world that people go in and don't come back out of. *A fucking witch????*

Frustration rushes through me, hot like a coal, and I crouch back on my heels before the sign, burying my filthy face in my equally filthy hands. Unfairness and anger course through me, burning. When I look up, my rage beginning to build upwards, all I can see through my blurry eyes is the fog, and vague shapes of the trees behind it.

Fog and tears.

I drop my head back down to my hands, finally admitting defeat. I'm never getting home. I'm lost in the fucking South Gate woods, and I'll be just another statistic. Maybe that thing will come back to pick me off. Hell, maybe I'll see the gate. Maybe my parents will finally feel bad for moving me here. Maybe they'll forgive me. Maybe Makani will-

It's thinking about Makani that finally makes the back of my throat tighten up, and the tears come hot and fast as I let go, finally. Thoughts of my best friends and how much I miss them, how shitty this move is, combined with how *horrible* I feel for hurting Mak finally break through the abyss I'd shoved it all down into.

I allow the full bodied, ricketing sobs to crash through my windpipe, my anger and unfairness, my secret that I've been holding tightly onto breaking me at last.

"Well, shit." Tyler's voice echoes somewhere around me.
As I whip my head up, a few things happen almost immediately.

The first, immediate thing: the layer of pine needles and brush that line the path in front of me is on fire.
Literal fire, despite the bucketing rain.

A small, contained fire, as if someone had started it on purpose. A real, legitimate fire. I can feel the heat of it on my skin.

And where my had been, his arm was charred and waxy, blackened and burned skin-

I choke on my sobs, Makani's arm burned behind my eyes.

The second thing: Tyler is back, standing at the treeline, and she isn't staring at the fire. She's staring at me, a look of true shock on her-

Holy shit- her *beautiful* face.

Finally standing out in the open, I can see how truly striking she is. Ethereal is a better word for it. Between her chocolate colored hair that just skims her hip bones, those deep, oceanic blue eyes, the smattering of freckles across her cheeks and raised chin, her thin, willowy body…. Those eyes that are looking *through* me right now…

I realize I'm staring and shake my head slightly, tearing my eyes away from the way she's looking at me now. That smirk is back in full force, like she knows. The faint, subtle scent of roses glides under my nose, like the fog is carrying it.

Tyler is fucking *beautiful.*

The third thing: The moment I stop crying, my anger subsiding along with my tears, the fire dies out.

The smell of smoke and blackened leaves are all that remain.

Charred remains, like Makani's arm.

Like what I did.

What *I* did.

And the fourth thing that happens: A swift drop, like the drop on a rollercoaster surges through me, my entire body immediately going tight and my eyes blinded with stars.

The same feeling I felt the day I burned Makani rushes through me, and I tilt my head back, gasping.
Finally.

And oh my god,

It feels *delicious.*

But it doesn't last. Tyler darts out, grabbing me by the elbows. She utters something quickly in words I don't understand, and just as quickly as it started, the feeling subsides.

I want to scream at her. How dare she, how dare she.

But my legs start to shake, and then they give out instantly. I know that if she wasn't holding me I would've fallen.

With that euphoric, otherworldly high comes an equally otherworldly low. I feel completely used. Completely spent.

For a moment, we just stare at each other. Neither one of us say a word for what feels like a full minute. My head starts to spin hard, and I consider the possibility of passing out. I've never passed out in my life.

Tyler doesn't release me even once I stop shaking. "You did that." She says.

A statement, not a question.

I think of the shed at Saxon Beach High School, and that dumb, stupid dare that changed everything.

I think of my hand tossing the lighter onto the shed. I think about how that anger that came out of nowhere started to consume me, filling me with this violent, aggressive burning. I think about how I'd *wanted* the shed to burn like I was.

And it had, because I'd told it to.

I think about how I'd felt something the others didn't that day. Mak saw my eyes the second before I'd grabbed him.

And he looked afraid of me.

I think of that fucking shed, and how good it had felt seeing it ablaze. *I* had set it ablaze. Whatever that feeling was, whatever happened that day was my doing. That unearthly, God-like haze.

Thoughts of that day, and of what I did race through my head like wildfire, and I let them.

I burned my best friend.

I set that shed on fire.

Me.

The secret I've been hiding from everyone since that day finally echoes in my head, reverberating with Tyler's words: *You did that.*

I did.

The shed caught fire because I'd told it to.

And burning Makani was my consequence, because I'd let myself get consumed in that haze.

My head is ringing.

But I'm done keeping this secret.

I look at Tyler, the fog still hiding most of the trees and area surrounding us, but not her. No, I can see her perfectly, from the constellations of freckles that coat her nose and forehead, to the wells of blue, that tumbling abyss that is her eyes.

Those intense, searching eyes that are looking at me right now like I'm something she'd lost long ago and finally found.

"Yeah." I whisper. An answer, for more than just her. "I think I did."

CHAPTER FOURTEEN

TYLER

Insomnia runs in our family, deeper than the roots of the pine trees lined up outside my bedroom window. My grandmother says it's the remnants of a curse passed down from another years ago, the result of a Lane woman who must have committed an unforgivable breach of magic, who used her gifts for something that went against nature. The equivalent of breaking a law or something, I guess. Like reanimating something that was dead. Or crafting a totally non-consensual love spell.

Or maybe, some Lane woman down the line decided to dive into some dark, heavy shit. Some type of black magic, for lack of a better word, and whatever force gives us our gifts cursed her for practicing it.

My grandmother once had a little sister named Mira. Mira apparently had gifts similar to my own: she could read others' thoughts. She could move things without lifting a finger. She had the Sight. She could get things out in the forest to come when

SUMMERHILL

she called and do things for her. Rabbits, birds, spiders, and all creatures of the earth flocked to her. She had many familiars, and she was powerful. She only grew stronger the older she got, her gifts excelling all normal standards. And Mira really, really liked to fuck with people.

She knew she was better than the average human. She'd been given these gifts, after all. Why not use them? Eleni's mother called her daughter a prankster; Eleni called her sister a bully. Like a kid who kicked kittens when no one was looking.

By the time she was fifteen, she started to grow curious. *Why* couldn't she use magic against those who harmed her? *Why* was it so wrong to hurt others with the gifts she'd been given? *Why,* she wanted to know, couldn't she summon things that would do her bidding for her.

Eleni said it was this comment that had her mother scared.

One day, Mira decided to find her own answers, since no one would tell her. It was always no. Never an explanation, Eleni said. Their mother always ended conversations Mira brought up with a firm, unwavering *no.* You just didn't, that was why. It wasn't until Mira turned sixteen that Eleni discovered why.

Mira was powerful, that much was apparent. So powerful that she wanted to see just how far that power went. How much her gifts could *really* do. She'd been studying all those months her mother kept telling her no without telling her why. Studying, and researching. A few months after Mira turned sixteen, she summoned something.

Successfully.

Something dark, something old. A demon.

A king, actually, a demon king under the command of Solomon. It was something she'd found in a book, an ancient, anonymous grimoire depicting seventy two demons and how to summon them. I looked it up one time after Eleni first told me about her sister. It's a real book: The Lesser Key of Solomon. No one knows who wrote it.

Mira summoned one of those things, and not just to see if she could. She wanted to see if she could get it to do her bidding, to combine her own gifts with something even more powerful.

Mira wanted to rule.

But the thing she summoned was much, much more powerful than a sixteen year old witch.

And much smarter.

Eleni never told me what happened to her sister. She only talks about her as a cautionary tale, usually to remind me not to ever dive into dark, old magic, or take my gifts for granted. She always uses the term 'black magic' as an umbrella term, but the shit Mira got into definitely falls under that.

It *always* involves darker magic if it's negative, according to Eleni. Can't seem to keep your plants alive? Can't sleep? Trouble making friends? Can't kick that cold that you've had for weeks? Dark magic. Always dark magic, and always the conjurer's fault.

Aka, a Lane woman's fault.

Five years ago, when I turned thirteen, I morphed into something new seemingly overnight.
I shed all my baby fat- what little was left- and grew three whole inches. My hair grew and grew and grew, until it skimmed my waist. My skin cleared, then stayed clear. Eleni nearly had a heart attack: my new body was distinctly, unmistakably fae. I grew tall, lithe. My features were prominent, sharp, and ethereal. My eyes were bluer, my hair darker, my skin whiter. My skin began to take on a clean, floral smell, like roses had taken root in my body.

Seemingly overnight, I began to resemble something graceful, something just short of beautiful.

Suddenly, boys paid attention to me, more than they ever had. It wasn't in the teasing, taunting way of years past. No, this time was different. This time around, they paid attention to the newer, sharper edges of me. The parts that made me look older and more cunning than I was, and made them forget that they ever called me names. The worst part is that for a time, the small, naive bit of me that remained relished in it.

When a harem of prepubescent teenage boys began to follow me home, though, my grandmother stepped in. She thought I'd put a spell on them, you see. She couldn't see why they would begin to just pay attention to me like they were.

Nevermind that I was growing up, my magic truly taking root: the better of a grip I got on it, the more beautiful I felt.

It didn't matter to Eleni. She was insistent that I put an end to it, less they fall violent. Which is why, at thirteen, I got the speech we all get.

Lane women aren't compatible with love.

And they never have been. And they never will be. Violence, death, and misery befall every Lane woman who shoots her shot at love.

I didn't believe her at first. What an outdated, bullshit idea. Right?

But then she told me how my parents died.

Right after my parents were married, they were killed instantly in a plane crash on the way to their honeymoon, not even two days' wed. I was three years old, and had been staying with my grandmother for the week. I'm not entirely sure I believe in the curse at all. I'm not exactly prone to just believing things people say, or doing what they tell me to.

All it's really done is make damn sure that I never go looking for love.

So it's the curse I'm turning over and over in my head as I pace my darkened room at a quarter to midnight, since sleep has decided to evade me once again.

Like it has been every night for weeks now. Every. Single. Night.

Night is supposed to be my favorite time of day, as one who possesses innate magic. It's the best time for any sort of spell. Midnight, traditionally, is where the line is drawn. An in-between time. A liminal, non-existent space. A time that is neither here nor there, neither night nor day, light nor dark. It's the best time for anything magical, period. Finding portals. Casting. Seeing. Reading cards, getting answers.

And since I am nothing if not a Lane, midnight is when I usually find myself most awake, charged, and alight.

Sighing, I quit pacing my darkened room and fold myself in a heap on my unmade bed. Wreaths of dried herbs, flowers, and pine needles stick to the frame of my bed, and a few fall from the movement. I pluck bits of tree from my hair, my gaze wandering to my window.

"This is such bullshit." I hiss to the empty room. As if someone, anyone, will hear me and suddenly fix it.

Honestly, though, in this house, someone might be.

I'm not even *tired,* and I've tried everything. Every charm I know, every incantation, every spell, *everything.* I *should,* as a practicing witch, be able to craft the simplest sleep aid. I should, in theory, be able to do it with my eyes closed, by now. I'm eighteen. I was doing *such* complex fucking spells at fourteen. Eleni was elated.

But sleep- sleep has evaded me, despite my best efforts. Instead of accepting defeat, though, my restless, stubborn brain is telling me that it must mean something else.

I stretch across my bed in the dark, my vision uncannily decent. Witch-light, or witch-eyes, my grandmother calls them. Another one of my gifts.

I reach below my bed for two long, angular mirrors, grabbing a spare white candle while I'm at it. Full length mirrors, the kind that usually sit on top of a dresser. Crossing my room, I grab the chair from my desk, and then another one from the corner that I keep by my door for when I need to stuff it under the handle in order to lock it.

I set the two chairs up to face each other, placing the mirrors on either one. Then I close my eyes, willing my witch-light to snuff out, and my window to shut. It closes softly by an invisible force. By my magic.

In my now pitch black room, I can barely see my hands in front of my face. I will the candle to light, and it does.

Going only by candlelight, I take a seat in between the two chairs, taking my 'throne.' Trying to calm my frustrated breathing, I reach deep to find that state of serenity that works best when trying to See. It never does well to try and look when angry, I've learned. It just messes with the outcome. If you try to find an answer while angry, you receive- get this- an angry answer. Attempting this ritual with a clear mind usually always gets me a clear answer.

Once I can breathe evenly, I close my eyes. When I open them, I do my damn hardest to just stare straight ahead.

Technically, the Three Kings ritual might fall under my grandmother's umbrella of Bad Magic That You Are Never To Mess With. On either side of me, just out of the corners of my eyes, shadows begin to move in either mirror.

In one is a Queen. In the other is a Fool. I am their King.

But from *their* point of view, I could just as well be their Queen, or their Fool. Hence the title: The Three Kings. No one knows who is who.

Technically speaking, this is darker magic. It's a ritual that a conjurer can perform when they need answers. You're supposed to never look at either one of the mirrors, never let your candle go out, just stare straight ahead until you get your answers.

I've never looked at the mirrors when doing this, even though I want to. Mirror magic is always sketchy, and I know that.

I'm not that fucking stupid.

Feeling just the tiniest bit stupid right now though, I exhale deeply and ask my question aloud.

"Why can't I sleep?" I say aloud into my pitch-black room. Asking an in-between question at an in-between time, to two in-between things: mirrors. I should, in theory, get an answer.

I close my eyes again. I know I'm not alone.

And then, a deep, scratchy voice to my left chuckles.

"Why will you not open your eyes?" The voice says. It sounds like loose gravel, like something grating against something else. Raspy and jagged, like it's throat doesn't work properly.

I swallow hard, and ask my question again.

To my right, another voice speaks. The shadows out of my line of vision grow bigger.

"She's afraid." This one's voice is smooth, like a pebble that's been washed up by the sea. Something deep and cold. Something that's seen unknown things, something that knows ancient knowledge.

That's got to be the king.

With a shaky, thin feeling, I realize this means that they either think I'm a Queen or a Fool.

If I'm their Fool, then I need to make this quick.

The faint, dull buzzing that is my magic begins to spread in my chest, in that space beneath my heart. My legs go limp, and my next breath comes out ragged. I open my eyes, staring straight ahead in the dark, ignoring the mirrors on either side of me.

"My eyes will stay open. Now, why can't I sleep?" I say clearly, firmly. I might be their Queen, and I might be their Fool, but they will respect me regardless.

I keep my tone respectful, though. This is not the place to be my cocky, brash self. If I want secrets answered, I'll get them. But the things on either side of me right now are from somewhere that I don't even want to know about. It won't kill me to be polite.

To my left, that grating, gravelly voice speaks again.

"You are blind to what's coming." It chuckles again, and my skin starts to crawl. I swear at myself internally.

To my right, whatever thing lies in the mirror starts to grow. And grow. And grow. It takes every fiber of my willpower not to look. I want to look so badly. But I know that if I do, I'll be no better than Mira, chasing an unclean spirit for answers.

I'm not that fucking desperate.

"You will rise, and then you will fall." That smooth, old voice says.

Then, to my right, I hear trumpets. Trumpets, and bells. Clear as day, and slowly growing louder. Trumpets and bells, announcing something that is coming. Something- or someone.

My heart feels thin and papery in my chest, and I'm starting to think this was a really, really bad idea.

"Got it. Thank you." I say, ready to end the ritual.

But from both the mirrors to either side of me, the shadows move quicker, jerkily. I feel myself grow nauseous.

The voices from both mirrors speak in unison.

"You will rise, then you will fall."

Grating, loose gravel, like the tongs on a fork scraping down a dinner plate, combined with the old, smooth voice that knows things both unseen to man and great knowledge of the world. I cover my ears despite myself, the voices and trumpets too much.

Quickly and before any weird shit can happen, I thank them for their time, and will my witch-light to return to my eyes. I shut my eyes tightly and use my magic, willing the blanket from my bed to drape over both mirrors. Immediately, I feel alone. Whatever was here in the room with me is gone.

When I open my eyes, I breathe heavily. That was a complete bust, and now I have to use the last of my fucking sage to cleanse whatever those things were from my room. I grab my last little nub of blue sage from my dresser, about to light it, when a very, very audible *'plink'* sounds from behind me.

I turn around slowly, facing my closed windowsill. My room is still dark, and I'm not one hundred percent sure that I really heard something.

I was two years old the first time I heard things go bump in the night, and four when I realized it wasn't just my imagination. I never ran for my grandmother, and I never cried. These things just sense me. They always have. When they realize I can sense them, too, they always leave me alone.

I don't scare easily, anyways.

At the second *'plink',* I realize that it's coming from outside. I cross the few steps it takes to get to my window and wait, leaning my ear against the shutters.

A third one, and this time, my window vibrates against my head. It's a pebble. Someone is throwing fucking sea pebbles at my window in the middle of the night. I unhook the latch, swinging it wide open, and peer down.

And when I see what's throwing the pebbles, I let loose a string of curses that would make even the saltiest of sailors concerned.

"What. The *fuck.* Are you doing here.*"*

Down on the ground, clutching a fistful of smooth white sea pebbles, is Morgan Van Devon.

I look down at her, and she looks right back. Neither of us say a word for a few moments, both properly stunned. She's not even dressed how she normally is. She looks like she's on some secret mission: a dark, inky black flannel, loose black jeans, and a black beanie. Combined with her deeply tanned skin and honey-colored hair, she nearly blends into the trees. Morgan looks like she wants to stay hidden.

She tucks a loose strand of hair behind her beanie. Maybe it's just her complexion… but if I didn't know any better, I'd say Morgan looks almost flushed. I can't tell if she's embarrassed, shy, or just unsure of what the hell she's doing.

We break the silence at the same time, overlapping each other in angry, rushed whispers.

"I said, what the *fuck* are you-"

"Relax, Tyler, I need to talk to you!"

At that, I stop short. "You're telling me that you, Morgan Van fucking Devon, need to talk to me? What could you possibly have to say to me, Morgan? Got some more shit to talk?"

I rest my elbows on the windowsill despite myself. Why is she here, at this hour? Despite the instant, pissed-off energy that rises in my chest like helium, I can't help my curiosity. The one person who probably hates me the most in this entire godforsaken town is at my windowsill in the middle of the night. This is so out of character for her.

Morgan sighs, tucking that escaped hair behind her ear again. She looks up at me, her concerned expression piercing through the night. "Look," She says quietly. I almost have to strain to hear her. "I don't want to be here any more than you want me here, but we have a paper due in English in two days. We got assigned together today. I don't know where you were," She rolls her eyes at this. "And I don't know if you particularly care about your grades, but I do. I just can't sleep until it's done."

Her choice of words almost makes me choke.

I just can't sleep until it's done.

Stupid fucking Three Kings ritual. Maybe that's what they meant, that I'm 'blind to what's coming' or whatever. Maybe that's why I couldn't sleep. I was blind to Morgan Van Devon showing up at my window like some fucked-up Romeo.

After this monologue, she falls silent, staring at her shoes.

I'm struck speechless again. At school and everywhere else, she's confident. Outspoken. Self-assured, a leader. But right now, she's staring at her shoes like she's shy. Or nervous.

I register her words. I wasn't aware we had anything due together, but she was right: I don't particularly care about my grades, and I did miss school today, choosing to skip with Felix and muck around town instead of showing up to more foul shit written on my locker, or finding another dead bird carcass shoved into my desk. It isn't like Eleni cares about my grades. It isn't a shocker that Morgan cares, though. I'm sure her perfect parents expect nothing less.

Quick, hot anger flares again when I think about her mom and the way she treated me after the spell debacle. I bristle visibly, the memories heating my chest and igniting my fury towards her again.

If I wasn't a liar, I'd say that I felt bad that she winced.

"Are you even allowed to be here?"
I can't help myself. The urge to be a complete dick to her is impulsive. "Won't mommy ground you?"

Morgan looks up at me again, and this time all shyness is forgotten. Anger paints her features clearly, making her look much more like the Morgan I envisioned.

"Lay off, Tyler. I want an A on this paper, so we have to work together. She doesn't even know I'm here, anyways. I snuck out for you. You want to maybe stop being difficult and just let me inside?"

My eyebrows raise into my hairline. She's bold, I'll give her that much. She's defying her mom for a *good grade.* The sweet powers that be would put us together for an assignment, just to test my patience. Christ.

I lean farther out the open window, my chin resting on my folded hands now. I summon the rest of the angry buzz in my chest, summoning the remainder of my lingering magic from the ritual: my ragged breath, my shaking limbs, the faint buzz of my magic. I will my voice to catch on the breeze, to carry through the night air and float down to Morgan's ears perfectly and clearly. And when I speak, I know that she'll hear my voice in my personal favorite tone: the one that's silky, the one that's smooth and seductive. A little cocky, a little sensual. Rose petals and fresh sheets, lilting, haunting beauty on the wind, coiling through the chilly breeze of the night and into her ears, wrapping around her throat.

"Why didn't you just knock on the door?" I smile, and not in a nice way.

Maybe I'll let her in. Maybe I won't. If she's anything like her mom, this entire thing is going to be fucking torturous. If she's anything like her mom, I might just tell her to fuck off.

I see the exact moment that my words reach her ears when she noticeably blushes and looks away. Huh.

Anyways.

But she doesn't need to say a word. I see the answer in her movements: she's embarrassed. Embarrassed to be at my house, embarrassed to be anywhere near me. Whether that's for her own concerns or her parents, it doesn't matter to me. The slight respect I managed to find up for her is instantly doused with my anger again.

I reel the rose petals and silk back, slamming steel walls down in their place. "Whatever, Morgan." I scoff down at her, hoping she knows exactly how I feel about her, about this. "You can come in. I'll meet you down there."

Fuck you, Morgan Van Devon. Fuck you and your stupid fucking mom who hates me for something I didn't do. Fuck this insomnia bullshit and stupid mirror rituals and partner homework assignments.

You know what, while I'm at it, fuck Summerhill, too.

Fuck you, Morgan. But you can come in.

Chapter Fifteen

Niamh

Tyler doesn't move, doesn't speak a single word. The thick rain starts up again, dousing the rest of the heat that had ricocheted through my body before she grabbed me.

We stand there staring at each other almost for too long, directly into each other's eyes. It feels strangely intimate. Tyler's deep, lulling blue eyes seem to look right through me, like she sees everything. Her dark eyebrows and freckles are shocking against her pale skin, giving her the appearance of something otherworldly, something almost elvin. She's striking. And I am positively *filthy*.

We look at each other for so long that I can feel a line being drawn, and then crossed. I can't quite put my finger on what exactly it is, though. All I can think of on a repetitive loop is that she knows.

She knows, and she didn't run away screaming like my old friends did.

Tyler's dark, rain-slicked hair clings to her skull, her clothes finally as soaked as mine, and yet somehow, she's still just as striking as she was before. So beautiful, and so striking, that I have the same thought for a third time: she looks nearly inhuman. And yet I can't tear my gaze away from those inviting, endless blue eyes.

I shake my head slightly, pulling myself out of my thoughts. Focus. Focus, Niamh.

"That," she finally says, letting go of me and taking a step back, "Was unexpected."

Her voice is softer than before. All raw honey, smooth lengths of silk, and fresh rose petals. She takes another step away from me, closer to the South Gate sign, then looks me up and down.
I don't know why with every step she takes away from me, it feels like there's a cord in my chest, pulling me with her. Tugging me.

"You've done that before, haven't you." She says. Another statement, not a question. She knows.
I swallow, my throat dry as ash in my mouth. Images of Makani's arm blare bright in my head, along with the way the shed burned when I told it to.

I shut my eyes, trying to squeeze the memories out, but they glue themselves behind my eyelids.

"Once." I say quietly, trying to get some moisture back in my mouth. "Right before we moved here. It's…. It's why we moved here, actually."

Tyler doesn't prompt me, doesn't beg me for the story.

Which is exactly why I find myself spilling the entire, horrible event out to her, sharing my secret truth amidst the bucketing rain in the dark of the South Gate woods. The words tumble out without me trying, and funnily enough, the deeper I get into the gritty details of that day, the lighter I feel. For the first time, I tell somebody exactly what happened that day at my old high school.

For the first time, I tell somebody exactly what *I* did that day.

For the last few weeks, I kept that secret under lock and key, hidden away deep in the darkest abyss of my heart. I was determined to tell no one, to bury whatever…. My ability is. To forget it happened. No one could know. No one could *ever* know.

But now, Tyler knows.

And she's the only one who does.

She doesn't say anything for a second after I finish, but after a few moments of looking at me, she smiles. It widens, and begins to stretch.

Amidst the rain, I can smell the air turning sweet, almost overwhelmingly so. Sticky and strong, like roses or fruit left out in the baking sun. Along with it comes something earthier, something distinctly smokier.

Cinnamon.

Her smile keeps growing, and growing, and growing, wrapping from one ear to the next one. I blink as my stomach drops, and there's a normal smile in its place. A gentle, probing one. A knowing one.

I must have imagined it.

My inner voice rolls her eyes, telling me to relax. The shadows behind her are just messing with me. All of today is messing with me, honestly. It's all finally catching up with me, I can feel it. My mind has seen and dealt with *way* too much today.

But I can't just leave yet. I need to know.

I *need* to. I know she knows what I am. Or… what it is. Or why. She has answers; I can see it perfectly in her eyes.

Those intense, searching wells of blue that she could very easily use as a weapon if she wanted to. Some deep, gut feeling tells me that if she wanted me to do something, all it would take is one look from her. People with eyes like that are cunning, and very lucky. My sister calls them scorpio eyes. Seductive, inviting, and intense. Aine's always joking when she refers to her own, but Tyler definitely has the same ones. But better. Sharper.

She leans against the South Gate sign again, the same position as when I first saw her.

"The way you felt when you burned your friend. Tell me, Niamh. How good did that feel?" She finally asks, leaning against the post lazily. She's dropped the sensual, rosy voice. Her tone is curious now, still lilting. And those eyes- they're glimmering, shining, giving away just how curious she really is to hear my answer. Her long blue skirt hangs low on her hips, showing a thin, pale strip of stomach and bone between the waistband and her oversize sweater.

I swallow, hoping my thoughts aren't as loud as they sound in my head. For fucks sake, Niamh. Get a fucking grip. This is not the time to be staring at the most beautiful girl you've ever seen in your entire existence right now.

Right. She asked me a question. Okay. Shit.

And then guilt and shame flood my exhausted, battered body as I think about my answer. Because the way I had been feeling when I burned Makani…. It was something that felt so good, so *powerful*…. It didn't feel like it was humanly possible.

But the way Tyler's looking at me right now tells me that she knows my answer anyways.

"Like…. Magic." I breathe. The honest, raw truth.

She laughs softly, shaking her head at the ground. "You're something."

For everything that could've come out of her mouth, that was the last thing I expected. "What?"

She looks at me pointedly, her voice cutting through the ropes of rain, carrying through the trees like the breeze. "Do you think just anyone can do what you just did, Niamh?"

I shake my head, looking behind me. The fog is rolling in again, like it wants to hear what she has to say, too.

"What you have is called a gift. You were full of emotion that day back home, right? Anger? And I'm going to take a wild guess and say just before you saw me, when you were on that path today that you were overcome with that anger again. What you can manifest that anger into...."

She trails off, looking at the woods behind her. "Most people get angry, or sad, or overwhelmed, and they shut down. People like you and I, and others like us are different. Anger doesn't break us down. It awakens us. It's a gift, Niamh. A gift that can be learned,"

And then her half-smile returns, all quirked up to the side, "And mastered, if you work on it. Clearly, your gift has something to do with fire. How very interesting."

My heart pounds wildly against my ribcage as she talks, so loud and so fast that I have to force myself to inhale and exhale so I don't pass out. My vision feels spotty, and I can feel my breathing start to get too fast. How does she know all of this? She makes it sound like I'm…. some witch, or something.

"Niamh. Breathe." She says. And then she steps forward, closing the gap between us. With one slim, milky hand, she grabs my muddy forearm again.

The feeling comes back abruptly, instantly. And

that deep, burning heat

that fire

  slips

   out of

    my ribs

falling down into my stomach

then even farther.

My legs start to shake, and the hair on the back of my neck stands tall, like someone just ran their mouth

     and tongue

          over it

down and behind my earlobes, running down the small of my back. Heavy, burning heat. Someone's mouth.

Someone- something- is trying to unwind me right now.

Instantly I'm back in my memories, thrown right into the very second the shed had caught fire.

The heat rushing down my back and spine,

Oily and thick,
Pooling between my legs.

And I remember just how *good* it had felt, being overwhelmed with that heady, tantalizing desire. It consumed me, just like it was right now, and

And then it vanishes, completely. My frustration rises just as quickly.

"What the fuck was that?" I demand sharply, angrily yanking my hair off the back of my neck, trying to give my skin some air. I can still feel the ghost of whoever's mouth was on me, and it's making me irritable now.

"Magic."

Her voice snaps me out of my irritability. "I'm sorry?"

Tyler grins, as I realize it was her. *She* made me feel it again. When she sees the recognition on my face, her next words are quick, as if she's growing excited.

"Magic is addictive solely for the way it makes the conjurer feel. Tell me, Niamh. Why do people do crazy things when they're in love?"

I blink, considering this. I don't really know, because I've never been in love. I dated one guy back in Saxon Beach when I was fourteen, and I broke up with him after a week when he told me he loved me. Which, besides being the Chernobyl of all love bombs, I realized that I just wasn't a fan of his tongue in my mouth. I felt nothing. Definitely not desire.

That was also around the time Indie and I got drunk together by ourselves without the guys. Like any stereotypical teenage cliche, we ended up making out. But that was when I had another realization about myself. Realizations like how kissing girls feels more like breathing, and kissing boys feels more like work.

So based on my limited experience, I'm not sure that I know the answer to her question. Instead, I think of all the movies I've seen, the books I've read. I think about what my dad has gotten books published about: all fantasy shit, elves and dwarves and orcs and whatnot. All full of temptatious, forbidden romance, with winged men who slew entire kingdoms to save their bonded mate or whatever. Ridiculous, not-like-real-life love.

"Because love can… make you do crazy things?" I try lamely. Crazy things like kingdom-slaying. Engaging in battles of epic proportion. I don't fucking know.

Tyler rolls her neck, the scent of roses and cinnamon drifting with her movement. In her eyes, something flashes quickly, but it's gone before I can really catch it. She's quick, and guarded. If I had to guess though, it looked an awful lot like grief.

Or anger, disguised as grief.

But why?

"Because love feels *good,* Niamh. Those happy chemicals feel really, really good. It feels so good that it's addictive. Having a connection so deep and so true to another person feels *good.* Tying your soul, your essence to another human…. It feels like nothing else on this plane of existence. People do *anything* to feel that once they've found it once. It's addictive. Magic feels like love, Niamh, which is exactly why it's dangerous. Like anything addictive, it can be deadly. If you don't control it, it controls you."

Before I can even open my mouth, she continues.

"People who use tarot cards, crystals, or say they practice are all liars. They're playing at something that is beyond them. Real magic is innate, Niamh. You're either born with it or you aren't. This gift you have- this ability to start fires? You think that's crazy, just wait. That's probably not even the brunt of it. You could do so much more, Niamh, because you have *real* magic. And it feels good, huh? Like being seduced? That's because magic mimics love. It mimics lust, it mimics desire. It mimics everything that is designed to make people crumble. I saw it all over your face. That *need?* That's *magic,* Niamh! Magic that you were somehow born with."

She sobers up quickly, her expression guarded and stony once more. "You just have to learn to control it before you succumb to it like you keep doing. Because it will control you. I've seen it happen. It eats people if they can't put a leash on it."

What she's saying....

Makani's arm. I did that, I know I did. But she's implying that it happened because I couldn't control it.

Emotion clogs my throat, and I feel like the wind's been knocked out of me.

What *is* this? I should've never left Saxon Beach. Ever. This is *not* happening.

This is not happening. Fuck *no.* No w-

"This is real, Niamh."

Tyler's voice carries a bite as she stares at me, her face not all that far from her own. "You can either acknowledge it and make it yours, or let it destroy you. Let what happened to your friend happen again, and again, or worse. Having the gift is *rare,* Niamh. You're special."

My face heats up, embarrassment brimming with it. "It feels strangely like you're reading my mind, and I don't appreciate it."

Then I realize what I said, and the realization feels like cold water being dumped over me.

"Wait. Can…. are you?" I let my question trail off.

Tyler just grins at me like I finally got it. "Your fire isn't all that exists. There's different kinds of magic. I have several gifts- being able to see into people's minds and grabbing ahold of their thoughts is just one of them. Maybe if you learned to harness your own, you'd be able to read mine, too."

The way she says it sounds like an invitation. An offer.

As her eyes lock onto mine, sapphire blue onto bright green, images flood my head one by one, accompanied by the feeling of a petal-soft breeze enveloping me.

Images of Tyler and I, sitting side by side in the woods, working together. Doing *magic* together. Images of burning, roaring fires, of incantations, of being able to do things I couldn't even fathom…

Images of me, strong. Confident. Not held down by the tether of home anymore. Not sad, not angry, not guilty.

Powerful.

"So you can teach me?" I find myself saying, something resembling excitement coating the insides of my heart. Strangely enough, I don't feel as scared now. I don't feel the need to cling to my disbelief. The Niamh that Tyler just showed me… that's who I'm meant to be. Strong. Powerful.

If Tyler's right, and this… *gift* that I have is true, real magic…

Then I want to use it.

Her eyes flash when she sees the decision in my eyes, and I find myself staring way too long at hers again.

"Yeah, I can teach you, Niamh."

She turns on her heel to leave, heading for the trees behind the sign. With her back to me, I can see just how long her brown hair is, skimming her waist. Just how elegant her walk is, lithe and graceful. Exactly how her hips dip and curve exactly in the right places, her waist-

NIAMH, my inner voice screams, banging her head against the wall. *CHILL!*

"Wait- Tyler!" I call before she's out of sight.

This is so, so much bigger than me. Bigger than I can understand, but she knows.

Tyler's silhouette disappears from view, but I can hear her voice from behind the trees, carrying through the rain and mist.

"I'll see you around, Niamh. Follow the path, you'll get home fine."

I watch the space beside the South Gate sign for a long, long minute after she's gone. For what, I'm not sure. Moving shadows, girls hiding behind the trees. Anything abnormal, anything to convince me that I'm asleep, or dreaming, or hit my head when I fell. I totally could have. It's a possibility for sure. I fell, clocked my head against a rock. Ran into a pine tree while I was running.

Sure. That's plausible. But Tyler…. Could I have made an entire *person* up?

Something at the depth of my deepest, truest thoughts say no.

I follow the path like she told me to, and sure enough, less than five minutes later, I'm standing at the edge of the woods. Standing, somehow, at the edge of *the fucking East Gate woods*. Staring right at my front porch, at our cozy little house. Someone has a fire going, based on the smoke coming out the chimney.

And crazier still, somehow it's still light outside, not quite sunset. The rain's let up to a gentle mist, the fog gone.

What. The. *Fuck.*

Too exhausted to even consider how any of this is even possible, I take one last deep, heaving breath, and don't let it go until I'm safely inside. I turn around once.

I look back one time after I step onto the porch, staring back at the treeline of the East Gate woods, watching the colors of the sunset paint the trees orange.

There's nothing there. I don't know what I expected, really, but still.

"Niamh?" My mom calls from somewhere inside. "Is that you?"

I kick my disgusting, ruined Vans off at the door, heading towards the kitchen, remembering too late that I look like death run over. My parents are going to have a fucking aneurysm.

"Yep!" I muster enthusiastically. "Sorry I missed dinner, I-"

And I stop in my tracks, frozen in disbelief. The kitchen table is set, not a single plate having been used yet. Steam rolls off the pasta still in the pan, and the salad hasn't been touched. The dinner rolls are stacked in a neat little pile, not one out of place.

My dad, clad in his soft sweater and reading glasses, is sitting on the edge of the kitchen table, a book in hand. He smiles up at me for a second, then wrinkles his nose when he really looks closely at me. Setting his book down, he frowns.

"Niamh MacKenna. Do I want to know?"

If I say nothing, he'll worry and it'll be a repeat of back home. If I tell him the truth, he's going to ship me off into a world of medication and psychotherapy.

So I aim for humor, and... Tyler. I feel like if I tell them I was with a friend, it'll make them feel like I'm adjusting better.

"My bad. I was hanging out with a new friend after school and took a spill on that big hill coming home through the East Gate. The woods are gnarly."

I go to snag a dinner roll, feigning innocence, but he smacks my hand away playfully.

"Absolutely not, what with those crusty hands." My dad says, wrinkling his nose.

"You're crusty."

He flicks a pine needle off my shoulders, and I roll my eyes. My mom walks into the kitchen, then, and also does a double take upon looking at me. "I'm glad you're making friends, but good lord, Niamh. Please go shower. I just set the table two minutes ago, we'll wait for you."

When I don't move, she leans forward, assessing me. My dad glances at me from under his eyes, all traces of humor gone.

I try to ignore the pointed, concerned look they give each other.

"What happened to you?" She asks me, her voice dripping with suspicion.

I ignore her, turning to the little yellow wall clock we just hung up. It's shaped like a book. My dad loves it.

It's only five o'clock.

But it *can't* be five, because I left the school at four, and I was on that path for at *least* two hours, between being chased and then talking to Tyler. It should be well past seven at the very least. It should be late. It should be dark outside.

Dark like it was in the South Gate woods.

But no, the clock sits right at five. Five oh one, to be specific.

Shaking, I head upstairs, but not before making the mistake of looking out our living room window that spans an entire wall, overlooking the woods. The sky is a deep crimson now, flecked with layers of deep reds, golds, and tangerine. It's beautiful, truly.

But it should've been done setting over two hours ago when I was walking home.

"Niamh?" My mom calls impatiently from the kitchen, snapping me back to the present. "I don't hear a shower running."

"Sorry." I force out from the stairs, swallowing the fear that rises up my esophagus. "It's been a really long day."

"I don't care." She calls back at the same time my dad yells after me "You smell."

And with that, I clomp upstairs quickly, heading straight for my bathroom. Peeling my disgusting, muddy, rain-soaked clothes off feels like shedding a fucking skin, and stepping into a hot shower quickly becomes high up on the list of Things I'll Never Take For Granted Again.

But all throughout my shower, as I comb pine needles out of my hair and scrub my body with soap three separate times, the fire I started in the woods keeps prodding the base of my skull, reminding me that it happened. Reminding me that *I* happened.

Makani's charred arm happened. Tyler happened. *I* happened.

Tyler calls it magic, and I'm inclined to believe her.

Magic exists. I watched it happen today. I *made* it happen. Tyler said that for me, anger doesn't break me down.

It awakens my magic.

Magic exists. Tyler has gifts, too. She has magic too.

Whatever it's called, it exists.

Whatever *I* am...

I exist.

When I finally step out of the shower, that thought alone blares through my mind, blinding everything else.

I exist.

I exist.

I exist.

NOVEMBER

CHAPTER SIXTEEN

TYLER

From the journal of Tyler Iris Lane

Sunday, November 3rd

(my 18th birthday!)

<u>To Form A Temporary Alliance With An Enemy:</u>

Crafted on a Sunday, during a full Hunter's moon.

A charm for myself, because the powers that be are throwing Morgan Van Devon into my life once

again.

<u>Ingredients:</u>

- Sea salt for protection (Not that I'll need it)

- Bay leaves (for cleansing & banishing)

- Fresh lavender sprigs (for calming)

- Lavender oil

- A single shard of Tigers Eye

- Thyme (for courage in this fucking endeavor)

- Chamomile (to relax and calm my rage)

- Peppermint (for soothing my hatred)

- Three citrine shards, charged under a full moon (for positivity and light)

- 1 blue candle

- An entire box worth of white tealight candles

- A small length of string

- 1 small glass vial

Instructions:

- Cleanse the vial with sea water. (I dipped this in the ocean just off North Gate beach.)

- Drop all ingredients into the vial. Top it off with the lavender oil.

- Light the blue candle, (Tonight, so it can charge & work for the next two days I have to be with her) repeating this phrase;

"Morgan, you're a cunt. I hate you and wish you would leave and take your entire snarky, entitled ass family with you."

I'm kidding. I can't put that in a charm.

"Against my will, I'm bound to you.

Strength and tenacity, I will see through.

My patience and tolerance I will duly wield,

A temporary alliance formed as this jar is sealed."

"I Will It So."

- Repeat this for the next two days, and try to actually mean it.

CHAPTER SEVENTEEN

TYLER

I float down the stairs gracefully, light as a spirit. Not literally floating, unfortunately. I haven't mastered that one yet.

It's pitch black in the hut, and if I didn't have my witch-eyes, I know that I wouldn't be able to see a thing at all. If I wasn't a Lane.

Fortunately, though, I am, and my eyes track the corners of furniture and paintings on the walls like a cat, clearly making out all the edges and swirls of color. I smile to myself as I glide down the stairs. I might have insomnia, but midnight truly *is* my time. I was made for the night. I was built for it.

I stop right at the front door, kicking my muddy boots aside. My tangled, unbrushed hair trails down into my pile of muddy things that I left by the door, and I swear. The ends look like I dipped them in wet mud, and are probably filled with bits of petals and leaves too. I can't walk into the woods without bringing bits of them home with me. Whatever sect of forest I go into, bits of it cling to me, weave their way into me, like the woods can't bear to let me go.

In the darkened hallway, standing behind the still-shut door, I glance down at myself. I'm in a simple navy blue tank top- my favorite one- but also the same one that was just laying on the floor for at least a week. My skirt is clean at least: a dark, oak colored thing that brushes the floor, just skimming the tops of my bare toes. I look like a faerie. I look like a tall, strange but beautiful thing, made up of pine and rose petals and the dark, plucked straight from the South Gate woods. I look fine.

Then I shake my head, wrinkling my nose. Why the fuck do I care? I remind myself, again, that I'm about to open my front door for *Morgan Van Devon.* And, on principle, I hate her.

I curl my fingers around the doorknob, and open it.

My first, immediate thought is that she's taller than I remembered.

Morgan stands at least five nine in her all black getup, nearly as tall as her brother. Up close, it's easy to see that she stole his clothes. Her black jeans are a couple sizes too big, that inky flannel swallowing her lean, muscled dancer's limbs whole. And up close- the closest I've ever actually been to her, I realize- I can easily see the shyness that paints her features. A gentle, innocent shyness.

Morgan? Shy?

That soft, tender expression on her face that seems to be innate surprises me more than I'd like to admit. Morgan is *shy.*

I snuff my surprise out quickly before I can allow myself to feel anything other than hate for her. She made my life fucking miserable. I don't owe her a scrap of anything less than my rage. It is shocking to me, though, considering she is the *last* person I'd ever expect to be shy, or gentle. Because none of the Van Devons are *shy,* or tender. No one in that entire fucking family is *gentle.* They don't get shy. They just get their way, they just get what they want.

Which, apparently right now, is access to the hut, and to me.

My anger simmers again, my magic bubbling beneath my heart, and I breathe easier.

"Morgan." I nod, attempting politeness.

I've never been this close to her, not even at school, where I always see her from afar. After the spell incident, I purposely kept it that way. We've never once interacted.

Despite myself, curiosity starts to take over. I war with it for a second, then two.

After three beats, I give up and stop fighting it, and my anger towards her is instantly replaced by something fresh and airy.

The space between us in my doorway grows sweet, and fresh, like a garden after the rain. It smells exactly like the space where my magic rests: at least, how that space smells right now. Because that little nook where my anger, my brashness, and my secretive, lying heart usually lies... that space where my magic lays coiled up like a dragon....

It currently smells like springtime.

Like the month of May. Like wildflowers, like gentle, cleansing rain.

Dumbfounded, I just stare at her. My witch-eyes have completely adjusted to the dark by now, two twin orbs of blue piercing through the dark, and I can see her as if it were the sunniest noon.

Morgan doesn't stare back. She steps past me into the hallway, her shoulder brushing my own, trailing almond-scented shampoo in her wake. The scent hits me strongly, and I blink profusely, again shocked.

Shaken the tiniest bit, I shut the door and pivot to face her.

I can see how tan she is even in the dark. Her silky, amber-colored hair falls just past her shoulders, sleek and shiny waves below that dark beanie. Her tan fingers, each one with about three rings apiece, carry a hulking spiral bound notebook and a planner. Despite that gentle face, along with her comes an air of authority, an

'I'm-supposed-to-be-here' attitude. Her dark, too-big clothes hide her figure, but she moves fluidly, with all the grace of a dancer. Elegant, slow. Graceful.

Poised, careful.

That's *my* fucking thing.

But it isn't until she finally meets my eyes that I can see how absolutely nervous she is to be here.

Her eyes are deep, deep like my own, and just as intense. A rich, honey colored brown, filled with that gentle, tender shyness. Warm. They're so, so warm. But she's nervous.

If I reached inside her thoughts right now, I know what I'd find.

I wonder if she's feeling it, the energy in these walls. Every nook and cranny of the hut is stuffed with restless, angsty energy, courtesy of my own magic. It's not my fault. I was born like this. Lanes are not known for being gentle and kind.

It isn't my fault that I've been gifted the rage that is unique to an eighteen year old girl.

I wonder if Morgan can detect the hum of each and every word I've uttered in this hallway alone. I wonder if she can sense the presence of years upon years of lingering, old magic, magic that predates even my grandmother. I wonder if the shadows in the corners, the ones that are oddly shaped and bent wriggle when she looks too closely at them.

I wonder if she can pick apart the subtle differences, the ones that tell her this house is full of things that aren't normal to the average person.

She just stands tall, looking me directly in the eyes. She stands gracefully, remaining poised.

Only her eyes betray her nerves.

Grudgingly, I find respect welling in my chest. The fresh, dewey smell vanishes, leaving behind a stamp: one of almond shampoo and honey. I want to kick myself. She is the *enemy,* damnit. She hates me. Her whole family fucking hates me. They all think I'm some desperate, fucking weirdo *witch* who used magic to try and get at their precious daughter.

So I shove that newfound respect down, because I don't respect Morgan Van Devon. I don't even *like* her. The thought of her family being so insistent that I tried to spell her in order to make her fall in love with me is comical. I don't even want to be *around* her.

Morgan nods towards the dark, winding staircase, her voice shaky.

"I was hoping to at least get this paper outlined tonight. We can do the rest tomorrow and Saturday. I'm guessing your room is up here?"

And then she starts up the staircase without another glance at me, without waiting for an answer.

I shake my head to clear my thoughts. Morgan Van *fucking* Devon is in my house. Morgan Van Devon is heading to my room. My room.

My room. Shit.

My room that's still set up for The Three Kings ritual, not to mention full of miscellaneous herbs, spell candles, and other various magical objects, incantations scribbled down on napkins and scraps of paper.

Shit.

"Hey!" I whisper-shout after her, abandoning all grace and tearing up the stairs. Fuck, I do *not* need to wake up Eleni right now, not for this. And why didn't I think to clean my room, even a little bit? One step in there and she's going to see exactly what a witch I am.

Then again, why do I care? It's not like she doesn't know what I am.

I beat her to my door and stand there for a second, my chest heaving, trying to decide what to move. Amidst the moonlight that spills in through my window, I can see the clutter perfectly: the two chairs with the covered mirrors resting on top of them. The new tarot cards that are scattered across my bed, open journals splayed on the carpet. The candle wax that dribbles down every surface, pools of it still warm.

The colored glass jars holding incense sticks and bundles of dried rosemary that line

my windowsill, along with the numerous scattered shells and sea stones. Sweaters,

skirts and moth-eaten knitted blankets all stare out at me from the floor, piled in

corners sloppily. My open window that Morgan threw pebbles at just minutes before

sifts chilly night air through the room, sending goosebumps up both my arms. The

dried bundles of rowan berries, sunflowers, and rose petals that hang upside down

from my window, all tied together with a thick, woven string stare out at me.

If Morgan wasn't sure I was a witch before, there's definitely not going to be a

single doubt in her mind now.

I quickly shove the chairs towards my desk, stuffing the heavy mirrors back

under my bed. Then, while I shove some of the clothes back into my hamper, I catch

my own piercing gaze in the glass of my window.

I look okay, actually. The second I walked into my room I felt myself relax, and

as a result I look more like myself and less rattled. Wind blown and earthy, like the

forest floor and the bluest sky all at once. My hair falls clean down my back, the bits

of dried forest and petals gone. My skin glows white, the moon itself reflecting in my

face. My eyes are dark and deep, a trench in the bottom of the sea, a siren's song, and

my thin collar bones jut out from my chest, perfectly complimenting my skirt that

hangs just off my hips. I look otherworldly.

I'm not just stunning. I'm fucking celestial.

The brash side of me smiles, and I let myself smirk and tear my gaze away from the glass.

As I hear her footsteps steadily climbing, I ask myself, again, why the hell I care what she thinks all of a sudden. This is *my* house, *my* room. My happy, safe little corner. Why do I give a fuck what *Morgan,* of all people, thinks? I'm running around tossing dirty clothes into baskets and stuffing them in corners. I don't even do that shit for Felix, let alone myself. It's not that I care about impressing her. It's not that I care what she'll tell people.

I can't put my finger on the reason. It almost feels just within reach, hiding just under the surface, but not close enough for me to grab.

Names have power, I've known that much since I was a toddler.
And this name eludes me.

I have just enough time to shove the tarot cards and loose spell pages behind my pillow before Morgan is standing in my doorway.

Energy crackles through the air, palpable and real. My pulse begins to race.

I stare at her, bracing myself for a comment as she scans the length of my dark room. I wait for her to say something nasty, something biting, retorts already brewing in my chest. I anticipate it, the ugliness that she must harbor towards me, the disgust and annoyance she must feel towards me. She must: she avoids me at school, doesn't say a word while her entire family acts downright nasty towards me, or while everyone at school makes my life miserable, writing me off as something disgusting.

Instead of a nasty comment, though, or a look of disgust, all I get is a stare back. Her eyes; those warm, sweet, honey-jar eyes meet mine head on, full of swirling, tender curiosity. Not disgust, not malice. Curiosity. Her eyes are gentle, searching. Just as intense and searching as my own.

She doesn't say a word, and I don't offer anything. The almost sweet, childlike curiosity in her eyes is unwavering. Morgan just looks around my room, then back at me, soaking it all in. Soaking *me* in, almost like she's trying to look inside me.

After a minute, the air in the room shifts.

"Your room smells like cinnamon." She finally says, her voice soft. Quiet, gentle.

I blink. It does, I notice instantly. I don't know how I could've missed it before: the air beneath my nose is all cinnamon and nutmeg, undeniably spicy and earthy. Warm, penetrating. Scent is such a thing with me: when Felix is in my room, it always smells of rain, of wet asphalt, and the smell of the harbor in the mornings. Clean and bright, refreshing. On the rare occasion my grandmother makes her way in here, she always brings notes of citrus, of the cayenne and clementine tea she makes every winter. As her gifts mostly pertain to healing now, that's no surprise. She always smells of the things I associate with her magic, teas and tonics that banish your sicknesses and warm your insides. And by now, I'm so used to my own scent- those fresh roses that seem to follow me everywhere- that the cinnamon is immediate and shocking, yet not unpleasant. It's almost overwhelming. The smell of it coats the inside of my nose, filling me with warmth.

I stare at Morgan for what feels like too long. "It does, doesn't it?"

She doesn't say anything else, but instead looks away, letting her eyes trail the length of my room again, taking everything in. I watch as she sets her notebooks down gently on my floor, then starts to pace. To my- again- surprise, she doesn't blanch or gasp at the very obviously magical objects, all my collected totems and trinkets. She doesn't linger on the puddles of colored candles, or the half-scribbled spells in broken latin.

No, what Morgan is interested in are all my baby pictures. My band posters. My dozens of potted plants, my books. The sticky notes bearing random phrases that Felix likes to leave me, the scribbled song lyrics on my furniture and walls. The non-magical things. The normal-girl things.

She soaks them all in with a reverence I've never seen on anyone before, that gentle, probing curiosity. Her honey-jar eyes roam over all the colored glass bottles and the seashells on my windowsill, the handful of shiny crystals and smooth stones in awe, like she's never seen such fascinating trinkets before.

The look in her eyes is worshipful, near glowing.

She runs her tanned, ringed finger down the edge of a baby-blue picture frame, the peeling, faded one that boasts a three year old Tyler in a high chair covered in chocolate cake. Eleni had snapped the picture after I'd smashed my entire face into it, laughing so hard that I'd inhaled the damn thing.

"Cute." she says, her eyes twinkling.

I can't tell if she's making fun of me or not: everything I had previously thought about her keeps getting tossed out the fucking window with every minute that passes. I opened my front door tonight expecting a rude, self-righteous, uptight girl. I expected a miniature version of her mom, to be honest. Someone hateful, someone who was disgusted with everything that I am.

This girl with the gentle, tender expression and the childlike curiosity in her intense, searching eyes is nowhere near what I expected.

This girl that's making my room smell like cinnamon.

Cinnamon and honey-eyes, cinnamon and almond shampoo.

Shaking my head and inhaling sharply, I summon my brashness, my arrogance, my acting-like-a-dick attitude from the reserves. The coiled, angry magic beneath my heart starts to hum, but it's weaker. Almost as if asking me *why* I feel the need to be obstinate.

I huff at her, willing my eyes to look sharp. Sharp and predatory, reminding her that we're enemies, and this is a one-time thing. I don't need her niceties.

"Fuck off." I say, finally.

Chapter Eighteen

Niamh

Bright and early Saturday morning, marking my fourth official week in

Summerhill, I wake up abruptly by hitting my head on the ceiling as my phone trills

loudly in my ear.

Swearing profusely, I have half a mind to silence the call. I know who it is

before I even open my eyes fully, because she stole my phone at Thanksgiving a few

years ago and changed her ringtone to her favorite song. Which, naturally, I know all

the words to now. There's only so many times you can hear the same Goo Goo Dolls

song.

But if I decline it, she's just going to call back. So, holding my sore head, I emerge

from my cocoon of blankets and pick up on the fifth or sixth ring.

My big sister, Aine, shrieks immediately into my ear, her low, raspy voice far

too awake.

"Niammhhhhhyyyy! How are you!! I miss you, you little shit."

My sister is the complete and polar opposite of me, and not just because she has her shit together and doesn't stress our parents out. She's six years older than me, has never once touched a surfboard, and her preferred idea of fun involves a paintbrush and *oil pastels*. I used to call her a fucking hippie as a joke, but I'm not really sure it's a joke anymore.

I tuck the phone to my ear and crawl back into my warm pile of blankets, the rain out my window already forcing me into hibernation.

"I miss you too. How's Santa Cruz?"

Aine sighs. "It's flooding right now. The Capitola pier is so fucked. My work gave us all time off because it's too unsafe to drive anywhere along the coast. It's so bad."

Aine moved to Santa Cruz four years ago and started working for a huge artisanal coffee company while she went to college. Within three years, and after acquiring several patchwork tattoos and a lip ring, she became the extroverted, creative, beautiful manic pixie dream girl that most girls only dream of becoming. Standing six feet tall with my dad's long, wavy red hair and green eyes and a fair-skinned complexion, Aine has always been the most beautiful of us three

MacKenna siblings.

"Damn," I mumble into the phone. "That's rough."

I hear scuffling, then some voices in the background, someone telling someone

else to give them a second. When she comes back, her voice is slightly breathless.

"Sorry. Addy's here. I just told her I'm on the phone with my little sister."

'Addy From Seattle', her girlfriend of the last three years, was a result of the

coffee shop job. I met her at Christmas last year, and she's exactly like Aine, which is

probably why I liked her right away. She took tequila shots with Indie and I on

Christmas Eve and described my taste in music as "whiny boys who can't really sing

and name their songs really obscure things like 'Mercury's In Retrograde And My

Girlfriend Says I'm A Dick.'"

I told her that she just didn't have the emotional capacity to listen to music as good as

Hot Mulligan, and being from Seattle didn't make her an expert on emo. She later

told Aine that I was cool. I about died.

"How's Addy?" I ask her, smiling despite myself.

"Shut up. I want to talk about you. How are things there? How's mom and dad?

School?"

I burrow deeper into bed, my smile fading. It's not like I can tell her how I'm really doing or what's really going on. It's not like what happened the other day in the South Gate woods- any part of that, honestly- is something I can just tell her over the phone casually. What the hell would I even say? Hey, Aine, miss you too. So guess what? Since moving here, I discovered that magic is actually *real!* And even cooler- I can start fires with my mind because I'm a witch, according to this beautiful girl I met deep inside the woods. Other than that, something that sounded like it came straight from one of gran and granda's stories chased me home the other day and tried to crawl inside of me, and I was so scared I pissed myself. But yeah, what's new with you?

Yeah, I think the fuck not.

This is something I can't tell *anyone.* Aine won't understand. No one would. Except for Tyler.

"I'm good. Mom's mom. Dad's finishing his last draft of the book, so he's been in a great mood."

I try to make my voice sound upbeat and not forced. She's got a really good bullshit detector.

"School?"

SUMMERHILL

I debate on what to say so that she won't see through my lies. The last two and a half weeks were positively torturous. Aside from trying to forget about whatever chased me in the woods that day, I've been taking the longest possible way home from school, walking along the scrawny highway instead of cutting through the woods. Combined with constantly thinking about Tyler but not seeing her anywhere at school, trying to play it cool in front of Zeke, and trying my damn hardest to get in with Marlo and all her surfy friends, I've never been more grateful for a Saturday morning in bed.

"It's good." I say simply. "I've been hanging out with these two kids every day. They surf too."

I don't know why I don't mention Tyler.

Aine sighs, and it's a frustrated one. I can hear her bullshit detector going off through the phone. She's always been good at reading me when I don't want to talk- it's like some weird sixth sense thing. Or maybe she's just intuitive, I don't know.

"Are you just telling me what I want to hear, Niamh? Don't lie to me."

My head starts to pound. I can't do this right now. Thoughts of Tyler's words to me swarm my thoughts: *what happened to Makani will happen again, and again, and again if you don't learn to control it-*

233

I swallow hard. I can't tell Aine. I can't tell anyone, other than the one person who already knows.

So I do exactly what she asked me not to, and I lie to her.

"No." I force my voice to sound genuine, keeping my tone upbeat. "I just woke up, and it's been raining here every day. And I miss-"

I trail off, the fucking lump in my throat more prevalent than ever before. I miss Makani. I miss Booker. I miss Indie. I miss my best friends. The hole in my chest widens to a cavern the longer I think about it. I could've told *them* anything. The four of us had no secrets between each other.

But now I'm keeping a gigantic secret from them, and none of them will even speak to me.

Aine's voice softens as I trail off, swallowing hard to keep from crying. "I know you miss them, Niamhy. I'm sorry."

I'm silent for a few moments, but I force myself to get out of my blanket cocoon and sit up. I look out my little triangle window, staring through the stained glass at miles and miles of pine trees that are the East Gate woods. Today they look exactly how my dad described them in his stories: a world shrouded in fog and mist, the tops of the towering pines barely visible. A mysterious place hidden behind a veil of fog, rain, and the sea. A cape just a few minutes away from the rest of Maine, but a whole other world entirely. Cape Summerhill, a place where things... *happen.*

"I know you miss them, and I am sincerely, sincerely sorry, but you are such a little gaslighter, Niamh. Don't tell me nothing's wrong when I can tell something else is bothering you. Just say you don't want to talk about it. You don't have to talk to me, I love you no matter what. But talk to *someone,* though, okay? It doesn't help to keep shit inside."

"You're obnoxious." I deflect.

"Because you know I'm right." She chirps back.

She is right. I consider her advice, and the only person that pops into my head is Tyler. I could, and should talk to Tyler. She's the only person in the world who truly gets it and knows what I can do. What I am.

A witch, I guess?

"I will." I tell her, and this time I mean it. I'll have to go find her, though. I have no idea where she lives, and I haven't seen her at school. The only place I've seen her at all was in the South Gate woods that day, and I haven't been back there at all. Since that day I've been taking the long way home, trekking through town and then alongside the highway, turning my ten minute path through the woods a thirty five minute trek.

But it's been worth it, if only to avoid whatever was in the woods that day. Just thinking about the way it tried to speak, that unused, scratchy voice:

Friend?

Floods my body with the same paralyzing fear I felt that day.

"Good." Aine says. "I know this sucks. But you'll be eighteen soon enough, you'll graduate, and then the entire world will open up for you. Go to Puerto Rico. Go to Fiji. Go surf somewhere for a month. It doesn't have to be college, Niamh. It doesn't even have to be a job. Just go do something that makes you happy. I know you miss them, and miss home. But don't stay in that mindset. There's no growth there."

Once again, she's right. There's no growth in missing what I won't get back. But easy for *her* to say. Aine is undeniably beautiful, has a job she loves, lives in a cool fucking city, and has a sexy ass girlfriend. She isn't impulsive. She doesn't do stupid things that get her in trouble. She didn't lose all her best friends at once, and she sure as shit isn't lonely. Aine curated a perfect life for herself at twenty three.

Pitifully, I think about the future I had envisioned for myself before we burned the shed. It was going to be even better than Aine's: surfing as much as we wanted the second we all graduated. A trip somewhere, one way tickets only. We'd debated Barbados, Costa Rica, and Nicaragua. Before I'd moved to Summerhill, Makani and I were still competing in local events, a couple regional ones. Had one of us gotten a big sponsor, that future would've quickly become a reality. And the best part is that it would've been the four of us, living it together.

I shove those thoughts down before Aine can call me out for them.

"You're right." I trill into the phone, still staring listlessly out at the forest, feeling sorry for myself. The image that jumps into my head then as I look out at the trees is from one of my favorite movies, Coraline. That scene when she dons her yellow raincoat and heads out into the woods with Wybie, looking for slugs. The ghost of a smile crosses my face, and I make a promise to follow in Coraline's footsteps today. But instead of banana slugs, I'm going to find Tyler, and get answers.

In the background, I can hear Addy saying something. My sister yells at her to shut up, but I can tell she's smiling.

"God, it never gets old hearing that. I love that phrase so much."

"You're such a Scorpio." I shake my head, even though she can't see. "Always having to be right."

"*Hey.* I can't help it if I just *happen* to be right all the time!"

She trails off then, sighing. "I love you, Niamhy. Have a beautiful, beautiful day. And think about what I said." She says it gently, as if she means it.

Aine hangs up, and I sit there for a second with my phone still tucked under my ear, imagining how different my life would be if I was my sister instead of me.

Getting off the phone with my reckless, wild little sister, and climbing back into bed with my hot ass girlfriend. Spending my days roasting artisanal coffee and dressing like I frequent hipster kava bars every night. Going to hyperpop shows at the Catalyst and traipsing around downtown Santa Cruz on the weekends, surrounded by equally indie-artist friends who love me.

Damn.

It's almost sad enough to make me want to crawl back into bed and sleep all day, but I've never been that kind of person. I've never once wished to be someone other than *Niamh.* I like myself. I liked my old life, I liked my old friends. Nothing else mattered except for them. I didn't give a shit about things like how I dressed, or my grades, and definitely not making other friends.

Everything's turned upside down since then, it seems.

With that parting thought, I decide to take charge, actually get out of bed, and do what I told my sister that I'd do: find some answers.

I swing my legs out of bed, my dad's old sweats nearly falling off of me. I take one glance in my floor-length mirror at my bedhead and look away. My eyes are their normal, mischievous bright green, crusted with sleep, and my face is still tan and freckled. My hair, however, is a problem. My hair looks like a very, very attractive cotton ball. Tufts of mussed-up curls and waves stick out all over. The only solution is a beanie. As for clothes, I pick roughly the same version of what I've been wearing since I moved here because it's fucking freezing, pulling on a thick black hoodie bearing the words SURFING IS A CRIME, baggy black corduroys, my last remaining pair of clean Vans, and my favorite beanie. I look like a fucking ninja, or a spy. A spy with hair so blonde that I'd never make it trying to go around unseen. I don't know why I care so much about how I look all of a sudden. I didn't before.

But thoughts of Tyler ring through my head.

Tyler, and her effortless, graceful limbs. Tyler and her strong jawline, her perfect button nose. Her constellations of freckles, her slim, pale fingers. Tyler and her deep, pulling blue eyes that look right through me.

Tyler and her eyes that I've definitely, definitely thought about when trying to fall asleep the last few weeks. Tyler and her eyes that I've thought about too much, and not just when I'm trying to sleep.

Shaking that thought away, I'm about to head downstairs and make some breakfast when my phone pings again.

I take one last glance in the mirror and fluff my hair over my shoulders, disguising my bedhead of white-blonde curls and waves underneath the black beanie right as it pings again. Satisfied at last, I grab my phone, half hoping it's Makani. Or at the very least, Booker or Indie.

It's from Marlo, sent in a group with another unknown number. Smiling, I open the thread.

We're picking you up at 6 tonight! Wear something warm. :)))

The other number must be Zeke. My heart feeling light and fluttery, I shoot her a text back, biting the inside of my cheek.

Sounds good super hyped

Slamming my door excitedly, I run down the stairs, feeling lighter than I have in over two weeks. The prospect of shitty alcohol and a house party is enough to boost my mood. This feels normal. Old Niamh is STOKED.

My phone for a third time as I jump off the last few steps. I stop at the bottom and fish it out of my pocket, expecting it to be Marlo again. Or maybe, hopefully the unknown number that might be Zeke.
But it isn't.

It's Indie.

My heart immediately jumps into my throat. I come to a full halt at the bottom of the stairs, every other sound in the house fading away. A dim roaring begins in my ears as I open the text, my mouth going dry.

hey.

That's it?

hey could mean any number of things, besides being the single most anxiety-inducing text a person can ever receive.

Breathing suddenly feels too difficult, like my throat shrunk to the size of a straw. I stare at the typing blue bubble as my phone pings again, then a third time, then a fourth.

Listen dude. You gotta stop texting us.
Mak doesn't want to hurt ur feelings, but he doesn't want to talk to u again.
What you did was fucked Niamh, and you know it.
Booker and I r done too. We're trying to b supportive of Mak. Good luck w/ ur new life. Stay out of ours.

I'm going to throw up.

I'm going to throw the fuck up and lose my shit. I can't do this. I can't do this.

Fuck. Fuck. I can't do this. I can't handle this.

I was not made to withstand this level of pain.

Images of Indie and I flash through my head. Every memory I have of the two of us, all the way back to kindergarten. All that we've done and shared together. Tears, thick and choking and all- consuming slam into my throat, cutting off my air supply. If I open my mouth, I'm going to succumb to them. With strength I don't feel like I really have, I try to do what I always do and slam the lid on the painful feelings.

It doesn't work.

But then, my inner voice wakes up and takes a look around.

No, she says. Fuck this.

Anger rears up in me then, so violent and so aggressive that it almost scares me. It replaces the grief entirely, so potent is my anger. My hands start to shake, my phone nearly slipping out of my grip.

I echo what my inner voice said: fuck this. I did *not* spend the last twelve years of my life with these people, cultivating the type of friendships most people never have, just to get a fucking *text message* that it's over, like a shitty breakup. This is more than that. I thought what the four of us had was worth more than a text.

Indie's seen the parts of me that I never show anyone. The bad, the ugly, the messy, the reality. She's seen me on my best days and my worst days. She was the first person I kissed where it actually meant something. She was the first person I wanted to tell all my good news to the second anything happened. She was with me when I won my first surf contest, and right by my side picking me back up whenever I lost one. It was her house I always ran to and stayed at for days whenever my mom became too much. She's been there for it all. Indie is-

Was-

My best friend. One of three.

This is not happening.

My head starts pounding, every throb in sync with my bright, angry heart. I'm not just angry at her- I'm livid.

Absolutely the fuck not. I'm worth more than some shitty *text message.*

I start to type back a response, my hands shaking so bad that I misspell words, but before I can hit send, Indie's message goes green.

No.

I send what I have of my reply, but it doesn't go through. *Message Not Delivered,* the screen reads.

That same consuming, tidal wave of anger rolls through me like a freight train, my entire body vibrating with it. Not sadness at all. Not the crushing, incurable grief that's been weighing me down for the last few weeks whenever I think of my friends, of what I accidentally did to Makani.

No, all that I feel is rage. Pure, undiluted anger rears its fiery head, and my chest starts to buzz. My clothes start to feel too hot on my skin, my face starting to feel like it's burning...

....And then Tyler pops into my head.

I think about what she told me: how if I don't learn to control my gift, I'll just keep starting more fires. How if I don't keep my anger in check- my magic, in check- I'll keep hurting people.

Thoughts of Tyler and all that she told me dull the haze long enough for me to take a real look at my emotions, to see what's really happening right now.

The hand that's holding my phone is glowing red and hot, as if I'd touched a stove. My phone *itself* is hot.

I touch my face. It's burning, but not like a fever. It's burning like.... Like the same way my chest is starting to buzz. A dull, faint buzz, like there's something inside that's trying to wake up.

I'm still angry, but I think about what Tyler said. To control it, to master it. I have no idea how, so I do the only thing I can think of.

I ignore Indie's last words to me and the anger they brought on. I ignore the dull buzzing feeling in my chest, and my burning skin. I ignore it all, and sit down on the stairs.

And I take one deep, soothing breath.

Then another.

Then a third.

When I lift my head up, I glance out the giant window in the living room, staring out at the misty trees. I think about Coraline and Wybie, looking for banana slugs, and then myself, looking for Tyler.

Looking for answers to my…. Gifts.

Not just a gift. Magic. I can do magic.

I'm a witch,

And so is Tyler.

I wonder if she's out there right now.

Sitting there, just breathing deeply, I wonder what Tyler would tell me if she were here. Based on my sole interaction with her, I have a nagging feeling that her poised, controlled self would probably tell me to control it. I can see it clearly in my head: she'd smirk, looking at me with those eyes that get whatever they want. She'd tell me in her silky, lilting voice to control this feeling and reign the fire in, to tame my magic. She'd tell me to control it before it controls me so I don't burn someone again, or worse. Like burn down our house. Or something else.

I nearly choke at my next thought.

Like my mom and dad, probably on their second cup of coffee in the kitchen. Images of flames engulfing the living room, trailing to the kitchen within seconds. My sweet, innocent dad. My dad, probably fully ignoring his coffee right now to re-read the latest draft of his book. My mom, asshole that she can be, probably pouring him a new cup and listening to him ramble excitedly.

I can't hurt them. I couldn't live with myself if I did.

Stay in control, Niamh. I tell myself, still breathing in and out. Deeply, thoughtfully, like you do when you're trying not to throw up after too many drinks. *Control this, Niamh.*

I open my eyes, looking around. The hallway is dark and dim, the natural lighting from the window leaking onto the stairs, all gray and misty. My throat still feels like a paper straw, but I force myself to keep breathing, trying to control the anger before it controls me.

Finally, my thoughts come easier. The anger dims. My chest stops buzzing, and I feel its absence like a missing limb.

I controlled it. That buzzing, that anger… that was the magic, and I controlled it. I didn't let it consume me.

I look down at my hands. They're normal, skin colored now. Not glowing red or hot anymore. Smiling ridiculously, my thoughts start to flow normally again.

I can feel like shit and dwell on the facts: I lost them. I lost my three best friends in the entire world. I lost Mak. I lost Booker. I lost Indie.

All because of something I did, something that I couldn't control.

I didn't know what it even was.

I lost them, and it feels like fucking *shit*. This is easily the worst thing that's ever happened to me, and it *hurts*. But what am I going to do about it? Am I going to sit here and let it ruin me?

My inner voice shakes her head *no.*

I stand up and wipe my sweaty hands on my pants. My face is cool, and I can breathe normally.

No. I'm not going to let Indie's shitty breakup-like text destroy me. I miss Saxon Beach. I miss my old life. I miss my friends. But everything changed the day we set the fire. It awoke something in me, changing everything. I'm not the same Niamh I was before the fire.

I have gifts, and I'm going to use them.

I'm a…. Witch, I guess. I'm a witch.

And I'm going to control this ability of mine. I won't allow Indie to ruin me. Summerhill is my new life now. My dad was right all along: this *is* my chance at reinventing myself. I don't want to be that angry, grief-stricken, weighted-down girl forever. That's not who I am.

That isn't who I need to be anymore.

And in that instant, still staring out at the East Gate woods beyond the window, I know that Tyler's right.

I have a gift. I have an innate, deep store of magic inside me that not everyone else has. I'm special.

I'm not going to run from it anymore.

I have a gift, and I'm going to learn how to fucking use it.

CHAPTER NINETEEN

NIAMH

On the dock in town, I sit with my feet dangling off the edge, musty blue sk8-his untied. The dirty laces dangle in the murky water. It's shockingly not as cold as I thought it'd be today, and honestly somewhat soothing to stare out at all the sailboats and skiffs that line the foggy harbor. The fog is thin today, nothing like the impenetrable kind last week. The sky is gray, but it's mild, like the sun might finally poke through. I feel hopeful.

I peel my hoodie off, my long hair tickling my bare arms in my gigantic black RipCurl t-shirt. I lean back on my hands, absorbing the smell of the breeze: sea salt, brine, and fish. Shockingly, I realize that in just over four weeks, the smell of Summerhill has become soothing instead of aggravating.

"Niamh!"

I whip my head around, smiling at the approaching voices.

Marlo and Zeke jog over to me, excitement in both their eyes. "Hey you. We're about to go SURF." Marlo trills, her face alight with excitement, looking more like Zeke's twin than I've ever seen her. Her joy is contagious, and I find myself itching to get in the water for the first time since leaving Saxon Beach.

I'd taken the long way to town again this morning after wussing out on finding Tyler in the woods. After inhaling a piece of toast and feeding my parents a lie about hanging out with friends, I'd jogged behind my house, determined to find Tyler.

Then I'd stood at the treeline, staring into the dim lighting of the East Gate woods for a solid ten minutes, working up the courage to get on the goddamn path.

But the memory of what happened last time stopped me.

That voice, whatever it was. That scratchy, inhuman voice.
Friend?

Standing there, looking into the trees had made me nauseous, the hair on my arms rising quick and fast had risen quick and fast. Nausea, and fear.

So I told myself to try again later.

Which is exactly how my cowardly self ended up at the harbor forty five minutes later, sitting with a paper cup of coffee in hand from *Cape Cafe by the Bay,* watching sailboats. Not a bad way to spend a Saturday morning, honestly.

But I needed to find Tyler. Back at the cafe while I waited for my drink, I'd asked the bored, disengaged sixteen year old who took my order if he knew a girl my age named Tyler, or at least her last name. Something, anything I could go off of. I described how she looked and everything, but the barista had never heard of her, which meant I'd have to go back into the South Gate after all.

Fuck.

"Come with us!" Marlo is saying, pulling me from my thoughts. "My dad has a ton of extra boards if you didn't bring any. Maybe if you keep hanging out with us, you'll get a custom."

She winks at me right as Zeke runs up, scooping me up into a gigantic hug that lifts me clear off my feet. Despite my half-assed protests of spilling my coffee and laughter, he holds tight.

"Hey." He breathes into my hair, setting me back down. "Dude, of course she's coming. She's never even been to North Gate beach before. It's such a fun right, Niamh. Wait, you're goofy. FUCK. But still. I-"

Marlo cuts him off. "Breathe, brethren. But seriously, Niamh, come. It's Saturday, so North Gate might be kinda packed, but it's supposed to get sunny within the hour. Let us christen your first surf in Maine properly with a crowded beach break."

Well, shit. I'm torn. My board bag, still packed tight with all my shortboards, is lying in the corner of my room, collecting dust. And surfing with Zeke and Marlo sounds fucking wonderful. But Tyler….

"I'd love to! But there's something I have to do first."

I say it happily, and I mean it. If I can go find Tyler and meet them later, that would be perfect. Then I recall the day I met them, and the gigantic blue and yellow logs they carried.

"I don't longboard," I say, looking at Zeke with faux panic. "Will a fish work?" I think of my custom fish that Booker sold me years ago. 5 '5, robin's egg blue, with beautiful, expensive keel fins. I haven't surfed it in ages, but it's a fun, speedy board. I look down at my wrist, checking my tide watch. I finally got around to setting it to Maine's settings. Yeah, my fish would be perfect for the tide right now.

Zeke's smile only grows, his entire tanned, freckled face lighting up again. "You are so fucking cool."

I smile up at him, that joyful, happy face making my heart feel funny. "Why?"

"Because you're new and beautiful and you surf, and because I'm taking a fish out too."

He smooths his shirt, hefting his backpack up higher on his shoulders like he didn't just call me beautiful.

I stand up and finish my coffee in one go, trying to occupy my mouth so that my smile doesn't take up my entire face. Out of the corner of my eyes, I can see the way Zeke's eyes trail the cup leaving my mouth, resting there for a beat after I throw it away.

"I gotta do something really quick, but I have to run home and grab my board and wetsuit anyways. Do you guys wanna meet back here?" I ask.

But Marlo's already gone, heading in the direction of the North Gate woods, yelling over her shoulder to meet at theirs in an hour, and all at once I'm left alone with Zeke.

Before I can say a word, he swipes my phone from my back pocket, typing something into it. I watch him while his head is down.

The way his coppery, sun bleached curls stick out from under his pink beanie. The way his badly sunburnt, splitting lips are pursed in concentration.

The way his tanned, strong face is so focused, his eyes perpetually smiling even though he isn't looking at me.

If happiness was a person, it'd be Zeke.

When he hands it back, I see a new contact.

Zeke Torah #1 Surf God & Niamh's Favorite Twin

(207) 716-4945

5575 Mirror Ridge Rd, Summerhill, ME 04401

"Dork." I smile up at him, pushing a stray blonde curl out of my eyes. He turns those joy-filled, golden eyes down at me right as the sun finally peeks out from behind the clouds. On his face are all of the things that I associate with happiness, written clearly in his expression;

The sky back home, and how blue it got the closer to summertime.

The smell of banana sunscreen on saltwater-kissed skin.

The billions of watermelon slices my dad would cut up every fourth of July.

Cannonball contests in our old pool.

Sunflowers.

The ocean.

Genuine, undiluted happiness on his face, just from looking at me.

"You love it." He smiles down at me. "So we'll see you in an hour? How you gettin home?"

I hesitate instead of answering him right away. I don't want to tell him that I'm purposely about to go into the South Gate woods now that I know about his childhood friend that went missing. I really don't want to upset him. I don't want that beautiful, radiant look on his face to disappear.

So I lie to him, and hate that I'm doing it. The secrets I'm keeping from more people than just him keep adding up.

I point vaguely East, and he furrows his brows. "What do you mean?" Even though I'm pretty sure he knows exactly what I mean: cutting through the woods. I feign indifference, then make to leave. "It's just a shortcut through the East Gate that my dad told me about. I take the same path home every day."

His face loses its cheerful glow, replaced instead with concern. I know what he's thinking before he can say it.

"I'm not going near the South Gate." I say quietly, my words halting even the breeze. It isn't totally a lie. I'm going to enter the woods at the East Gate. He doesn't know that I plan to end up in the South Gate.

"Is your *house* near the South Gate?" Zeke asks suddenly.

The sky that was sunny not five seconds ago darkens all of a sudden, a cloud passing over the harbor. It looks like incoming rain.

I glance back at the woods, at the North Gate where my first surf awaits. My first surf, and my only friends in the world.

I hate that I've become the type of person that lies to my friends. I never lied to Mak or Booker or Indie. Never, until the fire.

And now I'm lying to everyone. Everyone, except for Tyler.

Beautiful, elusive Tyler.

I can't tell Zeke the truth.

"Nah," I lie to him. "It's in the East Gate. But I should head out now so I don't make Marlo wait."

I shrug carelessly, hoping he'll buy it. I can't really afford to lose the only two friends I've made in this town, especially not the one who is endlessly, relentlessly chipper. Especially not the one who looks so happy every single time that he looks at me. I need Zeke's bright, happy-go-lucky attitude more than I thought I did.

The way he looks at me isn't bad, either.

Thankfully he nods, seeming to accept this answer, and lets me go with the promise of seeing him in an hour. I wait until he's completely out of sight, swallowed by the trees of the North Gate before I dart onto the path.

I tell myself not to be a fucking wuss.

I tell myself that I have magic in my veins.

I tell myself that if that fucking thing comes near me again, I'll burn it.

I fail to believe it, though.

After twenty minutes, I know that I'm heading into the South Gate woods. I would've been home by now otherwise.

My pulse is racing, quick as a hummingbird's wings. Going up a slight incline peppered with closely-knit pine trees, I breathe heavily as the darkness starts to swallow the rest of the sky. It blows my mind how truly dark it gets in here. The tall, majestic pines start to completely block the gray sky from view, the temperature along with it. It's isolating, cold.

Lonely.

Once again, I'm alone on the path, trekking through the woods.

My inner voice raises her eyebrows at me, as if to say *are you really, though?* Fear starts to nestle around my heart, curling around inside like a dragon. I can only pray that whatever was on the path last time isn't around today.

Or that it found someone else to be its friend.

After thirty minutes of not seeing the South Gate sign, my house, or anything familiar, I abandon all sanity and purposely try to get lost. I take wrong turns, blazing my way as far off the path as possible. I hop over little creeks, and pass not one, not two, but three faerie rings, ugly brown toadstools in three perfect circles. I tear my jeans in two different places, stub my foot on a boulder, and release strings of curses that would outdo my mom's.

But I almost cheer when after ten minutes, I see a familiar, crudely-drawn sign.

The South Gate sign.

I could cheer. I fucking found it. I sprint the last few steps, coming to a stop in front of the sign and inhaling shakily. It's so dark I can barely see it, but it's definitely there. This is real. I found it. It wasn't a dream. I didn't hit my head. This is real.

This is real, I tell myself. I'm in Summerhill, Maine. I'm in the South Gate woods.

Everything that's happened is real.

"So you came back."

I nearly tweak my neck as I whip my head around looking for her petal-soft voice. There, standing in the treeline behind me is Tyler.

She's wearing a deep, cobalt-blue skirt and a thin brown tank top today, still barefoot, still completely and utterly ethereal, and holding what seems to be a thick, leather-bound journal. Her mane of dark brown hair hangs loose and spills over one shoulder, the ends just brushing her bony hip bones. The thin brown tank top hugs her thin frame, her collar bones sticking out from above the neckline.

But what I really notice are her eyes, the same eyes that are smirking at me right now. God, she doesn't need anything else, truly. Those eyes are enough on their own. She doesn't need fancy clothes. She doesn't need makeup. She doesn't need jewelry. Her deep, tugging blue eyes alone, so intense and alive…

They make her simply striking. Honestly, I've never seen a girl so…

Say it, Niamh.

My inner voice is steepling her hands together, peering out at me from behind. *Say it.*

Fine, I tell myself. If only to shut my inner voice up.
Tyler is easily the most beautiful girl I've ever seen. That strong, sensual mouth, her freckles, her eyes, her thick, dark hair and eyebrows, contrasted with her porcelain skin….

Tyler isn't just striking. She's ethereal.

And those ethereal, intense eyes of hers are still looking right into my own, still smirking obnoxiously. If she's reading my thoughts right now, I'm fucked.

I meet her eyes, then, and my mouth goes dry. I feel like I got the wind knocked out of me, strangely enough, and it only intensifies the longer she looks at me. It's like she's…. Assessing me. Like she's seeing through me.

And it is *thrilling.*

"Hi." I rasp out, smoothing my hair down, grateful that this time, at least, she's seeing me in clean clothes and my hair not streaked with mud and pine needles. "You said you could teach me. I'm ready. I want to learn to control it."

Tyler's eyes spark amidst the darkness of the woods. "Why just control it when you can master it?"

She crosses the few steps it takes to reach my side and sits down, patting the space in front of her. We sit with our backs against a single pine tree, facing the South Gate woods beyond.

With her next to me, the South Gate doesn't feel as cold. Instead, they almost feel *alive.* They quiver with possibility. Anticipation.

The corner of my left knee touches her right, and the feeling of not getting enough air in just increases. She's quiet for a second, placing that hulking journal on the ground in front of us. Then she looks over, placing her elbow on her knee, chin in her hands, and looks at me.

For some reason, I almost expect something to happen. Almost.

But nothing does.

"Let me show you something, Niamh. May I?"

MAY YOU??????

The way she says it makes my heart skip a few beats, and she totally knows it from the way she's smirking at me, the way her eyes seem to darken.

That measured, petal soft voice of hers wraps its way into my skin and under my veins. All at once I feel dizzy, enchanted. I just nod, my tongue suddenly unable to work. If she'd asked me to jump, I'd ask her how high.

Wait. What?

I scrunch my nose up at the thought, looking at her suspiciously. When she laughs- a genuine, true laugh- I get the vague sense that I passed some sort of test.

"Good. It's all about control, Niamh. Control is what gets you to master your magic. Fight the thoughts that don't taste like your own, stay in control. You're a natural, though. This is good."

Then she gets up and sits directly in front of me, both of us cross-legged on the ground, my back still against the tree. She reaches out gently, placing both palms flat on my knees. My mouth is drier than it's ever been, my heart once again that of a hummingbird's wings.

She shuts her eyes, and I find myself doing the same.

"Dimiserunt Eam In." I hear that silky voice whisper, raising the hairs on my arms.

I sneak a quick look at her. She's deep in concentration, her breath rising and falling evenly. Feeling no better than a dude, I tear my eyes away from her chest, instead watching the way her pulse flutters erratically beneath the pale, nearly translucent skin of her neck.

I stare at it way too long, unable to look away until she whispers the strange words twice more.

"Is that latin?" I whisper. The smell of roses wafts towards my face, tickling my cheeks like strands of hair. It's as real and potent as if a field of them were growing under my nose.

"When I tell you to, say it with me." She says by way of answering me, eyes still shut. "It's easier to call upon your magic when you can reach it calmly, most of the time. Yours works when you're angry. That must be your gift, Niamh."

"Anger… is a gift?"

"For you, yes. I told you before; it's different for everyone who possesses magic. For you, anger is not an inhibitor. It's a gift. It's literally what allows you to tap into your magic."

It makes sense. I mull over all the times I've started a fire… and yeah, she's right. Every time I've been consumed with it, I've been able to tap into my magic, to reach into that well that exists somewhere in my chest, hiding.

"Is anger your gift, too?"

Her eyes are still shut, but she smiles, amused. "No, mine aren't tied to any single emotion. I can call upon them at will. That's what I'm going to show you right now. This time around, I'll just give you a taste. We can work on you reaching this on your own next time."

I like the sound of there being a next time.

With her eyes still closed, she releases one hand from my knee. Cool air pools in its absence. After a second, she hands me the journal that she'd brought with her. Up close, I can see how it's quite literally falling apart, loose pages threatening to fall out, candle wax stuck to the leather cover.

"Open that to the page on candle magic and read it to me. Do not read a single other page. I'll know if you do." She commands, then places her palm back on my knee.
I do as she says, unwinding the brown cord that holds it together, trying hard to focus with her hands on my knees.

Her journal is fascinating, even though I'm careful not to read a single entry. The thing is bound together with various scraps of ribbon and string, random scraps of information scattered about like she'd tossed new ideas in on a whim. Flipping through it quickly, I find that there's really no rhyme or reason to any of the entries;

various, rushed writings in slanted, thin handwriting, sketches of herbs and flowers and what looks to be their uses, half-finished poems, certain charms and their outcomes. Pages upon pages are filled with words I don't understand, with things that look like runes accompanying them in chicken scratch. Spells in languages I don't understand fill twenty pages at a time, thoughts and observations on various crystals and visions fill another ten. Multi colored candle wax, taped-in pine needles and sunflower petals, concerning red stains, and incense sticks line the pages, stuck in like an afterthought.

The entire book smells like rosemary and rose oil, and certain pages stick to my fingers as I flick through, potent enough that I know the scent will cling to my fingers for days.

Finally, I find a page that's filled with penciled drawings of candles in every color and stop, marking it with a sticky finger. Skimming it quickly, I learn that each candle color can have a different use, depending on what your intent is. A breeze starts to whistle through the South Gate as I try to read, blowing my curls into my face. I brush them away absentmindedly and keep going.

Tyler's only written notes on a few of the colors, so I read the ones with the most underlined and bolded letters.

RED: Passion, love, and desire. Strong color. Don't use red unless this is something you're serious about. Red is a color not to be used lightly. Love spells??

PINK: Also for love, but a gentler kind. Think friendship or platonic, light hearted love. Puppy love. Can be used for platonic affections.

BLUE: A healing color. Good for healing spells, soothing, calming etc.

GREEN: Money spells and luck. Works better w/ money spells, but you must be <u>super</u> clear w/ your wording. Better used for luck to be on the safe side.

YELLOW: Joy, happiness, etc. Good for manifesting happiness and joy, brightening your life. (I don't think I've ever even used one of these.)

BLACK: <u>DO NOT</u> use these unless you really, really need it and mean it. Great for binding or banishing spells, but <u>STRONG.</u> This color works exceedingly well when used for banishings... be <u>very</u> <u>sure</u> before using.

WHITE: A great all-around candle, sort of like an umbrella. Can be substituted for any color you need but don't have at the ready, even black. A good cleansing* color. (* can be used as a substitute for salt)

    I shut her journal after, my brain turning all the new information over and over like cloth on a loom. Interesting- so candle colors play a direct role in magic. I guess it makes sense. What it has to do with me, though, I have no idea. But I'm sure Tyler's mysterious, vague self will tell me in time.

    "Niamh." Tyler says softly.

    "Yeah."

"Say it with me now, and stop thinking so loud. I'm not vague, I'm guarded. There's an inherent difference."

I huff out a little breath at the fact she keeps dipping into my thoughts, but I do as she says anyways. Trying to match her deep, even breaths, I repeat her strange chant, tripping over my tongue until my voice aligns with her own;

"Dimiserunt Eam In."

The words feel foreign and strange on my tongue, like rolling marbles around in my mouth. My voice shakes as I repeat it again with her, realizing that I have no idea what it means. What if I just pledged my soul to some demon? I wouldn't know any different- I'm just doing what Tyler told me to do.

She keeps going, though, and I keep matching her word for word. The more I chant, the more that a faint, gentle buzz begins to grow in my chest: a buzz, a humming, something that feels distinctly hot. Hot like when you sit too close to a bonfire, searing. Something.... Something distinctly red. Yes, that's it. The color red.

Tyler keeps whispering under her breath, and her palms on my knees begin to grow warmer, and warmer still, just like how my hands were this morning. The buzzing in my chest grows into a dull roar, akin to a rogue wave, a wave much bigger than the rest in the set.

It builds. And builds.

It builds until it's so bright and so loud that everything else fades away: the South Gate woods, Tyler, her hands on my knees, my own body.

"Dimiserunt Eam In. Dimiserunt Eam In. Let Her In." She whispers, her silken voice barely audible.

"Say it." Tyler says. A simple command, no room for arguing.

I feel like I'm outside my body, fully outside the realm of controlling my tongue, but I try to listen to her.

When I speak, my words come out stronger, clearer.

"Dimiserunt Eam In. Let Her In."

And then the rogue wave breaks, the buzzing consuming every inch of my skin, the roaring all I hear.

And then, like a rollercoaster, I drop.

It's better than it's ever been before. *Stronger* than ever before. Stronger than the day with Makani, stronger than the day on the path, stronger than this morning, even. The magic that fills my body right now is…. God-like.

The heat glides over my skin quickly, flames licking my body like hot oil. My skin grows warm quickly, but not unpleasantly.

The heat that's spreading deep in my stomach is definitely, definitely warmer.

I feel the drop in my lower stomach first, the fall almost like a tug. I feel it so intensely and so quickly that my mouth parts open and a low, mangled breath escapes, a broken, jagged gasp for air. I don't have it in me to care if Tyler heard or not: all I can feel is the same deep, burning *want* that I felt the first time. A deeply rooted, insatiable desire, something that's making my body writhe and buckle.

The overwhelming, burning urge to release the power that's settling in my chest and winding its way through my body right now is growing, steadily and quickly, like the rollercoaster is climbing again.

My breath hitches, my body going tight in anticipation. I don't know if I'll survive another drop of magic. I don't know if I'll be able to handle it. Already, the magic surging through me is enough to have my eyes rolling back, all my muscles tight and coiled, begging for release. Anything. Any kind. Another drop might be…. bad.

But I want to feel it again.

With that thought, the increase of magic pauses, as if holding its breath. It settles into my chest, burning and coiled tight, then starts a slow, gentler drop.

I inhale sharply again, but it sounds less like a grasp at oxygen and more like a moan.

All at once, I know what I need: someone's mouth on mine. Release in the form of soft, curious lips exploring my own, slim, deft fingers wrapped tightly around my chin, tentative, gentle kisses that quickly turn greedy and deep, consuming. I need someone's warm, sweet breath against the shell of my ears, trailing the dips of my collarbones. I need hands on me, need to feel somebody on me aggressively, shoving me agains-

Wait a fucking second.

The vision halts, the magic along with it. As if waiting for permission before continuing.

"Good."

Tyler's voice pulls me out of the vision entirely, the powerful, consuming magic disappearing like smoke. Once again I can feel her hands on my knees, grounding me back in the present. I can feel the bark of the pine tree against my back, the chilly, thick forest air on my face. The darkness of the South Gate woods feels alive and thick like a blanket, but comforting, too. Not terrifying like it normally does, but understanding. Seeing.

Like it felt what just happened, and enjoyed it.

"You fought the images that weren't yours. You stayed in control beautifully. Good job."

Across from me, Tyler's grinning like a Cheshire cat, pride written openly on her sharp, freckled face.

All at once, the lack of magic floods my body, and my legs start to shake beneath her palms, completely overexerted. I feel…. oddly used, and dissatisfied. Honestly, it feels like how I felt every single time I hooked up with a guy back in Saxon Beach: dissatisfied.

The urge to be alone and…. fix it is overwhelming. The lack of magic leaves me feeling like I was teased, for lack of a better word. Like somebody wound me up, then left.

I'm lost in my thoughts and sheer frustration when I realize Tyler could be reading my thoughts right now, and I shake my head, trying to get the images out. For fucks SAKE, Niamh.

"How do you know which images weren't mine?" I croak out.

Tyler's dark eyes glimmer across from me. Her face isn't all that far from my own, and I cringe at the idea of her reading my thoughts. Jesus christ.

"Because I put them in your head, Niamh. Tell me- who was the person that came to mind for you in that little scenario?"

"I-."

The answer is I don't know, and now my face is on fire.

It isn't that I've never had sex before or anything. It isn't that I don't know where that scenario was headed. There were four guys back home, and they were nothing special. I'd only said yes to the first because I was bored and curious, and the other three times in hopes that it might be more fun than the first time. But time and time again, it was never anything special. It was nothing like... God, it was nowhere near as passionate and intense like whoever the person kissing me in my head just was. That.... Yeah. If that's how magic tries to consume you, no wonder other witches have succumbed to it. Without Tyler just now, I could have succumbed to it. And I would have done so willingly.

But I don't know how to answer Tyler's question, because it isn't that. It's that the person in my head felt distinctly feminine.

Soft and gentle. Cautious, curious. Gentle, sweet, holding me first as if I might break, but then pushing me hoping that I would. So, so intense, kissing me with a passion and fervor that I didn't think existed in real life. Whoever the person in my head just was, they kissed me like they needed me.

And it was definitely a girl.

But I've been kissed by plenty of girls, and never like that. Never in that greedy, profound way, like it wasn't just enough to have their mouth on mine; it was like they needed to to slip inside my skin.

So no, I can't answer her, because I've never kissed a girl like that before. I don't know who the person in the vision was; and based on her attempt at looking innocent, a completely fake smile pasted onto her face, Tyler knows.

The combination of lack of magic, her amusement, and vague questions, her vague *everything* gets under my skin, turning my words sharp and biting.

"I don't know." I bite out, realizing that my harsh tone just gave away my unspoken truth anyways.

And yet despite being short with her, I can tell Tyler is so utterly pleased with herself just the look on her face. She's dropped her innocent eyes, determination and excitement flooding her features now.

All of a sudden she stands up, helping me to my feet. My legs are still shaking, just enough to remind me how that power felt. What it could do.

"Don't be embarrassed. That vision was just an example of how *my* magic feels. I just let you into my direct channel of it. That's how I feel whenever I cast."

Good god. If that's how she feels whenever she does magic…. How does she stay in control?

"How long have you known about your gifts?" I ask her all of a sudden. It must have taken her years to master this, and she doesn't look any older than eighteen or nineteen.

Tyler doesn't answer my question, instead picking her journal up from the dirt and thumbing to the very back, where a slim red candle is nestled against the last page. She walks a few feet away, then crouches low to the forest floor, setting it upright against a few stones.

"Okay. Next lesson in control. I want you to use what you're feeling right now, the embarrassment, the frustration, all of it. Pool it all together into a ball, and use your magic to light this."

I stare at her, then at the little red candle in disbelief. "How?"

"Allow the emotions to get strong enough to almost override you, but not quite. Try to envision them mushing into a ball, feeling them all. Remember, anger is your gift. Use it. Feel it, let it sink in, but instead of letting it consume you, try and just…. extend it out, towards the candle. Think to yourself what you want to do with that energy: light the candle."

She allows her gaze to drift over to the candle for approximately three seconds. Her eyes darken, some emotion I can't place pooling in them. But then I see it.

Grief, stark and raw and shocking pools beneath her eyes, the shadows dimming her fair skin.

The candle sputters alight.

Tyler snuffs it out with her fingers, her eyes calm again, all while my mouth drops open. Even though I'm shocked and impressed, the urge to ask if she's okay overrides my excitement.

"Don't." She says simply without looking at me.

Okay, then.

"You can do it, Niamh." She says, breaking the tense silence. "I promise you, you can. Just control it. You can."

Her voice is measured and soft throughout our little area, and doing very odd things to the hairs on my arms right now. I'm definitely still bothered by her magic earlier. That drop…. Fuck. That was way, way more intense than mine. That's got to be it. That's why I have goosebumps right now. No way is it just her voice.

"You can do it, Niamh." She whispers into the dark.

Her voice prompts me into action.

I do what she says, taking everything from the last few minutes: the embarrassment at the vision, and her totally knowing why. The frustration from the magic leaving my body, that unspent, restless feeling stuck beneath my skin, the taut, tugging feeling still lingering in my muscles, and what happened with Indie this morning.

I add Tyler's lilting, petal-soft voice into the mix.

And finally, finally, I allow myself to feel all of it at once. She's right- it almost overwhelms me. The embarrassment, the sadness, the grief, the restlessness, and that deep, deep *anger...* almost. They almost get me.

But they don't get the chance, because I do exactly what Tyler said, squeezing my eyes shut and winding the feelings together into a thick ball. The mental image of a hacky sack comes to mind, growing bigger and bigger by the second. An enormous, tattered hacky sack made up of my magic; activated and awakened, because I'm in control of it.

And when I open my eyes, I hurl it at the little red candle.

It doesn't just light.

No, the candle bursts into flames, shooting high up into the air like a bonfire, illuminating the South Gate woods around us. After a second, it calms, and where the candle once stood tall, a shortened, half-melted version rests in its place. A little red tealight candle, essentially, instead of the pillar it used to be.

Although obviously smaller, it remains lit, flickering softly amidst the trees.

Tyler just looks at me, her face bathed in the candle's orange glow. An expression I've never seen on her before coats her entire face, the candlelight only magnifying the intensity of it in her eyes:

Joy.

She's looking at me with pure, undiluted joy.

But it's different from the kind of joy Zeke looks at me with. It isn't a happy, bubbly joy because I'm the new girl who's cute and witty and surfs. It isn't a cheerful, childlike joy.

No, Tyler is looking at me with a joy that says she's found someone just like her. It's dark and intense, almost twisted.

But addictive.

The way she's looking at me right now… Her eyes are pure ardor, those twin blue pools so intense and so magnetizing that I almost want to look away. It's like she's looking right into me, like she's seeing it all. And fuck, it is so addictive.

So I don't look away, because even though it's intense, I feel like a challenge. I just set a fucking candle on fire. I just controlled my magic. Pride and power surge through my chest, giving me a strange sense of confidence that I didn't know I lacked.

So I don't look away.

Deep, sea-floor blue meet bright green. Tyler doesn't look away either. She just looks at me like she knows: we're one and the same.

Like she's seeing me.

And with a jolt, and as the feeling of an enormous, leaden weight leaves my shoulders, a true, genuine smile works its way onto my sweaty, flushed face, mingling with the confidence swirling through my chest.
Tyler *does* see me. She just did. She saw exactly what I'm capable of. And she's the only one who does.

She's the only person who just saw me do what I can do-

Magic-

Every fiery, intense bit of it, and she *isn't scared of me.* She doesn't look even close to terrified right now.

No, Tyler looks *elated* as she stares into my face.

CHAPTER TWENTY

TYLER

"What rhymes with this?"

Morgan looks over at me from her current position: laying on her stomach sprawled out on my bed, with her chin resting over the edge. She's kicking her feet back and forth, her tan, bare arms dangling over onto the floor where her gigantic, spiral bound notebook laden with sticky notes and annotations sits. Excessive.

This is the third day in a row that Morgan's been at my house, sneaking over late in the night to do our project. As odd as it feels, tonight I've started to accept it. Yeah, she's the daughter of the woman who's made it her mission to turn the entire town against me. Yeah, she's never spoken a word to me before this project.

But Morgan's alright.

Her honey-colored hair spills over my mattress, trailing down her arms. Those amber, honey-jar eyes are trained on said notebook, specifically at the packet detailing our assignment that's due tomorrow. When I don't answer her right away, she looks back down, her pencil makes its way into her mouth. She starts to chew on the eraser as I think.

But as I think, I find myself looking at her- and I mean really looking at her. Studying her. She's deep in concentration now, unaware of my scrutinizing gaze. The fact that Morgan Van Devon at my house, in my *bedroom* for the third day in a row is truly baffling to me. Since that night, she's come over happily, not a single ounce of fear on her gentle, innocent face.

I'm not easily surprised, and yet Morgan Van Devon is continuing to surprise me.

The first night she showed up at my window, I questioned her morals. I questioned her motives, and her character. I was short with her. I didn't give her an inch. Her mom hates me, always trying to turn everyone against me: who's to say Morgan's would be any different? It just couldn't be possible that she's actually a decent person. No fucking way. And yet, for the third day in a row, I find myself with Morgan Van Devon, and not hating it.

She's actually…. Kind. She's sweet, and thoughtful. Those gentle, curious honey-eyes continue to take me in, and not shy away in fear. Not a single drop of hatred or disgust crosses her features at all. I can't remember a single time where someone other than my grandmother or Felix has looked at me like that.

The last three days, hatred or fear has never once crossed her face when she looks at me. That gentle, sweet curiosity does, though, relentlessly.

Morgan looks at me like I'm fascinating.

Even more surprising to me is the fact that since the first night she showed up, the act of reading her thoughts didn't cross my mind once. Not even after she left, as I watched her all-black-outfitted self quietly slip out my door and run home well after two in the morning. Not once did I consider slipping into that tan, curious little head of hers.

Maybe it was the fact that she surprised me. Maybe it's the fact that she doesn't hate me at all. Maybe it's the fact that, over the last three days, I haven't felt the need to be a dick to her anymore. Actually, I haven't felt the need to be anything other than myself. Maybe it's the fact that she's actually a good person: maybe that's what caught me off guard.

Or maybe it's that after she left that first night, when I was in bed trying in vain to fall asleep, the smell of almond shampoo, honey, and cinnamon lingered on in my room like a restless spirit. The smell of cinnamon still has yet to leave- if anything, it's grown stronger, especially heady when she's in the room.

Curious.

"Um…" I say, tearing myself out of my thoughts, finally. "Bliss?"

She looks up at me and smiles. "That's perfect. Our poem is going to be so good. Definitely A-plus worthy."

And then she looks back down, taking the pencil out of her mouth and scribbling furiously in her notebook with it, acting like she didn't just smile at me for the first time ever.

Out of nowhere, my chest begins to burn. Not burning like my magic- burning like something just plowed into me.

And it started the second she smiled at me.

Alarmed, I sit up and frantically rub at the space in between my ribs, willing myself to breathe. This isn't normal at all. This doesn't even feel remotely similar to my magic. This feels like…. Panic. Or anxiety. Or something.

She smiled at me. That was all. So what the hell?

Morgan, oblivious to this, finishes writing whatever she had been so excited about. With a deep, relieved exhale, she tosses the pencil down and flips over onto her back. With a sigh of contentment, she stretches her entire body, pulling her arms above her head and pointing her toes, stretching out fully across my bed. Every single muscle; every lean, lithe part of her, the parts built from years and years of dance are on display. The tight, smooth muscles of her arms, her strong, tanned legs, every bronzed muscle pulled taut beneath her thin green tank top and shorts. Despite the consistent rain and fog, she somehow manages to stay brown year round, blaming it on her Arabic blood when I'd asked.

Morgan closes her eyes, releasing a deep, tight exhale as she arches her back just slightly, getting every last ounce of her stretch in.

I can't explain why I do it. I really can't.
But when she arches her back, my eyes immediately glue to her hip bones and the small of her back, and the way they arc off my bed in one smooth roll.

The restless, fluid way they rise, then fall gracefully back down onto my comforter.

I don't know why I fixate. I have not a single fucking clue.
But even stranger still, the oddest, most searing feeling overwhelms my chest and skin, feeling like I've been doused in cold water and then burning hot immediately after. A shudder runs through me, and I feel a blush work its way up my neck to my face, my stomach flipping.

What. The. Hell?

I wonder, dizzily, if I'm sick.

I don't know why I just fixated on her fucking hips. Her back, the steep curve that runs from the base of her spine to...

Jesus, Tyler.

I don't know why I looked.

Or why it made me feel.... Something. I don't know. I don't know.

Morgan sits up then, yawning, and begins collecting her things. She adjusts her sage-green tank top, fiddles with her few necklaces, and then smooths her amber hair across her head.

"Alright. It's done."

She hops off my bed, gigantic notebook tucked under her arm, and I stand up too. Hastily, jerkily, my face still red. I will it to calm down, hoping it works before she looks too closely at me.

I'm flustered.

I don't *get* flustered. I don't *care* enough to get flustered, about anyone, or anything.

But my response to her is definitely, without a doubt, flustered. "O-. Okay. Yeah."

What the *fuck,* Tyler? It's like I can't formulate a single sentence around her right now. I'm definitely sick. Or something. I'm losing it. And I have no idea why. Morgan crosses my room, fiddling with the small crystal on her longest necklace. At closer glance, it's a nearly translucent pink stone. Three nights ago, I thought it was just quartz.

But no. It's a rose quartz. Morgan Van Devon, daughter of proclaimed witch-hater, is wearing a rose quartz.

If she notices my newfound awkwardness, she chooses not to comment on it.

"So... I'll see you in class, then?" I ask her, my mouth finally catching up to my brain. Well, almost. I hadn't meant that to be a question.

Morgan looks up at me, and holy fuck, her eyes are *golden.* Amber and honey and tangerine sunsets all molded into one. Bright and gentle, those curious, sweet eyes unafraid and penetrating.

The smell of cinnamon floats through my room, stronger than ever.

"Yeah, Tyler."

My name on her tongue brings the searing, burning feeling back full force, and I rub at my chest absentmindedly.

She pauses, as if thinking something else. The silence in my room grows thick, but it isn't awkward. More alive than that. It feels like nervous energy, a thoughtful silence.

"What?" I find myself asking her. Anything. Anything that will keep her looking at me like that: gently, unafraid, like she doesn't just see me as Tyler, the witch.

Anything that will keep her looking at me like she wants to ask me something else.

"I just…" She trails off, then looks down again at her feet. When she looks back up, there's a new look in her eyes.

Nervousness.

"We can hangout again…. If that's something you'd want to do."
She says softly. Then she goes quiet again, looking down and spinning one of her dozens of tiny rings around on her finger. "I'd like to."

The cinnamon in my room grows overwhelming.

Fuck.

Holy. Fuck.

Why my heart is racing right now, I have not a single fucking clue. Combined with my burning, too-tight chest, I should be concerned. But I'm not.

I feel elated.

Morgan Van Devon wants to hangout with me again. She isn't afraid of me. She *wants* to see me again.

I roll the thought over in my head again and again. She wants to see me again. *She wants to see me again.*

She doesn't just want to do this project and dip. She wants to see me again.

I swallow hard, tucking a strand of my long, night-brown hair behind my ear. I will my skin to calm down, to not look flushed. I will my hands to calm down, to not shake. I will my chest to breathe easier.

I have no idea what's happening to me right now.
She wants to fucking see me again.

"Yeah. I would love that. I mean. Yes. Yeah."

My voice holds none of its cocky, silken cadence. No, what comes out is awkward. Nervous. I want to crawl into a hole. Tyler, you fucking idiot. What was *that???*

As I walk her to the door, I feel faint, like I might pass out.

And when she says goodbye, heading home again well after two in the morning, I watch as she looks back at me not once- not twice- but Three. Times.

The thoughts buzzing around my head are deafening.

Morgan Van Devon wants to be my friend.

She wants to be around me.

And for some unknown reason,

I cannot fucking wait to see her again.

I head back upstairs, Willing the door to my room to close behind me. It snicks closed, and I slide down against it, sitting on the floor in a heap. I still feel like I can't breathe properly, my chest burning, my skin flushed.

And I have no idea why.

Slightly panicked about this, I get up and walk over to my open window, hoping in vain that the sea breeze will help.

Bracing my hands on the windowsill, I close my eyes. The night air cools my face, the smell of the South Gate, of the ocean, of brine and mist and pine filling me completely, soaking into my pores. My hair falls all around my face as I lean over my hands, the strands tickling my cheeks and down my waist. My hair smells like Summerhill: brackish and crisp, like the acres of woods just beyond the hut.

But then, amidst the smells of Summerhill, something else coats my skin. It's the same sea air, the same pine trees, but with it now are…. Fuck, what is that? It's sweet, sticky...

Honey.

Unmistakable notes of honey, and that cinnamon.

And what else is that- roses?

As if saying "duh," the smell intensifies.

Yep. Roses. Roses, cinnamon, and honey cling to my hair like glue. I grab a chunk that's skimming my waist and bring it to my nose, inhaling deeply. The three scents cling to my hair like I had dipped it in them.

"What the *fuck* is going on." I whisper under my breath, almost nervously. Something happened. Or is happening. I have no idea. Between the weird physical sensations that started when Morgan was here, this smell, and just…. Everything… I have no idea what's happening to me right now.

It reeks of magic to me.

I drop my hair and brace my forearms back on my windowsill, dropping my head in between my open hands. Breathe, Tyler.

I take one breath. Then another. Then a third. On the third breath, I look up, staring out at the darkness of the South Gate woods.
But something out of the corner of my eye catches my attention first.

There, on the carpet below my windowsill, lay three shiny, new pennies, facing heads up. Lucky pennies; the glinting copper so fresh they seem to glow.

It's only then that I know undeniably that whatever is happening to me is of magical origin,

Because magic is very good at coming in waves of three.

From the journal of Tyler Iris Lane

Thursday, November 7th

<u>It Always Comes In Threes:</u>

I make my wishes in threes, my promises in threes, tell my truths in threes. I seem to collect shells and stones and sea glass by handfuls of threes. I'll see shooting stars three nights in a row, I'll find dandelions in bunches of threes.

Three dried sunflower bouquets are strung above my windowsill.
Three dried roses are taped above my bed. The petals sometimes fall off, and I'll wake up, just to find three of them tangled into strands of my hair.
And today, I found three shiny pennies on my floor after Morgan went home.
Three times Morgan Van Devon has come over,
And three times today she made my skin feel hot and cold, my chest feel funny, and my words jumbled.

Threes. It's always in waves of three. Magic is so, so good at that. It always comes in threes.

Tonight, after I found the three pennies, I went to bed and nearly sat on three red rose petals. Three <u>fresh</u> rose petals, dewy and wet as if they'd been plucked fresh from the garden.

Eleni and I don't even _grow_ red roses. We don't grow roses at all.

I found three more of them sticking to the ends of my hair before I finally fell asleep.

It's always in threes. It's always come in threes. Magic loves the number three. It's an in-between number, it's holy, it's divine. Magic always works in threes.

But what I want to know is why it's happening to me right now, and why it's seeming to stem from Morgan.

Or, more specifically,

Who's doing it?

Chapter Twenty One

Niamh

There is something to be said about the level of drunkenness that makes you start to forget things and recall time differently.

Just walking into Kai and Colin Bohdie's enormous, sprawling house was a journey in itself. Zeke and Marlo had picked me up, as promised, rolling up to my driveway in a beat up, faded blue Ford that I could only assume was their dad's. Both of their longboards sat in the bed, along with several pillows and a gigantic comforter.

I didn't have the heart to tell them why I'd bailed on our surf earlier. After what happened with Tyler... I just couldn't bring myself to go surf with them. It didn't feel right after what happened with Tyler. Which is how I found myself spending the rest of the afternoon with her instead, working on various different things, loving every second of it.

Thankfully, they'd both accepted my lie of my dad needing me for something, and when Zeke had walked up to the door to pick me up, he made sure to introduce himself to my dad personally, promising to keep me safe. Besides that being a complete lie, I wanted to melt into the floor. Guys back in Saxon Beach didn't do that.

And besides, I didn't need protecting from anything. This afternoon alone proved that if anything, I'm the one that could protect Zeke, now.

Kai and Colin Bohdie's parents owned a gigantic, wide cabin right on the water's edge in the North Gate, so far North that the causeway was within walking distance. It sat nestled in between fat clusters of pine trees, the golden, twinkly lights of the house lighting up the Atlantic in front of it. Between the light rain that began to fall when we pulled up, the fog that began to rise up from the sea, pooling all along our feet, and the glinting, nearly hidden moon, along with this being my first party since back home… A large, energetic bundle of excitement had begun to grow in my stomach the second I'd stepped out of the car. Marlo had passed me her enormous glass handle of Fireball as we'd driven the eight minutes to the Bohdie's, but it wasn't enough to quell the nerves, *especially* once we'd walked in and I'd seen just how many people were here.

But now, I look around now happily, all my nervous excitement completely gone. I'm cocooned in a warm, gentle blanket of bliss, finally having reached the level of drunk where everything feels perfect and breezy and nothing really matters. I can't even think about everything with Tyler, or what happened with Indie.
Thoughts of my old friends glide off my back like the rain falling outside.

All that matters is what's right in front of me, which happens to be a sticky, soaked table covered in blue solo cups. Gentle golden lights from the ceiling wash over the giant, sprawling living room, bathing everyone in soft, buttery tones. It doesn't come close to matching the chaos of the room at all. The Bohdie's house is decorated spaciously, all golden yellows and wood, with sliding barn doors and wide, floor-to-ceiling windows. A house made for hosting lavish dinner parties, social events. I'm not sure Kai and Colin's parents envisioned their house would become famous for hosting the raucous, absurd parties that their sons are now known for.

Zeke snakes his arm around my waist, pulling me in for a brief, squeezing hug before taking his second shot. He sinks the last cup, causing the two random guys at the end of the table to groan and swear.

"Fucking hell, Zeke. How is that the third fucking time, dude?"

Always eloquent is the surfer boy.

Zeke introduced me to our opponents well over an hour ago, and I've already forgotten their names. Both tall, both with deep, cutting neck tans, both with long, sun-bleached hair and wide, delinquent smiles that tell me they know they can have whatever girls they want. They'd looked at me with those same smiles until Zeke had wrapped his arm around my waist and not let go.

They both look exactly like every other guy in the room, and most of the girls, too. Upon walking in, I could tell right away that the surf community of Summerhill really isn't all that different from those of Saxon Beach, similar in the way everyone here seems to brim with the youthfulness and obstinance that comes from hours in the sun and water, from defying those telling us to spend less time in said sun and water. It's comforting knowing that even across the country, the people I'm surrounding myself with now aren't all that different from those back home. Every adult back in Saxon Beach save for my dad called Mak, Booker, Indie and I troublemakers. Which we were, definitely. Aine and Cian liked to say that us four were the Z-Boys reincarnated. I always enjoyed that, my parents not so much. But it's just how everyone under the age of twenty was back home. Here's the thing: in my opinion, it's not having a neck tan and pterygium in both eyes that makes you a surfer. It's the rebellious, carefree attitude, and the innate urge to rebel. Nobody we hangout with back home acted how their parents wanted them to. We all just wanted to surf and have fun. We were all of one mind, in that way: just surf and have fun, and fuck everything else.

And everyone here seems to be following the same mindset.

Zeke hands me a third kombucha, tipping the rest of his beer into his mouth, his hand still wrapped around my waist. He's been finding little ways to touch me for the last hour and a half, and I feel *really* good. Like deep down, everything is perfect good. I look good, I'm warm, and people have been coming up to me the entire time I've been here asking me about myself and making me feel important and shiny.

Where am I from? What kind of boards do I ride? How do I know the Torah's? Did I have any sponsors back home?

I'm relishing in feeling *good,* for once, no longer terrified or hateful, finally, finally feeling like Summerhill could be enjoyable. At Marlo's behest tonight, I wore the hugely oversized, forest-green corduroy pants that she let me borrow. They hang low on my hips, trailing over my favorite pair of Vans sk8-his. Marlo's jeans swallow my legs completely, and paired with an oversized black t-shirt and my favorite black Rip Curl beanie, I feel more myself than ever. I'm comfortable, I'm myself. My arms are still tan from back home, my white-blonde hair is falling perfectly down my back in defined, loose curls for once, and I know without having to look that the alcohol is bringing out my tan complexion and freckles in a way that makes me look cheerful and approachable.

I feel *good.*

I finish my second kombucha and lean into his side hug. "Sorry." I say sheepishly to the guys across the table, after having kicked their asses for a third time now. Fuzzily, I try to sort through my sluggish thoughts, their names just out of reach. Wait. Maybe... I think one of them is Kai.
And then I remember. Kai Bohdie is the one on the right. *The* Kai, the one Marlo has a thing for. Yeah, he's cute. No wonder what she sees in him. His dark brown hair peeks under his beanie, just falling below his ears. His baby blue and gray flannel

bring out the icy blue of his eyes perfectly, and the silver nose hoop brings it all together.

Damn, I find myself thinking. Kai *is* cute. I wonder where Marlo is?

The other guy's name still evades me. Archer? No. The other one is…. Fuck. Arch….? No. Ash? Asher. Yeah. Asher and Kai, I remember now.

Zeke squeezes me again. "Get fucked, Ash."

I lean into his warm, strong side hug harder than I should have. I've only known him for a little over four weeks, but I'm already so happy to be his friend. I like being around him.

I *like* him, I realize in my happy, blissful-drunk brain. I like Zeke. I like how he feels. I like how he hugs me tightly, and how his face completely lights up when he sees me. I like the way he smiles with his eyes, I like that he always asks how my day is and cares to hear my answer. I like the way he's chipper and happy and caring. I like how he's sweet, and he seems to really want me around. None of the guys back in Saxon Beach treated me how Zeke does, and it feels fucking good.

I like Zeke.

"Zeke." I say, in a rush of adrenaline and happiness, my face hidden away in his side. "I'm really glad I moved here."

At my words, he pulls away from our hug and looks at me, the absence of his body against mine leaving me cold.

I swear to God, his entire face erupts in light. His golden, hearth-warm eyes are sparkling amidst the dim lighting, and that tan, chipper face is completely aglow. His smile is a supernova, a mile wide, and reaches every single corner of his eyes, the little crinkles in the corner coming out full force. He's looking at me like he doesn't know what to say, and my heart feels like it's freezing and melting all at once.

Zeke's looking at me like he likes me, too.

"I'm really glad you moved here too, Niamh." He finally says, that supernova smile stuck to his face. He swallows like he wants to say something else, his eyes flitting between my mouth and my gaze, and despite the billions of other sounds filling the room, despite the laughter and music and shouts, all I can hear is my rapid heartbeat.

His look is enough to make me wonder if he's going to kiss me, and enough to make me question whether or not I'm going to kiss him back.

But the moment is shattered when Marlo's excited, squealing voice carries through the room, screaming my name with a ferocity I've never heard from her before.

Marlo crashes into the room, literally, running down the stairs and jumping off the last three at a speed I can only imagine must be Fireball-fueled, two other girls trailing after her. Her simple, shimmering black dress clings to her tiny body, complimented perfectly by her black tights and white doc martens. Combined with the added few inches from her shoes, her long auburn hair cascading down her back, and the simple makeup that causes her aqua eyes to pop, she looks stunning. Perfectly hyper and perfectly stunning. Except as she reaches me, I can see that black dress is slightly off shoulder, her eyes too bright. Her pupils are enormous, and her cheeks are flushed. When I meet her eyes head on, she smiles at me, a wide, too-excited, manic grin. A quick glance at the two girls behind her show similar looks. Smiling despite myself, I wonder what exactly they were doing upstairs.

"NIAMH. ZEKE. Oh thank God I've been looking for you guys fuck okay we're playing Dare or Drop upstairs let's GO!"

She says this all in one excited, quick breath, like her thoughts are running too fast for her mouth to catch up. Zeke rubs a hand over his face, groaning something under his breath about Kai being a fucking idiot. I don't have time to comment, because Marlo's wired self grabs my arm and pulls me along with her towards the darkened staircase. I turn and grab Zeke's hand before I lose him.

We ascend the stairs in complete darkness, leaving the golden lights of the living room behind, but I can hear the twins perfectly as we head upstairs.

Zeke's now-excited, upbeat voice. "Yo, who's playing? This game's actually really fun, Niamh."

"Have you ever played Truth or Dare, Niamh?" This voice Marlo's breathless one, her sweaty hand clutched in mine.

"Of course. Why?"

We follow Marlo upstairs blindly, three entire flights of stairs in total. I can hear Zeke explaining the rules of the game to me, gathering that it's something like truth or dare, but it isn't. I'm trying to retain the information, I really am. But I'm more hyper-focused on the way his hand still hasn't let go of my own. His strong, calloused hand.

".... So it's just like truth or dare, except the rules are a little different. If you don't get it, Marlo's better at explaining it. She kinda helped invent it."

I blink amidst the dark, trying not to trip as I follow the faint glow of Marlo's white docs. "I'm gonna be totally honest with you right now. I didn't retain an inch of that."

Zeke snorts behind me, and I hear him swallow his beer. "That's because you helped yourself to the Fireball in the car."

"Fireball *you two* forced me to drink!"

"First off, it was Marlo's Fireball. Second off, 'forced" is a harsh word. I would never. Consent is sexy."

And it's *this* comment that has me twisting my head around sharply to look at him as we reach the landing, following Marlo towards a room that's lit up with blue LED's.

She heads inside the room, but I stop before going in. Zeke pauses too, leaning his back against the wall lazily, carelessly, in a way I've never seen him before. He props one foot up, his knee propped out, and I fixate on the way his hand is wrapped around the glass neck of his beer as he tilts it into his mouth amidst the dark. The blue lights from the room illuminate his face, and it's all I can do to not stare. So instead, fueled by liquid courage, I meet his eyes.

"Oh yeah?"

And in my head, I can picture it so clearly that it almost feels real. The word 'yeah' is barely out of my mouth as he grabs me in the faintly-blue darkness, pushing me back into the wall where he just was. His hands find my hair and cup the back of my neck, and he kisses me quickly and rushed like he just can't wait a single second longer. His hip bones dig into my stomach, pressing me tighter against the wall, forcing sounds out of me that I've only made alone for the last few months. Those rough, calloused hands around my neck, then roaming under my giant t-shirt, running those hands along my sides and the small of my back, pulling me closer to him. I want it, I realize. I want him. I want to know what his mouth tastes like. I want to know what he feels like, I want to know how those hands-

but my vision is shattered when he just looks at me like 'duh' and says "Of course, Niamh" in a surprised voice, then tugs me by the hand into the room.

I don't know what I expected, but there's nothing special about the bedroom. My guess is that it's either Colin or Kai's by the looks of it. Upon walking in, it's hard to see in the dim blue lighting, but I can make out surf posters and trophies littering the walls and every flat surface. Spare fins, dirty shirts, and boards rest on the floor. A queen-sized bed is shoved in one corner, neatly made. A couple dozen people sit on corners of the bed, a few cross-legged on the floor. A few six packs of hard tea sits in the middle of the room, and in the middle of it all stands Marlo, walking around pairing people up in twos.

"So Dare or Drop. Does everyone know the rules?" A blonde guy that was on the floor a second ago is standing, taking a count of everyone in the room.

Kai Bohdie comes tearing up the stairs a second later, bursting into the room with urgency and slamming the door behind him.

"You were not about to play without me, fuckers." He smirks, his grin cocky. Marlo's stunning face floods with color even amidst the blue light, her big pupils growing bigger. Our eyes meet, and I smirk at her.

"Relax, we haven't even started. I'm pairing people up right now. Who do you want?" She says, as if she doesn't care that he might pick someone else. So she's going for the nonchalant angle. I glance sideways at Zeke, who's rolling his eyes.

Kai doesn't answer her right away, instead walking over to the desk in the far corner of the room. He bends over it with his back to us all, sniffing loudly once, twice, as if we don't have a clue what he's doing. After this, he returns to Marlo's side, this time with a frantic, excited look in his eyes.

I shake my head internally. There were always the scant few that dabbled in coke at parties back home. I had way too big of dreams for myself to ever partake. Young up-and-coming surfers who want sponsors don't get the option of doing drugs and acting like cracked-out idiots. I know Indie and Booker had done it a couple times, but Mak and I were pretty straight edge for the most part. We had goals.

I hope Marlo isn't just doing it for Kai's approval.

"Yeah, you're with me, Marlo." He rubs his silver nose ring with one tanned finger, sniffing again. "Alright. Everyone play before?"

He still hasn't even looked at her. Poor Marlo. Zeke was right. Based on my first impression of him, he's not exactly the greatest guy. Come on, Marlo.

One of the girls in the corner looks over at me and then back at Kai. A muscular, bleach-blonde girl in a crop top and flatbill hat, with about six necklaces and six earrings apiece. She smiles at me, her eyes lingering on mine for a beat too long. "I don't think Niamh has." She offers. Her eyes rake me up and down, and I feel my pulse speed up. She looks like Indie a little bit with her style and intense eye contact.

She looks like Indie enough to have me wondering if her gaze is a little more than friendly, and I force myself to look away, nervous.

Kai's wide, overexcited eyes swing over to me, and then I really feel my pulse begin to flap its hummingbird wings. He looks me over, and then fixates on Zeke's close, almost protective proximity to me. We aren't touching, but he stands close enough to me to make a statement.

Kai smiles like he has an idea. A bad one.

"Dare or Drop. Okay. So it's just like truth or dare, dude. The game master offers up a dare to the room within a certain time limit, right? Whoever completes the dare successfully first wins, and then is the next game master. If you fail and run out of time, you're fucked. You're dropped from the game, along with an article of clothing."

He smiles wickedly.

My heartbeat is frantic, and before I can say a word, Marlo finishes pairing people up and addresses the room. "Who's the first game master? I nominate myself and Kai."

The blonde girl in the corner giving me eyes protests along with a few others. "No dude, Nat and I are first. We won last time after jumping off East Cliff, remember?

"THAT WAS A FUCKING TIE, LAYLA!" Kai shouts at them, but he's laughing. "Ryan and I hit the water before you guys." He throws a middle finger at her and another blonde girl in a thick fleece jacket and beanie who I presume must be Nat.

The cute blonde girl, Layla, throws him double middle fingers. "Fuck you, Kai. We *jumped* first. And it was so fucking cold. And the surf was so fucking big. That was such an ass dare. East Cliff is like fifteen feet off the ground."

Marlo laughs, interrupting the two of them before it gets too heated. "But you did it, didn't you, you badass. But Kai's right, he and Ryan technically won last time. Sorry, Layla. Rules are rules."

"Rules are rulesssss, braddah." Kai drawls out. Layla glares daggers at him, but she's either over it or not trying to argue with Marlo.

"Congratufuckinglations." She bites out, but smiling again. Kai smiles at Marlo, mouthing 'you're the best' to her then stands up, eying the whole room with a frantic, excited smile. He uses his empty beer bottle to point at all of us, pacing back and forth with one finger on his lips, as if trying to think of the worst possible dare. People around the room start whispering, debating what he'll pick. I'm wondering myself: back home, truth or dare was mild. The worst I'd ever had to do was jump off the Saxon Beach pier naked. Not the worst thing in the world, especially since Makani and Booker jumped in after me.

I catch snippets and tail ends of conversations, still mostly floating in a blissful, happy

drunk haze, still thinking about Zeke's hand in mine just

minutes before.

And my little daydream.

Jesus.

I shift my weight slightly, my breath catching, trying to dislodge the memory,

and what it did to me.

But then the pair to my right, a girl and her boyfriend whose names I already

forgot, say something that sounds suspiciously like "South Gate" and "woods," and the

happy, floaty feeling leaves my body in one quick, sickening tug. Nausea burns my

forehead and gut quickly and violently, and I force myself to breathe through my

nose.

Kai must have heard it too, because he stops pacing. Slowly, he faces the room,

setting his empty bottle down and grabbing a new drink from the box on the floor.

He rubs his nose, clears his throat, and then a big, maniacal grin fills his face.

"Alright, fuckers, Dare or Drop: find the gate and take a picture to prove it."

At his words, the room goes completely, utterly silent. Even Marlo's face falls.

Zeke stiffens next to me, and I don't have to look at him to know he's not happy

about this.

"Kai." Marlo says, her voice a little strained as she looks over at her twin. She sets her hard tea down and touches his arm gently. "That's not even real. It's just an urban legend. Pick something else."

For a girl who knows the origin story of that urban legend like the back of her hand and believes in it, I'm impressed at her nonchalance.
But Kai shakes his head, ignoring her pleas. He surveys the room with that same too-big grin.

"Nah, it is real. That's the dare for this round. Colin swears he and his chick saw it last year. It's totally real. He said it's exactly how they say it is in the stories, too, like thirty or forty fucking feet tall. Bigger than a fucking house. I swear to God."

The room is still silent as everyone weighs the dare. I look around, gauging everyone's faces. It's obvious that some people find this a complete joke. They swap smiles, eyes rolled. Some people mumble under their breaths, looking at Kai with annoyance.
Next to me, Zeke opens another beer and drains the whole Corona in almost one pull. He schools his expression into vague annoyance, running a hand through his coppery curls, but his eyes give him away. He's pissed. Pissed that this is just a joke to Kai, to everyone. His friend went missing, and he isn't over it. If it were any one of my friends, I don't think I'd be over it, either. I wonder if the rest of them even know. I wonder if they even care at all, or if Miles became just another statistic, another ghost story to them.

Zeke's obvious anger and discomfort forces my drunk self into action. I reach behind him for the fourth hard kombucha I'd stashed and crack it open. After one crisp, bubbly sip, I stand up, pulling Zeke up with me.

"Let's go win." I say to him and him only, clearly and loud.

I tell myself this is just another dumb dare, just like the stupid ones I used to do back in Saxon Beach. This is nothing different. And the South Gate woods won't be nearly as bad with Zeke there. I won't be alone. Nothing will hurt me. Plus, other people will be there too, all playing the game. We'll be fine. This is just another dare.

The room erupts in hollers, some "oooooooohs" from the guys. Someone behind me calls me ballsy, and others look at me with incredulity on their faces. I ignore it all, instead grabbing us both a tea from the box on the ground, then facing Kai head on. On top of everything else, on top of the adrenaline, I feel the room spin dangerously. Water might be smart at some point.

"What's our time limit?" I ask him, my voice hard, thinking about Zeke's missing friend, and how unbelievably ignorant Kai is about it all. I can feel Zeke's eyes on me, completely shocked.
Kai tilts his head at me, then looks out the open window to the balcony. The night is pitch-black now, the chilly sea air wafting in creating a trail of goosebumps on my bare arms.

"Two hours." He says simply, that shit-eating grin never leaving his face. "I hope you two are ready to lose your clothes. Then again, maybe you are."

He says this last part directly at Zeke, then mimes some obscene gestures at him. Zeke's eyes flash dangerously, and before this can go south I grab his hand, rubbing my thumb in comforting strokes over the back of it as I tug him towards the door.

"Hey." I whisper up at him as we make our way around people. "Ignore him. I have a plan. We're winning this."

Zeke's eyes soften in a silent thank-you, and we're both out the door before Kai can say anything else to piss him off.

I can only hope that my plan works.

CHAPTER TWENTY TWO

TYLER

From the journal of Tyler Iris Lane

Saturday, November 27

Just a little poem;

Whoever made you took their time.

Likely an artist,

Maybe a musician.

Because they added all the key details that only those with a painter's hand or a guitarist's heart

would notice.

Such as your honey eyes-

Sunset amber, sweet caramel,

Filled with a depth and warmth that speaks volumes without you trying at all.

The artists would have a field day trying to paint those.

How could they possibly capture everything in one frame?

One look at you from those eyes and I'm ready to sink to my knees,

Or voice exactly what it is that you do to me.

(it's a lot of things.)

The space between my ribcage-

That deep, cavernous space,

It cracks in two when you look at me.

Your voice was made for using; frequently and openly.

Any songwriter would be drawn to you- how could they not?

Your laugh is something akin to superglue for me-

It pieces me back together when I didn't know I needed it.

It smooths over my rough edges, soothes the jagged parts.

But, really-

The most beautiful sound to leave your lips is the way you say my name.

CHAPTER TWENTY THREE

NIAMH

"Zeke." I manage to get out as we finally pause to catch our breath. We're at the edge of the Bohdie's yard, where a run-down, squat wooden fence divides their enormous backyard and the North Gate woods beyond.

Both drunk, both giggling slightly, we'd torn out of the house with a few other brave pairs and all branched off once we'd left the safety and warmth of the party. Most people got in their cars and headed for the South Gate woods, which is something like a seven or eight minute drive from the Bohdie's house. Shockingly, Marlo and Kai are not one of the groups that head for the South Gate. Despite his affinity for stimulants and kind of being a dick, I hope Marlo is finally completing her mission.

I think of the way Zeke's been looking at me all night.
I think of my stupid little fantasy upstairs.

And then I think of the cringey, awkward way that he responded to my 'yeah?' which was meant to be a come-on.

At least one of us is getting some.

He pauses and looks over at me, his hands braced behind his head. "Do you really believe in the gate?" I ask him quietly, seriously.

He doesn't answer right away, and I hope I didn't cross a line. Fuck. Maybe I did. His friend went fucking missing in there. He probably wants nothing to do with this place. Goddamnit, Niamh. I kick myself internally, hoping that I didn't just open some deep ass trauma wound in the guy.

I gaze out at the treeline of the North Gate woods instead. It's black as pitch already, and I can't imagine how much darker it must be inside. My breath already fogs in the night air, and I'm grateful as hell for the winter coat that is Fireball and hard kombucha.

I exhale heavily. If we head directly forward, we'll be in the North Gate woods. If we enter the treeline at the right, veering away from the ocean, we'll be directly walking into the East Gate- which is where my plan comes in.

If- *if* I'm right, and I hope that I am, we can enter the East Gate woods and get on the path I take home from school. And *if* we can find that path….. Hopefully whatever has been leading me directly into the South Gate will work for a third time.

I doubt Tyler's awake right now, but if somehow she's around, that'd make our odds even higher.

And *if* all that goes according to plan…. Then maybe, just maybe, we can find the gate.

Zeke still doesn't answer me, but instead pulls his salt-stained gray hoodie off in that effortless way guys do and hands it to me without a word, ever the selfless gentleman. I still have the first one he gave me, and this one is no different- it still smells of sage, of saltwater. Goddamn.

He tugs the sleeves of his thin green windbreaker down over his thumbs, adjusts his blue beanie, and then offers me a small, sad smile. His breath fogs in the air like my own.

"Yeah, I do. I'm sure Marlo told you, but my friend Miles went missing when I was eight. He was biking around one day and just never came home. His family lived near the South Gate, and that's where they found his bike."

His voice catches on the word 'bike,' and I fight the urge to hug him tightly.

"His little bike was all they found when they combed the South Gate woods. They never found him. They never found anything at all. So in my eight year old head, I was sure the gate had taken him. There was no body, nothing. Obviously there's a lot of things that could've happened to him. He was fucking eight. But to never find his body, and just his bike? I don't know, Niamh. To me, that screams something weird, something maybe we can't explain or see. Like a gate, somewhere in the woods, where anyone who walks through it doesn't come out the other side. A gate to nowhere."

His words give me chills, and I look at him, weighing how heavy his eyes are, feeling the weight that he must have been carrying from that after all these years. How fucking traumatic must that have been for an eight year old kid?

"I'm really sorry, Zeke." Is all I can think to say.

He squeezes me into a hug, resting his chin on top of his head. "Thanks, Niamh. It's okay. I just don't fuck with the South Gate woods. Actual people go in there and don't come back out, and everyone's just left wondering. They never find bodies, they never find anything. Locals here have so many names for the gate and so many theories that it almost makes you wonder, you know? The gate's like Summerhill's version of the Bermuda Triangle now. I don't see a reason to go near a place like that. But of course Kai would."

"I'm gonna be super honest with you, dude. Kai's kind of an asshole."

He grabs my hand again as I pull us into the woods, entering at the East Gate. The last silver of moonlight is instantly swallowed by the towering pine trees, and the thought of us entering another world entirely hits me as we leave behind the bass and lights of the party, instead entering a place that's cold, stale, and silent.

Strangely enough, I'm not afraid. Thoughts of what's happened to me the last two times I walked on the path don't seem to penetrate as deep.

Maybe it's because Zeke's here.

Or maybe it's because I'm still fairly drunk.

Or maybe, maybe, it's because after the last time I was here, I learned how to control my magic, and now I feel less like a reckless, angry girl, and more like a weapon.

Zeke just snorts as we trailblaze our way towards anything resembling the path. "Yeah, well. It isn't my place to tell my sister who she can and can't sleep with. That's weird."

"Fair enough. So Marlo's type is obnoxious, cocky coke addicts?"

Zeke chuckles despite himself, and the lighthearted sound seems to ring through the darkness. "Yeah, she needs to check herself. The cherry on top is that his taste in music is shit, too. She can do so much better, but what do I know? I'm only her identical flesh and blood."

"His music taste is probably better than yours, though."

"Says the one who listens to songs by whiny, sad little white men from the midwest who still live in their parent's basements."

"Fuck you, dude."

"It's okay, Niamh. Just admit that midwest emo is trash. Acceptance is the first step to recovery."

"If you're gonna talk shit about Modern Baseball or Hot Mulligan right now, you can let go of my hand."

His grip tightens.

Our banter fades into silence as we keep walking, and nothing penetrates it in replacement. Nothing: not the sound of birds, a creek, mountain lions, nothing. The East Gate is just…. Dark, and growing darker.

Shadowy and silent, and completely without noise, the spaces between the thickly-clustered pine trees black as ink.

And as we trample through the forest at a slight incline, sidestepping brush and fallen trees, jumping at every single noise made between the two of us, of course my brain thinks of Tyler's stupid story about the witch of the woods: how she can change her shape, how her veins are full of pine needles and rot. Honestly, what she described sounded less like a witch, and more like a demon.

After a few minutes of using our phone lights to see and laughing hysterically every time we stumble in our tipsy hazes, our fear coated by the last of our drinks, I spy a stretch of dirt just ahead that closely resembles the path. Excitement growing in my chest, I pull Zeke towards it quickly. He doesn't argue with me, and as we approach it, I see that it *is* the path.

Fuck. *Yes.* My plan is working.

We head onto the path, and I don't have to question whether or not we're headed South- I can just tell. I don't know how, but I just know. Amidst our quiet chatter about Marlo and Kai, about the huge swell we're about to get next week, I can feel the air shift. All around us, it gets steadily quieter, the noise fading away again. It almost feels as if the farther along we go, the more…. Paused, everything feels. Like someone pressed pause on the world around us.

Nervously, I realize that we haven't come across anyone else since we left the party. If we are in the South Gate woods, shouldn't we have seen another group? Despite having an hour and a half left, it feels weird to not see *anyone.*

I'm about to comment on the lack of others as we wind around a particularly thin cluster of pines, farther apart in proximity than the rest of the forest has been. It's so dark that I can barely see in front of us, Zeke's tinny phone light barely illuminating the trunks of the great trees, but distantly, I wonder if we're approaching a clearing.

I open my mouth and turn to Zeke, a sarcastic, tension-breaking retort already on my tongue when he stops dead in his tracks beside me, then whispers my name once, in one breath.

And when I look forward, following his frantic, wide gaze at whatever he's looking at, the words die on my tongue instantly.

Because we did reach a clearing: a dark, wide clearing, the towering pine trees forming a perfect circle, slightly at an incline.

And there, right in the center of it is the gate.

My heart drops deep into a cavern somewhere in my stomach as I stare at it, my eyes unblinking. My mouth runs dry, and the thin, shaky adrenaline that floods my body kind of makes me feel like I could throw up. My head pounds in sync with my heartbeat.

The gate seems to stare back at us, looking exactly how everyone describes it, save for one detail.

It's much, much bigger than a house.

Thick, strong iron bars stretch into the tips of the trees, their sharpened tips nearly disappearing into the branches. The way it just stands there feels horribly sinister, like it's holding its breath, waiting.

And it feels *old.*

The gate in the woods stands wide, wide open, identical down to every last detail from the stories. Standing alone, unattached to anything else, like it's growing up from the ground. Both giant halves of it stand wide open, inviting us to walk through.

It really is fucking real.

The gate that swallowed Abigail Summers and Miles whole-

It's real.

The Demon Gate, Satan's Doorway, Solomon's Gateway, Solomon's Key, whatever it's called- it's fucking real.

I let go of Zeke's hand silently and pinch my arm, then I rub at both of my eyes until everything's fuzzy and staticy.

Nothing changes. The gate still stands alone, ominous and silent.

Without thinking, I reach down and take Zeke's hand again as if to anchor myself. It's fucking *real.*

My inner voice is tiny and hiding, but she repeats the same thought on a loop.

The gate in the South Gate woods is fucking real.

All the stories were true.

As I try to get a grip on myself and my heart rate, I look around the area. We seem to be in a huge, dark clearing, and yet oddly enough, the moon isn't penetrating through the trees. I look up, and my heart drops into my stomach again.

There is no sky. It's black. Where the stars and the moon should be is completely black, like a tarp is covering the sky.

And the second I look back down, the clearing goes dark, too, like the second time I walked the path home, like the day that thing followed me.

Fear coats my throat as Zeke curses next to me. The only reason I can see anything at all is from the weak glow of our phone lights. Zeke's outline next to me is barely distinguishable, and the rest of the forest is completely gone. I can't even make out the outlines of the trees. It's impenetrable.

And yet all around us, I get the vague feeling that the trees are all standing on guard, watching us pant and grow more and more afraid in the dark. Unnerving still is that even without light, even amidst the unnatural darkness that's swept through the clearing, the gate seems to glow with an old, ancient energy of its own. It's not even that it's glowing- it's more so that the dark seems to leave it alone, so that it's the only thing we can see.

I think of my gran's stories about places back home in Ireland. Places that exist outside of the normal realm of rules, outside of time, places like faerie rings, like castle ruins. Places like court cairns, like abandoned cottages in the woods. Like faerie mounds and stone circles. Places that aren't bound to the rules of Earth, or to this plane of existence at all.

Places that are older than other worlds, than time itself.

The gate feels like this sort of place.

And yet, at the same time, it feels older. Older, and just as unbound.

Without thinking, I shut off my phone light and let go of Zeke's hand, taking a step forward, swallowed instantly by the dark. Immediately he calls after me, and I can hear the tremble in his voice.

"Niamh!" He calls out into the dark, whispering. *"What are you doing?"*

I ignore him and walk closer. Then closer.

Finally, I stand right in front of the gate, close enough to touch it if I wanted to.

The air around the gate seems to still, as if holding its breath.

Waiting.

"I just want to see it." I say in a voice that doesn't sound entirely like my own.

As I look directly up at it, I can see that it really is taller than they described it. It towers over me like it wants me to know that it's here, and that it's not going anywhere. That it wants its presence to be known, that it belongs.
And that we do not.

The closer I step towards the open doors, the more I can feel an energy, a sort of static vibrating all around it.
It tastes old.

Then, as if waking up from a trance, I realize that I'm close enough to walk through it if I wanted to. My toes are nearly touching the line that separates one half of the gate from the other. The side Zeke and I are on, and whatever lies on the other side.

I can see clearly through to the other side. It's the same darkness, the same dark shapes of trees and woods.

But somehow, by some innate sense, I know that whatever lies on the other side is not the South Gate woods.

I don't even think it's Summerhill.

"Niamh do not fucking touch it."

Behind me, I can hear Zeke's furious, terrified whispers.

"Where do you think they all went?" I ask him, my quiet, still not really-Niamh sounding voice carrying through the clearing.

There might not be a witch in the woods, but there is sure as shit a gate.

Zeke's voice sounds farther away now. "I don't know, Niamh, but can we get the fuck out of here? This doesn't feel right. Fuck, Niamh, *please* get away from it."

I turn around, trying to see him in the dark, and go to walk back to wherever he is when the air stills again. Really stills, this time, without a doubt.

As if someone pressed pause on the air.

So still, the slight breeze that had carried from the ocean nearby halts.

So still that my breath stops fogging in the air.

So still that it feels like the air in the clearing just... died.

Dead air.

Instantly the feeling of *wrongness* washes over me, setting all the hair on my arms and neck up. It's too quiet, too still. It isn't natural.

Something's wrong.

Unease fills my entire body, along with that same quick, choking fear. I walk quickly away from the gate, fighting the urge to run and slam right into Zeke, who's wide, fearful face I can barely see in the inky darkness. His tan is gone, his face fully awash in a sickly, pale color. His eyes tell me everything I'm feeling, too: something is wrong, and we need to go. Now.

He takes my hand, and I grip it tighter, anchoring myself to him amidst the dead, silent air. We shouldn't be here. I shouldn't have gone closer.

My thoughts echo on a loop: we shouldn't have gone looking for this.

"Niamh." Zeke whispers, his voice shaking on every syllable. He feels the gate's presence, and he's afraid. "Let's fucking go. Now."

But I don't leave yet. "Does it feel weird here to you?" I ask him quietly. I try to keep my voice low to the ground, as if to keep the gate from hearing us.

I can't explain it, but the *air* feels different. I want to know if Zeke feels it too.

Dead air.

I look through the gate. Nothing ripples, nothing looks back at me. It's the same South Gate woods on the other side. The same trees, same inky darkness, but I know it isn't.

Like a mirror, it's just reflecting back at us what we want to see. Whatever lies on the other side of that gate… it's not whatever we're seeing right now.

With that thought, the smell of animal carcass floods the clearing, and I hear Zeke's breath catch. It's happening again. Whatever the thing was that day, it's here.

The slow building, bubbling fear bursts in my chest finally, and my muscles tense, ready to run.

I back away from the gate, my heart starting to pound too hard, too fast. I can sense it. I can *feel it*. It's here.

"We need to go. Now." I manage to get out, though my windpipe feels like it shrunk. I don't want to scare him, but I also don't want to stick around a second longer just to see if that *thing* still wants to be friends.

Zeke nods and backs away from the clearing slowly, slowly, but not before he pulls his phone out.

I hear the shutter of his phone camera go off once, twice, then a third.

Three.

Three pictures of the gate.

Three pictures to prove it really happened.

I had forgotten that we're still playing the game. Three pictures of the gate, three pictures for us to win Dare or Drop.

Zeke's fingers are shaking as he shoves his phone back into his pocket, his face still absolutely petrified. He must sense it too; between the dead-animal smell, the unnatural darkness, and the way the sky just... Isn't there at all...

"Okay. Yeah. Let's get out of here."

We turn to leave, when

A branch

breaks.

Somewhere. Somewhere. It could've been behind us, maybe in front of us. It breaks loudly, a reverberating snap that echoes through the otherwise deadly still clearing. The gate doesn't move, just watching it all.

Zeke tenses next to me, and I flinch as another too-loud snap echoes through the clearing. We're surrounded by a ring of trees, I think randomly. We're fenced in.

Caged in.

And then a third snap, like someone is walking loudly through the woods and towards us, not caring if we hear.

Walking loudly, like they want us to know that they're coming.

And somewhere,

without knowing how,

I can hear something moving.

Something chitters in the direction of the gate, something that sounds like a small animal, but also not. Something that's snarling, but almost joyfully. Chittering to itself, playfully so. Above us.

No- around us.

No- behind us?

And I know what it is, and I'm rooted to the spot, held in place by that same fear.

The thing that tried to speak to me that day on the path is back.

"Fuck you guys. This isn't funny, Layla." Zeke's voice, while shaky, rings loudly out through the clearing.

I want to clap my hand over his mouth, silencing his voice. He seriously thinks it's Nat and Layla, or some other group playing Dare or Drop? He seriously can't tell that whatever is here with us is *not human?*

As if in response, a lilting, girlish peal of laughter rings through the trees.

And this time, though, it's easy to pinpoint its origin. It's coming from behind the gate.

From behind it, somehow, even though I can clearly see through it, and there's nothing there.

Another peal of laughter, light and feminine and silky amidst the dead air.

A horrible, awful feeling begins to build in my stomach. Something's going to happen. Something is going to happen, and I can't stop it.

I squeeze Zeke's hand, willing him to shut up, to not provoke whatever is about to happen. The air seems to resume normal: our breaths start to fog again, the breeze starts to move again. I can smell the sea and the pines again, but with it is still that smell of animal carcass.

Of rot, of death.

And then it speaks, that horrible, scratchy voice wrapping its way through the entire clearing with urgency. It speaks better this time. Louder. As if it's been practicing.

Friend.

It isn't a question, this time.

Tears well in my eyes as nausea, fear, and adrenaline all take hold at once, battling for dominance. I gag with my fear and panic, and Zeke whips his head around, trying to see where it came from. I just shake my head and beg him to be quiet while trying to keep the contents of my stomach inside, trying to fight the panic begging to take control. I can't run. I can't move at all.

"No." I choke out to whatever it is, wherever it is.

And then it speaks again.

Such fun.

It coughs, raspy, a mouth full of gravel, then tries again.

Such fun. We will have.

"WHAT THE FUCK IS THAT." Zeke yells.

The thing breaks off again and coughs, as if choking on something gravelly and sharp. But it keeps trying.

This time, it speaks clearly.

Miles doth need a friend to play with.

That laughter that rings through the trees this time is a little boy's.

"Miles?" Zeke chokes out, his voice warbled with emotion.

"Hello, Zeke."

The voice isn't raspy, and isn't old anymore. It's young and bright, brimming with the youth of an eight-year-old. Brimming with the childlike joy and excitement of a little boy. His laughter carries on the breeze again, that decaying, rotting breeze.

A little boy's bubbling laughter amidst the death.

It sounds happy. Like it's learning. Similar to the way the more you ride a bike, the better you get at it, up until you master it, and never forget how to ride.

Zeke has tears pooling in his eyes, threatening to spill over. "Miles?" He asks again, his voice breaking. In response, another peal of Miles's bright laughter rings through the clearing.

Jerky, stilted movement from behind the gate catches my eyes. From one end of the gate, the shadows look oddly deformed, oddly... person shaped.

No. Little boy-shaped.

With jerky, stiff movements, whatever was standing behind one corner of the gate peeks out from behind it, an odd, small, boy-shaped shadow. The only difference is that it won't show its entire body.

All Zeke and I can see is a small, pudgy little hand gripping one corner of the gate, and what looks like a small face hidden in the darkness.

"Zeke," Miles calls out. "Please, come play with me. I miss you."

But then the shape that looks like Miles starts to cough, hacking like it's trying to expel something. That same gravelly, rough cough, like there's rocks or dirt in its throat.

After it clears its throat, the shadow-shape grows clearer.

The shadow shaped like Miles has more definition, now: that's definitely a little boy hand, dirty fingernails, baby fat and all.

But the face peeking out from behind the gate is not Miles, even though I've never even seen a picture of him.

Because the face peering out at us has two pairs of glowing, white eyes, wide as discs, and pupiless.

Zeke swears louder and fouler than I've ever heard him before, and as his grip on my hand tightens, I know he's going to run the second before he bolts, pulling me with him, unmooring me from my frozen state.

As we sprint out of the dark clearing, tearing through the South Gate woods, that still air follows us. That decaying, dead smell trails us, clinging to our hair and skin.

It's still as we run, so still and immobile that the sweat on our faces does not dry as we run. There's no breeze. There's no natural air at all.

Dead air dead air dead air

The voice in the back of my head tells me to pick it up and not look back, but I do anyway.

I look over my shoulder as we sprint, my long hair whipping in my face, mingling with the sweat and the tears and the alcohol seeped into my pores. All I can see for a second is that same pitch blackness, the trees so thickly grouped together that it's hard to tell what direction we're even going in.

But then out of the corner of my eye, what I see causes me to trip, and if it wasn't for Zeke's death-grip, I would've fallen for sure.

Just out of the corner of my eye, standing like a watchdog, there is a horse.

No.

Not a horse.

An enormous, black billy goat.

A black billy goat with those same milky, pupiless white eyes, watching us flee.

CHAPTER TWENTY FOUR

The two in the forest run, and the thing that looks like a black goat watches

them go

lets them go, more like

after they escape, it trots back to the dark clearing

watching from

wide

blank

eyes

the thing wearing the skin of a goat chuckles

it loves this clearing, this little pocket of the world

places like this are its favorite

the gate was here long, long before anything else ever stood

the gate was here before the people of Summerhill were ever born

long before anyone was

long before the mere idea of a human being was even a blip of an idea

and the gate will be here long, long after they leave

and it will stay here with it

The goat licks its black lips, smiling amidst the dark
chittering to itself

it sheds the skin of the goat

returning to the mere mass of shadow it prefers

An oddly shaped, jagged shadow in the corner

with a great big set of white eyes

why would it leave when the way their fear tastes is so delicious

so vibrant and so alive was their fear tonight that it almost sustained it enough to give it enough strength

almost

their fear

their life

gives *it* life in turn

the oddly shaped shadow peeks out from around the gate

sliding up and down its iron bars like oil

it smiles to itself

it knows it spoke well tonight

it had been rusty

but it was getting stronger

oh how the copper-haired boy ran when it spoke to him through the voice of
his friend

Miles

and oh how it had tasted his fear thick on its three tongues when he and the
girl had realized that it was not Miles at all

but something else

it wasn't as hard as it had anticipated

it hadn't taken the form of another for so long and yet

it hadn't been so hard after all

it seemed it was not as rusty as it thought

the little boy's essence was still stained on the gate like residue

even nine years later

all it'd had to do was

    lick

        some

            up

it decided then as it spoke to them in the voice of Miles

that it liked the taste

       and the

          flavor

of little girls much better

it had learned that girls were far more susceptible to finding the gate the gate calls to them like a moth to a flame

coaxing them through

calling to them

and with each little girl the gate takes

the stronger the thing that currently looks like nothing more than an oddly shaped patch of shadow grows

until one day

one day

it may be free

free to stop wearing its victims like a second skin

free to take its *own* form

the one that isn't compatible with this planet

free to leave these woods

free to explore other places where things like the gate in the woods exist

free to find other places like Summerhill

other strange powerful pockets on this planet

where things that

                              eat

live

one day

it cannot wait for that day

it thinks to itself

chittering and snarling

jumping from one branch to another as nothing more than a scribble of
darkness

and oh it likes the way *her* fear tastes

the girl with the white-blonde hair is so full of it

fear of herself

fear of losing her friends

 fear of never being loved or seen for who she really is

oh she is *rotten* with fear

and it knows that she will taste

                              divine

when it finally gets her

the scribble of shadow watches through white saucer-eyes from high up in the
trees as the girl full of fear runs away

she runs with reckless abandon

holding onto the boy as if he'll anchor her

it watches her

but it leaves her alone

she has a greater purpose

and yet

it thinks to itself

angrily slithering up and down the gate like oil

it is sick of waiting for more little girls

the little girl with the twin sister those hundreds of years ago

my
how

                   delectable

she had been

she was not it's first meal

but its first in *this* world

before they arrived and built this town

it waited alone in this little pocket of the world

this little pocket of woods

for

so

long

　　　and it was ravenous

then there was that angry brash girl years ago

the girl whose life essence still lives on

clinging to the woods like smoke after a fire

and oh she had been so

                    so

                         so

                                   mouthwatering

so full of fear and magic

                    so

                                        delectable

so

                   succulent

was she

that it was still picking remains of her from its three rows of teeth

it had feasted on her alone for weeks

it was even able to leave the forest for a time

able to slink around their little town and pick through their world

to learn the way they spoke

and walked

and behaved

so that it may better

feed

but its last *good* meal was so long ago

that it almost forgets how little girls taste

and yet it thinks the girl

Niamh

that was her name

might taste even better

it needs her alive for a time longer though

so it lets her and the boy escape

and when another pair stumble upon the gate an hour later

another twin

another girl this time

and another boy with her

it

          licks

its lips

and the gate stands tall beside it

waiting

what a fun coincidence it thinks

that this girl is the twin to the very boy it just let escape

it smiles

and it tries on its new skin this time

one it hasn't used in years

where the path of jagged shadow had been now stands a hunched over

wizened old lady with dark hair and dark eyes

a mere hag in the woods

and as the twin girl and the boy with her see the gate

and their fear floods the clearing

giving it strength for the second time that night

it asks them in its new gnarled voice if they believe in the witch of the woods and oh how strong its voice is this third time around

while they scream it sheds the hag

and slips back into Abigail Summers' skin

it can never get hers right though

it can never seem to add

    her

           eyes

or her

    perfect

        baby

   teeth

    but it can never seem to get the eyes or the teeth right with any of its skins

anyways

its true eyes are a blank white that are too big and cannot blink and it has far too many rows of teeth

so when the two in the clearing see what they think is Abigail Summers

and when it asks them in her perfect child voice if they should like to come

play

they scream and try to run

The thing wearing Abigail Summers just smiles Abigail's almost perfect child

smile

and it takes them instead

and

it doth

eat

December

CHAPTER TWENTY FIVE

TYLER

From the journal of Tyler Iris Lane

Wednesday, December 12th

A Story;

Once upon a time, two girls fell in love against all odds.

Over the course of just a few months, two girls went from complete and innate enemies to being unable to live without the other.

The first girl was secretive, brash, and impulsive. She was jaded, rude, and easily provoked. Raised in a town that shunned her for something she was born with, she learned to guard her heart with anger and a sharp tongue.

Her name was Tyler.

She hoarded secrets like a dragon with jewels, and was just as fiery. She told lies without trying, letting them roll off her tongue with a smile. She was quick to make blunt, cutting comments, and she rarely apologized.

She was a girl filled with power, power she knew she possessed. It ran in her family, and she reveled in it.

She could see things others could not.

She could make objects move without lifting a finger.

She could bend and shape her voice at will.

She could hear the thoughts of others without them knowing.

She could also reach into that in-between place, the place that was neither wake nor sleep, night nor day, living nor dying, and pull out visions of things to come.

They all called her a witch, but she was so much more than that. She was still a girl, with feelings she held as tight to her chest as she did her secrets. She still felt, and deeply so.

She was so much more than her gifts. She was so much more than just a witch. She was still a girl, who underneath it all, wanted to be loved, despite all that made her different.

The girl who unwound her was an enemy, at first.

A girl with a dancer's body, lean and lithe, made of almonds and warmth. A girl with eyes made of honey and amber, with skin that tasted of sun-warmed strawberries.

Her name was Morgan.

And Morgan's gentle, honey-jar eyes saw right through the brash, angry girl, saw her right down to her core. They saw her with curiosity and warmth, with kindness. They saw underneath the anger and the bitterness, beyond the rage and the sharp tongue.

The girl with the honey-jar eyes saw beyond the gifts: she saw the girl underneath, who wasn't nearly as fiery and untouchable as everyone claimed.

She didn't see Tyler, the witch.

She saw Tyler, the girl,

the girl who just so happened to be born of magic.

And magical was the perfect word to describe what Tyler was feeling the more time she spent with Morgan, because despite everything she'd ever known, she was falling in love with her.

They'd grown up in the same town their whole lives, fed the same lies about the other all their years:

Morgan's family was adamant.

Tyler Lane is a witch.

She tried to put a nasty spell on you.

Stay far away from her, Morgan.

Tyler's grandmother was just as harsh and biting.

The Van Devon's have it out for us.

People like them always have.

Best to stay far away from them.

And so the two grew up with an innate, hard-bred feeling their entire lives, sure the other was the enemy based on what everyone told them. It's what their families and friends told them, after all. It's what everyone told them.

It never occurred to them to think for themselves for once.

Until one day, nearly nine months after Eleni Lane had mistakenly delivered her a love jar, Morgan found herself having to seek Tyler out.

She'd never had the desire to see her before. Not once. She was a witch, after all. She was odd and crude and harsh, and cared for no one but herself.

So she'd been told.

And yet the second Morgan found herself at Tyler's window that night, something changed.

Morgan had never met somebody quite like Tyler, and not because she was a witch: no, that wasn't it.

She had never met somebody so deeply, truly genuine, somebody so unapologetically themselves.

Tyler wasn't angry and rude at all, to Morgan.

She was thoughtful.

She was caring.

She was, of all things, gentle.

She was gentle with Morgan,

She was sweet, with Morgan.

And so utterly, truly herself.

Witty, sarcastic, able to make her laugh without really trying. She was clever. She was a good listener.

And the way that Morgan looked at Tyler when she spoke.....

That look of reverence, of awe, of... want

was Tyler's undoing.

If Tyler was roses with no thorns,

the midnight sky, swollen with stars,

rose petals and silk,

dandelion wishes and shooting stars,

lucky pennies and gold coins,

the light the moon casts over the sea at night,

and the deepest, darkest part of the ocean,

then Morgan was sunflower petals and ardor,

cinnamon and wild sage,

honey and candied almonds on sun-warmed skin,

sweet, love-soaked eyes,

and the sun's rays on the hottest June day.

If Tyler was crafted from intensity and passion, the very look that shone in her eyes every time she looked at Morgan, then Morgan was crafted from devotion and ardor, and lovingly made,

just for Tyler.

Despite the odds against them, Morgan Van Devon and Tyler Lane fell deeply, truly in love.

And whether it was the result of a misplaced spell or some other force entirely, something brought them together despite all that was against them.

A town that hated witches, magic, and anything they were unable to explain away with logic,

an overbearing mother, monitoring her only daughter's every breath,

and a lineage of women born with magic, doomed to fall once they fell in love.

Despite it all, Tyler and Morgan fell deeply, completely in love.

One might even call it magic.

Chapter Twenty Six

Niamh

I wake up with a crash of anxiety- no, a semi-truck of it- plowing into my

chest. I also have no idea where I am.

I'm also not wearing clothes.

With a jolt, I sit up and cover my chest, trying to get a grip on my surroundings. My

head pounds in sync with my rapid heartbeat, and for a second, the leaden weight in

my chest spreads and deepens, cutting off my air supply. Okay. Okay. Anxiety. Shit.

Okay. You got this, Niamh. You're okay.

I press my knuckles to my bare sternum and breathe deep. After a few deep, six

count breaths, I start to soak in sweet, fresh sea air.

Wait. Sea air?

Then I see where I am: in the bed of a pickup truck, surrounded by pines and elms, with the ocean just to my left. It's early, probably not even five.

I glance down at my watch, the only thing I'm wearing at all. Six thirty in the morning. Okay, so I'm in Summerhill. I'm still on the cape. Okay. That's a good start.

But why am I outside at six thirty in the morning, and where the fuck are my *clothes?*

I sit up fully, my entire body- my very exposed, naked body- cold and stiff as hell in the bed of a faded, beat to hell blue Ford.

Zeke and Marlo's truck.

The bed of it is strewn with a thick, warm comforter and a few pillows, their longboards pushed to the side. My phone lies underneath Zeke's blue board, my house key perched precariously on top of it.

But what really sticks out to me is Zeke's sleeping, sprawled-out body next to me, also lacking clothes.

Instead of feeling excited about this, my heart drops like a stone into my stomach, my mouth going dry.

I don't…. I can't remember a thing. I can't remember getting here, I can't remember ever taking my clothes off…

A different kind of fear floods my body now.

Fear of the person next to me.

I choke on the thoughts, and combined with my hangover starting to show its teeth, I feel like I'm going to throw up.

Which I do, wrapping myself in the comforter and jumping out of the truck, heaving, which is what prompts Zeke to sit up groggily.

"Niamh?" He says confusedly, running a hand through his mess of curls. His golden eyes are dull and crusted with sleep. When he sees me and what I'm wearing, his eyes widen and graze over me, but he tears them away quickly. Maybe out of respect, maybe just out of concern, I don't know. At the moment, I'm not sure I trust him. My little daydream about us last night is a fading memory, the space in my mind where desire for him existed just hours before is currently replaced with roaring, nauseating fear. All I know right now is that I woke up to a boy I've known for less than three months in the back of a car, both of us completely naked, and I have zero recollection of getting there.

Which also means that I was unable to give an *ounce* of consent. I don't remember being that drunk, but clearly I must have been.

The thought has me heaving again, sheerly from fear.
After a minute, the nausea finally dulls, but every cell in my body is on alert. I wipe the back of my mouth with my hand then pull the blanket around me tighter, still

freezing in the early morning air. We're parked exactly where we arrived at the Bohdie's house last night, at the base of their lengthy, paved driveway that leads to their beautiful, enormous house. Cars still line the driveway from top to bottom.

Flashing lights from the top of the driveway catch my eye, seeming to come from the house, but I ignore them for the time being. I want answers, and now.

"Zeke." I say, my voice curt. I do my best to sound stern, but it's hard with nothing more than a comforter covering me. Zeke finds a pair of boardshorts somewhere buried under their boards and shimmies them on, yawning. "Do you want to explain to me why I just woke up here? And like *this?*"

I don't mean to be a dick to him. I don't mean to speak to him sharply, I really don't. But I can't remember a single thing, and now I don't really trust him. It hits me, then, the second semi-truck revelation of the morning: I *don't* know Zeke. Not at all.

And he doesn't know me, either. He doesn't know who I am inside, doesn't know what makes me tick, or makes me *me.*

But Tyler does, the little voice in my head whispers.

Zeke can never truly know me.

Only one person does, and that one person is the only one who ever will.

Zeke's face loses its sleepy, hungover expression and sharpens immediately, his eyes flashing in surprise. When he speaks, his tone is just as sharp as mine, and heavily defensive.

"Jesus, do *you* want to explain it to me? I don't remember how we got here, either, Niamh."

The bite to his voice hurts me more than I expected. On top of my pounding head and aching chest, his defensiveness is almost too much. I can't do this right now. It's too much, I'm exhausted and so, so very hungover, and I don't have any patience. My bar for being tolerant and kind is gone.

"First off, don't fucking snap at me. I think I'm allowed to be a little upset when I just woke up in the back of some guy's car with no recollection of getting there and neither of us have fucking *clothes on.*"

Zeke laughs, but it's humorless. "So I'm just 'some guy' now? Wow. Cool. And seriously, Niamh, that's your first thought? That's the kind of guy you think I am? Nice. I thought… whatever, dude. You know, if you would've looked around, you'd probably have a fucking answer for yourself."

He gestures to the side of the truck, and I crane my neck around to see what he's pointing at. There, written on the driver's side window with what looks like surf wax is the giant, bolded words: **U LOST!**

"When you lose Dare or Drop, you lose your clothes, too. We probably got back hammered as fuck, and Kai took our clothes. It's not that big of a deal, dude."

"That's really convenient, Zeke."

I hate that I'm still dragging this on, despite the fact that he might be right. But I just don't trust him.

Zeke scoffs and looks away from me, a disgusted look on his face. I scoff right back at him, running a hand through my hair incredulously. He's seriously going to turn this on *me?* What the fuck?

Dull, hazy anger begins to rise, but another clear, ringing thought darts through my head, cutting clear through it.

The gate.

"We saw the gate." I say out loud without meaning to.

My fear and anxiety towards him vanish for the moment, instead swallowed by the growing certainty: we saw it. We saw it, we fucking saw it. We saw the gate in the woods.

And as the memories flood back in, I remember that something saw us, too.

Miles. Or- whatever had looked like Miles.

Even as I think his name, I know without a shred of doubt that whatever we saw last night was most definitely not Zeke's missing friend. His eyes....

Those enormous, pupiless white eyes.

Whatever that was, it saw us. It *talked* to us.

Zeke looks back at me, still disgusted, but it's fading quickly as recognition grows in his sleepy eyes. He looks wildly around the bed of the truck, searching for something. When he finally finds his windbreaker from yesterday, he fumbles around in the pockets for a second before pulling out his phone.

It's cracked in three different places, but the screen is still functioning. He looks up at the Bohdie's house for a second, where faint noise is coming from now, and the flashing lights are continuing to grow, but tears his gaze away and trains it back on me.

"They think we lost the game," He says tonelessly, "but I doubt anyone else got these."

He unlocks his phone, and I sit precariously on the edge of the tail bed next to him as he opens his photo library, pulling up the three shots he'd grabbed last night right before we'd run. Our proof that the gate is real. Fuck winning Dare or Drop with these: we could use these to warn people.

But when he opens his camera roll, clicking on the photos, we both gasp in disbelief.

The photos are there- all three of them. But there's no gate.

Just an empty ring of trees in a dark clearing.

Where the gate had been is merely an empty spot.

There's nothing there.

Zeke laughs, but it's the kind of laugh that sounds more like he's trying not to burst into hysterical tears. "No. No fucking way. We saw it. We fucking saw it. Right? Right, Niamh? Right? Miles was there. Miles was-"

His voice trails off, and I shove aside whatever anger I feel at him right now and lean my head on his shoulder.

Him, Marlo, and Tyler are all I have. I can't lose anyone else.

Despite the alcohol I'm sure is seeping from my pores, Zeke still manages to smell like sage. Clean, wild sage and sea salt. His horrible bedhead is endearing, his curls springing up in corkscrews and tufts all over. Despite it all, the sight of him hunched over trying not to fall apart in clear, obvious pain kills me.

I still want an answer for why I woke up naked in his truck. If it really was Kai and the others, I'll accept it and apologize. But I still don't trust him the same way. But an answer can wait. There's more important things to deal with right now.

"We saw it. It was real." I whisper into his shoulder, trying to reassure him.

We sit in silence for a few minutes after seeing the pictures, pondering what the actual fuck happened last night.

We saw the gate. That much was certain. It's real.

And something else was there with us. Something that tried its damn hardest to look like Miles. That was real, too.

The memory of that lilting, feminine laughter coming from the gate causes every hair on my arms to rise beneath the comforter. The fact that it's early in the morning does nothing to comfort me, or take away the fear that still lingers in me.

Zeke took the pictures, then we ran.

I remember seeing a goat as we ran away. A big, black goat.

With another roil of nausea, I remember how the goat's eyes had looked: too big, too white. Eyes that don't belong to goats.

But after that, everything goes fuzzy. I can't remember how we got out of the South Gate woods, or how we ended up all the way back in the East Gate, all the way in Zeke's truck, parked back at Colin and Kai's house.

Which, speaking of. "Do you see that too?" I ask him, lifting my head from his bare shoulder.

Because at the top of the Bohdie's driveway, the lights are still flashing. And then, tearing past us well over the speed limit, a Summerhill police cruiser speeds up the driveway, red and blue lights flashing.

Police.

There's police at Colin and Kai's house.

Zeke springs up, his face alarmed. "The cops are here." He says anxiously.

"And? They're probably busting the party, right? Aren't their parents out of town?"

Zeke shakes his head and starts for the driveway, tying his boardshorts in a tight knot. I almost want to laugh at the sight of him: disheveled, beheaded, barefoot, with nothing but a pair of crusty boardshorts he found in his dad's truck. But the situation kills the laughter before it can ever reach my throat.

"The Summerhill PD do jack shit. Something happened."

And he starts to jog up the driveway, leaving me behind.

CHAPTER TWENTY SEVEN

TYLER

From the journal of Tyler Iris Lane

Sunday, December 16th

Another poem

(inspired by the one we had to write for class that first time she came over.)

Sun-drenched skin and honey lips

Amber eyes and restless hips

All of her, all of this

Feels exactly and perfectly

Like bliss.

Okay. I can't believe I'm writing this right now. But I think I love her. And I think she loves me, too. It's in the way she looks at me, like I hung the fucking moon, and all the stars. She sees the parts of me that nobody else does. She hears the things I don't say.

She looks at me like she loves me.

We've been inseparable since the first day she came over. That was over two months ago. And the way she looks at me now...

I don't know if I can live without it.

I taught her some basic magic tonight because she was curious and had been asking, just a little bit about candle magic and herb usage. Real basic stuff. She took to it easily, naturally. We wrote our wishes on bay leaves, soaking them in rose oil and patchouli, catnip and cinnamon. Under the glow of a red candle, a pink candle, and a yellow at her behest, we spoke our wishes to the stars, blowing the mixture of bay leaves and herbs out my window onto the breeze.

Afterwards, this.... God, it was nothing like I've ever felt before. It didn't even feel like magic- this <u>glow</u> started in my chest, something deep and profound. It felt... bigger than my magic, somehow. Stronger, if that's even possible. It felt more tangible, like a weight, but not a bad one.

It felt like a cord, pulling me to her.

And when she kissed me after that... It felt like sealing a promise. It was in the <u>way</u> she kissed me- it made my heart feel like it was going to explode out of my chest. So full of need, of desire, and this strong, undeniable want. She kissed me like that, and...

Okay, fine. I reached into her mind for the first time. I couldn't help myself. I had to know what she was thinking. It wasn't a lot. I reached in for maybe ten seconds.

But Jesus christ.
When I did read her thoughts, plucking them out with two slim, nimble fingers, she was thinking the same thing over and over.

The same three words, on a loop.

"I need her."

My magic might have popped out then, my chest burning bright. My eyes might have started to glow, turning more purple than blue. I might have accidentally pulled fresh rose petals from strands of her hair, kissed her with cinnamon on my tongue, all of which had just made her laugh. I asked her what she was thinking, acting like I didn't know, and she'd just kissed me again, her cinnamon-flecked tongue meeting my own, melting me. Claiming me,

Promising me, with three new words, this time.

"I'm yours, Tyler."

CHAPTER TWENTY EIGHT

NIAMH

Marlo and Kai never came home after the party.

While we all thought they'd been hooking up upstairs while the rest of us left to go play Dare or Drop, it turns out that they'd left, too.

Three days ago, the small, fully unprepared force that made up the Summerhill Police Department found Kai Bohdie's enormous, lifted Ford f350 deep in the South Gate woods.

It was too far deep to have just driven inside, offroading.

It was so far into the uncharted, unmapped parts of the South Gate woods, so deep that the trees barely had room to breathe between each other.

So deep that the hundreds upon hundreds of pines clustered so closely together would have made it impossible for a giant Ford f350 to have driven inside.

Marlo's phone was still lying in the passenger seat.

Kai's keys were still inside the ignition.

And yet Marlo Torah and Kai Bohdie were nowhere to be found.

I push my disgusting, rank hair out of my face, bits of pine needles and tree sap clinging to my towheaded strands. I still haven't showered, not since the party. After picking me up and bringing me home from the police station- the second time in my life my parents have had to do that- I curled into a ball on my bedroom floor and stayed that way.
Fetal position day and night, no food, barely getting up for a sip of water. Trying to come to terms with everything that's happened in the last seventy two hours.

Fact: Zeke and I saw the gate.

Fact: We weren't alone.

Fact: We both woke up unable to remember anything, but somehow escaped the gate.

And now Marlo is gone.

And while I've been laying curled in a ball on my floor doing absolutely nothing about it for three days, something in the back of mind has been telling me to find Tyler. At the very least to warn her, since she's always hanging out in the South Gate. She could be in danger. Whatever that... thing is... Fuck.

I can't handle Tyler being in danger, too. Even though Tyler, of all people, could probably hold her own.

I should still warn her.

But now, three days later I find myself sitting at the breakfast table, the literal last place I want to be. My mom and dad sit side by side, both looking at me with poorly-veiled concern on their faces.

I'm so goddamn sick of that look being directed at me.

"Niamhy." My dad starts. He puts the draft of his latest book down on the table, and I focus on all the cheerful, crisp highlightings and annotations sticking out of the pages instead of his face. I can't take the sympathy coming from those bright green eyes right now. I can't take the look I know he's going to give me, because it's the same one he gives me every time something awful happens. When my grandparents on my mom's side died. When Cian had to be hospitalized his sophomore year of high school. When he told me we were leaving Saxon Beach and moving to Summerhill.

"This is very, very serious. I know the Torah's well. Jimbo and Heather are good people, and I know you've been hanging out with their kids, too. You're friends with Marlo, right?"

His kind, prompting voice puts tears in my eyes, and I brush them away angrily, my throat clogged instantly. I hate that his voice alone reduced me to tears so quickly.

"Yeah," I say through my tight throat. "Her and Zeke and Tyler are literally my only friends, dad."

My mom clears her throat, and I brace myself for whatever's about to come out of her mouth right now.

"So what happened, Niamh? You were there. You were with her."

Her tone is curt, barely hiding her impatience. This is nothing new, she always talks to me like this, and yet it doesn't make it hurt any less. If anything, her tone right now just makes me feel even shittier for talking to Zeke how I did that morning, accusing him of assaulting me after we both woke up naked. That biting, harsh tone is the exact one I used on him, not even giving him a chance to explain himself. I've been flirting with him for close to three months, spending all this time with him, and then the second something went wrong, I bit his head off. And... It's entirely my fault.

All these months I've let him think I was this cute, witty surfer girl from Saxon Beach who doesn't have a care in the world. I've been letting him see the old Niamh, never letting him see the angry, reckless side of me. The *real* me.

I've never once let him see who I really am. I've been lying to him all this time, letting him like the idea of me: the old me.

God, I am such a piece of shit.

Anger rears up bright and quick, along with racking, horrible guilt. I look up at my mom with every bit of contempt I can fit behind my crusted, sleep-deprived eyes.

"Exactly what I told the police that morning, Mom. Zeke and I can't remember how we got home. Everyone left the house to play that game, but after that I can't remember anything else."

My mom tuts under her breath, zero sympathy in her eyes. "Well. Maybe you shouldn't have had so much to drink."

Before I can open my mouth to protest how fucked up and insensitive of a comment that was, considering Marlo is *fucking missing,* my dad puts his hand on her thigh.

"Shawnie." He says, his gentle warning to her. His tone conveys everything he doesn't say: your daughter's friend is missing. We moved her all the way across the country. She's had to completely remodel her entire life at seventeen. Give her a break.

I glare daggers at my mom, but try to reign it in. "We were all drinking. That had nothing to do with it."

"So what was it, then, Niamh?"

I swallow hard. My mouth tastes like bile and death, and I want nothing more than to go to sleep and not think about any of this. Talking to the Summerhill PD three days ago hungover as shit was enough to make me never want to drink again, nearly chuking in their lobby after answering hours worth of questions enough to make me contemplate every hard kombucha I'd downed.

Three days ago, I told the police, the Torah's, and everyone else who asked that my guess was as good as everyone else's: that she and Kai left to play Dare or Drop like the rest of us, and got lost. The police from the mainland that came by yesterday didn't have any other questions for me, either. Just where, and why. They seemed to accept my answer, despite the fact that Kai's truck was just… in the middle of the fucking woods, just like Miles' bike had been all those years ago.

I told the police exactly what they wanted to hear, and it was a lie.

Despite what I told everyone, I think I do know what happened to Marlo and Kai.

It was never the gate.

I mean, maybe. The gate in the woods definitely has something to do with it, sure. The fact that the urban legend of a gate just appearing at random in the woods definitely has something to do with it. But I think we've been wrong all along.

Finding the gate with Zeke three nights ago just confirmed what I've been thinking ever since the first time I walked on the path.

It's never been the gate. The gate isn't what's taking people.

It's whatever's in the woods *with* the gate.

Whatever that *thing* is..... *That's* what's causing people to disappear. Because every single time it's spoken to me in the woods, it's sounded lonely, like it's been that way for a long, long time. Like it's been.... Asleep, or hibernating or something.

And in my gran's stories, things like that usually wake up hungry.

A favorite of my gran's was a story she called The Skinny Man. The tale was definitely told to keep my dad from getting out of bed, but now I'm not so sure.

According to my Gran, after the wee hours of midnight, the veil thinned juuuuuust enough for spindly, skinny things to slip through the cracks. Things like The Skinny Man.

He climbed down chimneys and landed in a heap, all long, gangly limbs. He had long, spindly arms, and long, spindly legs that he used to crawl on walls and ceilings like a spider, or a snake. He had long, sharp nails, and long, needle-sharp teeth with no eyes. The Skinny Man was a type of demon, or entity, I guess, created to keep wayward children in bed after they were supposed to be asleep. Because if The Skinny Man caught you out of bed after you'd already been tucked in, he ate you. Or-worse-he dragged you by your limbs back to whatever hole he'd crawled from.

The Irish are fucking weird. I've always thought my gran was kinda mean for telling my dad stuff like that when he was a kid, but he turned out okay, I guess. He writes some weird shit, but he's mentally sane.

I look up at my parents, finally, but mostly my dad. If anyone's going to take me seriously about this, it would be him. My sweet, gentle dad, whose fingers are always stained with ink and pen. My dad, who writes tales about orcs and elves and faerie courts. My dad who buys me journals and books, who's never once raised his voice at me. My dad, who's told me stories of Summerhill since I was a baby.

"Dad?" I say thickly. It's now or never. "Do you remember that story you used to always tell Cian, Aine and I about Summerhill?"

His eyes scrunch in confusion, and he rubs the back of his freckled neck. His shiny red hair gleams in the early light of the morning. It's sunny today, for once. Bright, eager sunshine illuminates our kitchen, so very much the opposite of how the entire town is feeling. It should be pouring today. It should be fucking storming, it should be miserable.

"Ahhh… which one, Niamhy?"

I look at him, praying that he'll listen. "The one about the gate."

My dad, to his credit, sits up straighter. He looks at me as if truly seeing me: yeah, I look like microwaved death. I look like I need a shower, a decent hairbrush, and maybe some water. But at a closer glance, I'm also covered in forest dirt, and I smell like pine and….

Rot. I smell like death. As if whatever had been in the South Gate that night hadn't been willing to let me go, so it latched its death smell onto me.

Latched onto me maybe, just maybe, as a warning.

Just like maybe, just maybe, it had taken Marlo and Kai since it couldn't get me and Zeke.

"Yes, I remember that one." He says. He gets up and pours himself a cup of coffee, then sits back down across from me at the table, giving me his full, undivided attention. The easy, bubbly sunlight shining on him and his gentle, calm face make

my throat feel a little less tight. He hasn't told me I'm crazy yet. He hasn't gotten mad

at me. Maybe he'll believe me.

Hopefully.

Hopefully.

"Zeke and I…. we saw it, Dad. We went looking for it, and we found the gate."

And then I'm breaking down, sobbing like I haven't done since I was a toddler.

Sobbing with the weight of all of it: the day Makani, Booker, and Indie left me at our

high school, right after I'd burned Mak. Leaving Saxon Beach. The thing in the

woods that's seeming to latch onto me over and over and over. Arguing with Zeke.

Losing Marlo.

I cry so hard that I begin to swallow more snot than saliva, until my face is so puffed

and red that it stings. In between my gulping, breaking-down tears, I tell my dad

everything.

Everything, except for my gift. Everything, except for that.

I tell my parents about the thing in the woods, about seeing the gate. I tell them

about meeting Tyler, and about becoming close with the Torah twins. I tell them

about how not having Makani, Booker, and Indie started to hurt way less once I met

Tyler, Zeke and Marlo. I tell them about how fucking terrified I am of the woods,

because no matter where I seem to go, I end up in the South Gate, and whatever else is in there has seen me, and wants to be my friend. I tell them about how Zeke and I took pictures of it to prove it, and they didn't show up.

My dad looks at me after I finish, and for a minute, the only sound in the kitchen is my gasping, ugly sobs. He waits for me to finish, and then takes a deep, steady exhale.

But it's my mom who speaks up first with the most disgusted look on her face that I've ever seen her make.

"Niamh, I've tried to give you a pass. I've excused your behavior time and time and time again. Every single time back home, every *single* time. You have no regard for consequences. Aine and Cian were *never* like this. You just can't accept the consequences of your actions, can you? You can never take accountability, and now you're going to guilt trip your dad who loves you more than anything with his *own* stories? You're just going to put the blame on anyone but yourself? Really? Instead of just admitting that you're all underage kids who got trashed and now someone's missing because of it, you're going to blame it on a ghost story? I can't believe this."

She looks at my dad and shakes her head, that disgusted look still etched onto her face. "Side with her all you want, Aidan. I'm going out for breakfast."

Then she turns to me one last time. "You're almost eighteen years old, Niamh. Start acting like it."

And with that, she grabs her keys and thick raincoat then leaves the kitchen. The front door slams loudly, and I flinch.

My tears flow freely now, and all I feel now is sorrow and guilt. Sorrow for myself, for Marlo, for Zeke. Guilt for everything I've done, when all I've wanted was to be a good friend, and yet somehow I keep fucking that up.

I feel sorry for myself, and it consumes me.

My dad sighs after she leaves, then passes his cup of coffee to me across the table. I don't touch it, instead letting the steam cloud my vision. Notes of blueberry and nutmeg waft from the cup.

"Niamh, what have I always told you about your mom?"

I ponder this, snorting back tears and snot. "That she isn't from somewhere like you and gran and granda. She doesn't think like us."

"Right. I love your mother more than life itself, but the fact is, she doesn't see things how we do, and that's okay. She's not from Ireland, and she's not from Summerhill. She isn't from places where weird things can happen. Do you understand what I'm trying to say?"

"I think so?"

"Where I grew up, Niamh, it wasn't a question of whether or not unnatural things happened. Irish people are full of weird stories and quirks. Your grandparents used to scare the shit out of me with theirs. I'll never forget the time I walked into a faerie ring near these old church ruins by our house. Your granda nearly gave himself a heart attack sprinting to grab me."

I laugh a little, picturing the event clearly. Sounds right.

"Your mom isn't like that, though. It's not how she was brought up, and that's okay. She's very rooted in reality, Niamhy."

"You literally make a living writing fantasy books."

"You know the phrase opposites attract?"

I snort. "Sure."

My dad rests his chin in his hands, smiling at me. "My point, Niamh, is that I believe you."

My body jolts to attention. What? I must have said it aloud, because he smiles softly at me.

"I believe you. Stories don't just pop up out of nowhere. Look at the Jersey Devil in New Jersey. Look at the Night Marchers in Hawai'i, the Bunnyman in Virginia. Look at Ireland: how many faerie stories did gran tell you as a kid about changelings? Everywhere has a story, Niamh. It would be shocking to me if Summerhill did not. Whatever's in those woods... I don't know, my love. Kids went missing in there even when I was young. There are places in the world where things happen that we can't explain away. The South Gate woods have always struck me as that sort of place."

I swallow my fear, soaking in his words. "It was fucking scary, dad. It felt... old. Like it didn't know how to talk right."

"And I believe you. But if the Torah's kid is anything like her parents, she'll be okay. I need you to promise me something, though."

I'm already halfway out of my seat as he says this, ready to take the world's fastest shower and go find Tyler. My dad's belief in me finally shook me out of my depression hibernation, and I know exactly what to do.

Find Tyler.

If anyone can find her, it's Tyler.

Tyler and *I.*

I have a gift, too, and thanks to her, I know how to use it now. And maybe… maybe if I combine my magic with Tyler's, we can find Marlo, somehow. There's got to be some sort of seeking spell, or finding spell. A spell for lost things.

The thoughts bang and collide through my head rapidfire, and I nearly ignore my dad until he says my name sharper than he's ever said it before.
I stop, surprised, before I tear out of the kitchen. "Yeah?"

"Niamh, I need you to promise me right now that you won't go looking in those woods for Marlo."

This causes me to fully stop in my tracks.

"Dad." I say thickly. "What? She's my *friend.*"

But he just stands up and grabs the manuscript of his book off the table, looking from it to me with a look in his eyes I've never seen before.

"I'm going to put my foot down this one time, oh willful, feisty daughter of mine. I believe you, which is exactly why I'm going to say this. Listen to me very carefully right now, Niamh. Do not go into the South Gate woods again looking for Marlo Torah. Don't go into the South Gate woods, period. Because I believe you, and that means that this thing has already seen you twice now. Do not give it the chance to get close to you a third time."

I swallow hard, thinking all the way upstairs, all the way into the shower.

And as I pull pine and fir needles out of my hair, scrub my body twice, wash my hair twice, I think about how much I've changed in a little over two months. Because the old Niamh would've done anything, *anything* for her friends. Anything in the world, and that much hasn't changed.

I'm going to find Marlo, just like I would go find Makani, or Booker, or Indie, or Zeke.

Or Tyler.

But the old Niamh wasn't a liar. That trait is new.

Because as I step out of the shower and pull a brush through my hair, seeing my wide, bright green eyes in the mirror and the sheer determination and grit in them, I know that I just fully and completely lied to my dad.

I am going back to the South Gate woods, because this thing will *not* take Marlo. I won't let it.

And I might be the only one that can help her.

My anger flares in my chest, burning bright red, brighter than the candles Tyler's been having me light while we practice.

I'm sorry, dad.

But I'm going back into the South Gate, despite how utterly fucking terrified I am. But I won't be alone.

I'll be with Tyler.

CHAPTER TWENTY NINE

NIAMH

For the first time ever, Tyler is waiting for me.

I haven't even stepped a foot into the woods yet, let alone stepped off my front porch. As I close the front door quietly, hoping that my dad won't hear it and ask me where the hell I think I'm going, I hear something. Like paper rustling, or maybe the wind blowing through the trees. Faint rustling.

Hopping off the last three steps of our porch, I stand in the driveway, looking around for the noise. There's nothing in the treeline to my left or right, but in the East Gate behind me...

I walk around to the back of our house, keeping low beneath our giant windows. Once I take a closer look, I can see her.

It's Tyler, lying on her stomach in the treeline.

She's got her face buried in her journal, writing furiously as I approach her. I wonder how the hell she knew where I lived. I've asked her time and time again if she wanted to hang out at my house instead of the woods, but she always says magic works better in nature.

When I'm close enough to catch wind of her rose petals and cinnamon scent, she looks up at me. Those deep, all-seeing blue eyes darken when she looks up at me, her freckled face smiling gently.

"Hey, Niamh." She says simply in that melodic voice, then goes back down to her journal. I sit next to her cross-legged, adjusting my oversize black hoodie over my fingers, then pull the hood over my wet hair further. Combined with my black dickies and Vans, I feel like a ninja today. Maybe I picked this outfit out subconsciously. Like if I *look* like a ninja, speedy and shadowed, maybe whatever's in the woods won't see me.

Idiotic.

"Hey." I say to her, not ready to waste even another second with small talk. Marlo's already been gone for three days. "Something happened, and I need your help. Please."

Tyler doesn't look up, and I force myself to give her a second, recalling her mysterious, lilting way of conversation. She usually talks after she's had a minute, even if her answers are vague and guarded. So instead of pushing her, I stare at her while she writes: the way her dark, shiny hair spills over both of her bony shoulders, pooling down to the small of her back. The way her bare feet are up, kicking back and forth. The way her deep, sapphire blue tank top hugs her thin torso, the straps disappearing under her sheet of hair. She's in jeans today, baggy blue jeans that look like they might fall off of her.

"Your friend's missing." She says while still writing, shaking me from my trance, my face going red. Bits of pine needles stick to the strands of her hair that pool on the ground, and I force myself not to pick them out.

I don't even question how she knows about Marlo. I've never seen Tyler at school, and she doesn't hangout with the surfy crowd. Maybe she just heard from her parents or something.

"Yeah. My friend Marlo. She-"

And then my phone buzzes in my pocket.
Once. Twice, then it starts to ring when I don't answer the texts. Tyler doesn't look up, still scribbling in her journal with one hand. With the other, and without looking, she reaches over and pulls something from under my shoe, wedged under my foot and the ground. She holds it between two fingers, studying it, then she tapes it onto the page she was writing on.

A single, fresh rose petal.

"Are you going to get that?" She says simply as my phone keeps ringing.

I furrow my eyebrows, then pull it out of my pocket. *Incoming Call from Zeke Torah #1 Surf God and Niamh's Favorite Twin.*

I stand abruptly. I haven't heard from Zeke since the morning after the party. He hasn't texted, he hasn't called, and between our argument and Marlo being missing, I've tried to give him space.
So this I'm taking as a good sign. Maybe he has news, or maybe he can help us look for Marlo.

The thought hits my head right after I pick up. I've never introduced him and Tyler. And now that I think about it... I'm not really sure I want to.

I excuse myself and stand up, walking a few paces away into the treeline. The sun hides behind the clouds, and as I stand in the shadow of two pine trees, Tyler just a few feet away, an odd, tightening sense of discomfort begins to grow in my chest.

Something feels off.

He doesn't say anything for a second, so I try to fill the silence. "Hey, Zeke. I'm glad you called. I-"

But then he cuts me off. "We're going to start a search party for Marlo and Kai in an hour. I can pick you up in twenty minutes."

I adjust my grip on the phone, looking at Tyler back in the trees. She's not writing anymore: she's sitting up straight now, staring at me with an unnerving, too-wide grin. Is she listening?

"I... I can't, Zeke. I'm with a friend right now."

As soon as the words come out, I cringe at how bad they sound. Fucking hell, I didn't mean that how it came out. I'm literally about to go look for Marlo, just like he is... but with someone who might know where and *how* to look. Someone who might know where she actually is.

Zeke's silent over the phone. So silent I wonder if he hung up.

"Hello?" I whisper.

"No, it's cool, Niamh. Go hangout with your friend while my *fucking sister,* your *friend* is missing." His words are hateful and sharp, and he sounds just like my mom.

My heart breaks at his tone of voice, snapping the tether of all flirtatious feelings towards Zeke once and for all.

I thought I knew him. I thought he was gentle, kind, and cheerful. This angry, hateful boy who's so quick to be defensive is not who I thought Zeke was at all. This boy who talks to me just like my mom does… that's not who I want anymore.

Maybe I never did at all.

But before I can say anything else or try to defend myself, his voice raises, his anger continuing.

"You know what, who the fuck are you even with right now, Niamh? Who's more important than your *missing friend?*"

His second hateful sentence gets my own anger boiling, and I can feel my chest start to heat up. I've always hated being yelled at. It always makes me act defensively with meaning to and do things I wouldn't normally.

But now, when I get angry, I can burn things without meaning to. So when I respond to him, I'm just as angry, but my voice stays calm, my breathing even. I stay in control.

"I'm with my friend Tyler, Zeke, who I actually was going to introduce you to today. We're about to go look for M-"

"Oh. Okay. *Tyler.* Tyler, who I've never once heard of. It's cool. Go hangout with *Tyler,* Niamh."

"I've been friends with her just as long as you!" I burst out in disbelief. Zeke doesn't reply to this. After a second, I hear a dial tone.

Shocked and scoffing in disbelief, I stalk back to where Tyler's laying down in the grass again, anger and frustration contorting my features clearly. I don't even try to hide it. Makani, Booker, and Indie aren't ever going to speak to me again. Marlo is missing. Zeke is being an asshole.

All I have is Tyler, now.

"He's just jealous, you know." She says, still buried in her journal, kicking her feet back and forth.

I wipe away the few angry tears that escape before the frigid air turns them icy. I don't know how the fuck Tyler's in a tank top and barefoot right now, or all the time, for that matter. December on the East Coast is actually cold. Not like Saxon Beach, where I was still surfing in a bikini this time of year.

"What?"

Tyler closes her journal and sits up fully, facing me. Her bony knees bump the edges of my own, her jeans swallowing her legs completely, her tank top hugging tight to her thin chest and hips. She trains her sharp, assessing gaze on my face, watching my few escaped tears. Today, I see that she's wearing a necklace, the first time I've ever seen her wear jewelry. A thin silver chain hangs down her chest, a fat pink crystal on the end. I don't know much about crystals, but it looks like rose quartz, maybe? Huh.

She toys with the crystal as her eyes never once leave my face. "He's jealous, Niamh. I don't know how else to word it."

"Of.... you?"

She smirks, and the way her mouth quirks up in the corner combined with the way she's looking at me causes a strange, warm feeling in my chest. She never once breaks eye contact, never once blinks. She just looks at me like she's seeing me. The feeling in my chest is not all that different from magic.

"Why else would he be pissed that you're spending time with me and not him?"

I want to say he has no reason to be. I want to say that I don't understand why he would be jealous, because Tyler is just my friend. Zeke doesn't even know I'm bisexual- he's never asked. Just another way I let him like the idea of me. And that's what Tyler is, anyway: a friend.

But for some reason, the words don't come out.

For some reason, the words don't find a place outside my mouth at all. The word 'friend' sticks to the inside of my throat, then dries up and withers there.

I swallow hard and don't reply to her right away, trying to deal with the weird buzzing in my chest, along with the way she's looking at me right now.

"Um." I say eloquently. "My….. fuck. Okay. Look."

And I tell her what happened: the same story I told my dad, minus the tears and snot. Minus the complete breakdown.

"So I was wondering if you could help. I think… I think whatever's in the South Gate woods is angry that Zeke and I saw the gate and didn't walk through it. And maybe when Marlo and Kai went looking for the gate, it saw them and took them instead." I look at her in earnest, my eyes wide and begging. "You're the only one who I thought might know what to do." I say quietly.

At this, Tyler's face perks up. "Ohhh. So you need me, is that it?"
She tucks a strand of chestnut-colored hair behind her ears, smirking up at me. It isn't her usual smirk, flirtatious and witty. This one looks somewhat sad, a little more guarded.

"You know," She says, sticking one thin, pale finger west, in the direction of town. "They only like me when they need me."

And then she turns back to her journal, once again writing something I can't see as if she didn't say anything important.

I can only assume 'they' must be Summerhill, and for the zillionth time today, I feel like the world's shittiest friend. God, I hope she doesn't think that's how I see her. I know she doesn't care much for Summerhill or its people because of how they treat her, but I'm not them. Not even close. Without thinking, I reach out and poke her thin, pale arm, trailing my finger down it gently.

"I don't only like you when I need something, just so you know. You're my friend."

Tyler doesn't say anything, still on her stomach writing. After a second, though, she stops, but still won't look at me.
So I speak softer, really trying to get through to her. "You're cool, Tyler. You're patient. You're understanding, and you're gentle. I think you're great."

From my vantage point above her, I can see something like pain flash across her face instantly and violently. I balk, wondering what it was I said wrong.

Her voice is quiet and low when she speaks, but she finally looks up at me, covering her journal with both forearms. "You'd do anything for your friends, wouldn't you, Niamh?"

And yeah- there's definite pain in her eyes. Raw, stark grief, an emotion I've never seen her display before. Since the day I met her, Tyler's been cocky, coy, and confident. Smooth and lilting, ethereal and mysterious. Never... sad. In the entire three months I've known her, I've never once seen her truly sad.

It shocks me, and deeply. But she's right- I would do anything for my friends, even if they wouldn't for me.

"Yeah, I would." I say firmly. I don't like seeing her sad. It makes me feel like the world is falling out from under me.

"Hey," I say gently to her while trying to maintain eye contact, trying to not look away from her intense, all-seeing gaze. Trying to reach through the walls she's had up since the day I met her. "Are you good?"

"Good?" She laughs without humor.

"I mean…. Like, are you okay? You seem kinda sad. It's super out of character for you." I try, teasing gently.

Tyler stiffens, and then wilts in front of me. Her shoulders drop along with her head, and I hear her breathe shakily through her nose while her face is hidden away from me. Completely, thoroughly sad.

"Yes." She finally says from behind her curtain of hair. "You just remind me of someone when you look at me like that."

I don't know what to say to this, so I don't say anything. It never occurred to me that Tyler has a life outside of what we do together. It never once occurred to me that she probably has other friends, a family, maybe siblings... maybe a boyfriend, I don't know.

The thought fills me with a deep, burning feeling that takes me a second to place.

Jealousy.

I shove it down, fighting the urge to comfort her again. I need to focus. Marlo is what's important right now. My friend is what's important right now. If she's in the South Gate somewhere…. If she's afraid…. If that *thing* has her….Then yes. Yes, I would do anything for her. I'd do it for Makani. I'd do it for Booker, for Indie, for Zeke. I'd do it because I love my friends, even if they wouldn't do it for me. Even if they all hate me, even if they want nothing to do with me, I'd still do it for them.

After a second, Tyler stands up, brushing the grass and dirt off of her stomach. I go to pick up her journal and hand it to her, but she snatches it up before I can touch it, eyes flashing.

It almost feels like she's hiding something.

"Let's go find your friend, then." She says, a definite edge to her voice. I cross and uncross my arms, my wet hair dripping down my neck. I know the cold is causing my freckled cheeks to go rosy, my green eyes probably super bright. I look at her with what I hope isn't a pitiful, begging face.

"Do you want to come inside for a second? I kind of told my dad I wouldn't go back into the woods at all. If he could meet you, though, I think he might feel a little better, at least knowing I'm not alone."

Her back is to me, already halfway into the treeline, but I can see the muscles in her back stiffen.

"I'd rather not." She bites out.

I'm quiet, wondering how the hell I've made her this upset within twenty minutes. Wondering how the hell I keep making *everyone* upset. First my old friends, then Zeke, and now Tyler, somehow.

I can't lose Tyler, though. So if she doesn't want to come inside, fine.

"Do you want my help or not?" She says, her voice fading the deeper into the East Gate she goes.

Fuck. Shit. Okay. I guess I'm coming. "Yeah, wait up!" I call after her.

I look back at the house once as I jog to catch up with her. I tell my dad sorry in my head.

I have to find Marlo. I have to help my friends. If I can find Marlo, then Zeke won't be mad at me anymore. If I can find Marlo, then maybe Tyler won't act weird and sad anymore or think I'm just hanging out with her because I need her.

The more I think about it, finally catching up to her, the sunlight slowly getting swallowed by the woods, the more I realize that she's absolutely right. Like she always is.

I do need her.

CHAPTER THIRTY

NIAMH

Zeke keeps texting me the deeper we walk into the East Gate woods, and I keep ignoring him.

He tried to call me once about ten minutes ago, but before I could pick up, Tyler just shook her head at me and said something completely true, something that had me turning my ringer off entirely.

"He'll never truly get you, Niamh."

It stung, because I like him. I do- even though I hate arguing with him, even though I hate how quickly he jumped to getting defensive. Even though I don't trust him the same anymore, Zeke is still my friend.

But Tyler, like usual, is one hundred percent right.

Zeke can never really, truly get who I am inside. He never will. When my three best friends in the *entire world* saw what I was capable of, they bailed. When they saw my magic, they abandoned me. They left me completely on my own, abandoning everything we had. Why would Zeke, a guy I've known for less than three months, be any different?

After she said that, I fought every instinct telling me to apologize and make things right, turning my ringer off and shoving my phone in my back pocket. Maybe he was going to apologize, maybe he wasn't.

I don't care. Tyler's right, and I'm done being nice. Being angry feels much, much better.

Powerful.

After a few more minutes of walking in silence, I know we're in the South Gate woods without having to ask. I've grown to recognize how the trees here swallow the light, how the path grows darker and thinner, like the woods don't want us to find our way out.

But for the first time, I'm not scared in the slightest, because I'm with Tyler, and I know how to use my magic now. If that... thing comes anywhere near me or Tyler,

I'll fucking burn it.

Despite the darkness that's only growing thicker and the slight fog that's begun to rise, Tyler must be able to see just fine. Every two or three seconds she stops, plucking things from the path in front of us, pocketing them. I can't see that well in the dark, but every time she bends down to the path, the smell of roses seems to emanate from her ahead of me.

Fresh and dewy, like there's a handful being held right beneath my nose.

The farther South we head, the more I realize that I had absolutely no plan other than finding Tyler and asking for her help. She knows about magic, and nothing seems to scare her. Other than asking for her help though, I have zero plan. I don't know where Marlo is. My only theory is that she and Kai somehow found the gate, and that thing took them.

And if *we* somehow manage to find the gate again... I have no idea what I'll do. All of this is resting on Tyler, who's vague, mysterious self seems to have a plan. I'm fully relying on her.
With a jolt, I realize that Tyler is all I have in the world right now.

She stops again, plucking something up from the path. Every movement seems purposely slow and smooth, from the casual way she bends over to grab whatever it is, to the fluid, graceful way she stands back up, tossing her hair over her shoulders lazily.

Irritation flares up. I know I'm just upset about my argument with Zeke, but I can't help it. My anger has been boiling just under my skin all day, and she's deliberately stopping.

"Do you have to keep stopping every ten seconds?" I bite out, my chest starting to burn.

Tyler whips around, her eyes flashing amidst the dark. I can see the twin orbs of blue, piercing and intense look right through my own.

Instead of shrinking from her intense gaze, I match it, willing my green eyes to hold hers accountable. When I don't back down, she steps closer to me, closing the gap between us. Wordlessly, she hands me the object she'd picked up, dropping it into my palm.

It's a fresh rose petal. A red one, from the looks of it. A single crimson rose petal, the color of bright blood. As I stare at it, she reaches into her pockets, pulling them out by the handfuls.

Roses in the South Gate woods?

I have no idea what it means, and I open my mouth to ask her when she turns around and keeps walking, her voice carrying over her shoulder.

"Do *you* have to keep fretting over that guy who won't leave you alone?" She says up ahead of me. Her thin, willowy figure is paces ahead of me, yet I can *feel* that stupid smirk on her face.

Fuck this. Who is she to ask me that? And when was the last time I heard the word *fretting?* I'm so *sick* of this, so sick of the arguing. Tyler is all I have left, and now she's getting on my last nerve when I'm already stressed out. I am so goddamn sick of this entire fucking shitshow I've been dumped into. I didn't ask for any of this. I can feel my anger flare up in my chest, my magic bubbling and roiling beneath my skin like a tidal wave.

And god, it feels *good.*

But I reign it in, because starting a forest fire is the last thing I need right now. It only hits me a second later as I keep following her that maybe she's egging me on. Maybe she wants a reaction.

Well, I tell myself. If Tyler wants a reaction for whatever reason, she's gonna get one. I'm fucking *sick* of this.

My irritation grows, and I don't fight it at all, my hands starting to glow red at my sides. I'm fucking sick of her mysterious, vague answers, sick of her know-it-all, lilting voice. Sick of her acting all high and mighty and wise when really, she's just an outcast. I've never once seen her outside of the woods, I've never seen her at school, and she doesn't ever go into town because she hates them. So what if she knows about magic? She's a loner.

She's obnoxious, actually. She tells me things, then withholds the knowledge because she *knows* I'll keep coming back for more.

If Aine were here, she'd call that kind of behavior manipulative.

"Hey." I say sharply to her. I'm not sure what sort of reaction she's trying to get, but I don't really care at the moment. I'm fucking pissed.

Tyler turns around and leans back against the closest pine tree, crossing her arms. That smirk that I expected shines clear on her face, and I force myself to take a deep breath through my nose. I can barely see the trees around me or the path beneath me, and yet somehow, Tyler stands out clearly, as if what little light there is bows only to her.

I force myself not to look her in the eye. If I look into her eyes, I'll get lost and forget why I'm mad. It's the effect she has on me: looking her in the eyes pulls me in. She's that intense. Tyler knows exactly how to use her eyes as a weapon.

I need to focus on something else.

My gaze drifts to her pale stomach, where I can see exactly how low her baggy jeans hang on her thin hips. To where her blue tank top has risen up, and I can see the exact point on her body where her waist begins to curve. To her smooth, slim shoulders, her collarbones, and lower, where I can see just how cold she really is.

Fuck.

If she wants a reaction, she's going to get one. I inhale deeply, and then lift my gaze to meet her eyes.

A challenge.

She's been challenging me since I met her, hasn't she? It's what she does, because she knows it works. And look where it's gotten me- where *she's* gotten me. I know what I am now. I know what I can *do* now.

I have a gift. It isn't a curse. I'm not crazy.

I'm magic. I have *magic* beneath my skin, and I know how to use it now. I'm an angry person, but that doesn't make me dangerous.

It makes me powerful.

I can start fires, if I want.

I can burn things down.

Tyler's face is alight while my thoughts race, and her smirk only widens into a smile, like she knows exactly what's running through my head.

Fucking hell, she can read my fucking thoughts.

I force myself to wipe my mind blank, to not think of anything so she won't see what I'm about to say. I will my brain to go blank, my magic humming in my chest as I do it.

When I speak, my voice is raspy, my anger poorly concealed. "What is your problem, Tyler? Why are you pushing me so hard?"

She rolls her neck, her eyes closing. She's still the only thing I can see clearly amidst the dark. The darkness of the South Gate woods don't seem to have a hold on her.
They don't seem to touch her at all.

With her eyes still closed, she yawns, relaxing back into the tree. "Is that all?"

"I- No. No, actually. What's your fucking deal with Zeke?"

She opens her eyes then, and the look she's giving me is pure, undiluted apprehension, like she's debating something within herself, and can't decide which way to go. I wonder if she's still thinking about earlier- about whoever it was I reminded her of.

The feeling from earlier crashes back into me, causing an odd, tight feeling in my chest that mingles with my magic. Jealousy.

She sighs, then uncrosses her arms and stretches. I hyperfixate on the way she raises her long, pale arms above her head and inhales, the way that strip of bare stomach rises until I can see all the way to her ribs, then higher, her tank top just barely covering her. I hyperfixate on the way she looks at me while she stretches, watching me watch her.

Like she totally and completely knows what she's doing.

"Maybe because I know pushing you is the only way to get you to act, Niamh." She says, yawning again as she arches her back like a cat. "Maybe it's like I know you or something."

"Do you?"

I say it without meaning to and instantly kick myself. *Fuck.* Good job, Niamh. Push away the literal last person you have. Push away the *only* person in the world who knows what you are and doesn't shy away from it, the only person who really knows you. The only person who hasn't left you yet.

But instead of getting angry, the apprehensive look in Tyler's eyes disappears, and quicker than my mind can comprehend she darts forward and grabs my chin with her slim, pale hand.

I stand there on the path with her fingers wrapped around my jaw, my pulse quickening unlike ever before.

This is different from how I felt when I saw the gate. Different from how I felt when the thing in the woods first talked to me. This type of fear….. It almost feels like excitement, if I really look at it.

Because this isn't fear at all.

I feel like a rabbit standing before a lion, except the lion is beautiful and has sapphire-blue eyes that see all the way into you, seeing everything you don't say. A lion that you know is primed to kill, and very well could. But it's a killer in the same way that a siren is a killer: beautiful. Magnetic, intoxicating. Beautiful in the way that those who hear the siren's call are unable to look away, unable to say no.

And they don't really want to say no, either, because seeing a siren is the best thing that's ever happened to them.

Tyler might not be the thing in the woods, but every inch of her feels predatory right now with my chin gripped tightly in her fingers. I'm a rabbit, a lamb. I'm the *prey.* I'm the fucking prey right now, and she knows it, too. She looks at me with aggression in her eyes, with raw, burning power.

I breathe shallowly, my eyes blinking far too fast.

"I'm not going to answer your own questions, Niamh." She says softly. Her mouth is just mere inches from my own in the dark. I can smell the roses on her fingers, the cinnamon on her breath.

I've never been this close to her, and it's shocking to my senses. Being this close to her is like standing in front of a bonfire: she truly radiates magic, her fingers nearly buzzing with it. It's intense- she's intense. Between that and the way the misty rain dots on her face, coating the hundreds of freckles on her nose and the crescent-moon shaped scars lining her jaw in little drops, it's almost overwhelming.

Tyler radiates pure power, this close.

I don't know how I didn't see it before.

I wonder if she can tell how hard I'm shaking beneath her grip. "What do you mean?" I whisper, almost directly into her mouth as she holds tight.

I'm the preyI'mthepreyI'mtheuckingprey holyshit

Humor fills her deep, pulling blue eyes. "Because you can answer your own questions without me doing it for you. You don't need me to tell you that your little boyfriend isn't it for you."

"Zeke isn't my boyfriend."

Tyler's eyes flash dangerously, and her freckles start to glow like stars. Her hand grows warm against my chin, the blues of her eyes going so dark they look almost violet in this lighting.

When she speaks, the cinnamon on her breath carries all the way into my mouth, which causes my legs to go limp on their own accord, as if my brain short circuited at the thought of her mouth so close to my own.

All I can think right now is that I've never, *never* felt anything like this Zeke. Not with anyone, not even close.

Tyler drops her smile, but the mischievous, know-it-all look rests behind her eyes still, her voice cocky and assured.

"No, he isn't, is he. You can't bring yourself to feel a goddamn *thing* for him in real life, other than the fake scenarios you create in your head. You play games with yourself, thinking maybe, *maybe* today will be the day you'll want him in the way you think you should. Maybe, *maybe* today will be the day that he lights a fire in you and makes you *want.*"

The way she puts emphasis on the 'maybes' is what sets me off.

"You don't know what the *fuck* you're talking about." I rip my chin out of her hand, anger finally reaching a crescendo, and I push her.

Hard.

I've never shoved anyone in my life, but I shove Tyler away from me, hard.

And it feels *fucking good.*

She doesn't budge, despite her thin, gangly limbs. She should've gone flying with the way I just pushed her. I'm strong: all those years of surfing have kept me lean and muscular, along with having a natural athletic build. Tyler should've stumbled, at the very least, but she doesn't.

Instead of deterring me, this only makes me angrier.

So I shove her again.

Tyler just smiles at me like she's bored, and I grind my teeth together, nearly seeing red at the little *smirk* on her fucking perfect, beautiful face. Fuck her. I don't care what she's doing. This feels *good.* This exhilarating, bright anger feels *good.*

So I shove her a third time, doing exactly what she taught me. I let everything coming to a head all at once, consuming me:

The way my mom spoke to me this morning.

The way Zeke yelled at me, cursed at me, turning into someone I didn't even know.

The way Indie just cut me out of her life over a text message, not even hearing me out.

The way Makani looked at me that day.

The way I lost my three best friends, and now Zeke and Marlo, too.

The way everything is just so, so *unfair.*

So fucking *unfair.*

I take all of it, every burning, bright inch of it, ignoring the slick, oily feeling starting to trickle down my arms and legs. I ignore the magic's call completely, molding all of it into a ball. Then I hurl it at her, all my magic at once. Every single bit of it.

And finally, finally, she flies back a few feet, pushed backwards by an invisible force. Tyler's back hits the pine tree she was leaning against minutes before.

I smile, panting. Holy shit.

I don't have it in me to feel bad, because fuck, that felt *so. Good.*

Tyler's eyes widen in surprise as she catches her breath, and then not even ten seconds later the biggest, most elated look I've ever seen on her glides across her face like summer lightning, a smile that I've never seen her wear before.

And it's *beautiful.*

The way she's looking at me right now is fucking *beautiful.* There's no other word for it. Her smile, her eyes, they say it all. The look of awe in her eyes right now, trained on my own…

It's like she can't get enough of me. Like she's proud, and in awe, and surprised. Like summer lightning, it comes and goes, quick and strikingly beautiful.

I cross the few steps it takes to get to her, no room for shame or guilt over the way I pushed her. No, I get right the fuck in front of her, ignoring the way her glowing, star-like freckles are smattered across her milky cheeks, her nose, her chin. Ignoring the way her eyes seem to darken the closer I stand to her, yet remain impossibly bright at the same time. Ignoring the way those deep, expanseless pools of purple-blue are looking at me with that same awed look, that look of wonder that's doing very odd things to my chest right now. Ignoring the-

But I'm unable to ignore the way that the air suddenly starts to smell aggressively and unmistakably like roses. Roses, and something spicy. Cinnamon. No. Cayenne? Roses and something hot, something that burns.

I lean in close to her face, my anger still simmering just below my throat. I guess I didn't throw *all* of it at her.

"Don't talk about Zeke as if you know him. You've never even met him."

Tyler just smirks, crossing her arms over her chest while managing to make leaning back against a tree look effortless. Even though I'm standing over her, angry as hell, I'm starting to get the sense that I'm losing a battle of wills here.

"Who was the person you saw in the vision I gave you that first time, Niamh?" She asks me, her voice smooth and cool, that ever-present smirk only growing as she looks up into my face. "Tell me- was it Zeke? Was it a boy at all, Niamh?"

I glare at her, because besides her clearly looking into my mind right now, she's totally doing this on purpose. She's purposely trying to make me angrier, to make me act out. I'm still not even sure why, or what reaction she's trying to get out of me. Whatever she's doing, though, it's working. Her lilting, beautiful voice and her vague, avoidant questions and answers are doing nothing but stoke the flames again, and I want to make her snap.

I want to make her break, and I want to win.

I want to beat her at her own game.

So I say the exact opposite of how I feel, the exact words that I hope will hurt her, even though they're a complete lie.

If she is reading my mind right now, she'll know that.

"Fuck you, Tyler. You don't know me."

And *that* is finally what gets her mad.

She darts her hand out and grabs the back of my neck, pulling me to her with surprising, shocking strength for someone so thin.

Her eyes are nearly purple in the darkness and too bright, snapping with anger. She's got me close enough that our noses nearly touch, and I can see the way her chest is rising and falling quicker, like she's trying to control herself, and failing.

My pulse is so fast, it's nonexistent. I feel like I can't breathe.

"Except I *do* know you, Niamh, better than anyone. Look me in the eyes and tell me that isn't the truth."

Her voice is dangerously low, carrying on the breeze with a soft, silky lilt. It's intoxicating. She's intoxicating.

And right.

She's right, like she has been since I met her. She *does* know me better than anyone.

And she's the only one who ever will.

She's right- and very, very close to my face. So close that I can count every freckle on her face, so many clusters and patches that they outrank a sky full of stars. So close that I can see the dozens of tiny, crescent-shaped scars that trail along her jaw. So close that I could press my forehead to her own.

And then, as if reading my mind, she does exactly that. The rain continues to fall around us harder now, soaking through her thin tank top thoroughly, droplets snaking down her face, but I can't feel it at all. All I can feel is her forehead against my own, her hand wrapped tight around the back of my neck, and-

Magic.

Magic floods my body, and this time I can name it for what it is: it's the same feeling I got the day she merged her magic with my own, giving me a taste of her own power. The day she let me inside her well of magic, and I felt everything that she does on a daily basis.

Being this close to her, physically touching her floods me with that same addictive, intoxicating feeling. At this point, I don't even know if it's magic or just her.

Whatever it is, she's right.

I don't feel this with Zeke.

I've never felt anything like this with anyone.

Zeke might be charm, joy, and cheer.

But Tyler is power.

Desire.

And being *seen*.

She's magic.

But she feels like magic because she's Tyler.

So I do exactly as she says and look into her purple eyes amidst the darkness, her face the only thing I can really see.

And then I kiss her.

CHAPTER THIRTY ONE

TYLER

From the journal of Tyler Iris Lane

Tuesday, December 20th

I've been finding rose petals, shiny pennies, and little yellow sunflower petals everywhere. I keep sticking them in the pages of my journal, and there's so many that the smell of roses is now permanently stuck to my fingers. This is the result of teaching her basic, simple magic. Things that people not born of magic can try and attempt. Key word, <u>try.</u>

And yet Morgan took to everything I taught her easily, naturally. And combined with my own gifts...

Fuck. Doing magic with her is unlike <u>anything</u> I have ever felt before in my entire life. Introducing her to my world, to who <u>I really</u> am... I feel so seen. She makes me happy, she gets me.

I love her.

(I'm just going to scribble my thoughts down right now since I'm already thinking about her)

She calls me a romantic, but she doesn't know the half of it.

How could I be anything else, when it feels as though my hands were the perfect size to hold her hips?

As though every inch of me and every inch of her were made to compliment one another?

How could I be anything else, when just the way she looks at me causes my heart to jack up its speed, or fall out of my chest?

How could I be anything else when songs sound louder, sweeter, and deeper when they remind me of her?

How could I be anything else when holding her in my arms feels like the only place I'm content to reside forever?

How could I be anything else when she places her lips on mine, and seals all her kisses with a promise:

"I'm yours."

Chapter Thirty Two

Niamh

If I am made of anger, unfairness, and the smell of the ocean after it rains,

Then Tyler is made of magic, pure honey, and roses.

She kisses me back the second my lips touch hers amidst the dark like she expected it, pulling me to her tightly by the back of my neck. Her tongue meets my own, deepening the kiss, and causing my breath to catch sharply. The cinnamon that was on her breath earlier tastes ten times stronger, mingling with notes of wildflower honey.

Kissing her feels like I've been wandering around aimlessly, and have finally been found.

I press her further back against the pine tree I shoved her into, all my anger melting away and into something else: something just as strong, something that binds the air around us tight with notes of cinnamon and cayenne.

Something that smells and tastes exactly and undeniably like magic.

Tyler pulls me closer and closer into her as if she still can't get close enough to me, until my hips are pressed tightly against her own, my stomach against hers. She pulls me into her until I'm fully taut with her, and the feeling of her body against mine has my hands grabbing sloppily and hurriedly for her, any part of her, because I *need* my hands on her: her waist, her neck, the small of her back, anything. All the thin, sharp parts of her, all the parts that I've looked but haven't touched, my restless hands against her restless hips. She mirrors my movements, antsy to touch me, as if she can't get enough of me, either.

Tyler kisses me as if just touching my skin isn't enough for her.

As if holding my neck tightly in her hand with the other one snaked around my waist beneath my hoodie isn't enough. As if having her hands touching my bare skin isn't enough. As if just kissing me isn't enough: it's as if she wants to be within me, underneath my skin.

Within me.

Tyler kisses me like she already knows the answer to her question: she *does* know me better than anyone, and I do need her.

Because she kisses me like she needs *me* just as badly as I need her.

After a second, I pull away for air, the only sound reverberating through the entire forest both of our heavy, restless breaths. She looks at me amidst the dark with that same wonder in her eyes, and I know it's reflecting back in mine. Her eyes are darker than I've ever seen them, either from her enormously dilated pupils, or the near-purple of her irises just swallowing up the light. She's still glowing as brightly as if we were standing under the sunniest noon, and not deep in the bowels of the South Gate woods. Her face is flushed, her skin a gentle pink instead of the usual gaunt white. Her freckles stick out, and amidst the heaving of her chest, she looks more alive than I've ever seen her.

Ever.

Tyler radiates with power, so much of it that my body begins to shake. So much of it that the air around us seems to warble and bend, as if the forest itself is caving to her will. As if kissing me gave her strength.

As if *I* gave her strength.

That thought alone has me leaning forward again, reaching for her because I need her, because I need to feel that close to her again, need to feel that wanted again, need her to look at me like that again-

And like she read my mind, Tyler grabs both of my hip bones in her slim hands and flips me so that it's my back against the rough bark of the tree, until I'm the one breathing heavier. My eyes widen, stunned, but I don't care where she wants me. She can put me wherever she wants: I'm fully consumed with something I've never truly felt before, something heady and intense, something that makes my entire body *want* in a way it never has before.

Something that tastes like lust, like magic, but feels more like need. Because that's what it really is. I *do* need her. I need her, and not just to kiss me. I need to feel as close to her as possible, because she *is* the only one that knows me. I need her the way I thought I needed Zeke the night of the party.

Tyler pulls her face away but keeps her body tight against mine, pinning me between the tree and herself. With her mouth still hovering just above my own, she runs one hand along my waist, the other hand starting to trail down my stomach with two slim, pale fingers. She presses her lips to my ear then trails her mouth down my neck, and I'm so consumed by this alone that I almost miss the quiet, silky words she whispers at the base of my neck;

"Let me try something, Niamh."

I nod furiously, trying not to lose it. After a second, and with another kiss pressed to my neck, my stomach tenses and my chest goes tight, starting to burn in that familiar way. I can feel her well of magic starting to merge with my own. I don't know how I know that's what she's doing- I just know.

And holy. Fuck. This merging... it is unlike *anything* I've ever felt before. Unlike *any* magic her and I have done, period. This is.... This is colossal.

It's a bright, vast forest fire, towering flames of orange and crimson mingling with reckless, rogue ocean waves amidst a night sky peppered with stars.

Our combined magic burns my chest, sliding all the way from my searing heart to right between my thighs, right where her own thigh is pressed tightly between mine.

I feel like I might die. And if she touches me, I might really die.

Tyler's amused smile interrupts our kisses, like she can't help herself. "Can I help you, Niamh?" She whispers into my mouth, her lips a ghost on my own.

I nod furiously, the combination of our magic and just her in general starting to unwind me. Tyler laughs softly, like she knows. She can read my mind, goddamnit. She fully and completely knows what she's doing to me.

Motherfucker.

"Tell me." She says in a petal-soft, silken voice, a voice that is only making me want her more. A voice that comes off so silky, so full of promise, dripping with ardor that makes me think that she might be as good with her mouth as she is with her words.

Despite just wanting to give in, to tell her exactly what she wants to hear, my innate urge to be stubborn and fiery shines through, and I scoff against her mouth, hoping to regain some semblance of composure.

Though the smile that's growing on her face is telling me that she knows *exactly* how I'm feeling.

"Why don't you read my mind, Tyler." I say, my chest heaving.

And it is her own name on my tongue that gets her.
Tyler's eyes flash dangerously, and she slams me back into the tree with that unnatural, shocking strength, causing me to cry out. She kisses me fiercely, tightly, as if branding me. As if showing me *exactly* what she just saw by looking into my mind.

Tyler kisses me like she wants to get underneath my skin, like she wants to make me hers.

Silk. Silk, roses, and need. She is all of these things, and I want her.

Now.

I'm sick of waiting.

I wriggle out from her tight grip and drop to my knees, my back still against the pine tree, ready to show her exactly how badly I want her.
But Tyler just laughs, and while standing over me, she shoves me by my shoulders to the ground, and not all that gently. I fall back onto my elbows, looking up at her with shock.

"Sit down, Niamh."

My brain short circuits. Holy mother of fuck, I am sat.

Tyler drops to her knees in front of me, trailing gentle but sure kisses up my bare stomach while leaning over me. Her hair falls on either side of my hips.

I try to breathe regularly, but all that comes out is small bursts of air, shocked, sharp exhales which only grow stronger as she straddles my chest, her bony knees on either side of my hips. And when she uses one slim, pale hand to untie my stupid shoelace belt, and dips the other into the waistband of my pants, I can't help my reaction.

My back arches off of the forest floor on its own accord as she touches me, the sound that leaves my mouth just short of sinful.

I've hooked up with girls before. Not a lot, but enough. And it has *never,* not once, caused me to feel like this. Not once.

Tyler inhales sharply, her dark eyes popping open in surprise when she feels just exactly what reaction I'm having to her.

"Fuck, Niamh." She exhales, her mouth slowly dipping back to my own. She kisses me again, this time hurriedly, frantically while simultaneously moving her

fucking

HAND.

Slowly and gently, like she knows exactly what she's doing.

"This. Is what. You're doing. To me." I manage to get out, my hips rising up beneath her bodyweight to meet her hand, to get her closer to me. My sk8-his dig into the dirt as my hips buck, my head falling back to the ground. I *need* her closer. I need her.

As if reading my thoughts, she presses against me tighter. My sounds reverberate through the forest, and I do not care. Not a single thought about where we are or why we even came here enters my brain. I do not give a single fuck about anything other than Tyler in this moment. Nothing has ever mattered as much as her, as this. Nothing. I've never felt this level of intensity, of *want* like I have with her.

She feels like magic.

And as she continues her gentle movements, our combined magic in my chest begins to heat and expand, growing bigger and bigger, very similar to the steady feeling that's rising between my legs as she moves her hand on me, then in me. I can't help it when her name falls off my lips again, then again, reverberating through the South Gate woods.

Her name on my mouth only prompts her to go faster, kiss me deeper, pressing her fingers tighter against me when I whimper every time she pulls away.

Then, she ohmyfuckinggod ohmygod *omygodohmyfuckingod*

withdraws her hand, and instead dips her beautiful, perfect lips to my stomach, using one hand to pull all her hair to one side. My own hands fall to her face, her head, twining my fingers in the night-dark strands. Tyler trails her tongue down to my waist, unbuttoning my dickies with the same hand that was just inside me, pulling them down farther, just past my thighs.

And when she dips her mouth back to my skin and her tongue runs over me I ohmyfuckingjesu

*fucking hell*jesuschrist

I can't think.

My voice is nonexistent. "If you keep. Doing that. I'm-"

And so she keeps doing that, but after a second she ever-so-slightly lifts her head up, and I whimper without meaning to.

But she just smirks at me, then lowers her mouth to my right thigh, running deep, soft kisses over my legs and my lower stomach, running her tongue back down onto me.

She looks up at me once, just once.

And I swear, I see stars.

But then,

as she dips her mouth and her hands back to my thighs, still teasing me, still not taking my clothes off fully, something makes her stop.

With a small, slight jerk, she gets off of me and backs away from me, looking horrified with herself.

I'm on my feet instantly. "What??"

She just shakes her head then grabs her hair with her hands, looking frenzied and panicked, like she's about to cry. And then she does- bursting into panicked, gut-wrenching tears that trail down her beautiful freckled face, pooling in her sapphire eyes and spilling down her cheeks in rivers.

And she's mumbling under her breath, so quietly that I have to strain to hear her.

"I can't. I can't." She repeats, her sobs turning just short of hysterical.

Tyler's crying harder than I ever have in my life, harder than I knew a human being was capable of, and it splits my heart in two. I don't know how to console her, considering I currently feel like a tightly wound spring, but I shove my lust aside and try to ask.

"What's wrong?"

I know it isn't something I did- her reaction when she touched me is enough to convince me of that. But clearly something happened. Something internally, maybe, that she's now coming to terms with. When I ask her, though, she looks at me as if remembering that I'm still standing right there.

And what she says to me slams a wall down on my desire quicker than if I'd been doused in cold water.

Tyler shakes with her sobs, completely, utterly broken. She lifts her eyes to mine, and there's no apology in them: just stark, honest truth.

"There was a girl, a long time ago. Her name was Morgan."
I can't fucking breathe.

I stiffen, my body suddenly tight again, but not with need this time. Slowly, I button my pants back in place, re-tie my shoelace belt. I smooth my curls down, plucking stray pine needles from the ends. I try to compose myself, struggling to breathe through the boulder that's now lodged in my chest, struggling not to let the jealousy that her words just spawned overwhelm me completely.

She said a long time ago. A long time ago, not now.

The thought allows me to breathe a bit easier.

I stare at her, the taste of cinnamon, of her mouth still sharp on my tongue. "You were in love with her, huh."

And I know it's true just by looking at her. Just by seeing the damaged, broken look in her always-confident eyes, horrified with herself because she'd almost had sex up with a girl that wasn't *Morgan.*

Whoever this Morgan chick was.

You remind me of someone, she'd said earlier. She'd meant Morgan. Great. So I remind her of some ex that she's still clearly very much in love with.

Tyler just looks at me, tears spilling down her cheeks. She doesn't bother to wipe them away, and despite everything I'm feeling towards her right now, I fight the urge to wipe them away for her, to kiss them the second they spill over her eyes. She'd probably rather it were Morgan, anyways.

"So how long ago was this, exactly?" I bite out.

I groan at how much of a dick I'm being. I might be an innately angry person, but she's hurting. And she's my... Friend. I guess. She's my friend, and I'm being an asshole.

Although I don't really fuck my friends. But to each their own, I guess.

Tyler looks at me, her mouth opening and closing. Then again. Then a third time, like she's debating telling me something. But after the third time, she shuts it and backs away from me.

"You're not going to want to see me again if I tell you." She whispers, her voice cracking. "And I don't want that."

My anger flares up, and I realize that I'm only becoming more and more comfortable with it. So comfortable that I don't shy away from telling her how I really feel, how she really hurt me. Just because she's afraid to lose me doesn't mean a thing. I need honesty.

"You know what, Tyler? Cool. If you've been secretly seeing some chick this whole time, and I just happened to get in the way, by all means, don't let me be a problem any more. In fact, I-"

But she cuts me off with two words that freeze my ranting completely.

"Fifty years."

I blink at her, my anger vanishing like smoke. "I'm sorry?"

She can't mean that. She's still fucking with my head, goddamnit. She turned me on, wound me up, teased me, and now she's *still* fucking with me. What is her *problem?*

"Fuck off, Tyler."

I turn around, ready to go find Marlo on my own. Screw Tyler. Maybe I don't need her.

Maybe I don't need anyone.

"Niamh." She says after me, and I can hear her following me. When she catches me, she tries to grab my elbow, forcing me to look at her. I don't turn around, instead ripping my arm out of her grip, disgusted by the same fingers that were inside me not three minutes ago.

"What, Tyler? What?" I say, exasperated, finally facing her. "What could you possibly have to say to me right now?"

"Have you ever asked yourself why we only hangout in the South Gate woods, Niamh?"

This forces me to really look at her. Her tears stop, leaving shiny white trails down her freckled face.

"Have you ever asked yourself why you've never seen me around school? Or why I don't know your friends, or why I didn't want to come inside your house today?"

Something horrible and heavy starts to build in my chest, my mind beginning to fog. I don't... No...

"I can't ever leave the South Gate woods, Niamh."

Something deep, deep in my stomach is trying to worm its way up, trying to tell me something, but I can't tell what it is yet. I'm not sure if I want to know what it's trying to say.

"I don't get it." I whisper into the dark, looking into her still-broken gaze. "You were in the East Gate woods behind my house this morning."

Tyler stares into my eyes, those deep pools of blue trying to get me to see. They grow shinier the longer she looks at me, as if she's fighting back tears again. But not for Morgan this time- for me.

"Because the path you take home every day is just an extension of the South Gate, Niamh. The gate makes it that way- *all* paths lead back to the South Gate, if it wants it to. It can change directions, it can mislead. You always end up at the South Gate sign every time you walk that path, do you not?"

My throat constricts as tears build in my eyes. The leaden feeling in my chest expands. "I don't get it." I whisper to her in the dark.

Even though... I think I do. I think I get what she's trying to tell me, because it's all starting to make a horrible, horrible sort of sense.

But it can't be.

Tyler looks me dead on with deep, watery eyes, and what she says next upends me and the world, tilting it on its axis entirely.

"I can't ever leave the South Gate woods, Niamh, because it's where I was killed."

CHAPTER THIRTY THREE

TYLER

December 20, 1973

Just after eleven o'clock on an unusually dry, cold night in December, a group of people set out to the Lane's cabin just outside the South Gate woods with one purpose.

Two of those people were Morgan Van Devon's mother, Cathy, and Morgan's brother, Jonathan.

The rest of the group were friends of Jonathan's and the Van Devon family, people of Summerhill that sided with them either through loyalty or fear.

The two aren't all that different, really.

And so, just after eleven on this frigid December night, The Van Devon's gathered up their people, a few supplies, and a few lanterns, then marched from the town of Summerhill all the way out to the Lane's cabin, where both inhabitants slept peacefully.

Eleni Morwen Lane slept deeply and without dreams. She'd crafted herself a sleeping charm that night, as she'd been plagued by anxiety all throughout the day that something terrible was going to happen. She had learned in her years as a practicing witch, and simply as Lane woman, that fretting about events that were to come was never wise: if anything, it made the outcome worse. Bearing through them like a great pine tree withstanding a storm was the only way to go about these things.

So she'd willed the anxiety in her mind to dim, crafted a simple yet potent sleeping charm, and she'd slept.

Her granddaughter, Tyler Iris Lane, was also asleep for once, but fitfully.

She too had been plagued by a constant stream of anxious, unwanted thoughts. Unlike her grandmother, though, Tyler had always believed in taking action against events that may come to pass. Tyler had never been one to sit around and wait.

But when all her attempts to See failed, her magic seeming to fizzle out just before taking shape, she was forced to abandon her hopes of seeing what was to come.

It was as if something was blocking her magic.

So instead, Tyler Lane laid in bed, slipping in and out of sleep. When she was awake, she fretted over her blocked magic, lighting the dozens of white candles placed strategically throughout her room in hopes of reaching through the block. She tried rationalizing. She tried chanting. She tried deep breathing, trying to remain calm, trying to reach that place of peace deep within her well of magic.

But thoughts of Morgan kept breaking through her concentration, and not in a bad way.

Tyler was going to take Morgan to her favorite cliff in the East Gate woods tomorrow, a spot called East Cliff. She was planning to officially ask Morgan to be her girlfriend.

And she was going to tell Morgan that she was completely, undeniably, and irrevocably in love with her.
She knew it was true. Every time they'd kissed, every time they'd stared into the other's eyes- Tyler's deep, piercing blues into Morgan's deep well of honey-gold, she knew it was true, and that Morgan felt the same way. She knew Morgan loved her back, and it filled Tyler with something she'd never truly felt before: joy.

They looked at each other like they had never found something so beautiful in their entire lives, and couldn't get close enough. She knew that Morgan was thinking the same thing, knew she loved her by the way that she kissed her. She knew by the way Morgan pressed her forehead to Tyler's own, trying to communicate telepathically with her. Tyler had never told Morgan that she could read the thoughts of others, and yet she always tried to get Tyler to read hers. It had become a game between the two of them: to press their foreheads together and guess what the other was thinking.

Tyler had never once cheated when Morgan had pressed her forehead against her own, but she never needed to.
Until yesterday, when she finally did.

They'd been laying on their backs in the grass of the South Gate just behind the hut, lying side by side underneath the open sky and watching as it grew grayer and cloudier, awaiting the storm that was coming. Morgan's head had been on Tyler's chest, her tanned, golden arms wrapped around Tyler fiercely, tightly.

And Tyler had never felt so wanted in her entire life.

She loved this feeling, and she loved this girl who held her with every bit of strength her arms possessed so much that she almost felt it might kill her. Gone was the secretive, brash girl that had worn a thick layer of armor her entire life. Morgan had unearthed the Tyler that lay beneath the armor:

A girl made of magic who possessed the ability to love deeper than the sea, wider than an entire sky full of stars.

Morgan had rolled over and propped herself up on her elbows right as the rain had started, looking at Tyler with that look of sheer awe and wonder in her honey-jar eyes that Tyler couldn't get enough of. That look of raw, pure love and adoration, searing through Tyler's heart.

Morgan had opened her mouth as if to say something, then shook her beautiful, tanned face, her silky caramel locks parting deep to one side. She'd reached behind her neck, unclasping the rose quartz on the silver chain that she'd been wearing for the last few months, and had placed it around Tyler's own with a soft, sweet smile.

Then she'd trained her deep, intense eyes right into Tyler's own, and the last three months had shrunken into this very moment, this very nanosecond.

Then she'd pressed her forehead to Tyler's, and squeezed her eyes shut in concentration.

And overwhelmed by the peace, the gentleness, and the sheer happiness that Morgan was radiating, Tyler had finally, finally listened to the buzzing in her chest, listened to her well of Lane-magic, and read Morgan's thoughts while her forehead was pressed taut with Tyler's own.

Morgan's inner voice was just as raspy, just as soft, just as perfect and sweet and honey-dipped as her true voice.
She spoke quickly, rushed, repeating herself in succession.
Quick, like she wanted to fit as much out in a single breath as she could.

IloveyouIloveyouIloveyou.

And Tyler had opened her eyes, her breath whooshing out of her in a single exhale, because for the first time in her life, she was truly stunned.

This beautiful,

Golden,

Hilarious,

Sarcastic,

Charming,

Perfect,

Perfect girl

Loved her.

Tyler didn't want to tell Morgan that she'd read her thoughts, not yet. So she'd simply kissed her, more gentle than she ever had before, and sealed her kiss with a promise, sealing it with their promise to each other:

"I'm yours."

Now, laying in bed trying in vain to focus, Tyler knew that she wanted to solidify it all. She wanted to make Morgan *hers* in every sense of the word. Even if Morgan couldn't read her thoughts, Tyler loved her just as much.

And so asking her at East Cliff was her plan, along with giving Morgan a few pages of writings she'd torn from her journal. Little poems and writings all about Morgan that she'd been amassing for the last three months, all pages that smelled like rose oil, just like the rest of her journal. Tyler picked the few that she was proudest of, wrapped them tightly up with a length of red ribbon, and stuffed them with a few handfuls of the red rose petals and shiny coins she'd been finding everywhere since that third day.

Since the day that they'd gone from enemies to something else.

Despite the unwavering, creeping feeling of something horrible about to happen, her blocked magic only amplifying the feeling, she told herself it was nerves. Tyler told herself to relax.

As much as she didn't want to admit it to herself, thinking about Morgan *could* very well be the cause of her not being able to sleep. It could simply be that thoughts of the girl she loved were keeping her mind restless.

Her mind, and her hands. She couldn't help herself- thoughts of Morgan's perfect, beautiful self had imprinted onto Tyler's brain, keeping her awake late into the night. Especially on the nights Morgan stayed over instead of sneaking home- those nights were Tyler's favorites.
Because Morgan was sweet, and gentle, and soft by nature- but not all the time. Not when it was late at night, and they were cuddled up in Tyler's bed together. Not when they were completely alone and didn't have to hide out loud.

No, Morgan was not sweet and gentle on those nights. She was restless, she was needy,

and Tyler loved it.

When the group of people arrived at the Lane's cabin just after eleven, they took no heed to the hour of the night, and no heed to the two women sleeping inside. They pounded on the door with rage emanating in their fists, their fury wafting through the cracks in the door and all through the house, making its way up into Tyler's room.

And Tyler Lane had shot up, images of her mouth on the little rose tattoo on Morgan's hip suddenly blasted apart as her body filled with adrenaline. Adrenaline, and fear as the smell of pure, undiluted anger filled her room.

Her safe, dark room, her room full of candle wax and sea shells and dried flowers that had begun to permanently smell of roses and cinnamon, catnip and honey-almonds- of *Morgan*- suddenly turned sour, the smell of their anger driving out the sweetness.

The smell of fire- of burning- began to override everything else.

Tyler sat up in her bed, paralyzed with fear as they yelled through the door and through their furious pounding that she'd forced Morgan into a homosexual relationship against her will. That she'd spelled her to fall in love with her. That she was a

desperate

fucking

lesbian.

That was Jonathan Van Devon.

They yelled that she'd coerced her with magic, that she should've been banished from Summerhill years ago, before she'd ever been born.

That was Cathy Van Devon.

They yelled that she'd changed Morgan, and put a spell on her.

This was all of them.

They yelled and screamed and raged all sorts of nasty, horrible things into the Lane's front door, then said that they were coming in one way or another, that she would *fucking*

pay.

And that they were going to put an end to all of this. They yelled that she'd done horrible things to Morgan, and she was going to pay for it.
For the first time in Tyler Iris Lane's life, her heart filled with fear.

Not fear for her life, but fear that something had happened to Morgan. Fear that something was going to split them apart.
And Tyler wasn't sure she could handle that.

Real fear has a way of slinking its way into your heart, either freezing your limbs along with it, or propelling them into action. Real fear, mortal fear, has a way of wrapping around your throat and stomach, winding dark tendrils into your mind, making you shake, making you
truly,

deeply afraid.

Real fear spikes your adrenaline into overdrive, short circuiting any sane, rational thoughts.

It was only then that Tyler knew this was real fear. Not just fear for Morgan anymore, but fear for her own life as they kept yelling, and as her front door sounded as if it were being smashed in.

Because once that fear consumed her, any thoughts of magic, of safety charms, or banishment spells left her brain, instead being replaced by an innate, primal urge to *run*.

So she did.

Had she stayed put,

had she cast a charm or two,

or had she awoken Eleni, who slept like the dead just down the hall from her,

Tyler Lane's outcome might have been very, very different.

But,

something in the trees that had been

waiting

so

patiently

and

been

hungry

for

so

long

tasted her fear on the wind as it trailed through her open window into the South

Gate woods below.

And when it caught a whiff of that fear, it grabbed hold of it,

and

told

her

to

run.

The woods had been her home, her muse, and her safe place for as long as she'd

been alive. As long as Tyler had lived in Summerhill, the South Gate woods- a place of fear and unease for everyone else- had been her home, her safe place. She knew the woods as well as she knew that she was made of magic.

So it was out her window and straight into the South Gate woods she ran to, the frigid temperatures of the night barely grazing her skin, barely laying its cold hands on her as she tore through the treeline and began the steady incline into the darkness of the South Gate.

Run was all she knew.

Nothing but pure, undiluted fear propelled her forward. She could barely see the trunks of the great pine trees as she tore by, barely feel the brambles and brush that scratched her and tore at her favorite sage-green skirt.

And yet, despite the primal fear that had grabbed ahold of her as she crashed through the trees, one thought kept circling around in her head, looking for purchase. She just wasn't sure if it was the mob on her heels, or something else that was making her see things amidst the darkness.

Things she couldn't explain.

After a few breathless, terrified minutes, Tyler slowed, and realized that she had never been this deep into the South Gate before. She'd never been this far from the hut, either. She recognized no landmarks, nothing to tether her to home. She was merely surrounded by darkness, black as pitch, and pine trees clustered so thickly together that they felt suffocating. She could barely see her hands in front of her face amidst this type of darkness, barely make out the trunks of the trees around her. Even the moon couldn't seem to penetrate through the pines at all.

Breathing heavily, looking around her, the mob was nowhere to be seen.
Maybe she'd lost them, she thought. But it was so dark she couldn't really tell.
Her magic still wasn't working, for some reason. Normally whenever she was in the
dark, she could still see clearly with bright witch-eyes like a predator of the night.
That's what she was, after all, wasn't it? She'd never been scared of the dark. She
wasn't some cowardly, spineless human who feared the unknown.

Tyler *was* the unknown.
Tyler *was* the thing that crept around in the dark.

But now, with her magic blocked and being this deep into the woods, she felt
slightly afraid. It almost made her wonder if she might actually stumble upon the
gate. She'd never seen it, but Eleni had.

And, she recalled with chattering teeth as the cold air finally sunk into her
skin, Eleni had forbidden her from going this far into the South Gate alone for that
very reason.
Tyler rubbed her bare arms up and down. All she had was the clothes on her back,
which were not nearly enough for the unusually cold night. It was dry out, so dry and
so cold that her breath fogged out in front of her, running icy fingers up and down
her thin limbs. Her favorite sage-green skirt and a thin white tank top were no match
for the frigid December air.

And to top it all off, Tyler swore she was seeing things.

Between the trunks of the towering pines, between the fear that coated her mouth like the sweat on her face, she swore she was seeing faces between the trees.

First, she thought she saw a little blonde girl in a dress darting between the trees, just out of the corner of her eyes.

If she tried to look at her head on, she disappeared into the dark.

Then in the other direction, she swore she saw something tall and spindly. Taller than a man, and thinner. Thin and skinny and all black with long, skinny arms, and long, sharp nails.

But when she tried to look at it, it disappeared.

And then, standing directly in front of her as if it had been there the entire time,

there stood a large, black billy goat.

It stood alone, looking right at her, but its eyes were all wrong.

Where beady yellow goat eyes should have been were two plate-sized, wide white orbs, two giant white eyes on the goat's face.

They stared at her, and they did not blink.

Tyler had never been afraid of the unknown before. She'd grown up seeing things others could not and hearing things in the dark that others could not hear. She had never once been afraid of them- some things could weave between life and death, but they could not hurt you. This she knew, even as fearsome as they appeared sometimes.

But Tyler was afraid now as she stared at the big black goat, because she knew, deep down, as sure as she knew that she was made of magic,

that it wasn't really a goat.

And then the black goat with wide, unblinking eyes spoke to her.

"Hello, Tyler."

The goat's voice was equally young and old, equally silky and rough. It sounded as if it were a great and powerful thing, old and ancient.

But mostly, it just sounded *old.*

Tyler choked, gagging on her fear, and then it was gone, as if she'd imagined it entirely.
She was alone in the trees, shaking with more than just cold now, and yet she could hear laughter ringing through the air.

Hollow, false laughter, as if it didn't belong to a human's throat, and never had.

Laughter that sounded, to Tyler at least, like something was trying to imitate what a human's laugh sounded like.

Like it was *playing*.

Tyler looked around herself in the dark, trying to control the panic that was steadily rising in her chest. She couldn't see, it was freezing,

And there was something else here with her.

In certain spots of the forest, unbeknownst to Tyler,

something

was

moving

In certain spots, the air was going

still

so still that it seemed

dead.

Because Tyler was right: something else *was* there.

Something old. Something far older than the woods, far older than Summerhill.

Something older than time itself.

Older than this plane of existence.

it follows her as she spins in circles

trying to see where she is

it circles her in the trees

jumping from branch to branch like a spider monkey

watching her

giggling through a childs mouth

the rage of the people on their way combined with her fear is simply too

tantalizing

too

mouthwatering

to resist

it slithers down a pine tree behind the girl and lands in a misshapen heap on
the forest floor

amidst the pine and fir needles

lying on its belly in the dirt

how ironic

it thinks

for it crawled into this particular world on its belly

crawling up from the darkness on its belly like some great snake

but it is no snake

it is many

      it watches the powerful

brash teenage girl

giggling to itself

it loves the way her fear tastes

so

       rich

    so

         glorious

   it thinks that maybe it likes the smell of her fear almost as much as it liked the

way the little girl with the twin sister had tasted those hundreds of years ago

that little girl had tasted so very good

and how her twin sister had screamed when she didn't come out the other side of the

gate was

        delectable

it had feasted on her fear alone for weeks

but she was so long ago

that it almost forgets how little girls

                      taste

and yet it thinks this one

           Tyler

                    might taste better

    it will

                eat

It felt old, this part of the woods. Old, and... wrong. It was darker than should've been possible, and Tyler knew she wasn't alone. Even the air felt strange to her- she couldn't see at all, and yet now, the trees she was surrounded by seemed to cluster in a circle, fencing her in.

Almost like she'd wandered into a clearing without trying to.

It was dark like someone had spilled ink into the air, and oddly still, completely void of a breeze.

And yet it wasn't these things that felt off kilter to Tyler. No, it was the way the air *felt.*

It felt dead.

She was in a clearing in the South Gate woods, surrounded by dead air and the dark.

Tyler was completely spent.

She could hear the crowd of people growing closer now. They'd be upon her soon, and her magic was still blocked, nothing more than a faint fizzle in her chest where normally a great, rogue wave existed.

And as much as it enraged her to admit it... without her magic, she was defenseless. She was truly alone in the woods with nothing to protect herself, and far away from Eleni, from Felix, from Morgan.

She was alone, and starting to become very, very afraid.

Tyler tried to catch her breath and think of what to do. Realistically, she was afraid and had nothing to defend herself. If her magic had been working, she would've had unlimited options.

She could fell one of the great pine trees, making it land on them.

She could disappear into thin air, and reappear somewhere else.

She could read their thoughts before they acted, and remain one step ahead of them.

She could hurt them, if she really wanted to.

She could do a lot of things, because they underestimated her. They always did.

And if they were coming here to hurt her...

Then she would show them just exactly how dangerous she could be.

But she could do none of those things, because her magic wasn't working.

The sheer size of the group unnerved her. One, maybe two she could handle easily with no magic. She was thin, and she was fast. But a group of roughly twenty people, all very, very angry, possibly with weapons?

This felt horribly like a witch hunt, she thought.

And she was the only witch around.

Tyler, in her growing panic, tried to chant under her breath as she looked in vain for a place to hide. The clearing of trees only seemed to grow as she spun in a circle, her panic worsening. Big, hot tears began to run down her face, mingling with the sweat from her panicked skin.

Tyler never cried.

And she didn't mean that she hadn't cried in a while, or in years. Tyler had never cried at all. Not once.

But she cried now as panic began its steady ascent into her mind and heart.

The only spell that came to her mind was an old one she'd found in one of her aunt's grimoires: one of *Mira's* old grimoires.

Mira Lane, her aunt who, at sixteen, had summoned a king of hell, one of Solomon's seventy two demons.

Mira Lane, who had taken it too far, who had been too obsessed with the darker side of magic. Mira Lane, who had questioned too much, who had dabbled with things that were far older and wiser than her.

The spell was old, and reeked of dark magic. Darker not as in evil, necessarily, but dark as in it came from a place that human beings were not meant to see. Places full of ancient, unseen knowledge, places full of answers that mankind should not know.

Places that only princes and kings of the pit should reside,

Places where things are made to lie on their bellies and eat dust.

The spell that came to her mind just then was one of Mira's, and Tyler knew that it was not something she should try. Her grandmother had expressly forbidden her to dabble in anything resembling what Mira had gotten into, and yet here Tyler was, alone in the dark, defenseless, and without her magic.
And all that came to mind was one of Mira's old, ancient spells.

From what she could remember, it was a cloaking spell, used to veil somebody from what harmed them, but not just from harm:
From death itself.

The spell was, indubitably, a protection from death.

A hiding spell.

Despite knowing that it wasn't a good idea, and despite the knowledge that her magic was not working whatsoever, Tyler knelt to the earth and placed one hand on her chest where her magic normally lay.
The other she placed in the dirt of the South Gate woods.

She took three deep, shaky breaths, and then she started to chant, her voice wobbling slightly.

"Keep Me, Keep Me, Protect Me From What Seeks Me. *Custodi Me De Morte.*"

She paused, waiting for a flicker of her magic to awaken.

Nothing.

So she kept going anyway, the old Latin rolling off her tongue easily.

"*Custodi Me De Morte. Custodi Me De Morte. Custodi Me De Morte.* I Will It So."

Protect me from death, she begged. *Please.*

The old Latin that Mira had translated in her journal all those years ago burned brightly in Tyler's head.

Custodi Me De Morte: Protect Me From Death.

And as the voices of the mob began to echo through the clearing, their shapes marching up the hill, and still not even a *flicker* of her magic working, a single, horrible thought buzzed through Tyler's head.

For a brief, fleeting second, she wondered if this is what her grandmother had always meant when she said that Lane women doomed themselves when they fell in love, that Lane women and love don't mix.

She recalled the Three Kings ritual she'd done a few months ago, and what the entities in the mirror had told her:

You will rise, then you will fall.

Had Morgan been the rise? Was this the fall? Was her grandmother right all along?

But the thought of Morgan resulting in this crushing, petrifying fear and this horrible, angry mob chasing her was too painful for Tyler to wrap her head around. How could something so pure, so *true* result in this? Morgan had been her one good thing in this life, her one sliver of sunshine in a world that despised her.

She refused to accept that this was the result of their love.

And so Tyler pushed that thought away, instead waiting for the rush, the tingling, heady sensation in her body that always accompanied magic work. She waited for her legs to shake, for her stomach to tighten.

Nothing.

Tyler swore under her breath, sweat and tears sliding down her cheeks right as the group of people reached her clearing.

Morgan's big brother Jonathan emerged from the treeline first.
Behind him in the shadows, Tyler could just barely make out Cathy Van Devon, still in her pantsuit and heavy, teardrop diamond earrings. The rest of the group trailed after her, Tyler easily recognizing classmates of hers and Morgan's.
Friends of Jonathan's. Friends of the Van Devons.
Residents of Summerhill, every last one of them.

The first and last words Cathy Van Devon ever spoke to Tyler Lane were the ones she uttered to her son as she handed him something Tyler couldn't see in the dark.

"Finish this." She said to Jonathan.

Then she hissed the word *witch* to Tyler like it was a slur, turned on her heel, and left.

Tyler couldn't see any weapons on anyone in the group amidst the dark, but somehow, this made her no less afraid of them.

Jonathan stepped forward a few paces.

Tyler forced herself to hold her ground, forced herself to cross her arms lazily, defiant. She leaned her back against the closest pine tree, her skin tearing against the rough bark, and smirked at him. They all saw her as a cunning, brash little witch. And she had been exactly that- until Morgan.
Until the parts of her that were buried underneath the anger and the bitterness were shown some kindness, some gentleness.

But she could still play the part that they knew.

"You fucking *cunt.*" Jonathan seethed at her. He wasn't that much taller or bigger than her- he was every bit as gangly as Tyler was, every bit as lean and sinewy, and yet his rage and his mottled red face made him seem bigger to Tyler. Anger had a way of making you seem bigger than you really were- Tyler understood that better than most. It gave you courage that you didn't really have.

"You know what you fucking did." He continued, his spit flying as he hissed at her. Jonathan's words matched his face in ferocity. Even amidst the dark, she could see how puce his face was. It was almost enough to make her wish it was darker. Behind him, somebody lit a lantern, which flooded the pitch-black clearing instantly with a dim golden glow. Not a lot- the darkness seemed to swallow the light immediately, the puny lantern barely making a dent against the inky blackness.

But it was enough for Tyler to see exactly how many people were there. Twenty five, at least.

And at least six of them, the ones she recognized as Jonathan's friends- all mean, cruel boys who couldn't think for themselves-

Those six all carried a length of thick, winding rope. Thicker than her bicep, and longer than she was tall.

It only took Tyler about five seconds to realize a few things, then.

1. They were not here to avenge Morgan for whatever they thought Tyler did to her.
2. They were here to hurt her.

Tyler knew why they were here then, because it all boiled down to the obvious, blaring truth: they were here to hurt her, simply because she was Tyler, and Morgan was Morgan.

Despite everything that had stood in their way, despite being raised as enemies for most of their lives, Tyler and Morgan had found each other, and fallen into a deep, rare kind of love: the kind that bridged two souls into one, making each other theirs until the end of time.

The kind of love born of magic.

But Tyler was a witch, and Morgan was a Van Devon.

Tyler was Tyler- a secretive, brash little liar.

And Morgan was Morgan-

Perfect.

Beautiful.

Everything.

She was everything Tyler had ever wanted, and everything that she didn't know she needed.

But Tyler was Tyler.

Flawed,

magical,

and different.

And the town of Summerhill just couldn't have that.

Jonathan took another step forward, his sun-kissed, long caramel locks just barely reaching above Tyler's own, just barely. He wore his work clothes, as if he'd come straight from the harbor in town: worn coveralls over a thick, stained black hoodie, and rubber fishing boots. The kind of boots you wear on a boat, the ones meant to repel fish guts and blood.

The ones that are meant to withstand a mess.

Tyler took in the rest of the group. They were all dressed similarly, as if they were about to go fishing.

And yet Tyler knew with a sinking, awful feeling that wasn't why they'd worn rubber.

"Whatever you plan on doing right now, just don't." She drawled, forcing her voice to sound bored and lazy, as if she couldn't care less that they were here.

As if they couldn't see the sweat on her face, the shaking in her hands.

As if they couldn't tell that she was completely fucking terrified of whatever they had planned.

The only thing she had going for her in the world right now was that while *she* knew her magic wasn't working, they did not.

Jonathan took yet another step forward until he was directly in front of Tyler. By some miracle, magic or not, she did not flinch.

"You know," he mused, rummaging in the pocket of his coveralls, "in the olden days, they burned witches. Fuckin strung and hung 'em. But I bet you knew that. You aren't dumb."

Before Tyler could even think of a response to this, Jonathan pulled a shiny blue Bic lighter from his pocket, along with a packet of crumpled up Marlboro's that he probably stole from his dad.
But it was the third thing he pulled from the pocket of his coveralls that solidified it all for her.

At first glance, it seemed as though he'd pulled a handful of squished, crushed up blueberries from his pocket. His fingers came out deeply, violently purple, his smile growing wide as he watched her face realize what they really were. Not blueberries at all, but elderberries.

Fresh, ripe elderberries.

Her grandmother's words began to ring in her ears, along with the dull hum of fear beginning to buzz in her head.

The first lesson in herbs she'd ever learned with Eleni as a child were imprinted in her memory permanently, as deeply rooted as the magic that ran alongside her blood.

"You must never ingest elderberries, Tyler. Since the medieval times, they've been used as a deterrent to magical creatures. They have the ability to dampen magic, or halt it altogether."

Jonathan's smile only grew as he saw the moment she recognized the berry for what it was.

"You might be a fucking dyke, but you aren't dumb. We can't have you casting any more little spells, Tyler. Not after what you did to Morgan."

Despite the fear that was beginning to climb up her throat, Tyler chuckled. They were so completely ignorant. They *still,* all these months later, thought that Tyler had sent Morgan that spell jar on purpose.

She couldn't help the next words that came out of her mouth.

"Is that seriously what this is all about? You think I fucking spelled your sister to fall in love with me?"

The thought alone was enough to cause her fear to subside for a moment, just long enough for some of her old self to poke its head back out. Enough for the brash, cocky Tyler to emerge.

"Here's news for you, dipshit. That spell jar was never for Morgan. It wouldn't have worked on her, because it wasn't ever *for* her, dumbass."

Jonathan's face grew red again at her tone, and she knew she should be afraid. She knew that it would be stupid and reckless not to be.
He smiled at her, their mouths nearly perfectly aligned. She could smell his last cigarette on his breath.

"That's a convenient story, Tyler."

He didn't put the berries away. Instead, he just watched her as she wilted, watched her as the color drained out of her face.

Because she knew now that no matter what the truth was, it didn't even matter. To the Van Devons, it would never be enough for Tyler to tell them that she and Morgan fell in love on their own accord, no misplaced spell involved. It didn't matter, because they would always see her as a secretive, brash, lying little witch. They would always see her as not good enough for their perfect daughter.

They would always, always see her as Tyler.

"Where's Morgan." Tyler had the strength to ask quietly, just to Jonathan.

He shook his head, popping a single berry in his mouth. "Somewhere you'll never find her again. My mom finally figured out where she's been disappearing all these months. When she wasn't in her bed this morning, she waited."

Tyler's face paled. Morgan had woken up in *her* bed that morning, sneaking back home well after the sun had risen, leaving Tyler trying in vain to fall asleep with the smell of Morgan all over her bed, her sheets, and her mouth.

"And the second she got home, my mom weasled it out of her. See, my sister isn't as good a liar as you."

He swallowed, then picked a thin berry hair from his teeth. "Yeah, Morgan's on the mainland now with friends from church. You won't be seeing her again, Tyler."

And it was right then she knew, as she tore her gaze away from the elderberries in Jonathan's outstretched hand, as she looked around her at the group of angry, vengeful faces amidst the dark clearing, that this is where it would end. Her visions, month after month of an angry mob chasing someone into the forest blared blindingly clear in her head.

It was her all along. *She* was the one being chased.

She thought again of the entities in the mirror:

You will rise, and then you will fall.

This was the end.

That primal, deep fear, oily and *real* clogged her throat like pills swallowed dry.

Or maybe it was the knowledge that Morgan was gone.

That thought alone nearly had Tyler on her knees, begging for it to be over already.

Without Morgan… she didn't want to breathe. She didn't even want to try. Without

Morgan, she felt untethered. A lost soul.

But Tyler forced herself to take a breath, forced herself to think clearly. No

matter what they said, she loved Morgan.

What they had was not wrong, or bad, or forced.

It was *real.* Whether or not their love was forged through magic, through a

spell jar, or completely natural,

It was real.

What she felt for Morgan traversed time, traversed stars. It was boundless and

infinite, and the single purest, truest thing she had ever known. It had bridged their

souls, it had bound them to each other.

The love Tyler had found in Morgan had changed her, and magic had nothing to do with it.

It was real, and it was hers to hold onto until the end.

And she could at least have that.

She could at least go while knowing that truth in her dark, secretive heart.

Thinking about waking up to Morgan just hours before...

The way her smooth, caramel hair had tickled her nose, her head tucked into the crook of Tyler's neck.

The way her hair parted to one side naturally.

The way her mouth parted slightly in sleep.

The way her sweet, honey-jar eyes fluttered gently while she dreamed.

The way she sighed with contentment against Tyler's bare chest.

The way that her thoughts flowed even in her sleep.

Tyler had dipped into Morgan's mind while she slept this morning, and even in sleep, her thoughts were clear:

IloveyouIloveyouIloveyou.

Remembering it all brought her comfort, and an instant, flooding warmth filled Tyler's chest like spilled honey. Not magic at all: just love.

Pure, true love, the kind that gave her strength and courage. With that love in her chest, the old Tyler emerged again- the brave, cunning, brash one, the one that didn't give a fuck about anyone else.

She reached a hand out, delighting in the way Jonathan flinched at her movement. With one finger, she flicked the elderberries from his open palm.

"Good thing we aren't in sixteen hundreds anymore. Burning witches is so archaic. This isn't the fucking Crucible, dipshit."

It was the wrong thing to say.

Jonathan's face was pure malice, pure rage as he breathed right into her face. "Here's what's going to happen, witch." He said pointedly.

He was still talking to her, saying some other things, but all Tyler fixated on were his eyes.

He had the same eyes as his sister. But where Morgan's were a soft, honey brown, full of sun and warmth and love...

Love.

Her last words to Tyler that very morning, right before she'd snuck out of her bedroom window, had been of love.

Her last words to Tyler, not even spoken aloud. She'd grabbed Tyler's face in her hands right before she'd climbed out the window, wrangling them both back into Tyler's warm, cozy bed. She'd sat in Tyler's lap, holding her face tight in her tanned, ringed fingers, and smushed their foreheads together in the dim, hazy pink and gold that was a true Summerhill sunrise.

And in the quiet of Tyler's bedroom, in the glow of the sunrise, with not a single sound other than their heartbeats, Tyler had reached into Morgan's mind with slim, deft fingers as their foreheads touched.

I love you. I love you. I love you.

Over and over, on a loop, as if she couldn't say it enough. Morgan's sweet, raspy voice had been both nervous and exhilarated, joyful and found.

And when Morgan had opened her eyes, Tyler knew that she hadn't ever needed to read Morgan's thoughts with her magic.

It was written clear as day in Morgan's eyes that she loved Tyler.

And where Morgan's brown eyes were full of love, Jonathan's were deep, dark holes that soaked up the light. There was no room for warmth, let alone room for love in them.

Not at all.

He was still talking to her. ".... and if you make this difficult or try to run, we're gonna leave you up there for a week. Got it?"

Tyler blinked at him, lost in memories of Morgan. Those memories gave her strength, even though she had nothing to save her now. She had no magic, she had nothing. Nothing but memories of Morgan, and the love in her heart.

"You're fucking delusional." She scoffed.

And that is when Jonathan grabbed her.

it watches everything unfold from up in the highest branches

a mere scribble of darkness pooled in the corner

a mere scribble of darkness with grinning teeth

and hungry white eyes

it watches from above as they string the girl up to the highest pine tree

binding her limbs tightly to its thick trunk

it watches as they shove crushed elderberries down her throat

and it watches as she screams

it smiles as it watches her buck and fight

never succumbing or giving in

it smiles as it watches her lose

and yet never once admitting defeat

it relishes in the way she tries to live

      it knows she will lose

but oh is it so fun to watch

      her will to live is so strong

her desire to remain alive so bright

      when she finally can bite and scratch and kick at them no longer

when her arms and legs are finally bound completely to the tree

it

      skitters

and

            jumps

through the darkness

resting atop the very tree she is tied to

and it looks down at her

staring at her head of dark hair

it stares down at her and grins

    then it crawls down the tree onto her head

    and pools itself behind her ears

Tyler knew with a dull, quiet finality that this is where it would end.

Jonathan and his friends had grabbed her swiftly and bound her to one of the great pine trees, just high enough off the ground that her bare feet couldn't touch. They'd shoved the handful of elderberries down her throat while tying her, thinking it would stop her magic, and they'd been right. When she'd retched into their hands, they'd just shoved her bile back down her throat and laughed.

And now, Tyler was bound completely to a tree, unable to move, her throat burning, her mouth tasting of vomit, and without magic completely. If her magic had any chance of returning, it was shot to hell now.

Yet now, as they all stood around the clearing, laughing and talking amongst themselves in the dim light, her raw, mortal fear had been slowly dissipating. Dissipating, and slowly being replaced instead by a new feeling:

Cold, deep, *old* anger.

The anger felt older than her, as though it didn't belong to her at all. It felt as though it had never come from her, and belonged to someone else entirely.
As Tyler lay there, bound to the tree, the cold feeling seeping down her neck, she had the strangest thought.

It felt, she thought, as though something had crawled onto her skin, and was trying to wear her.

Laughter rang through the treeline then, around her, above her, behind her. A childs laughter, bright and bubbly. She tried in vain to look up, but she couldn't move at all. Jonathan and his friends had her completely, fully immobile.

Tyler swore under her breath, craning her neck against the lengths of rope. But then something to her right, something just beyond the group of townspeople caught her eye. Just out of the corner of her eyes, right out of her direct line of vision, she swore she saw, for all the world,

a little girl.

The same one from earlier.

She stood behind some of the trees, her small, grubby child-hands braced on the trunk as if peeking out from behind. A small, cherubic blonde thing, in a faded white dress and apron that were very out of fashion.

Tyler noted the bonnet on her head, the petticoat on her waist. The little girl was not from this time- Tyler was smart enough to know that much.

And, just like earlier, she still couldn't see the little girl if she tried to look straight on,

but it almost looked as if the child had no eyes.

The little girl smiled brightly out of the corner of Tyler's eyes once she realized she had seen it.

"What ails thee, Tyler?"

The little girl's voice rang through the clearing, echoing all around her in the bubbly, sing-song voice of a child.

Her speech was stilted, and held a strange accent that Tyler couldn't place. Tyler blinked, fear holding her throat in an iron grip, and then the girl was gone. But that childlike laughter kept ringing through the trees.

And then,

the air went oddly still,

void of movement,

just like it had earlier.

Jonathan and his friends noticed it too, right as the air behind them started to shimmer.

And then,

as even their breaths ceased their fogging in the frigid, dry night air,

behind them, resting amidst the towering trees if it had been there all along,

stood an enormous, towering iron gate.

Tyler's mouth dropped open along with everyone else's as they took in the tall, imposing gate that appeared in the clearing behind them.

And yet, for Tyler, the gate that had suddenly appeared was the least of her worries.
She was still seeing things:

While Jonathan Van Devon and the rest of the group all stared at the gate, fear and shock now filling *their* bodies,

Tyler was seeing shadows slithering between their legs, and odd, jerky movement behind other trees. Shadows that were shaped wrong, not looking like regular shadows.

Scribbles of darkness that seemed to *move.*

She kept hearing chittering, like something was moving behind her. Or trying to, at least. It sounded like something was lugging along behind her, trying to walk.

But it was too heavy.

Tyler knew that there was something else here in the clearing with all of them besides the gate, but she wasn't sure what it was. Maybe, she thought, it was whatever that little pilgrim girl had really been. Or whatever that black goat really was.

Tyler had grown up with creatures of the dark, with things that could exist on different levels, different planes. Things like that were always old and liked the dark, and they usually always saw her, because they knew she could see them.

Whatever the thing in the South Gate was, Tyler knew it had seen her.

Because while everyone else was occupied with the gate, something was trying to wear her like a second skin right now.

Something was trying to climb inside her, and Tyler wasn't entirely sure she wanted to know what it was.

But god, she didn't want to die.

I don't want to die like this, she thought to herself with clear, resounding clarity. *Please, I don't want to die.*

She thought of Morgan.
She thought of Eleni.
She thought of Felix.

But mostly, she thought of Morgan, of how the world had finally, finally opened up to her. How life with Morgan had started to feel like the teaser trailer of a film: this is what your future could look like, Tyler, if you keep this beautiful, golden girl around.

Tears began to cloud her vision as she realized that future was slipping away through the cracks.

Tears that were quickly replaced by anger, by fury, and not entirely her own.

PLEASE. She begged in her head, growing desperate. *Someone. ANYONE. Save me. I don't want to die. I don't want to die.*

She began Mira's chant again, this time just in her head. Her magic was fully and completely gone by this point thanks to the elderberries flowing through her system, but she could try.

She could at least try.

Custodi Me De Morte. She uttered with her eyes squeezed shut, tears leaking out the corners. *Custodi Me De Morte. Custodi Me De Mor-*

And then,

Something answered her.

"Anyone?"

The smooth, stilted voice spoke to her from somewhere behind her.

No- not behind her. All that was behind her was the trunk of the pine tree.

The voice spoke to her from inside her ears, slowly and carefully.

"Dost thou wish to live?"

Tyler's spine stiffened, goosebumps coating her entire body instantly.

The voice was old, but as smooth as the sea stones that she loved to collect. Smooth, powerful.

Ancient.

The voice sounded like something straight out of Mira's grimoire.

Between Tyler's goosebump-ridden skin and the frigid night air, Jonathan and his friends could see just how very cold Tyler truly was, her thin white tank top leaving little to the imagination. They'd lost interest in the gate, and instead fixated on a new plaything: Tyler.

Tyler, and her very thin, willowy body.

In their minds, they knew that while she might be a fucking witch, and a faggot at that, they couldn't deny that her body was incredibly, intoxicatingly alluring. Those eyes of hers, that body of hers...

She might be a faggot, but she was pretty enough.

Jonathan and three of his friends stepped closer to her, smiling down at her chest, their eyes narrowing in on her chest.

Tyler bit her tongue so tightly she wondered if she'd drawn blood.

One of Jonathan's friends, a tall, sullen boy that she'd had a few classes with, took his wide, calloused hand and ran it down her collarbones, finding her breasts underneath the thick coils of rope.

Another one trailed a finger under the waistband of her sage-green skirt, laughing as Jonathan mirrored his movements.

She could hear them laughing to each other, and could hear Jonathan's low voice asking if this is what she'd done to his sister that morning.
And as their dirty, calloused fingers found their way inside her, their jeering, ugly mouths on her lips and ears, Tyler's soul splintered.

How *dare* they touch her. How *dare* they.
Just mere hours ago, it had been Morgan's hands in those places. Morgan's fingers, Morgan's mouth, every movement full of love and eager to please. It had been Morgan's mouth causing her legs to shake, her eyes to pop open.
It had been Morgan, all Morgan, and full of *love.*
The ghost of her body intertwined with Tyler's own felt like a mere memory. Waking up to her felt like a memory, now.

A memory that was being replaced with these dirty, horrible boys having their way with Tyler's body now.

Tyler's heart, soul, and body was Morgan's. Her body had been Morgan's that very morning- and now the last people to ever touch her would be these three, and not Morgan.

A single tear slid down her cheek as she struggled to keep her heart from completely shattering.

The smooth, old voice spoke again as her tears began to fall, dripping onto the hands of Jonathan and his friends.

"Dost thou wish to live?"

Their hands roamed over her freezing skin, grazing into her mouth, forcing her to taste herself on their dirty fingers.

And as they finally, finally got off of her, as all twenty of them began to throw freshly chopped firewood and kindling at her feet, she knew with certainty, with finality.

She, Tyler Iris Lane, was a witch.

And she was going to die.

The voice spoke a third time.

"Dost thou wish to get revenge on thee?"

The voice curled itself around her throat, resting itself behind her earlobes and her teary cheeks. If she arched her back and shifted her head to the side, it almost gave her the same feeling that magic gave her: that sensual, heady rush, that bloom of warmth.

Like if she thought really, really hard, and leaned just the right way into whatever thing was curled behind her, the voice felt like something resembling magic.

It a*lmost* felt like magic.

Almost- but not quite.

"What are you?" She asked it in her head, begging it to hear her, whatever it was.

And it did.

"I can save thee, if thou wishes." The voice breathed into the nape of her neck, curling just behind the opening of her ears. *"Thou asked to be protected from death. I can save thee, if thou wishes."*

A single tear slid down Tyler's cheek.

Some deep, primal voice deep inside her, buried beneath the ever-present thoughts of Morgan, beneath the bitterness, the brashness, the secrets, and the lying, buried beneath the armor she'd worn her entire life, beneath the gifts she was born with that were passed down from generation and generation of Lane women spoke to her.

Her inner voice told her with certainty: *this thing is not a friend.*

This was something she should not let in.
But Tyler did not want to die.

All she wanted was Morgan. She just wanted Morgan, and everything would be okay.

And she was so afraid. She didn't want to die, not like this.
Not like this.

And so, as the group of people continued to toss firewood at her feet, Tyler Lane shut her eyes, her tears freezing in the cold air.

"Please." She whispered.

And that was all it took.

it smiles

finally

finally

and it allows its grin to stretch wide

stretching from one earlobe to the other

splitting its mouth in half

it shows the girl

Tyler

its true face

its true smile

the one with three rows of needle thin teeth
and it's white eyes that cannot blink

and oh how she screams when it shows her what it really looks like what it's real shape is

she screams, and it

        climbs

     inside

       her

           throat

finally

   and

      it

        doth

            eat

Jonathan Van Devon stepped back and admired his work, wiping his fingers off on his coveralls. That lesbian bitch was tied to the tree, tight enough that she couldn't escape. The elderberries had been a good idea, too. He wasn't sure if they would work, but his mom had said to try anyway.

A pile of fresh kindling lay at the bitch's feet, and he laughed aloud at her blank, unfeeling face. She really thought they were going to kill her- he could see it on her bored, stupid face.

Fucking faggot.

They weren't going to *kill* her. She really was that dumb, he guessed. They were never going to kill her. They were just going to scare the living shit out of her, make her think that they were going to burn her, so maybe she and her weird grandma would finally fucking leave.
Summerhill was *their* town. There was no room for witches here.

When his little sister had finally slunk home that morning, and their mom had wrangled the truth out of her, finally, Cathay Van Devon's objective to her son had been very clear: make the witch pay.

His mom's exact words to him, in fact. Make her pay.

So Jonathan did what he was told. With his buddies and a few other scattered family friends, they'd marched to the Lane's pitiful excuse for a cottage, and then chased the bitch all the way to this clearing. They'd tied her, scared her, and now they were going to leave her here, and maybe come get her in a week. Maybe.

If a mountain lion didn't get her first.

If the gate didn't get her first.

Jonathan handed his cigarettes and lighter to one of his friends next to him, then stepped back from the pile of kindling. The giant, enormous gate behind them unnerved him, but he didn't care as much as he cared about the white, blank-faced girl tied to the tree. Taking a deep, sinful drag, he stared up at her.

She didn't say a word. Tyler Lane just looked at them, all of them, her wide, vacant eyes unblinking. In the dim lighting of the woods, they looked white. Combined with how pale she'd gone, the lack of blinking, and the dirt that coated her now, she looked downright disturbing.

Honestly, who was he kidding? The bitch *was* fucking creepy. He didn't know how his sister did what she did with that *thing*.

It didn't matter anyways. Tyler Lane fucking spelled his baby sister, turning her fucking gay.

The thought boiled his blood. Thinking about his sister with the girl on the tree boiled his blood so deeply, so thoroughly, that his anger seemed to surpass normal levels. So strong was his anger in that moment that, without thinking or really meaning to, he tossed his lit cigarette onto the pile of kindling at Tyler's feet.

It caught fire within a nanosecond.

The entire pitch-black, unnerving clearing lit up spectacularly, bathing everyone in vibrant shades of orange and yellow, bringing chaos with it. People began to shout, to step back as the kindling caught flame unnaturally quick.

Too quick.

It was unnaturally dry outside, and freezing, which left the South Gate woods dry, thirsty.
Or maybe just easily flammable.

Realizing what he did, as if being jolted out of a trance, Jonathan stumbled away from the fire as his friends grabbed his arms and pulled him back.

"What the fuck, Jonathan?" They shouted into the night. This hadn't been the plan, not at all.

Everyone began to step back, watching as the base of the great pine tree that Tyler was tied to began to smolder, the flames licking their way up its base.

But not one of them put an end to it.

Not one of them tried to get Tyler down.

Not one of them went to grab water.

Nobody, not a single soul in that clearing,

Not a single person from the town of Summerhill even *tried* to put out the fire that was going to kill Tyler Iris Lane.

And yet during all of this, Tyler still hadn't moved. She just looked down at the group through white, vacant eyes, not blinking as the fire began to reach the tips of her toes.

And when her too-big, white unblinking eyes found Jonathan's, she smiled.

Jonathan Van Devon would never forget the last thing Tyler Iris Lane ever said to him.

He would not forget it as long as he lived, which wasn't really that much longer, anyways. Rarely does someone who sees the gate in the South Gate woods live to tell the tale.

Nobody heard what she said to him but Jonathan himself.

From up in the tree, elderberry juice still coating her chin and the front of her shirt,

Tyler's wide,

too wide

white,

unblinking eyes searched the clearing.

Without moving her head an inch,

her white eyes searched,

and finally halted on Jonathan Van Devon's face.

Tyler's eyes found his own, and in the second it took Jonathan to realize that she had no pupils anymore, she smiled at him, and her grin

grew

and grew

and grew and grew and

grew some more,

stretching her smile from ear to ear, splitting her face completely in half.

Jonathan's heart nearly stopped as he saw the needle-thin teeth she smiled with.

Too many teeth.

Tyler's teeth were as sharp and thin as her eyes were white, and she grinned widely at him.

Joyfully,

gleefully.

The fire began to lick at her bare toes, then work its way up her feet.

And when she spoke to Jonathan, it wasn't in the lilting, bored voice he was used to. Gone was the lazy, measured cadence, the silken words wrapped in rose petals and sensuality.

Because gone was Tyler Iris Lane.

Tyler's voice now was filled with pine needles, black dirt, and rot. It was a voice that had seen things both young and old, had lived many, many millennia,

and would live many more.

A voice that had slithered in between different planes of existence as easily as shedding skin,

a voice that came from a place where things like it were made to lie on their bellies like snakes,

and went by many names.

A voice that, in its original form,

it was regarded as a king.

But to Jonathan, it was a voice that just sounded old. His human mind was unable to process or grasp what was really up in the tree.

All he knew is that he had tied Tyler Lane up there with his own hands, but what just spoke was most definitely not her.

And her-
it's-

last words to him were in that same old, wise voice, full of dirt and darkness.

"Tell me, Jonathan Van Devon," Not-Tyler asked him from up in the tree. "how do you plan to kill something that is already dead?"

And when it spoke, black dirt-

dirt that did not belong to the woods of the South Gate-

fell out of her sharp teeth like drool.

Whatever had crawled inside Tyler Iris Lane smiled that big, too-wide grin, those pupilless, unblinking eyes holding Jonathan's own, until the flames licked her smile right off of her.

That was when Jonathan Van Devon and the rest of them ran.

CHAPTER THIRTY FOUR

NIAMH

December 7, 2023

Tyler's story has me in tears before she's even finished.

Even though hearing the way she speaks about Morgan guts me completely and wholly, I can't help but feel my heart break just like I know Tyler's is all over again right now.

Morgan Van Devon, who would be in her sixties right now if she was still alive.

I'm jealous of a relationship that happened fifty years ago.

Tyler tells me everything, from growing up in Summerhill and how backwards they were, to how she and Morgan went from enemies to something more: lovers.

She tells me about Morgan's brother, Jonathan, and the things he called her, and she tells me in enough words what he did to her without having to say it, which causes my anger to flare up brightly.

And she tells me exactly what they did to her in the end.

They burned her to death.

Not at a stake, but it might as well have been.

By the end of her story, I'm fighting back sobs of my own.

Tyler is… dead. She's been dead the entire time I've known her.

Everything starts to make a horrible, chilling sort of sense now.

The day I met her at the South Gate sign, and her response to me asking if she was a local.

I used to be.

Asking her if she was okay whenever that brief flash of grief crossed her face.

Don't.

Tyler is dead-

and yet she isn't. She's still here.

And for a dead person, she certainly feels very, very real.

Thinking of her hands and her mouth on me earlier only boils my blood when I think about Morgan's big brother laying *his* hands on Tyler. My blood boils at what they did to her in general- at all of them.

My blood boils at the thought of Summerhill.

"You don't have to look at me like that." Tyler says finally, after I've been dead silent for the last few minutes.

I look at her head on, meeting her dark, swirling eyes. She's still Tyler. She's still the same girl I've spent hours upon hours with for the last three months. She's still the same girl that showed me exactly what I really am.

She's still the only person that knows me for what I can do.

She's still the only person who's ever seen me for what I really am.

But she isn't... alive.

Tyler is *dead.*

No- not dead.

Tyler was *murdered.*

She was burned like witches back in the day.

She was murdered.

The people of Summerhill fucking killed her.

I force myself to hold her gaze, and she leans forward, her tears slowly halting.

She steps closer, close enough to touch me. "I'm still me." She whispers, looking directly at my mouth. Her lips are just mere inches from my own, and I can still taste the cinnamon from her tongue, can still the roses on her skin, her fingers.

Can still see that beautiful, sensual mouth as she bites her lip. That beautiful mouth that I was moments away from knowing exactly what it was capable of.

I swallow hard, pushing thoughts of her mouth away, and will my pulse to calm down. This isn't the worst thing that's happened since moving here, but it definitely is the craziest.

I wonder if Tyler can tell how hard I'm shaking.

"You're still you, yeah. But you're not…. You aren't….."

"Alive?" She finishes for me.

My voice is barely a rasp. "How is it... possible?" I choke out.

Tyler looks away. If she's uncomfortable talking about her death, she doesn't show it. Her voice stays measured and calm, silky like I'm used to.

"Honestly? After Jonathan lit the fire, I don't remember... A lot. The gate was there, and I think... I don't know. I was seeing all sorts of shit that night. But everything kind of went dark for a long time after he lit the fire. I remember waking up and everyone was gone, and realizing that time had definitely passed. The trees looked different, and the air felt different, but I wasn't burnt at all. I wasn't even hurt. I didn't have a single scratch on me."

Tyler looks me dead on. "I think something kept me here. I don't know what- there's so many stories tied to these woods, I can barely keep track. I just remember waking up in that clearing... and I couldn't leave. Time kept moving forward, and I couldn't go anywhere. Every time I try to this day, I wind back up in the South Gate woods."

I can't breathe. "It's like you're tied to the South Gate."

"Exactly like I'm tied to the South Gate."

I take a deep, long breath, forcing myself to get air in. Tyler died.
No. Tyler was fucking *murdered.*

The Van Devons- No.

The people of *Summerhill* murdered her.

Tyler is not alive. Tyler is *fucking. Dead.*

Tyler is a ghost.

I almost laugh, because the thought of basically having sex with a ghost in the woods is so crazy and unbelievable that I almost want to cry.

But my hysterical laughter fades in my throat as I really think about it. She isn't a ghost, then. She can't be, because she kissed me. She had her hands on me, her mouth on me. I touched her, and you can't touch ghosts. Right?

I voice my next thought before I can think it through.

"So you're not a ghost?"

Tyler laughs. "You tell me, Niamh. I've been asking myself that for fifty years."

"But you still look eighteen."

"Good observation."

I give her a pointed look, and she laughs again. The tight feeling in my chest starts to ease. At least she isn't sad anymore.

My inner voice, still seething with jealousy, pipes up:

At least she isn't talking about Morgan anymore.

I shake it away, and then another thought crosses my head quickly.

"Tyler," I say with a sudden burst of realization. "What if whatever took Marlo is what kept you alive that night?"

I tell her the things I've been seeing and hearing, from the thing that sounded like Miles the night we saw the gate, to the enormous black goat. The thing that, apparently, can look and sound different depending on what it wants to appear as.

Tyler considers this. "I thought I was seeing things the night I died… but yeah, I saw a black goat. I think I saw Abigail Summers, too."

She swallows, her deep eyes widening slightly. "Their eyes didn't look right, though." She whispers to me.

The white, too-big eyes. Holy shit.

I look at Tyler, connecting the dots one by one. I know I'm right.

"What if all the people who've gone missing in the South Gate woods never actually went missing? What if whatever it is is *taking* them?"

I talk faster, starting to pace despite myself. "What if it's a demon, or some sort of entity, and it needs to feed? What if it's tied to the gate? Or maybe it came from the gate? Maybe people don't just walk through it- maybe it pulls them through it?"

Tyler exhales deeply, her voice still every bit as measured and calm. "If that's true, then it's definitely getting stronger."

"Why do you say that?"

"Think about it. It's been taking people since the sixteen hundreds, maybe even before that. If it took me that night... And now it just took two more when your friends went missing... I don't know, Niamh. It sounds to me like it's trying to build up to something."

She pauses, thinking. "Or that it wants something else, and it's just using Marlo as bait."

"Like what?"

Tyler looks me dead on, and what she says raises the hair on my arms instantly. "You, Niamh. Think about it. You're made of magic. You're powerful as hell, and it tried to get to you as soon as you moved here. You saw the gate, and now it took your friend. What if it wants you?"

I think about the three kids that went missing when my dad was little. Three little girls, he said, when I asked him.

I think about Miles.

I think about Abigail Summers, of Tyler, and of Marlo.

"It likes little girls." I whisper, my voice barely audible.

Tyler just stares at me while I process.

But then I shake my head, refusing to let this overwhelm me. "Well. Regardless, Marlo isn't gone. I refuse to accept that."

And I mean it. It had the others, but it can't have Marlo. It can't have my friends.

Tyler just cocks her head at me, as if trying not to illuminate what I know might already be true.

Marlo might already be gone.

"If you're right, it's only going to bait you." She says to me, running a hand through her long, dark hair. It pools over her shoulder, falling over her chest, and I have to look away.
She's heartbroken. She's still pining over a fifty-year lost love, and she doesn't need me to make her feel shitty right now, or worse, confuse her feelings. I don't need to get in the way of that.

Clearly, I'll never be Morgan.

I look around us in the dark, searching the spaces between the closely-knit pine trees. I notice the way the darkness seeps in, pooling at our feet, recalling the way the light can never penetrate through the branches anywhere in the South Gate.
If there was ever a place for something to exist in our world that was not, and had maybe never been from our world at all,

it was here.

It was in the South Gate woods,

it was in Summerhill.

Summerhill, Maine.

Cape Summerhill, shrouded in fog and darkness and rain, hidden amidst the cold Atlantic, where the harbor, the sea, and the forest intermingled.

Cape Summerhill, surrounded by hundreds upon hundreds of acres of wood, full of uncharted darkness and paths that mislead amongst the great pine trees.

Cape Summerhill, where, no matter where you go in the forest, you always wind up at the same spot.

Cape Summerhill, where hundreds of years ago, a gate appeared in the middle of the woods, and took the little girl that walked through it.

Cape Summerhill, where only fifty years ago, the residents burned a witch at the stake.

I look at Tyler, already sure of my decision. Despite how fucking terrified I am, despite the darkness and feeling of the air stilling around us,

as if it hears us

as if whatever is somewhere in the woods *right now* is listening to our conversation, and giggling at the thought of us thinking we know what it is.

Giggling at the thought of us trying to outsmart it.

I square my shoulders. I'd do this for Marlo, I'd do this for Zeke. I'd definitely do it for Tyler. I'd do it for my friends, because I love them.

Even if they wouldn't do it for me, I love them.

My inner voice cackles. *Hopefully love doesn't get you killed like it did Tyler,* it says. I tell it to shut the fuck up.

"Then we won't let it." I say to Tyler. She whips her head around sharply, her blue eyes flashing in the dark.

"We're both made of magic. We're capable. We're strong. We're powerful. We could combine our magic… We could…"

I think of everything she taught me, all her journal entries, stuffed to the brim with information and notes she's collected over the years. I think of black candles, black ribbon. I think of the page she'd shown me weeks ago on bindings, on banishings. Something about taking a picture of the one you wished to banish, rolling it up with black ribbon and banishing salt, then burning it and burying the remains.

"We could do a banishing spell. We could banish it from the South Gate woods and send it back to wherever it came from before it takes anyone else."

Before it tries to take me, I think.

Tyler's mouth opens and closes. "Niamh…" She says quietly.

"No."

I shake my head at her protests and point south, farther south. Farther into the darkness that's beginning to pool at our feet, deep splotches and scribbles of pure shadow beginning to cover my sk8-his.

"We need to move, Niamh." Tyler says cautiously.

"Yeah, we do, and we are. Because we're going to find the fucking gate, and we're going to stop this."

I grab her cold,

dead

hand, and pull her towards the treeline.

Her hand that was just ins-

Stop it, Niamh, I scold myself. Stop thinking about it. She wants Morgan, not you. Get over it.

I pull her off of the path, and into the dark of the South Gate woods.

To my surprise, Tyler doesn't pull away. If anything, her grip in mine tightens, and her magic dances over my fingertips, gold, warm light merging with my own violent, fiery orange.

A faint glow in my chest starts to grow, spreading up and out to my fingers right as a faint, orange light spreads in front of us, lending more vision in the dark.

"Nice. Witch-light." Tyler whispers. "Can you see better now?"

"Yeah."

She looks at me sideways and smiles, and I try to ignore what it's doing to my heart.

Shoving my feelings down, I smile back at her, and hand in hand we head deeper into the South Gate woods.

CHAPTER THIRTY FIVE

The thing in the woods picked at its teeth, watching from a nook high up in a great pine tree.

Much too high for a human to have climbed.

It liked its newest skin: this short, small teenage girl with the long auburn hair and strong body. She was athletic and stout with strong muscles, and she smelled of the ocean. It liked that strands of her fiery hair were streaked with blonde from the sun, from countless hours spent in the sea.

But what it liked most were her eyes.

Piercing, bright aqua, eyes that were so bright and so vivid, the whorls of seafoam green and turquoise alive and full of life.

It liked her eyes the best, because this time when it tried on the skin of Marlo Torah, it actually got her eyes right.

Gone were the days of milky white pupils that did not possess the ability to blink.

Unfortunately, it still couldn't quite get the teeth right. The thing that was wearing Marlo Torah's skin got her eyes right, no doubt about that.

But Marlo Torah currently had far too many teeth. Three rows, to be precise, and all needle-thin.

The thing that mostly looked like Marlo Torah smiled to itself. It wasn't worried. The teeth it would get eventually. It was the eyes that were always the problem. It simply couldn't go out in this world with its normal white, unblinking eyes- it would be too much of a dead giveaway that it was not human.

But now, after getting Marlo Torah's aqua eyes right, it knew.

It was nearly strong enough to leave these woods.

The thing that looked like Marlo Torah shrieked into the trees, positively delighted.

Then it shifted into black ink, skittering down the tree and pooling on the ground in a clump. The second it touched the forest floor, darkness began to spread over the ground like fog, spreading well into the South Gate woods.

It lay on its belly on the ground in its shadow form: a pair of colorless, milky eyes amidst a scribble of darkness.

It sighed to itself. How it missed having Marlo's human eyes.

But it would have to wait, because it could hear people coming.

It could smell faint, rising fear, hidden beneath determination and bravery.

It could taste their intentions on its thick, darting tongue-

Oh, it chittered to itself, crawling over the ground. How exciting.

Somebody was in the woods, looking for the gate.

The thing on the ground screamed, a loud, excited scream.

It was the two girls that carried gifts in their blood, the ones that held innate, magical abilities within their veins.

Two little girls,

two little witches.

Two little creatures of magic and power.

Two girls.

It *loved* the taste of little girls.

One was the girl that it had kept alive, tied to the woods just like it was, just like the gate was.

Tyler. Tyler Lane, that was her name.

The other was the girl that escaped with the ginger-haired boy.

Niamh.

Yes, that was her name. It knew her name well.

And they were looking for it, together, Tyler and Niamh.

The scribble of darkness slithered across the ground, chittering and screaming oh so *elatedly.*

It tasted their fear the closer they got to where it was hiding.

Darkness trailed them as the gate, somewhere nearby in the trees stood alone, waiting.

Waiting, sensing their presence.

Waiting, and pulling them closer to it.

Lulling them, calling to them.

It was just as hungry as the chittering, shadow thing was.

How exciting, it thought to itself as it tasted on their fear. They really believed that they could send it back to where it came from.

They thought, in their excited, zealous revelations about the gate, that they could best it.

They thought that maybe, just maybe, they could even *kill* it.

The jerky, shapeless scribble of darkness laughed into the pitch-black darkness, sending its laughter throughout the trees so that they may hear it.

It laughed in its natural voice: a smooth, old one.

Silly, foolish girls. You cannot kill something that was never alive in the first place.

It slithers into the dark heading farther south, heading closer to where the gate stands.

When it reaches the clearing, it shifts back into the skin of Marlo Torah once more.

The gate stands tall in front of it, the air around it all at once shimmering, and yet still, void of movement.

Still and dead, because air cannot truly exist here, this close to the gate.

Still and dead, because the gate

eats

all living things.

Where living, breathing things go when they walk through the gate, it has no idea. All it knows is that the gate was here before it, and the gate has a mind of its own.

Maybe those people die.

Maybe they get sent somewhere Else.

Maybe, it thinks, they get sent somewhere dark,

somewhere old.

The thing that looks like Marlo Torah smiles to itself, smoothing her auburn hair down. It likes her dress, too. Even though it looks so very out of place in the clearing- all dressed up, still in her clothes from the party- it likes her dress.

It likes her human skin, so supple and soft.

It hasn't worn a *fresh* human skin since the boy, Miles, almost nine years ago now. It will need to remember the basics that humans do when it sees Tyler and Niamh, and while it wears Marlo Torah at all.

Things like blinking, like breathing in and out.
Things like holding eye contact, like not standing so stiff.

It will need to act human when Tyler and Niamh arrive, because it needs them to believe that it is really Marlo Torah they are seeing.

How else will it get Niamh to walk through the gate?
It has tasted Niamh's fear:

She wants to save her friend.
So it would let her.

So strong is her loyalty to her friends that it knows that if she believed the only way to save Marlo Torah was to walk through the gate,

Niamh would do it.

It shivers in delight, screaming again. If it could have Niamh MacKenna...

If it could just

                                    taste

    her

It would be *free,* maybe, at last.

Free to explore the rest of their world,

free to find more

                        delectable

little girls.

Tyler Lane it already owned. Tyler Lane was already its plaything, and had been for the last fifty years. It kept her alive because she asked it to. It kept her alive because it had *begged* her to.

Please, she had called out that night.

She had called out, begging something to save her, chanting a spell that was much bigger than her.

Begging for something to hear her,

and then, something had.
Please don't let me die, she'd begged.

That angry, brash girl had been reduced to begging.

It wasn't the thing in the woods' fault that Tyler Lane had no idea what she'd let save her that night.

And now, it owned her life, it owned her body.

And, it realized joyfully, screaming into the darkness a third time, if Marlo Torah's facade failed, Tyler Lane would be the key in getting Niamh instead.

If saving her friend- saving the thing that *looked* like Marlo Torah but was not at all really her- was not enough to convince Niamh MacKenna to walk through the gate, then Tyler Lane would be.

Love and lust were very, very powerful tools. It knew this by observing Tyler Lane and the other girl all those years ago. It had been watching Tyler Lane- that powerful, powerful girl-for a long, long time.

And she had made it very, very hungry for just a little

taste.

It was Tyler who had taught it that you could get people to do the most absurd things if you offered even a taste of the two. Much in the way magic tasted like love, like lust,

when the two intertwined, they were the most powerful forces on this planet.

The thing that currently looked like Marlo Torah knew this, because it had watched as Tyler Lane kissed Niamh earlier. It had seen the look in Niamh's eyes as Tyler had pushed her against the tree, had seen the way her body woke up, had seen the exact moment that she became completely and fully Tyler's.

It had seen the way Niamh looked at Tyler in general, like she was the only person who truly saw her.

Niamh MacKenna was a fool.

Tyler Lane would never truly want her in the way Niamh wanted her to.

And this fact alone would be the key in getting Niamh MacKenna to walk through the gate.

It had seen the way Tyler Lane had intertwined their magic as they kissed, giving Niamh just a taste.

It had seen her make Niamh *hers* more than Niamh even realized.

Love was strength. Lust was power. Holding the two over somebody's head made you invincible, and made them yours whether they knew it or not.

Love and lust combined were nearly as powerful as innate magic, and Tyler Lane had barely given Niamh a taste of the two. Just a taste, because she would never want Niamh the way she wanted the other girl from all those years ago.

And a taste had been enough for Niamh.

Yes, it thought to itself. Niamh MacKenna would be its next meal. If Marlo Torah failed, it would simply wear Tyler Lane again like it had that night fifty years ago.

And then it would

feed.

CHAPTER THIRTY SIX

NIAMH

December 7, 2023

The darkness envelops us like a second skin the farther south we head. Tyler's hand in my own tethers me, though, and amidst the fear of what we might find, I can't get the image of what happened less than two hours ago out of my head.

We walk in steady, tense silence, neither one of us talking. Whether it's from fear of what we're about to try and do or something else, I can't tell- all I know is that I keep stealing glances at her out of the corner of my eye, watching how she walks with her chin up, as if defiant. Watching the way her dark hair spills over one shoulder, the way her pulse flutters in her exposed, pale neck. Watching the way that even in the darkness of the woods, I can see Tyler's face crystal clear: that perfect, sharp jawline dotted with those crescent scars, her sensual, always-smirking mouth, her pale, freckled face, and those intense, pulling blue eyes that always see right through me.

Tyler is fucking beautiful.

I swallow hard, looking back at the ground. I still can't get what *almost* happened an hour ago now out of my mind. The mental image of Tyler dropping to her knees in front of me… Her obnoxious, smirking mouth on my thighs… The way my heart short circuited and stopped at her words:

Sit down, Niamh.

I swallow harder and roll my shoulders back. Stop it, Niamh. I try to force myself to stop thinking about her mouth, to stop thinking about how her hand had felt…

Niamh. Focus. Think about… Morgan. Think about Morgan, Niamh.

So I do, and it douses my lust instantly.

Morgan Van Devon. Perfect, beautiful Morgan, with her caramel-colored hair that parted to one side naturally. Perfect, beautiful Morgan and her deep, warm-honey eyes. Perfect, beautiful Morgan that always smelled like almonds and honey. Perfect, beautiful Morgan with her perfect, graceful body, her perfect, beautiful mouth that probably kissed Tyler like she couldn't ever get enough of her. Perfect, beautiful Morgan with her little rose tattoo on her hip, her dozens of necklaces and rings she liked to wear.

Tyler had told me it all- and the way she'd talked about Morgan had left no doubt in my mind that she was still very, very much in love with her.

I look over at Tyler again, Tyler who still hasn't let go of my hand.

Fifty years ago. *Fifty* fucking years ago she was madly, deeply in love with someone. *Fifty.* Years Ago. Morgan would be in her late sixties by now, and Tyler was forever eighteen- and yet she still loved her just as much.

She loved Morgan enough to still feel deep, gut-wrenching guilt over kissing another girl.

Me.
As much as I want to be mad at Tyler, I'm not. I'm not mad at all.
I'm jealous.

I'm jealous of this Morgan girl, because the thought of Tyler with someone else…. It makes my chest tight, and I fucking hate it. So Morgan was her first love or whatever. She was *fifty* years ago. She was a lifetime ago.

I hate that I'm so in my head, hate that I feel petty and selfish and jealous. I was never like that back home. The old Niamh didn't care enough to be jealous or petty. Then again, I never knew someone like Tyler back home.
I never had someone who gets me like no one else does, or ever will.

The mere thought of this Morgan girl constricts my chest so tightly that it almost hurts to breathe, hurts to have Tyler's hand in my own, but her heart so very, very far away.

I had her goddamn tongue in my mouth an hour ago.

I have her hand in my own right this very second.

But I don't have her heart.

What are you trying to get at, Niamh? My inner voice whispers to me. And even though we're walking towards what could very well be a demon, or a monster or something...

My throat and my heart constrict as I answer my own question, just like Tyler always tells me that I'm capable of doing.

I might never have Tyler's heart, so long as Morgan still has hers.

But she had mine the second she saw me start that first fire that day on the path.

The second Tyler had looked at me with elation, with glee at what I could do, at what I really was.

I don't love her. I know that.

But I'm tied to her.

My soul burns in similarity to her own. We are one and the same, and magic with her... I know I will never find something like that anywhere else. I'll never find *her* in anyone else.

But, I think savagely, I'm not perfect, beautiful *Morgan.* I'm Niamh.

I want to shake Tyler, want to yell in her face, into those perfect, alluring eyes. *I'M RIGHT HERE.*

I'm not Morgan, but I'm *Niamh.* I'm not your fated love or whatever from fifty years ago, but I'm *Niamh,* and I'm here *NOW.* I'm right here, and I'm just like you.

"What are you thinking right now, Niamh?"

Tyler's quiet, silky voice echoes through the trees, penetrating deep in my chest, causing my pulse to race. I look over at her right as the trees start to thin out.

My pulse jacks up again, and this time not because of Tyler. This time, it's purely from fear. If the trees are thinning out... are we about to walk right into that clearing?

But my fear subsides as the trees don't lead anywhere. They get thinner and farther between each other, but there's no clearing. The air still feels normal, and I can't smell anything dead.

In fact, all I can smell all around me is roses and cinnamon. Still her.

Still fucking Tyler.

"Don't read my thoughts, please. Boundaries." I say to her, trying to coat my jealousy and pitiful, selfish thoughts in sarcasm.

Tyler looks me right in the eyes as we keep walking, her gaze deep and searching, but gently. "I wasn't going to. I was just curious. You're oddly quiet."

"Oh, am I? My bad, there's just so much on my mind right now. Where do you want me to start? With my missing friend? With waking up naked next to a guy that I thought I knew? With fighting with literally *every one of my friends I have?* With the evil demon thing we're about to purposely go find right now? With the fact that there's a fucking gigantic gate that just pops up in the woods at random and *eats people?* Or, get this, the girl that I've been spending all my time with is actually dead? Or even better, that same girl tries to fuck me in the woods, but is actually hung up on her ex from *fifty fucking years ago?*"

It all spills out. I wish I could say I felt bad, but I don't. My feelings are hurt.
We keep walking in silence for a minute, but Tyler withdraws her hand from my own.
My heart caves in on itself. Fuck, fuck, fuck.

"First off, I'm not hung up on her, Niamh." She says quietly, dodging a fallen tree.

I almost stop walking, and laugh tonelessly instead. "Seriously? That's what you chose to respond to? Not the rest?"

I open my mouth to say something else just as biting when she throws her arm out quickly in front of me and yells for me to stop, nearly knocking the wind out of my chest.

I almost walked off the edge of a cliff.

Somehow, without either of us noticing, we ended up outside of the woods. Properly outside, out of the grim darkness of the South Gate woods and into the open air, at the sea.

Well, not exactly the sea. We're at a foggy, gray cliff edge *overlooking* the sea- somehow, without noticing, we exited the South Gate woods and ended up at a dead end right over a cliff- a sheer, very tall one at that.

I look over the edge, peering down at the ocean. The spot reminds me of Santa Cruz a bit- whenever we'd visit Aine, she would take us up the coast to a little bakery that sat on the side of the highway. On one side were tall, rolling hills, and fields of sunflowers and pumpkins. On the other, just across the highway were miles of trees atop the cliff, the sharky, freezing surf below it.

Looking over the edge now, I can just make out a decent looking right that breaks almost touching the cliff- a right that looks just as cold as Santa Cruz water, and just as sharky. It looks deadly, right now.

A fall from this height would kill you the second you hit the water.

Staring mindlessly at the surf below, I wonder with a jolt if we somehow ended up at East Cliff, the spot where Zeke and Marlo's friends like to surf. But that can't be possible, because we just came out of the South Gate woods. Emphasis on *South*. I can't even comment on how this is possible, because at this point nothing about Summerhill is surprising to me anymore.

Tyler lets out a shaky exhale, staring out at the gray, churning ocean with her arms folded across her chest. The thick, dense fog hangs low in the air, enveloping the cliff edge, the grass, and the sky all in hues of gray, which just makes her seem even more pale, even more like some forest faerie or sprite than a girl. It clings to her, shrouding her partially in a thick, wet mist like a ghost.

Now she really looks more like a ghost than a girl.

Tyler walks over to the very edge and sits down precariously, swinging her legs over the edge. Every instinct in me screams to pull her back, to tell her to get away. But my feelings are hurt right now, so I bite my tongue.

Besides, she's already dead. If she fell, she'd probably just end up back in the woods anyways.

Fucker.

"I'm not hung up on her, Niamh." She repeats quietly without looking at me, just staring down at the sea.

SUMMERHILL

My anger and my wounded heart rear their ugly, ugly heads. I might not stoop to begging for her affection or her reciprocated feelings, but I'm sure as shit not immune to feeling sorry for myself.

I stand behind her, also staring out at the ocean. My arms stay crossed over my giant hoodie, my dickies are soaked from the mist, my sk8-his are trashed, and my hair hangs in limp, unruly curls over my shoulders, everything weighed down by the fog. I'm uncomfortable, wet, and angry. And jealous. Very, very jealous.

"It's cool, Tyler. Love is gnarly, I'm sure. Even if it was fifty years ago. I get it."

And then she's up so quick and grabbing my arm so tightly that I'm surprised I even have the time to grow a little bit afraid.

"No, you *don't* get it, Niamh. I will *never* fall in love like that again."

Her face is seething, every freckle standing out starkly against her bright, flushed face. Her eyes are black holes, and the pure anger punctuating her every word has me recoiling from her close proximity to my own. The bite in her words are sharp enough that they could draw blood. I almost want to look down and see if her nails digging into my arm pierced through my hoodie.
It wouldn't be the first time her words garnered a physical reaction in me.

Instead, I breathe shakily and force myself to meet her eyes.

Those deep, captivating blue eyes that I lose myself in every single day I look at her are bottomless right now, twin orbs that eat up the light.

No emotion lies in them right now other than pure, undiluted rage. And she isn't done.

"Ever again."

Tyler releases me and begins to pace the cliff edge, her fists in tight little balls. I know without having to look that her nails are piercing into her palms, and she's welcoming the pain.

Anger is a bitch, but sadness is worse. I know I'd rather be angry at her than sad.

She whips around after a second and gives me a look that terrifies me with its intensity.

"You *don't* get it. Love made me fucking *blind.*" She hisses. "It made me *weak.* Love got me fucking *killed,* Niamh! And all I did wrong was love a girl that I couldn't ever really have."

She laughs without humor, lost in memories. "We never could have been together, and yet somehow... I thought we could. I thought what we had would beat the odds. You don't get it: it was *transcendent,* Niamh. You think magic feels good? You think doing magic makes you feel all types of ways? Try really, truly being in love. *Real* love. I bent over *backwards*. I was a whole different person. I would've-"

Then she pauses, her hand to her mouth.

One sob.

She allows herself one horrible, heaving sob.

Just one, like if she allows herself to cave, she might never recover.

Tyler's thin, willowy body heaves again, the weight of another full-bodied, gut-wrenching sob coursing through her.

Despite kind of hating Morgan, my heart splinters in two watching her break.

Tyler sobs a third time, this time wailing through her hand.

Like her soul is trying to exit her body, like every thought about Morgan is causing her to shatter into pieces.

"I would've done anything for her." She chokes out, her voice thick with tears. "I would've-"

She stops and pauses again, breathing shakily. When she regains control, she braces both her hands on her knees, taking slow, even breaths. I can tell by the obvious tremor in those breaths that it's taking all of her willpower, every fiber of her being not to hyperventilate, not to give in to this heartbreak.

It's more than heartbreak, I realize. This is grief, in its rawest form.

Tyler looks at me, her eyes swimming with unshed tears, broken beyond repair.

One thought crosses my mind before I hear what she's saying to me:

I want someone to love me *that much.*

She's right- I *don't* get it. I don't get how she can still love someone all these years later just as much as she did back then, so much so that the grief of losing them is still just as fresh as if it happened yesterday. I don't get how she loves Morgan so much that the thought of being without her still tears her up inside.

I guess a love like that transcends time.

"You think you get it, Niamh? I don't think you do. What Morgan and I had…. It was more than every single star in the sky, Niamh. It transcended time itself. It could've crossed other worlds. It was like…."

She trails off for a second, looking for the words.

"It was like I was meant to meet her. Like meeting her was *it,* that was what I'd been looking for. Like being hers, and her being mine was what I was meant to have in this life. My reason."

A single tear slides down her cheek, her sapphire eyes finally spilling over. "I would've done *anything* for her. I would've sold the moon. Grabbed a star. Laid my life down. She was it, Niamh. She was my reason."

I don't have any words left in my mouth.

"You think you've done magic, Niamh, but that's real magic. That's where I draw all my power from. Thinking about her.... Red candles don't mean shit. Dried rose petals and catnip and bay leaf wishes blown into the wind don't mean shit. The full moon can fuck right off. None of that means anything without a source, without a muse. Morgan was mine."

The anger and the rage that was so prevalent just moments ago is gone. All that remains on her face now is a deep well of hurt and of grief.
A well so deep and so prominent that I genuinely wonder if the ocean has ever breached a depth greater than she.

A well so deep that I wonder if whatever Tyler and Morgan had was deeper than the sea itself.

Tyler's eyes betray her innermost thoughts, and right now, I'm surprised she's choosing to look at me.
I'm surprised she's showing me this much of her. She's been vague and guarded since the day I met her, biting my head off whenever I asked how she was doing.

Now I know why.

But then she stands, sniffing her tears away, and tucks her hair behind her ears. Composing herself.

Then she's back to pacing the cliff, as if she didn't just shatter into a million pieces.

"But that's that." She says, her voice clipped, still raw with her sobs. "Never again. I've had fifty years to think about this, Niamh. Fifty fucking years, and not a single day has gone by where I don't think about her. I will *never* give someone that kind of hold on me ever again, that kind of grip on me. Never, so long as I live."

My heart caves and folds in on itself, the words trying to roll off my tongue all sounding wrong. I want to try for some semblance of hope, of positivity, even though I know there's no point.

Despite everything she's saying, there's a little part of me that still wants her to see that *I'm* here. Her and I don't have any sort of love like that, and maybe we never will. But we have a similarity, a partnership. We have an understanding no one else ever will- sort of an I-see-you, you-see-me thing. I revel in it, because it gives *me* power.

And I know it gives her power, too.

I give her something, at least.

I'm right here, in the flesh,

and I want her to see me.

So I aim for a positive and cheerful tone, trying to at least sound a little upbeat. "Well, never say *never.* Not everyone is Mor-"

"Do not say her fucking *name."* She hisses at me, angry once again. Yikes. Okay. Wrong thing to say.

I shrink away from her, then cringe at myself for doing it. Tyler can be really fucking intense when she wants to be. There isn't a doubt in my mind that she'd hurt me if I keep pushing her. Maybe not intentionally, but still.

So I don't.

"See this?"

She mimes turning a door knob, locking it shut, then twisting her fingers in empty air over her heart.

Then she steps over to the cliff's edge, again closer than I find comfortable or safe. My heart in my throat, I watch as she rears her thin, lanky arm back, and tosses the invisible key with all her might.

Tyler looks over the edge, her eyes tracking the imaginary key as it falls to the churning, fog-covered sea below.

"Never again." She quips lightly, her voice all roses and silk again, lilting and lazy. "It's gone now, sealed by a watery tomb. The fucking ocean can have it. I will *never* give another human being that much of me again."

She trails off again, and I'm still a little afraid because I can't tell if she's going to burst into the kind of tears that might make *me* cry, or threaten me within an inch of my life. She goes for neither option, thankfully.

"It's just..." She tries again. "The things Morgan made me feel are things I can never put myself through again. That kind of love got me killed. And maybe... Maybe I wasn't strong enough to handle it. Maybe it was too big, too powerful. Too beautiful. We did magic together, you know. I taught her some things. One time, on our anniversary, we did this spell together, and all we had was a pink candle and some paper. And the way she looked at me... Like she fucking *needed* me..."

Tyler stops, taking a deep, steady breath, as if catching herself. "I never should have done magic with her. It made me weak. It deepened our love, it deepened what was already there. And that depth... Maybe I was never meant to have all of that inside me. I'm only human. As much as I like to think otherwise,"

Her voice cracks, along with my heart.

"I'm not invincible, clearly. When it came down to it, I cracked under pressure. My magic didn't even work the night I died, and I have no idea why. All I could think about that night was how much I loved her."

Tyler's voice cracks again, and I feel my own traitorous eyes start to water just watching her.

"Maybe it was just too much for my human heart to take." She finishes. She tries to speak again, but her voice is too clogged with emotion.

Tyler swallows, then tries again. And again. Then a third time.

"All I know is that what I had with her I can never have again with anyone. Because loving Morgan might've killed me, but it didn't break me. I'm still here, I'm still alive, somehow. But loving someone like that a second time would *actually* break me. I think I can only live through that kind of pain one time, as a lesson. A lesson to never do it again."

I don't answer her, because if I look at her, *I* might break right now.

Instead, I stare down at the churning ocean trying to swallow the lump in my throat, trying to swallow my jealousy and my own broken heart.

I wonder if she'll ever go back and dive for her lost key, if she'll ever eat her words and change her mind.

Or, if someone else might try one day.

Someone being me.

CHAPTER THIRTY SEVEN

NIAMH

December 7, 2023

I t feels too easy.

After composing herself and refusing to talk about it anymore, Tyler promptly heads back into the South Gate woods behind us. I watch her sullenly from the cliff edge with my arms still crossed, my heart still on the floor as the darkness begins to swallow her until I realize she's expecting me to follow her.

I shove my thoughts out of the land of self-pity as I follow her back into the woods, hissing at myself to snap out of it. So what if she had some astronomical fucking love? So what if she's vowed to never love anyone that much ever again? So what if this Morgan girl seems to be utterly, completely irreplaceable? I shouldn't give a fuck. Despite what she said, Tyler is *clearly* still hung up on Morgan.

So I shouldn't waste my time. She's my friend, and we're here to find Marlo and maybe send whatever this fucking thing is back to where it came from.

I manage to focus as we get back on the path, the thought of what we're attempting to find right now enough to douse my jealousy for the moment. Tyler walks a few paces in front of me, and I lift my chin, square my shoulders, composing myself. It doesn't even matter how much she hurt my feelings- if I lose her in the darkness of the South Gate woods right now, there's no doubt in my mind that we will not find each other again.

She doesn't say anything as we walk in silence, and I don't offer anything up. My feelings are temperamental right now, and so are hers. Clearly I'm not what she wants or needs. I'm not *Morgan.*

For fucks sake, Niamh. *Marlo.* Focus. Finding Marlo is what's important right now.

I'm about to break the tense silence and ask Tyler where exactly she thinks we should be heading to try and find the clearing again, but then the darkness lifts slightly, and besides being able to see Tyler clearer than I have since we entered the woods, it's light enough for me to see that we didn't find the clearing.

We've been in it this whole time.

I turn around in a circle, and it's exactly the same as it was the night Zeke and I were here. The path spit us out into the clearing perfectly: a wide, ominous ring of pine trees, the sky above us dark as pitch and without stars, despite it being the afternoon, and wide, open spaces between each towering pine tree.

Enough space for shadows to skitter and crawl.

The only difference is there's no gate here, this time.

This feels way, way too quick. We got back on the path five minutes ago. This feels easy.

Too easy.

I whip my head around, looking back at the tracks on the muddy path from my sk8-his.

My footprints go in circles.

We've been walking in fucking *circles* in the dark since we left the cliff. The path did exactly what it does best: it misled us.

"What the *fuck.*" I say aloud. Even Tyler has a look of incredulity on her face. "Where's the fucking gate?" I hiss at her, lowering my voice instinctively.

"Shut up, Niamh."

Tyler's sharp, pale face has gone still, and for once, I listen to her.

"This….." She trails off, then rests wide, uneasy blue eyes on me. Her eyes say exactly what I'm thinking, once again confirming what I know: she and I are one and the same. Two twin flames.

"This feels too easy, doesn't it?" She whispers to me.

I can only nod. There's no gate, but we definitely found the clearing…

Or maybe, my inner voice says, *the clearing wanted you to find it.*

The thought doesn't reassure me in the slightest.

A ring of thick, towering pine trees amidst the craggy dirt, clustered thinly together, and no moonlight whatsoever. The sky is black, like something plucked the stars out one by one. The hill in front of us is a steep, steep incline, more trees and darkness seeming to crawl down it.

Suddenly tasting panic on my tongue, I realize that if we had to run, there would be nowhere to go. If we tried to go directly forward, the incline of the hill would slow us down. If we turned around, we'd reach the cliff. If we went left or right, we'd risk running directly back into the South Gate woods.

Directly back into that *thing's* territory.

There's nowhere for us to run- and it is as that thought crosses my head that I hear it. A faint, weak cry, like a wounded animal. Like somebody- or something- is hurt.

Tyler whips around to face me, her eyes wide and curious. Not afraid, necessarily- but thinking. Planning.

"Did you hear that?" She whispers.

But I can barely hear her anymore, because I've already taken off running for the incline of trees at the edge of the clearing.

I recognize that voice- it's Marlo.

"MARLO!" I scream out into the darkness, not caring who hears me. "Marlo, where a-"

"JESUS!"

A tall, lanky body slams into mine mid-sprint, nearly knocking the wind out of me as we both crash to the forest floor in a heap. With my newfound vision, I blink dirt and fir needles out of my eyes, squinting at my assailant. The smell of sage, of clean sheets, and sea salt assaults my senses.

"Zeke?"

And in the dim lighting, I can see that it is him. Zeke sits up on his elbows, rubbing a hand over his face. It comes back dirty, and he scowls at me like I purposely knocked him over, yet the relief in his eyes at seeing me- not disgust, not anger, not even frustration-just sheer, stark *relief* warms my chest. That relief is brighter than I feel I deserve- he looks overjoyed. It's the way he used to look at me, like I hung the sun in the sky. Like I'm his favorite person, like I brighten his days just by walking in the room.

Zeke wipes his hands on his cargo pants, then re adjusts his black beanie on top of his mess of gingery curls. After he's sufficiently less disgruntled from our tumble, he proceeds to envelop me in a thick, suffocating hug. The words that come out of his mouth as he crushes me into his arms shock me slightly, but also fill my chest with a deep, calming warmth.

"Niamh, I'm sorry. I was a fucking asshole, and that wasn't my intention. I'm so fucking sorry." He whispers into my dirty, tangled blonde curls.

I don't even ask what he's sorry for, because it doesn't matter.

"I'm sorry too." I breathe out.
Because I am. I let him like the idea of me, and that was my fault. I led him on for months, letting him think I was still the same rebellious, carefree Niamh from before. I was dishonest with him. Trust is earned both ways, and I fucked with his colosally.

We sit there on the floor of the South Gate wrapped in each other, easily the tightest hug I think I've ever received in my life, even tighter than the way he used to hug me. Even with where we are, even with everything that's happened between us, it feels like I'm putting a piece of myself back together. We don't say a single word, just hug on the ground for a few minutes.

It's everything.

"How did you find the clearing again?" I finally ask into the crook of his armpit, my voice muffled.

Zeke releases me but doesn't move, as if he needs to be close to me, as if he's just as happy to see me as I am him.

And in that moment, one thought crosses my mind, quickly, and then vanishes like smoke: so what if he'll never get me like Tyler does?

He keeps coming back for me, and he keeps trying.

The voice in my head smiles at me like I'm naive. *Is that enough, though?* It asks, and I know my answer immediately.

No, it isn't.

Because he'll never be Tyler.

"We sent out a search party for Marlo, but everyone pussied out when we got what they felt was too deep into the South Gate woods, so I went by myself."

Zeke pulls his black JanSport off his shoulders and dumps the contents out on the forest floor. Among the snack wrappers and empty boxes of surf wax: a giant, heavy-duty flashlight, two plastic bottles of water, a pocket knife, and an entire bag of flavor-blasted Goldfish.

"Nice provisions." I snort at him. "You're a fucking idiot, you know that? Why would you just go by yourself?"

He just looks at me, those bright gold eyes shimmering as he stuffs his supplies back into his backpack. "She's my sister, Niamh. She'd do it for me."

He doesn't need to say what we both know is true. He'd do it for me, too.

"I think I just heard her." I whisper to him in the dark. Helping him to his feet, we stand together, staring up at the incline of trees in front of us.

"So did I. That's where I was running before I smashed into you. Sorry, by the way."

"I accept apologies in the form of custom boards."

Zeke snorts, but we both fall solemn as we strain to hear Marlo's voice again.

But then someone screams my name. But it isn't Marlo-

It's Tyler.

"Shit." I say, my heart in my throat as I sprint back towards the clearing. No, no, no. Please God, no. Not her.
Thoughts of Marlo exit my head completely as thoughts of Tyler override her.

I can hear Zeke close behind me as his heavy backpack slaps against his shirt. I didn't even wait for him.

"Who is that?" He asks, panting as his long legs catch up to my strides.

"My... friend. Tyler. We were looking for Marlo, too."

If he's bothered by the fact that the same Tyler from our phone call earlier is here, he doesn't say it.

The second we reach the other end of the clearing, I notice immediately that the air feels different. Thick and choking, but it's still now. Dead still, like the breeze was put on pause.

Completely dead.

The dead air is back.

I brace myself, waiting for the stench of animal carcass, of rot, of death to reach my nose, but nothing. Just still, oppressive air,

because the gate is here.

In the *maybe* five minutes after I ran into Zeke, distracted, the gate showed up.

I stare up at it with Zeke for a second before remembering Tyler screaming my name. I whip my head around in the dark and spot her instantly just to my right. Reaching her side, she seems fine at a glance. She's looking up at the gate too, her eyes wide and shocked.

"That's the Tyler you've been with?" Zeke exclaims. She just looks at him sideways with a look on her face that tells me she doesn't even want to *try* and be nice to him. But it's not Tyler, or Zeke, or the goddamn gate that I'm concerned with anymore. Because on the dirt in front of her, looking dazed, but very much uninjured,

is Marlo.

"MARLO!"

Zeke launches himself at his sister, pulling her into one of his heavy, crushing Zeke-hugs. He kneels in the dirt, holding her coppery hair and tiny, petite body to his chest. After a beat, she returns the hug, but stiffly.

Marlo sits up, rubbing her eyes. She's still in that beautiful, form-fitting black dress from Kai's party, the fabric making her skin glitter in the night. Her white doc martens are scuffed and dirty and her shimmery tights are ripped at the knees, but otherwise her hair is perfect, not a single auburn strand out of place. Her face is blank as she looks at all of us without recognition, without blinking.

She's got to be in shock. Fuck.

Zeke pulls away from his twin, confusion and concern peppering his freckled, charming features as he grips her by the shoulders and bombards her with questions.

"What *happened* to you? Are you okay? Where's Kai?"

Tyler and I inch closer to each other instinctively as we stare down at her, staying quiet and observing while Zeke questions Marlo. As he hands her a bottle of water from his backpack, still asking her what happened, we both watch as Marlo takes it but doesn't open it.
She doesn't open her mouth at all.

With her beautiful, unblinking aqua eyes she just looks up, ignoring Zeke entirely, and instead looks right at Tyler and I.
I want to reassure her, want to tell her that it's okay and that we've been looking for her. I want to tell her that we never gave up on her, that we never once even thought about it.

But something dries the words in my throat.

A cold, creeping fear begins to build in their place, coming from a pit deep inside me- the same space where my magic exists, deep in my chest, somewhere alongside my heart.

And there, in that little spot, amidst my fiery gift, there is a small, quiet voice telling me to pay attention.

Zeke helps Marlo to her feet as she continues to look at us and ignore him. We all look at her in silence, the gate behind us watching.

The creeping feeling intensifies as I glance over my shoulder at the gate. I don't like this. I don't like the three of us just standing out here in the open. I don't like that Marlo won't even look at her brother, which is super unlike her, and I *really* don't like that the air is still and dead and the gate is here like it's just... waiting.

Finally, she talks, staring down at her shoes.

"I do not know. What happened." Marlo says quietly to the ground, enunciating each word with effort. "Kai is gone."

I catch Tyler's eye to my left, and Zeke catches mine. Both of them give me the same look in return: *what the fuck?*

Why is she talking like that?

But once again I answer my own question, which is something I'm just getting better and better at, apparently.

Marlo's talking like that because something isn't right.

My inner voice is trying to wake me up, trying to get me to see.

Something is very, very wrong.

Marlo looks back up, her freckled, shining face tan and rosy, her eyes bright. This time, it's me that she looks at directly, and combined with the gate standing tall behind her and her suddenly intense, serious gaze that is very, very unlike her, a feeling of deep unease begins spreading through my body like a virus.

The air crackles behind us, stilling harder, and Zeke snaps his head around to look at the gate. It's still there, towering high up into the trees, watching us.

Marlo coughs,

and then a deep, black fog-

no, not fog- shadows. Shadows. Pure, thick shadows, thicker than the fog that coats this entire cape begin to flood the clearing, spilling over the ground like mist. Thick, winding fog, starting to cover our shoes.

The little light that the clearing had starts to go out, mirroring the starless sky above us.

I know instantly that it's here. The thing... whatever it is.

It's here.

I look over at Tyler, trying to convey my rising, nauseating panic at what's happening, but she's looking at Marlo with a weird look on her face.

"Did you see the gate the night you went missing?" Tyler asks her, keeping her voice low. She speaks with her normal cadence: that lilting, lazy, careless tone, but I know her better than that by now. She knows something isn't right, too, but she'll play it cool until the end.

But then the smartest thought I've had in hours hits me, and I want to kick myself. If Tyler could just read Marlo's mind, that would help immensely.

When Marlo looks back at the ground, I nudge Tyler's shoulder. She looks over at me, and I tap two fingers lightly against my forehead, glancing back down at Marlo discreetly. Her eyes spark, and I know she gets it.

Marlo speaks again, still staring at the ground, at the darkness that's slowly covering her white docs. She seems completely oblivious to what's happening around us, or to the gate at all.

Completely oblivious to the slim, gentle fingers of Tyler Lane peering inside her head right now.

"Yes I did. See the gate."

Her speech is weirdly stilted. Stiff, awkward.

Zeke furrows his brows at his twin, taking a very small, barely noticeable step backwards. He knows, too.

Fuck.

"...Dude... Why are you acting like that?" He asks her, the shaky tone of his voice betraying his unease.

The air around us keeps stilling, and the smell of something rotting starts to slink into the clearing now too. Something sickly sweet, something that wiggles into my throat and makes me want to gag.

Death.

Marlo addresses her brother by staring at his shoes. With great, valiant effort, she speaks slightly less awkward- but it's still not how she normally speaks.

The sarcastic, quick-witted, hyper Marlo is just... simply not there.

"Acting like what? Brother?"

Zeke takes another step backwards, and this time Marlo notices it. She whips her head up, all five feet nothing of her seeming to stare right through Zeke, seeing right through his unease for what it really is: Fear.

Her aqua eyes flash, and her mouth presses into a thin line.

Zeke starts to breathe heavy, his tall, gangly chest rising and falling too fast. "Well, first off, you've never once called me *brother.* The fuck is that about? And you haven't blinked. Like at all."

Zeke looks at Tyler and I then, his voice trembling. "What the fuck is going on, guys?"

A sick, nauseating feeling like oil slides around my stomach, making my head spin. Oh, my god. Oh my god.
Oh my god. Oh my god. No. Oh my god oh my godohgod

Tyler takes a step closer to Marlo and looks down at her. She doesn't look afraid in the slightest- if she is, she's hiding it well in that lazy, careless gaze.

"Why won't you look at us when you speak?" She asks Marlo in her smooth, rose-petal voice. The voice that normally gets people to do what she wants. The voice that normally gets people to fold, to bow down, to listen. The voice she uses when she wants something.

I can taste hints of her magic in her words, cold, rogue ocean waves and roses, and when I see Zeke tilt his head out of the corner of my eye and sniff, I notice surprisingly that he can sense it too. Tyler's magic is that strong.

Marlo doesn't say a word, instead looking up at Tyler with an expression that I've never seen Marlo have before.

Malice.

That is sheer malice glinting in her aqua eyes right now, fully trained on Tyler.

Like the question angered her.

Marlo blinks once, twice, then a third time with great effort.

As if remembering that's a thing people do.

And then, very, very slowly, without answering Tyler, without breaking her eye contact, she starts to slowly, slowly back away.

Walking backwards, towards the gate.

Every step of her white docs crunches the dirt and leaves, echoing loudly throughout the silent, pitch-black clearing.

As she keeps walking backwards, Tyler, still maintaining eye contact with Marlo, whispers under her breath to me and me alone. I can barely see her, my witch-light or whatever she called it, seeming to sputter out.

"I can't read her, Niamh."

Tyler swallows hard while we all watch Marlo's retreating figure, watching the gigantic, ominous gate that she's slowly getting closer to. "I can't read her at all. It's like... there's just nothing there."

Goosebumps rise on my arms and legs beneath all my layers, and I see Tyler's are the same.

Slowly, barely moving at all, she shakes her head at me.

She knows.

Zeke looks over at the two of us, seeing our wide-eyed, fearful faces, and I see the exact moment that the recognition dawns in his golden eyes. His gaze darts back and forth between us and his retreating sister, who is almost to the gate. Even the way she walks is wrong- her gait is too stiff, too rigid.

Like she's never walked before.

Like she's just learning.

And oh, god, another memory hits me as I swallow hot bile that crept up my throat just now. Oh my god. Oh my fucking god.

The voice I heard on the path that day had sounded just like Marlo.

The way it spoke was as if it was just learning to speak.

I gasp out loud, but it comes out as more of a strangled breath. Zeke and Tyler both stare at me as the same oily fear that was sliding through my body rises and hits a crescendo, cutting off my air supply. My strangled breaths turn unproductive, mere wheezes at this point.

That day on the path- forever ago, it feels like now- that fear was nothing compared to this.

Nothing.

I stare at Marlo's retreating self, still slowly, jerkily walking towards the gate without breaking that furious, malicious eye contact with Tyler.

Her wide, unlinking eyes, the beautiful seafoam green and aqua blue are far too big. How could we have missed that?

They're too wide,

Too still.

They don't blink.

They're as still as the gate behind her.

Zeke slowly walks over to us without tearing his gaze away from the thing that looks but does not act like his sister.

"What the fuck is happening right now?" He whispers, his voice just as warbled with fear as my own. His head whips between Tyler and I, and panic: real, tangible, choking panic coats his face and eyes. "No, what the actual *fuck* is happening right now?"

The fear causes his voice to sound tight and raspy, and I look at him just long enough to see as his gentle, happy-go-lucky, bubbly demeanor crumbles right in front of me, his panic making him small.

It kills me.

It kills me, so I tell him what he already knows, because the second Tyler couldn't read her mind, it solidified what she and I already knew, too.

"That's not Marlo."

CHAPTER THIRTY EIGHT

NIAMH

December 7, 2023

The thing that looks like Marlo hears me.

I know it hears me, because it finally stops walking backwards with its stiff, awkward legs, and it smiles at me.

The second it grins, I immediately know why it didn't look at us while it spoke.

Because the thing that is not Marlo smiles, but it isn't Marlo's mouth that smiles at the three of us.

The real Marlo doesn't have three rows of crowded, way-too-many, sharp needle-thin teeth.

The first thought that comes to my mind is my Gran's story about The Skinny Man, the one that used to scare the living shit out of my dad. Unnaturally tall and skinny, with long, skinny limbs like a rope, long, skinny nails, and long, sharp teeth.

My breath gets caught in my throat.

"Do you like what you see, Niamh?"
Not-Marlo speaks clearly, this time, but it isn't Marlo's stilted, awkward voice anymore that leaves her mouth.

This is the voice of the thing in the woods.

It's no longer raspy like it sounded that first day I took the path. Gone is the struggling, barely-coherent rasping thing in the South Gate woods. This voice is smooth, and old.

Old and crooked,

a voice that comes from somewhere else.

A smooth, ancient voice,

a voice that doesn't need any more practice.

Not-Marlo is still smiling, watching us with her aqua eyes as the three of us become completely, utterly frozen with fear. Even Tyler begins to pant shallowly, and although her face is still schooled in a neutral expression, I know she's scared. She'd be a fool not to be.

I surprise myself when I speak up, despite wanting to run with everything in me.

"Where's Marlo." I say in a low, steady voice, half-hoping it won't answer in that voice that isn't Marlo's. Hearing the old, rotten voice coming from Marlo's throat is enough to make me want to ditch our plan entirely. Every instinct in my body is screaming to *get the fuck out of here now.*

"Gone." Not-Marlo says, chuckling slowly to itself. Her- *it's* laugh echoes through the clearing,

and then it *sheds.*

The thing that was inside Marlo *folds in on itself,* discarding her like a second skin, dissolving completely into itself.

Folding into *Marlo* like a vacuum from the inside out.

In her place stands the large, black billy goat, smiling.

Its horns are nearly as thick as the pine trees around us, but that's where the normal goat features end.

Because most billy goats do not have sharp, needle-thin teeth, or white, wide eyes that do not blink.

The goat looks at the three of us, but then focuses on Tyler next to me. The way it looks at her forces bile up my throat again, and I choke it back down, gagging.

It looks at Tyler like it wants to eat her.

And when it speaks to her, it speaks slowly and smoothly, drawing each word out in that horrible, ancient voice.

"How delectable has it felt to have been protected from death all these years, Tyler Lane?" It breathes, looking right at her.

I watch as a single tear falls down her cheek, and as her eyes lose their light.

And then the black goat sheds again, folding into itself.

This time, nothing stands where the goat was.

It's just gone.

With a horrible, gurgling noise not five seconds later, Tyler falls to the forest floor.

Her high-pitched, pain-filled screams pierce the silence of the clearing as she writhes on the ground, her thin body contorting like someone is burning her.

My heart contracts with each scream, and I reach for her, yelling her name as everything else dulls. I can barely hear Zeke's cry of *"NO, Niamh!"* as he grabs me and pulls me tightly to his chest, as if he can shield me from the horror unfolding in front of us.

I struggle against his arms as Tyler writhes on the ground, rolling and contorting in the dirt like she's having a seizure. I try to reach out to grab her again, but Zeke yanks me backwards with a muffled cry.

"Don't, Niamh!" He yells into my ears, and his voice echoes through the clearing, mixing with Tyler's agonizing screams. Mixing with what sounds like laughter ringing through the trees.

Miles's laughter?

A child's laughter, at least, high-pitched and bubbly.

Laughter that comes from the gate.

I can't think or care about anything else other than she's in *pain.* I've finally, after months of knowing her, heard her angry, sad, and afraid, but never once in pain. Never once. She might be stuck in the in-between, neither alive nor dead, but she can certainly still feel pain.

She's in pain, and he's holding me back from her.

I try to rip my arms free from Zeke, but he only holds tighter. He thinks he's protecting me, which I could laugh at if this wasn't happening right now. I'm the one that protects *him*. He has no idea what I'm capable of.

"LET ME *GO*" I seethe, trying to tear out of his grip like a feral animal. I buck and toss my body, but his grip is iron.

But then, after a brutal, agonizing three minutes, now on her belly face down in the dirt, she stops.

For a moment, Tyler just lies horribly, horribly still. If she wasn't already, I'd wonder if she was dead.

She doesn't move. She doesn't breathe.

But then she looks up at us, her face snapping up jerkily and quickly from the dirt. Mud and pine needles and sweat coat her face, but that isn't what causes the most gruesome, bloodcurdling scream to leave my own mouth.

It's the space where her beautiful, deep blue eyes were, the eyes I lost myself in, the eyes that looked at me like they saw me.

Her sapphire eyes are gone. In their place is a pair of white, too-big, unblinking orbs.

What looks up gleefully, happily, is not Tyler anymore.

"*Niamh.*" It says in the smooth, ancient voice, as if trying it out.

Then it speaks again, but it's Tyler's voice this time.

"Hello, Niamh."

She lays on her belly still, but with a few jerky, awkward tries, she manages to push herself up, clambering to her bare feet clunkily.

Tyler looks the same, physically. The same tall, lanky girl, the same ethereal, sharp features. The same thin, tight blue tank top, the same baggy blue jeans. The same long sheet of dark brown hair, the same freckles, clustered like stars. The same sharp, confident jaw, the same graceful, beautiful body. But her best feature- her eyes-

those are gone.

Gone, and replaced with the milky white orbs of the goat, wide and unblinking. The horrible white eyes of the creature it belongs to.

White, horrible eyes, bigger than the palm of my hand.

Not-Tyler smiles at me with the mouth that was *tasting me* just a few hours ago,

and inside that mouth are three rows of those needle-sharp, thin teeth.

Teeth meant for tearing things apart.

Teeth meant to

eat.

I scream again at the sight of her teeth, no longer fighting Zeke's grip, instead scrambling further backwards into him. At my sudden movement we both fall flat on our asses, and I don't even try to get up, instead scuttling backwards like a crab in my rush to get the *fuck* away from the thing that is not Tyler. I can hear Zeke's terrified, heavy panting in my ear as the thing that's wearing Tyler smiles bigger, and bigger, until her grin stretches from ear to ear, splitting her face in half completely.

"FUCKING CHRIST!" Zeke yells, scrambling backwards like me. I can taste his fear in his voice- it's palpable and potent, coating his pores thickly like sweat.

His fear, my fear. They reek like death in this place. Combined, they coat the air that stilled a third time while the *thing* was trying on different skins.

While it was playing with us.
While it played, the air went perfectly still for a third and final time.

The clearing goes completely dark, dark until I can't see at all anymore. I'm blind, defenseless.

The smell of dead animal,

of decay,

of death,

coats the trees around us like another layer of still air, piling one on top of the other. Coating it like it's replacing the very oxygen.

Gagging, Zeke grabs me tighter to him as we scramble backwards, and I grab his muscled arms, crossing them tight over my chest while the thing that's wearing Tyler stands directly in front of the gate, the darkness lifting *just* enough to make out her silhouette.

Whatever's inside Tyler smiles at us. A successful, gleeful smile, like it knows we're going to lose.

Like it knows we were never going to have a chance of defeating it in the first place.

Banishing spell my ass. I almost cry at the flimsy idea of it. As if some black candles and some string would've done a fucking *thing* against this. As if Tyler and I's magic could've done a fucking thing against this- against whatever this is.

Against whatever creature has the ability to wear humans like a second skin, but talks like it's from another time entirely.

I know with a sinking gut feeling that this is beyond my magic. This… being is from a different place, a different time. This thing is not human, not even close.

And it probably never has been.

It's glaringly obvious to me now, staring up at Not-Tyler in front of the gigantic, ominous iron gate.

What sort of creature exists alongside an enormous gate that stands taller than trees, and can appear and disappear at will?

What sort of creature takes little girls?

What sort of creature exists in the dark period?

The voice in my head is screaming the answer into my eardrums.

Something that comes from an even darker place than just the South Gate woods.

"You know," Not-Tyler says in the old, smooth voice again. "Abigail Summers tasted wonderful. *Savory,* truly. But Tyler Lane was always my favorite."

She- it- smiles at me, the white pupils still not blinking. Not-Tyler cocks its head to the side, considering me. Watching for a reaction, just like the real Tyler always does.

"I saved her that night, you know. She didn't remember that bit when she told you her story, did she?"

My eyes widen, my breath stuck as I stare at her.

"While Tyler Lane was being tied to the tallest tree, while those boys planned to burn her like the witches of old and she begged for someone to save her from her certain death, *I* answered."

Zeke looks at Not-Tyler, then at me, and I can barely see the tears that streak down his bright face as he struggles to understand. "What is it saying?" He chokes out into the darkness. "It killed her?"

His voice catches on the word *killed.*

"Tyler Lane died fifty years ago, stupid boy. The people of Summerhill tried to kill her, but I saved her instead. She *begged* me to save her. So I did."

Not-Tyler sighs, a deep, contented sigh, that horrible tongue licking those sharp needle teeth. "She was so powerful, so strong. So *angry,* so consumed with her feelings and her thoughts. She was powerful, and so unlike anything before."

It screams, a chittering, excited scream into the darkness, sounding like something between a growl and crunching gravel, and I fight the urge to clap my hands over my ears. It's a scream-laugh that belongs to something not of this Earth.

"I saved her, and then I ate her."

Not-Tyler picks at her teeth, leaning one shoulder against the edge of the gate in a lazy, airy gesture that is so *Tyler* that I want to scream at it.

Tears prick my eyes as its words register.

NO. No, no, no. Fucking *NO.*

I stand up, then, shoving Zeke's limp arms off of me.

I stand up, and I fight every instinct telling me to run

I stand up, shoving my grimy hair off my shoulders, balling my hands into fists.

I stand up, and feel my anger coursing through my body, the bright, fiery rage that's starting to warm my hands. Feeling the heady, hot rush of magic starting to slip it's oily hands down my limbs.

I fight it naturally, because not even the strong pull of magic could distract me right now.

I stand up, and I stare directly into the white eyes of the thing that's inside Tyler.

Inside the girl that found me, and saved me from myself.

"You can't have her."

My voice comes out rigid and unbreakable as my well of anger rises.

It took Abigail Summers hundreds of years ago.

It took three little girls when my dad was little.

It took Miles.

And then it took Marlo and Kai.

It would not.

Take.

Tyler.

It might have taken all of them, and it might have taken hundreds more before any of us were even born.

It might have been taking girls for even longer.

But it would not take Tyler, too.

My anger grows brighter, brighter, and brighter still in my chest, and when I look down, my hands glow bright red, penetrating the thick darkness. My magic is reaching a crescendo, and still rising as I only grow angrier, more sure of myself.

It could *not* fucking have Tyler.

Zeke, still on the ground behind me, swears softly under his breath when he sees my hands. "What the hell?"

I ignore him, because my legs start to shake as the magic revs up its dangerous pull. I force myself to concentrate on what's right in front of me as the sensual, tantalizing heat sweeps through my body a second time.

When it sweeps through a third time, oily and potent, images of Tyler come with it. The ghost of her mouth on mine, her tongue sweeping into my mouth, claiming me.

Images of her on her knees.

Images of her shoving me back against the pine tree, making me hers.

With a cry, I shove the thoughts away, and I stay in control.

What comes out of my mouth next shocks even me.

"You can't fucking have her." I growl, my voice cold. "Give her back, or I'll make you."

Tears slide down my face as my fear slips away, anger and sheer *rage* taking over.

I curl my fingers into my palms, my short nails biting into the skin. My hands are burning. If I wanted to, I could hurt it.

I'm strong enough, now, because Tyler taught me how to be.

With my next words, I start to do exactly what she taught me: molding all of my magic into one giant, fiery ball, ready to be launched. I know exactly where I want to hit it, too: right in those wide, unlinking white eyes.

"You can't have her." I say again, raising my hands in front of me. "Take someone else. But not her."

I realize too late what I just admitted to it, and to Zeke, too, betraying my deepest, purest truth.

I need her.

I need Tyler, and I'll fucking save her or die trying.

"I need her." I force out on my next breath, and my words carry all the way into the gate itself, floating in the still, rotting air.

Not-Tyler smiles wide, that horrible, terrifying grin taking up her entire face, and starts to clunkily, awkwardly walk over to me. Each step she takes away from the gate pulls the shadows along with her, the little lighting starting to dim.

"Silly." She declares, one foot lugging in front of the other like she weighs a thousand pounds, not a hundred. "Stupid. Girl."

"NIAMH!" Zeke screams from somewhere, but he doesn't run to my side. "RUN!"

I don't move, and when Not-Tyler stands nearly a foot away from me, I fight every single instinct that is telling me to run, to scream, and to kick her away from me. That isn't Tyler. That fucking *thing* is wearing her right now, and it's fucking terrifying.

But for once, my anger is stronger than my fear.

That thing might have saved her the night she died. It might be the very reason that she's still here, trapped in her eighteen year old body.

But Tyler isn't *gone.*

I won't accept it. I won't accept that she's just gone like the rest of them are.

Not-Tyler steps closer, until she's right in front of me, looking down at me. She- it- looks down at me with those white, palm-sized eyes and those needle teeth, all while Zeke is screaming my name in the background.

It looks down at me, and the tears roll down my face with reckless abandon, my body shaking like a leaf. Between my bubbling, roiling magic burning its way through my body and the fear that's beginning to trickle in alongside it, I feel like I might pass out.

Not-Tyler smiles at me. "Silly girl. I've been hiding in the skin of Tyler Lane since the night she begged me to save her. You thought you were friends with the girl you met in the woods? That was never her. I've been in her for fifty years, and oh she feels *so delicious.*"

She shakes her head of silky hair and runs her fingers through it longingly, like she's never felt such a thing. Then she trails one long, slim finger down her arms, shivering at her own touch.

And then she reaches that hand out and runs her finger down *my* arm, releasing a chittering, low growl at the heat that's emanating from my skin. I fight the urge to scream and shove her hand away.

"Come on, Niamh." She chitters to me from Tyler's throat. "You weren't recoiling at my touch earlier today."

I don't even think about what Zeke's feeling right now, because no. No, no, no. I don't believe that, not even for a fucking second. I *won't.*

It's just not possible. Tyler couldn't have been this…. Rotten, dark thing all along. She just couldn't have been.

That was impossible, because she was the girl that taught me what different color candles mean.

She was the girl that taught me how just the right amount of catnip and patchouli can draw a lover to you, and make them desire you.

She was the girl that showed me how to burn bay leaves with wishes scribbled on them in ink, willing them to come true.

She was the girl that showed me that my anger was not a curse, was not something bad at all, but a gift.

She was the girl that showed me that I'm made of magic, and didn't run from it. Tyler, not this *thing.*

Tyler is the one that sees me for exactly who I am, for who Niamh MacKenna truly, truly is: every angry, fiery inch of me,

and thinks it's beautiful.

Tyler, not this thing that's wearing her right now. *Tyler* is the one that looks at me like she sees me, gets me, and likes every single inch of me.

It couldn't have been this creature wearing her skin all these months. It just couldn't have been. I would have known. I would have *noticed.* It couldn't have been this… thing that's moving her like a marionette.

I refuse to believe that the girl who kissed me like she wanted to be within my skin, like she couldn't get close enough to me, was not really Tyler.

I refuse to believe that the girl who saved me was not really Tyler.

"You lying, manipulative fuck." I say simply to her, ready to release my magic in tenfold, right between it's fucking eyes. It's lying. It's lying, trying to get me to bend, to break.

I won't.

But then,

Not-Tyler speaks in Tyler's *real* voice, her rose-petal, sensual voice, the one that floats over my skin and makes my eyes want to roll back in my head. The smell of roses and honey pierce through the rot for a moment, stunning me.

And then it speaks to me,

and says the one thing that does break me, in Tyler's true voice.

"You will never be Morgan."

It might not be the real Tyler speaking right now, but it sure as shit sounds like her.

And hearing the words in her own voice shatters me.

"Oh, you poor girl. Did you really think you *mattered* to Tyler Lane? You could never be Morgan. Did you think she *wanted* you? You poor, stupid girl. She never wanted you. You will never be Morgan."

And with a quiet, dull *pop,* my magic fizzes out instantly, the giant ball of power that I'd been ready to hurl at it winking out.

Everything around me starts to fade, even the terrifying creature wearing Tyler in front of me. Her words from earlier echo in my head as my vision goes spotty.

"Love made me fucking blind, *Niamh!"*
"Love made me weak."

Everything becomes engulfed in a dull, fuzzy haze: the darkness of the clearing, the towering pine trees surrounding the three of us, the gate just feet away from me, Zeke screaming at the top of his lungs behind me, everything.

Everything fades, and the buzzing, glowing magic in my chest finally winks out completely as my legs give out and I slip to the ground, landing in a heap on my side.

Just like I did the day I met her.

Shallow, small sips of air start to feel like too much,
so I take one last breath.

And then,

She reaches into my chest cavity with hooked, skinny fingers, sharp, needle thin nails meant to cause pain, to draw blood.
They tear into my skin like paper, ripping my ribcage in two, exposing my heart to the elements.
My exposed heart- that stupid, piece-of-shit, worthless fucking muscle- beats once.
Twice.
Then a third time,
waiting in anticipation of what she'll do with it.

She grips my esophagus in other hand,
those claws digging into my jugular just tight enough to make me see black spots.

Gripping *just* tight enough to squeeze the air supply off a bit.

And despite it all,

I'm not afraid of her. Even though it isn't really Tyler in there, I'm not afraid.

I'm just broken.

It's right.

I'll never be Morgan,

and she will *never* want me that same way. It doesn't matter that what we have

is different, and special. The thing wearing Tyler is right.

I'll never be Morgan.

It broke me, in Tyler's own voice.

There's a lump in my throat,

all the things I wanted to say to her squished together into a little ball with all the

things she made me feel.

A little knot of hurt, perfectly lodged in my throat.

My eyes pool and threaten to spill over with it all as I lay there,

telling myself dizzily, angrily not to give in.

Do not cry.

Do *not* cry, Niamh. Do not give this thing the satisfaction of that.

I tell myself to breathe,

and I lie to my still-beating heart, telling it that it'll all be okay.

Even though I don't believe it,

And may never, not when it comes to her.

She squeezes the hand on my neck tighter,

digs the other hand deeper, feeling around with those jagged nails.

She reaches around my chest cavity and broken ribs for my heart, searching,

searching for the very last bit of me.

She got all the rest, I think.

Tyler got my mind, every square inch of it. My loyalty, my adoration, my respect.

She got my time, my devotion, and my curiosity.

She got my body, nearly every inch of it.

She got my heart, the very best part of me. That stupid, loyal, too-big heart.

Because I might be an angry, impulsive girl. I might be the kind of person that

damages property and steals from stores, all because her friends dared her to.

I might be the kind of girl that hurt her best friend in the world without meaning to.

I might be the kind of girl that, when she gets angry enough, can light things on fire.

And I might be the kind of girl that loves that.

I might be dangerous, or reckless, or a bad person for feeling that.

I might be all those things, but my heart is good.

I might be all of those things, and worse. I might have gone on to do worse things,

bad things. Seventeen year old girls who are prone to anger shouldn't be trusted with

fire.

Girls made of anger,

girls who have too-big feelings,

girls who feel everything so intensely have hearts like mine, and we're dangerous,

with or without fire. We know how to survive.

But my heart, while dark, dangerous and deep-

my heart is unfailingly loyal and coated in magic.

My heart knows how to love like like those only born of magic know how:

With all of me.

And that, I think, is the best part of me: the kind of heart that lies inside of me loves

unconditionally, deeply, and fiercely,

whether or not it's returned.

> She got all the rest of me, I think. Tyler Lane got all of me.

> I guess she can have my heart, too.

> "NIAMH!"

> I open my eyes, the starless, inky sky filling my vision.

Sitting up, despite the ache that's rolling through my heart, weighing it down, I look down and can clearly see that my chest is whole and intact.

I lay one dirty, filthy hand on my heart, and am greeted with its steady, calm beating.

I'm alive.

Nothing ripped into my chest,

nothing hurt me at all.

Nothing, other than her words.

I let her words consume me.

"NIAMH!" Zeke yells again, and I can hear him running over to me, but it's so dark that I can barely see him until he's basically on top of me.

The face that is so etched into my mind: his chipper, freckled face, his bright gold eyes, his happy, sunny features every time he looks at me.

That face is currently flooded with concern as he helps me to my feet, then crushes me into a Zeke-hug that tells me exactly how terrified he was for me. "Holy shit, Niamh, I thought she was going to kill you."

I don't have the heart to tell him that I would've let her.

Zeke lets me go, and at this close, I can see how he's really feeling: hurt. Despite everything that just happened, he's *hurt.*

"You love her?" He asks me, three words that spike the adrenaline in my body, flooding my exhausted heart.

I open my mouth, looking at him, and I don't know how to answer him. My hesitation causes him to look away, and when he turns back to me, tears roll down his cheeks again, fresh ones. He doesn't wipe them away.

"Answer me this." He says to me in the dark, his openly wounded face breaking my heart all over again. "I have no idea who Morgan is, or really, who Tyler is either. But answer me this one thing, Niamh. There's eight billion fucking people in this world. Are you going to let *one* fucking person show you what love is?"

I don't know what to say to him, because all I can think about is what that thing said to me. I'll never be Morgan.

And what Morgan and Tyler had… that seemed to be enough to show Tyler what love was. That one, astronomical love, the kind you find when you're young seemed to be enough to show her.

I look at Zeke, my voice coming out raw and shaky. "She sees me." I say, and he looks away, his muffled sobs covered by his arm.

"And I don't?"

I look at him as he wipes his face roughly on his jacket, eyes gleaming and sharp. "I don't know what rise that thing is trying to get out of you, Niamh, but you are not hard to love at all. Anyone who says differently can go fuck themselves."

I inhale deeply and look away from him. I can't do this right now.

He doesn't even *know* me.

And the thing inside Tyler is a goddamn liar, because I *know* that it wasn't in her all these months. I don't know how I know- I just do. It's lying to me, trying to bait me.

But it was right about one thing. I'm not Morgan.

I'll never *be* Morgan.

And I don't know how to get past that, because... Tyler loved someone too much, and it got her killed.

I can't help but wonder if I'm heading down the same path.

"Where did she go?" I ask Zeke quietly instead of commenting on his statement.

He looks around the clearing as if she'll suddenly just appear, also ignoring what he just said.

But there's nothing, other than the gate, still standing there, watching everything unfold. We're alone, and yet the air is still completely void of movement, the gate still looming over us. Waiting. Waiting, watching what we'll do next.

I can't imagine we'll be able to escape as easily as we did last time.

"She- it- it just sort of... I don't know. It just kind of... shed her." He says quietly, shivering violently while he recalls it. "But I don't know where it went."

Out of the corner of my eyes, I can see movement near the gate. My heart jacks up in my chest, fear rising like nausea. Zeke grabs my arm before I can bolt, but when I see what it is, squinting through the dark, I tear away from his grasp easily.

Lying in front of the gate, limp on the ground, is Tyler. I know in my gut that it's really her this time, and not the thing. I don't know how I know- I just do.

I'm up and running before Zeke can try and tell me not to.

When I reach her side and drop to my knees, my tears flow freely, deep, ugly sobs ricocheting out of me at the sight of her.

She looks pale as death, and not in her usual pale complexion. She looks void of pigment completely. Even her freckles seem to disappear, so pallid is her face.

Her eyes are shut, her chest not rising or falling. There's no movement at all underneath that blue tank top.

I cry harder than I have in my life, my body spasming.

I can't accept that she's dead. I won't. I told that thing that it couldn't have her, and I meant it.

I can't accept that she's dead.

And neither, it seems, can the clearing.

CHAPTER THIRTY NINE

It watches the broken girl with the white-blonde hair as she cries over the body of Tyler Lane.

It's slightly disappointed in Niamh MacKenna.

It had watched her as her magic stretched and grew, stronger than it ever had before. It had watched, drooling, as she had grown so powerful in those few minutes that she had almost forgotten how afraid she was.
It had pushed her until her magic started to warp the air around them, until it could taste that burning, deep well.

Oh, she was going to be

delectable

And when it told her in the voice of Tyler Lane, from the lips on Tyler's body that she would never be the one Tyler had loved, it had expected her to get angry. It had expected her to dip into her well of magic.

It had expected her to try and fight it.

Instead, she'd crumpled into a heap, allowing its words to break her. Instead, she allowed the words to swallow her, to crush her, to consume her fully. Much in the way her magic always had the desire to consume her.

She let it break her.

It chitters angrily, it's jagged, jerky screams echoing through the trees. It wanted to taste Niamh MacKenna while she was at her strongest.

It no longer craved her fear. It drooled over her power, now, her magic.

For hers was almost stronger than Tyler Lane's had been those fifty years ago. It didn't want to eat her or her fear.

It wanted to feast on her,

that magical, foolish girl.

She wasn't *so* foolish, though. The girl had seen right through its lies, calling it out.

It hadn't worn Tyler once since the night it had saved her from death.

It hadn't touched her, not once.

It had saved her, and then it had left her alone.

It just needed Niamh to believe otherwise.

Which is why, just moments before the ginger-haired boy had pulled her out of her grief and woken her up, it had shed the skin of Tyler Lane and shifted back into a shadow.

Into the scribble of darkness and a pair of white eyes.

It didn't kill Tyler Lane. It left her body there in front of the gate, but it did not kill her.

It just needed Niamh MacKenna to think it did.

And she would.

The girl exposed her feelings too quickly, too rashly. She had a heart just like Tyler Lane did all those years ago: too big, too deep.

 It knows her heart now.

It knows what she will do.

It coils behind the gate, slithering closer to where the body of Tyler Lane lies, to where the other two lean over her. Their fear, sadness, grief, and anger puncture the darkness and the shadows amidst the clearing like a knife through fog, and it smiles to itself as it sidles up to the gate, all those needle-thin rows of teeth shining through the oddly-shaped patch of darkness.

It was so, so close. It would feed. It would

taste

And this time, it would have more than a meal, more than just the *feast* that was Niamh MacKenna.
It would have not one,
not two,
but *three* meals tonight.

The thing slithering up and down the iron rungs of the gate laughs loudly, unnaturally, a gasping, gurgling laugh.
It never really learned how to laugh like a human.

It makes sure it sends its laugh out into the clearing for them to hear, then shifts its voice from the smooth, old one to the pealing, bubbly one of Miles. Then a third time, to the faint, girlish laugh of Abigail Summers.

It watches as Niamh MacKenna and Zeke Torah rip their heads up, searching frantically for the location of the different laughs. It watches as the fear slinks back onto their features, making its mouth water.

And then it slithers in front of the gate, and it allows them to

see it.

CHAPTER FORTY

NIAMH

December 7, 2023

I see it before Zeke does.

A wrong, out of place scribble of darkness, clinging to one thick rung of the gate like a spider.

The oddly-shaped patch slithers down towards the ground,
and this time, I give in to my instincts, and I scream.

When it hits the floor of the South Gate woods, sending up a cloud of black dirt, the scribble starts to grow.

It grows and grows and growsandgrowssomemore

until there is a little girl standing in front of us, directly between us and the gate. A little girl in a simple, stained white dress that falls to her feet, a simple, stained apron, and a bonnet that ties right beneath her chin, trapping her golden curls. Her cherubic face and sweet presence would be perfect, if not for her eyes and her smile. Abigail Summers was a seven year old back in sixteen sixty four. She was described exactly how the girl before me stands: a happy, polite child who loved her twin sister, who loved playing in what is now called the South Gate woods. She spoke only when spoken to, respected her father, and treated her twin with kindness. She was everything a little puritan girl should've been.

But then Abigail Summers walked through the gate.

The thing that stands before me now, wearing what is left of Abigail Summers smiles, as if delighting in my reaction to her.

The thing that looks like Abigail Summers has white, unblinking eyes, too big to be human eyes.

The thing that looks like Abigail Summers has needle-thin, sharp teeth definitely do not belong on a little girl.

"Niamh." She utters, a perfectly lighthearted, childish sing-song voice coming from those razor-sharp, predator teeth. *"Pray tell, what ails thee?"*

I don't answer her, instead standing tall in front of Tyler's limp body and Zeke's trembling form.

I have no plan. I have nothing. Literally nothing.

Nothing comes to mind, and I can't feel my magic at all.

Tyler couldn't feel her magic when she died, either, I remember.

So this is it.

This might be it.

I look at Zeke behind me. "Run."

I don't look back to see if he listens or not.

And then, to the thing wearing Abigail Summers, I square my shoulders and tell it with clear, resounding finality,

that it cannot have Tyler.

I can't feel my magic, and I can barely see in the darkness, but it can't have Tyler.

"You can't have her." I say clearly.

My voice echoes through the clearing, reverberating in the darkness all around us. Reverberating into the gate, not even a foot away from me.

Abigail Summers licks her lips, and her black tongue catches on one of her needle-thin teeth. Beads of blood run down her perfect, rosy chin, and I feel fear drill itself into my heart. It's a wonder it hasn't stopped at all yet.

"If thou want Tyler," She says in a low, guttural, and completely un-childlike voice, "then thou must come get her."

And the thing that's wearing Abigail Summers darts forward.

I shriek and try to grab Tyler's limp, lifeless body. She's heavy, completely deadweight.

And in the milliseconds it takes for the creature to reach me, the gate has somehow moved closer. I could reach out and stick my hand through it, if I wanted.

Right as she looms over me, Abigail Summers reaches one pudgy, dirty-child hand out and grabs Tyler's bare, muddy foot.
With shocking strength and speed for a seven year old- or what's choosing to appear as one- the little girl tugs her body easily across the dirt as I lunge for them both.

"STOP!" I scream at it, catapulting my body towards them both.

The thing wearing Abigail Summers snarls at me, the guttural noise clashing directly with her childish voice. "You can die just like she did." She hisses. "Over a girl she loved too much."

I lunge at her, but she sidesteps me with unnatural, inhuman speed. I don't care if she hurts me- *it can't have her.*

It can't have her it can't have her it can'tFUCKINGhaveher

and with a guttural, gravelly laugh,

a laugh as young as it is old,

a laugh that sounds like bells and trumpets,

like something regal, something wise,

a laugh that does not at all belong to a seven year old girl,

or to a human at all,

she

       tosses

Tyler

                            through

the

       gate.

The sound that comes out of me shatters the still air around us, piercing the clearing like a cork popping.

Because the second Tyler's body passes through the other side of the gate,

she vanishes.

Just a blink, and she's gone.

Simply gone.

The trees on the other side of the gate are the same ones around us.
It's the same penetrating darkness, the same clearing.

But this side, the side that Abigail Summers and I stand on is one world,

and the other side is very, very clearly somewhere else.

Somewhere else entirely.
I know what I'm going to do before I start breathing again.

I look at the thing wearing Abigail.
I look at the gate, that tall, towering, sinister iron gate that is so close now that my nose is nearly touching it.

I hear Zeke somewhere behind me, screaming my name with a ferocity I've never heard from him before.

And what I do is this.

I do not walk through the gate.

I do not sprint through the gate.

I do not fall through the gate.

What I do is *hurl* myself into it without breathing,

hurl myself into the unknown,

making myself another statistic.

I hurl myself through the gate,

      to Tyler.

Epilogue

Here's one last wrench for you.

Let's say Tyler Iris Lane and Niamh MacKenna went through the big gate in the woods. Let's say they both went through it, clear to the other side, and vanished. Let's say that they went through the gate- wherever that may have led to- and yet were both very, very much still alive.

Let's say they passed through the gate and vanished, just like everyone else did,

except they did not die.

So if they did not die when they passed through the gate,

then where did they go?

Acknowledgements

Since I was fifteen, I've had the idea for a story that would be called

SUMMERHILL.

I tweaked it over the last seven ish years, scrapping it, editing it, and then working on

other stories instead, temporarily abandoning it. One of these ideas ended up turning

into a full blown novel, and I ended up publishing *The Gig Harbor Suicides* at sixteen

years old. I never forgot my fifteen year old self's idea, though, and now, all these

years later, I can't believe what *SUMMERHILL* evolved into. What started off as

nothing more than the idea of "what if there was a giant, forty-foot gate that just

appeared at random in the woods?" developed completely on its own into a horror

story- but simultaneously a beautiful, deeply intense love story, one that weaves

magic and passion together, creating a love that is not bound by time or space.

SUMMERHILL became a passion project that, like most writers, I lost myself in

completely, forsaking everything that was not this book. Therefore, I'd like to thank

the following people for supporting the dream and the chaos.

First off, thank you to my Nonni and Papa. Thank you for loving me

unconditionally and truly, and always believing in my gift for writing since I was old

enough *to* write.

Another grandparent thank-you must go to my late Grandma Canter for

passing the gift of writing down to me, always regaling me with Irish and Celtic folk tales, and for all the tedious hours spent researching our family tree, which is where I found Niamh and her siblings' very, very Irish names.

Thank you to Claire for the BEAUTIFUL map at the front of the book, and for being such a supportive sweetheart throughout the whole process.

Thank you to Griffin for the insane cover, and for not getting mad at me when I kept telling you to make it "darker and scarier" :)

Thank you to Angela LaBella, my absolute best friend in the entire world of the last eleven or twelve something years. Thank you for always listening to me ramble excitedly about this book, for joining me on my manic coffee & sprint-writing days, and for supporting my every dream. I love you endlessly.

A HUGE thank you to the entire staff at OB Beans Coffee Roasters: Eddie, Dee, Ella, Josh, Callyn, Matt, Noah, Keenan, Maddy, Alexis, and Kelly. Building friendships with literally every barista in the shop while I worked was great. The constant encouragement and love was great. Also, the dozens of free lattes were super great. I love all of you.

Another huge thank you to all the staff at Crown Point Coffee- Lotte, Eli, and Aisha, and Cafe By the Bay- Eddie, Jennifer, Carson, Silas, and Mark for the happy faces and support I received when I came in and took up one of your tables for five or six hours to sprint-write. I'm grateful for each and every one of you.

Thank you to those three baristas at Bird Rock Coffee on Morena for being SO EXCITED about my book the day I came in after surfing and hyping me up to the max.

Thank you to the OG BETA READER, Hanne, for literally kick-starting this entire book and helping me realize that it was, in fact, a really good idea and needed to be written. I seriously could not have written this without you. Thank you a hundred billion times over.

Thank you to my beta readers, Cody, Kayla, Hanne, and Angela. You guys knew Niamh back when she was still Sloane aka SJ!

Thank you to Keanna Miller for showing me around Santa Cruz, which inspired a majority of places in *SUMMERHILL.*

Thank you to my cousin Sailor, who keeps my heart happy and joyful because she loves writing just as much as I did at fourteen. You are insanely talented, and I love seeing the way your mind works. KEEP WRITING.

Thank you to the insanely fantasy authors I binge-read while writing this book: Piper CJ, Sarah J. Maas, and A.K Mulford. Thank you for being the biggest inspirations ever and serving as a constant reminder to keep writing, because I want to look on the shelves one day and see my books amongst your own- but also for writing the sort of love stories that fuel my hopeless-romantic self.

Thank you to both Patty Lanham and Sgt. Orloff for being my real-life heroes and people I look up to most.

Thank you to my favorite movie in the entire fucking world, Stuck in Love, for reminding me of why I write, and why being a writer is the thing that gives me purpose more than anything else in the world: I want to move people. I want people to feel big things. I want people to feel something bigger than themselves. I want to write stories that move people.

And finally, I want to thank Ellie Barimo.

I will never not be grateful for what we had, and there will always be a part of you in me- a part that feels like the ocean and your old apartment, country songs and the color purple, forehead telepathy and brushing through shower-wet hair, and hearing you play guitar.

I hope you read this, and I hope you know that I couldn't have written Morgan and Tyler's story without you. That kind of love does exist, even if it doesn't work out in the end.

Critical Thinking

1. Do you agree with Tyler's belief that love makes you weak? Why or why not?

2. Tyler is an innately morally gray character. Based on her personality, her family, and the town she grew up in, do you believe she is truly good or bad? Why or why not?

3. Niamh's deepest desire is to be loved and seen for who she truly is, hence why she feels so strongly attached to Tyler. Do you think Tyler knew this and used it against her in the end? Why or why not?

4. Do you think Tyler being a Lane woman who fell in love is what ultimately doomed her, or do you think the entity in the woods had a plan for her all along? Why or why not?

5. Throughout the novel, Niamh feels pulled between both Zeke and Tyler. Do you think Niamh would have been better off with Zeke, who loves the idea of her, or Tyler, who might never want her the way she wants Morgan? Why or why not?

6. What do *you* think is on the other side of the gate? Explain.

7. One of the biggest themes of *SUMMERHILL* is big emotions and their consequences: anger, lust, fear, and love. Which emotion do you think is the strongest and impacted the character's actions the most? Why?

8. Do you think that love truly conquers all? Following the storyline of Tyler and Morgan, then of Tyler and Niamh, explain.

9. Niamh is willing to die for Tyler, even though she may or may not share her affections. Do you think this makes her weak or just extremely loyal? Why or why not?

10. Do you think Tyler meant to lead Niamh on? Why or why not?

11. Do you think the love that Tyler and Morgan have in *SUMMERHILL* exists in real life? Why or why not?

About The Author

Ashdon Byszewski, author of *The Gig Harbor Suicides* and *SUMMERHILL,* is a surfer, swimmer, scorpio, beach lifeguard/EMT, and pop punk/emo enthusiast who really, really loves to write. (Almost more than she loves the ocean!) She's a huge fan of rainbow-colored surfboards and queer representation in novels, and is very excited to have finally written one that showcases that herself. She lives in Southern California, and when she isn't in the water, she can be found holed up somewhere writing, in the mosh pit at a Knuckle Puck or Real Friends show, belting pop punk or lil peep songs in her car, or spray painting her shortboards very obnoxiously bright colors.

Stay updated on her latest works via Instagram: (@ashdonbski)